"YOU'RE KIRK, AREN'T YOU?"
THE HUMAN SAID . . .

Glissa's nostrils flared at the mention of that terrible name.

"The one who was captain of the *Enterprise,* aren't you?"

Glissa stared deep into the eyes of the man she knew as Sam Jameson. "No," she whispered. "No, not you." She let his hands slip away from hers.

Sam looked up at her as if to speak, but she shook her head to silence him, trying to suppress the shudder of revulsion that passed through her. "There is nothing more to be said. I will have your account closed out and book your passage on the next outbound shuttle. You should . . . you should leave here as quickly as possible. Before too many others find out." She had to look away from him. "The company will not be able to guarantee your safety."

The human said nothing. Glissa left him to join the other workers and explain what had happened for those who didn't understand Standard. As if the name Kirk needed translation.

As if the entire universe didn't know of his crimes.

Look for STAR TREK Fiction from Pocket Books

STAR TREK: The Original Series

STAR TREK: The Next Generation

STAR TREK ®

PRIME DIRECTIVE

JUDITH AND GARFIELD REEVES-STEVENS

POCKET BOOKS

New York   London   Toronto   Sydney   Tokyo   Singapore

The plot and background details of *Prime Directive* are solely the authors' interpretation of the universe of STAR TREK® and vary in some respects from the universe as created by Gene Roddenberry.

POCKET BOOKS, a division of Simon & Schuster Inc.
1230 Avenue of the Americas, New York, NY 10020

This book is published by Pocket Books, a division of
Simon & Schuster Inc., under exclusive license from
Paramount Pictures.

ISBN: 0-671-74466-6

First Pocket Books paperback printing September 1991

10 9 8 7 6 5 4 3 2 1

POCKET and colophon are registered trademarks of
Simon & Schuster Inc.

Printed in the U.S.A.

HISTORIAN'S NOTE

The events of this book take place in the final
year of the *Enterprise*'s original five-year mission.

space is infinite
without ending
all within it
just beginning

VULCAN CHILD'S KOAN

traditional

PROLOGUE

LE RÊVE D'ÉTOILES

Extract from *A Historical Analysis of the Five-Year Missions*
Admiral Glynis Kestell Tabor, Stellar Institute Press, Paris,
Earth

According to the records as they existed at that time, of the original twelve Constitution-class starships that had embarked on Starfleet's visionary program of five-year missions, five had already been lost in the service of the United Federation of Planets: the USS *Constellation* as the last casualty of an ancient war, the *Intrepid* in the Gamma 7A system, the *Excalibur* in war-game maneuvers, the *Defiant* in the Tholian Annex, and the *Enterprise* during the incident at Talin IV.

No one denied that these losses had been heavy, in lives and material, but among the dozens of planning commissions that set the Federation's long-term goals and policies, there was no serious doubt that the five-year missions would continue with new ships and new crews. Because, despite the high cost of such epic exploration and expansion, the returns these activities brought to the Federation were always greater.

In a period of only four standard years, the records showed that thousands of strange new worlds had been explored, hundreds of new civilizations had been discovered, and the

Federation's boundaries had grown to encompass a volume of space nearly five times that which had been charted as of stardate 00.1. Given these results, ways could always be found to commission new starships, and as for the new crews those ships would require, they were the secret of the Federation's unprecedented strength.

It was the same secret shared by all great political movements in the histories of a thousand worlds. The Federation was founded not by force, nor by expediency, nor in response to an outside threat. It was founded on a dream—a dream of greater goals and greater good, of common purpose and cooperation, but beyond all else, it was a dream to know more, a dream to explore to the farthest limits and then go beyond.

They called it *le rêve d'étoiles*—the dream of stars.

Like all profound ideas, this dream of stars was irresistible, and the Federation's planners were aware of its attraction. They recognized its presence in the more than twelve thousand applications Starfleet received for each Academy opening. They felt its pull within themselves.

But dreams alone were not enough to sustain the Federation's goals, and fortunately the planners also understood what else was needed and how to obtain it. They understood that throughout the worlds of the Federation there were beings in whom the dream burned brightest. Invariably, all of these individuals had known instantly where their destinies lay from the moment they had first looked up to the lights of the night sky. In every language in all the worlds, the words were always the same: the dream of stars. Not traveling to them, not stopping at them, but moving among them, ever outward, always farther, no end to space or to their quest. Or to the dream.

At Starfleet Academy, the planners were careful to set in place the challenges and the system that would guide the best of those called by the dream to the only position that they could hold, the position to which each had been born.

Starship captain.

There could be no greater embodiment of the dream, and it

was upon this foundation that the Federation was ultimately based and its future assured.

The system was not perfect. At the time of the Talin IV tragedy, the planners knew that for every Robert April or Christopher Pike the Academy produced, there would be a Ron Tracey or a James T. Kirk. But that was to be expected when dealing with exceptional beings whose very nature put them at odds with most definitions of what was deemed predictable or normal behavior. On the whole, the planners felt the system worked, and reason and logic—much to the Vulcans' chagrin—had nothing to do with it.

So the Federation's planners set their course for the future, building new ships, setting new missions, knowing that there would be no end to those who would volunteer to take part, because the dream of stars, once acknowledged, could never be denied.

But at that time, in the aftermath of Talin IV, what the planners did not yet know was that once that dream had been experienced, neither could it ever be willingly surrendered.

In accordance with the Federation's goals for the gathering of knowledge, it was a lesson the planners were eventually due to learn, and their system had already created the man who would teach it to them.

Once and for all.

Part One

AFTERMATH

ONE

☆

Humans, Glissa thought suddenly, as she caught the first unmistakable scent of their approach. *You can't live with them and you can't live without them, but by Kera and Phinda, you can certainly smell them.*

The short Tellarite shift boss looked away from the viewscreen blueprint she studied, then narrowed her deepset, solid black eyes to squint into the distance. All around her, she felt the thrumming of the thin air that passed for an atmosphere within the hollowed-out S-type asteroid. It was the pulse of the machines and fellow workers remaking its interior into a living world, a home for thousands. For Glissa, there was excitement in this job of world making, and fulfillment. Which is why the unexpected scent of humans was so unsettling. With them around, she feared the excitement would soon give way to drudgery.

The Tellarite twitched her broad, porcine nose as she tasted the circulating breeze, seeking more details of the human presence she had detected. In the soft, seasonless mists of her home world, natural selection had not been inspired to evolve keen eyesight. As an adult of her species, Glissa had long since lost the ability to see past two meters with any clarity. But she could hear with an acuity that surpassed most Vulcans, and could decipher scents and airborne pheromones at a speed and rate of accuracy to challenge all but the most sensitive tricorder.

It was those other fine senses that now confirmed for her what she had feared—the telltale odor of the dreadfully omnivorous humans came to her from what could only be her second-shift crew of rockriggers. Even Glissa's near-useless eyes could make out the brilliant yellow streak of the safety cable that linked the blurry figures. The cable traced a sinuous route around the wide yellow warning bands that marked the overlaps of the artificial gravity fields on the asteroid's inner surface. Spinning the rock to produce centripetal pseudo-gravity would make working inside the asteroid much easier, but until the final bracing supports were in place, the engineers didn't want to subject the shell to the additional strain. So, in the interim, the asteroid's outer surface was studded with portable artificial-gravity generators, creating both amplified and null-gravity zones within the rock. As if that crazy-quilt arrangement didn't produce enough strain on its own.

Glissa sighed and the sound she made in her barrel chest was deep and guttural—like the prelude to a particularly invigorating string of invective. But there was no such joy behind her sigh. She hadn't realized that the first shift was already over, let alone that it was time for the second to begin. And the lake-support pylons for the rock's eventual basin of freshwater supply were still not in place. They hadn't even appeared on the massive cargo-transporter platform waiting empty at the edge of the work site. At the rate her division was falling behind schedule, Glissa calculated she was going to have to endure at least another tenday of overtime before she had the slightest chance of taking a few shifts off to enjoy a good wallow in the communal baths on the rec station. And from the smell of things, it was definitely going to be another tenday of working with humans.

Of course, Glissa had nothing against humans personally, but not being from one of Miracht's ambassadorial tribes, she found it extremely unsettling to work with them. Who wouldn't have difficulty working with beings who could never seem to tell the obvious differences between time-honored constructive insults and improper personal attacks on their parentage, and whose lack of a sense of humor was second only to the Vulcans? Still, it took all kinds to make the worlds go round and, to be fair, she knew of few Tellarites who had the appetite to administer the monstrous bureaucracies that kept the Federation functioning.

She sighed again and rippled the sensitive underpad nodes of her hoof against the viewscreen's control panel—one of dozens of similar viewscreens that were mounted on light poles ringing the work site. After erasing the blueprint from the two-meter-by-one-meter display, she sniffed the air more slowly to determine which particular humans she had been cursed with this time.

The twelve approaching rockriggers were still too far away for Glissa to recognize any features other than their individual yellow safety harnesses and helmets, but she could identify most of them by their scents. Seven, thank the Moons, were Tellarites themselves—client workers from the Quaker commune that had hired Interworld Construction to reform this rock into a Lagrange colony. At least half the workforce on this project were client workers providing the commune with substantial labor savings.

But of the other five workers approaching, Glissa scented, all were human, and that was unfortunate because rockrigging and humans were never a happy combination.

The task of asteroid reformation was one of the few remaining hazardous occupations within the Federation that legally could not be done more efficiently or less expensively by drone machines. If the Council ever decided to relax the Federation's prohibitions on slavery to allow true synthetic consciousnesses to control robots, then perhaps the industry itself would be transformed. But until that unlikely day, rockrigging would remain the exclusive province of two basic types of laborers: dedicated client workers who welcomed the chance to literally carve out a world with their own bare hooves, and the hardcases who signed on with Interworld because they had exhausted all other options.

As far as Glissa was concerned, the hardcase humans who worked for Interworld—some fugitive, all desperate—might just as well be Klingons for all the honor and diligence they exhibited. But the making of worlds was honorable work for a Tellarite, and no one had said it would ever be easy. So humans, with their unique and unfathomable mix of Vulcan logic and Andorian passion, were officially tolerated by Interworld, even if it meant that Glissa and the other shift bosses did have to watch their language.

As Glissa turned back to the viewscreen to call up current work assignments and detailed plans for the second shift, the shift-change alarm sounded from speakers in the towering lightpoles that encircled the five-hundred-meter-wide work site. She looked up to squint at the wall of the rock four kilometers over her head, and could just make out the smeared constellations of the lightpoles surrounding the work sites on the airless half of the rock's interior as they flickered to signal shift change for those workers in environmental suits who could not use sound alarms.

Puzzled, Glissa checked her chronometer and saw that the change signals were on time. But that meant the second shift crew was also arriving on time, and in all the years Glissa had spent with Interworld, one of the few things she had learned to count on was that hardcase humans were never on time. It was almost a religion with them.

For a moment she was concerned at the break in tradition and order—few things were worse to a Tellarite than an unexplained mystery. She quickly retasted the air, but there was no denying the scent of humans in the approaching workers. She sniffed again, deeply, questioningly . . . and then the answer came.

Glissa raised her hoof to the unfocused form of the human who led the team and waved. "Sam?" she growled. "Sam Jameson?"

The lead figure raised his much too long and scrawny arm to

return the wave and Glissa felt a sudden thrill of hope. If Sam Jameson had been promoted to work as her second-shift team leader then there was an excellent chance that Glissa's division might make up for lost time. He had only been with the company for four tendays but had already proven himself to be a most remarkable being, human or otherwise.

"I thought I smelled the foul stink of your furless human meat!" the Tellarite blared deafeningly as Sam finally came within range of her vision.

"It's a miracle you can smell anything through the stench of that slime-encrusted *skrak* pelt you call fur!" Sam shouted back.

Glissa's huge nostrils flared with pleasure. Here, at last, was the exception to the rule: a cultured human who truly understood the subtle nuances of Civil Conversation. She could almost feel the hot mud of the rec station oozing up around her as she anticipated the rewards of meeting her schedule.

The Tellarite held out her hoof and Sam Jameson grasped it without hesitation, returning the proper ripple of greeting against Glissa's underpad nodes as best as any human could, considering how the creatures were crippled by the ungainly and limited manipulatory organs they called fingers. If Glissa actually stopped to think about it, it was a wonder any human could pick up a tool let alone invent one. They might as well have arms that ended with seaweed fronds.

As the second-shift crew gathered behind their team leader and began disengaging the safety cable from their harnesses, Glissa thought for a moment to come up with an appropriate statement of Civil words to convey her satisfaction that she would once again be working with Sam. She looked up at the human, nervously smoothed the fine golden fur of her beard, and hoped that her pronunciation would be correct.

"Damn it, Sam, why the hall are they punishing me by making you work my shift?"

Glissa could tell from the quick smile that crossed Sam's face that she had got something wrong. Odd that Sam's face was so easily read, though. The long, soft brown hair and thick beard

11

he wore certainly helped, making Sam look less like a dormant tree slug than most barefaced humans did, and much more like an intelligent being. Too bad about the puny down-turned nose though, and those human eyes, beady little brown dots ringed by white like those of a week-old Tellarite corpse . . . they could make Glissa shudder if she stared at them too long.

But Sam looked away to the iron wall beneath his feet and leaned forward, dropping his voice to a whisper low enough that only a Tellarite could hear him.

"Hell, Glissa," Sam said gently. "You meant to say 'hell,' not 'hall.'"

Glissa nodded thoughtfully, appreciative that Sam had kept this part of their conversation private. "Which one is the underworld and which is the corridor?"

"Hell is the underworld. Humans don't get too excited about corridors. At least, not in Civil insults."

Glissa decided she would have to start making some notes if she were to keep up with Sam. "But the 'damn it' . . . ?"

"Perfect," Sam said, still whispering. "Proper place in the sentence, good intonation, very impressive. . . ." But then he stepped back in midsentence, looked up from the ground, and raised his voice again for all to hear. "For a beerswilling, gutbellied warthog, that is."

Glissa's cheeks ballooned out into tiny pink spheres as she snorted her delight. She wondered if Sam liked mud wallows. Perhaps he might like to be invited to join her in one. For the moment, though, there was work to do, and clever repartee and Civil Conversation must be put aside. But at least with Sam Jameson taking part, she felt sure the excitement of her job would remain. There would be time enough for friendship later.

After the shift briefing had been completed—in record time thanks to the way Sam was able to reinterpret the shift's goals for the other, more typical humans on the crew—the incoming chime of the cargo transporter finally sounded. It was deeper than the sound that came from most systems, since to save credits this project used only low-frequency models—less power hungry but not certified for biological transport. As

Glissa watched the first load of twenty-meter-long, black fiber support pylons materialize, she felt certain that her division's schedule would finally come back on line within a few shifts. Sam Jameson didn't disappoint her.

Cajoling the Tellarite client workers with appropriate Civil insults and adopting a more conciliatory tone for the humans, Sam had the crew latch antigravs to the pylons and clear the pad in record time, load after load. Glissa was still amazed at how easily the rockriggers took his orders. Perhaps his secret was that he used a subtly different approach with each individual, acknowledging that each was worthy of individual respect. Perhaps it was the way he moved among them, never shirking his turn at heavy labor the way some other shift leaders did. However he accomplished it, Glissa was impressed, and saddened, too. For whatever Sam Jameson had been before he came to Interworld, she was certain of one thing: he had not been a rockrigger.

By the time the main meal break came, a full shift's work had already been accomplished and, under Sam's direction, the crew actually seemed eager for more. For once Glissa was able to sit down to her *tak* and bloodrinds without feeling panic over the swiftness of time. She wished that she might share her meal break with Sam—she had thought of something exceptionally vile to call him and was looking forward to an equally inventive response—but she saw that he, as always, took his meal alone.

The other humans on the crew sat together, talking among themselves, occasionally glancing over at Sam where he sat against a large boulder. On the other hoof, the Tellarite client workers stood around and stared into the distance. Through one of the hundreds of visual sensors which fed images to the viewscreens in deference to the limits of Tellarite vision, Glissa observed them sampling the air with twitching noses.

Then she saw what they were waiting for. Two Tellarite pups—barely out of the litter pen—waddled along a safety path, guiding a small tractor wagon stacked with food trays. In actual fact, the meter-long tractor wagon guided the toddlers through the maze of gravity warning bands and the viewscreen showed that both were securely attached to the wagon by their harnesses.

The pups' mother was one of Sam's team and she welcomed her offspring proudly as they brought food to her and her fellow workers. Glissa was impressed with the seriousness of the young pups and the way they wore their commune's ceremonial red scarves, at such odds with the puffs of white fur that stood out so sweetly from their round little forms, like softly shaped clouds captured in blue overalls.

As she watched them on the screen, she heard familiar hoofsteps approaching. It was Sam.

"Are our pups as appealing to humans as they are to us?" Glissa asked, seeing that he, too, watched the young Tellarites at their work.

"The appeal of babies is universal," Sam said. "But it's such a shame those two will grow up to resemble something as ugly as you."

Glissa grunted happily and gestured to the slight rise of a digger's ridge beside her. "I have never met any human quite like you, Sam." Glissa spoke without using a Civil intonation.

Sam paused, then sat down next to her, resting his arms on his knees and swinging his safety helmet idly from his hands as he watched the pups. They had finished eating and were now wrestling furiously, tumbling over and over each other with excited squeaks and snorts. "Then I suspect you haven't met too many humans at all," Sam said.

Glissa folded her food tray shut, remembering what she had heard about what humans thought of bloodrinds. "I have met many humans here. Just none like you."

Sam shrugged but said nothing. He glanced up to check the time readout on a viewscreen. There were still a few minutes left in the break.

"Why are you here, Sam Jameson?"

For a moment, Sam's eyes changed in a way too alien for the Tellarite to understand. "Why are *you* here, Glissa?"

"To build new worlds," the Tellarite answered proudly.

14

A new expression appeared on Sam's face, and Glissa at least knew human misery when she saw it. "As if there weren't enough out there to begin with?"

Glissa didn't understand. She tried another approach. "You are not a hardcase."

The human smiled sadly at that, but still there were undercurrents to his expression that she couldn't read. "What makes you think I'm not?"

"Interworld is not known for asking too many questions of those who want to be rockriggers. The human hardcases we get seem to be those who are one step away from shipping out on the next Orion freighter." Then she peered closely at him, suddenly recalling how little sense of humor humans had. "Perhaps I should point out that I have used the term 'freighter' in a sarcastic sense, if that makes my joke more logical."

Sam looked away from her, his eyes somehow appearing to be more reflective, as if their moisture content had suddenly been elevated.

"Are you all right, Sam?"

"I'm fine," he said, and smiled again with that same gentle sadness. "You just reminded me of someone I knew . . . a long time ago."

"A close friend?"

"I think so. Though he might not want to admit it."

"The human hardcases we get seem not to have friends, Sam."

The human took a breath and stared up at the far wall of the rock, but she felt he was looking at something else which only he could see. "On Earth, centuries ago, there was an . . . organization much like Interworld's rockriggers."

"They built things? Surely not worlds so long ago, but . . . continents perhaps?"

"It was a military organization."

"How human. No offense intended," Glissa quickly added because this was not turning out to be a Civil Conversation.

"None taken," Sam said. "It was called *La Légion étrangère*.

It was the place to go to when there was no place else. No questions asked. They didn't even need to know a real name."

"Sometimes . . . that is a preferable circumstance," Glissa said as diplomatically as she was able. "Is it preferable to you?"

He turned to her and his face was unreadable. "No questions asked," he repeated.

"Too bad, Sam. You look like a being who has many answers."

He shook his head. "One answer is all it would take, Glissa. And I don't have it." He hefted his helmet to put it on. "That's why I'm here. That's why I'm a hardcase."

Glissa reached out to him, to place a soothing hoof on his shoulder. What was the answer he searched for? What possible reason could bring him here? "Sam, if there is anything that—"

The asteroid shifted.

A field of pulsed gravity swept over the work site. Glissa saw the bright spots of the lightpoles undulate as local gravitational constants fluctuated wildly. She grabbed at the rock beneath her, feeling herself rise up and down as if caught in a raging surf. Gravity warning alarms erupted from a hundred speakers, echoing shrilly from the hard iron floor of the rock.

"What is it?" she growled.

Sam's strong arms pushed her down between two iron ridges. He had expertly, instinctively, hooked his feet beneath a small ridge overhang at the first ripple of motion. "Harmonic interference," he shouted over the sirens. "One of the gravity generators must have cut out and the others didn't compensate in time."

Sam looped a safety strap around a second overhang, then fed it through one of Glissa's harness clips, fastening her safely in place. "Don't worry. It's self-correcting. There'll be a couple more fluctuations as the fields spread the load but we'll be all right."

"The pups?" Glissa squealed, unable to turn her head to the viewscreen as a high-g wave slammed her to the ground.

Sam craned his neck to look over to where the client worker

had been eating and the youngsters had been playing. "They're fine, they're fine. They're still hooked to the tractor wagon." He grabbed onto Glissa as a low-g wave rippled back, sending him half a meter into the air. "See? It's getting weaker."

"How do you know so much about artificial gravity fields?" the Tellarite demanded.

But before Sam could answer, the asteroid shifted again as another gravity generator failed—and another, twisting the rocky shell in two directions at once. A low rumbling sound began, mixed with the shriek of tearing metal. Sam turned to the source, eyes widening like the face of the dead as he saw—"The lake bed!"

Glissa grunted with a sudden and terrible knowledge. "The pylons are not in place. The lake bed cannot—"

The first pressure siren wailed, drowning out the gravity warning alarms.

"No!" Sam fixed on something Glissa couldn't see.

"What is it?"

"NO!" Sam untangled himself from Glissa's harness and unhooked his feet from the rock ledge.

"Sam, what?"

"The children!" As Sam leapt over Glissa and scrambled away, the wind began.

Glissa struggled to sit up. The wind could only mean the thin lake bed floor had cracked in the stress of the gravity harmonics. And there was nothing beneath it except the vacuum of space.

The Tellarite heard the screams of her work crew mix with the wild screech of disappearing air and the clamor of sirens and alarms. She slapped her hoof against the nearest viewscreen control, calling up image after image until she tapped into a sensor trained at the lake bed.

"Dear Kera," she whispered as she saw the pups trailing at the end of their safety cables, only ten meters from a ragged tear in the rock floor through which debris and white tendrils of atmosphere were sucked into nothingness. "Dear Phinda," she cried as she saw Sam Jameson, crouching against a ridge near the youngsters, attaching a second cable to an immovable outcropping of metal.

Glissa switched on the panel communicator's transmit circuits. If she could send this image to cargo control perhaps they could lock onto Sam and the pups. Surely the risk of being transported at low frequency was better than the certain death of being sucked out into space. If only the pups' cables would hold. If only Sam would stay in position.

But the cables were anchored to the small tractor wagon and the winds were pushing it closer and closer to the fissure. And no matter how little Glissa knew of the real Sam Jameson, she knew enough to know that nothing could keep him from going to the pups.

Glissa called out coordinates to cargo control as Sam pushed himself up from the safety of the ridge and moved out into the open, slowly playing out his safety line, pulled taut by the force of the gale that blew against him.

He moved across the open lake bed in the finally stabilized gravity as if he were aware of nothing but the infants, now only six meters from the opening into space. Rocks and debris flew past him. Some hit him. But he ignored their impact and the blossoms of red human blood that they brought. Glissa had never been able to completely understand much of what Sam felt, but at this moment, his intent so fixed, his concentration so powerful, she was sure that the human felt no fear.

Sam reached the slowly skidding tractor wagon. Its in-use lights were out, its power exhausted by fighting the inexorable wind. He wrapped his arms around its sensor pod, trying to stop its movement. Glissa switched sensors and brought up an image of Sam as he strained against the impossible pressure. His cable was pulled to its limit. Glissa could see his arms tremble with the force he was exerting. But the tractor still slid forward. The squealing infants still slipped toward the inescapable pull of the vacuum.

Sam's eyes blazed, and of the few human emotions Glissa could recognize, she knew it was anger that lit his eyes. Then he reached to his harness and disengaged his cable. Glissa called out to him to stop though she knew he would never hear her.

The tractor wagon bounced a meter forward on the lake bed as Sam swung around it and began crawling down the length of the youngsters' cable. He reached them as they were only three meters from the fissure. And it was widening, Glissa saw with sickened certainty. Where was cargo control?

Two meters from the fissure, Sam had both round forms in his arms. He pushed against the gale and the floor. But where was he going? And then Glissa saw his plan. There was a smaller ridge almost within reach. With an effort which she would not have thought was possible for a human, Sam pushed the pups into position against it. If they didn't move, they would be safe as long as the atmosphere lasted. But how could he keep them there when the ridge wasn't large enough for him as well?

Glissa could only moan as she saw what the human did next. He *removed* his harness—his last hope for survival—and wound it around the infants, using its straps to tie them firmly into place.

"Please, no," Glissa prayed to the twin Moons as she saw Sam's fingers desperately try to dig into the unyielding surface of the metal ridge. She prayed to the mists and the mud and all the litters of heaven but it was the heavens that were claiming the human now.

Sam slipped from the ridge. He fell toward the fissure. Toward space. Toward the stars.

And he caught himself on the opening, arms and legs braced to hold on for a few more hopeless seconds.

Glissa caused the sensor to close in on Sam's face and fill a hundred viewscreens throughout the rock so his heroism and his sacrifice would be remembered by all.

What manner of human was he? What manner of being? He had no chance yet still he struggled. And on his face, an instant from oblivion, poised above an endless fall into the absolute night of space, *there was still no fear in him.*

Tears streamed from Glissa's small eyes because she did not know what she witnessed. He faced the stars and death with a

19

ferocious defiance she could not imagine. *They shall name this world for you,* Glissa thought. *I swear it, Sam. Sam Jameson. My friend.* And with that vow, the human's hands slipped for the final time.

The stars had won.

But the howl of the wind abruptly stopped as a near-deafening transporter chime overpowered the wail of the sirens and alarms.

Glissa peered closely at the viewscreen as Sam slowly rolled away from the fissure. Within it, the familiar glow of the transporter effect sparkled from the smooth metal walls. Cargo control had not transported Sam and the pups *out,* they had transported pressure sealant *in.*

Glissa tapped her hooves to her forehead in thanks to the Moons, then unhooked her harness and ran out to the lake bed to welcome Sam to his second life. But when she joined him, others had arrived before her. And she was shocked to see anger and disgust in their eyes.

The Tellarite pups, now only sobbing fitfully, were cradled by their mother and her fellow workers. The fissure had become nothing more than a long scar mounded with the hardened blue foam of pressure sealant. Sam sat slumped against the ridge that had protected the pups, his work clothes torn, blood streaming from a dozen wounds. But the humans clustered near him offered no help. They only whispered among themselves.

Glissa pushed through them and went to Sam's side.

"I'd think twice about doin' anything for 'im," one of the humans said. He was taller and heavier than Sam, and wore a punishment tattoo from a penal colony.

"What do you mean?" Glissa demanded as she knelt to cradle Sam's hands in her hooves. "He saved those pups."

"Use your eyes," a second human said. Female this time, as big as the one with the tattoo. "Didn't you see him on the viewscreens?"

"Of course," Glissa answered uncertainly.

"And you didn't recognize him? From the holos? From the updates? Before he grew the beard?"

Glissa turned to Sam. "What are they saying?"

The woman kicked a stone toward Sam. "Go ahead. Tell her what we're saying. If you've got the stomach for it."

"Sam?"

"That's not *his* name, Boss," a third human said scornfully. He was shorter, rounder, more compact, from a high-g world, and he moved forward to stand before Sam and Glissa. He glared down at the wounded human and the Tellarite beside him.

"You're Kirk, aren't you?" the short human said, and Glissa's nostrils flared at the mention of that terrible name. "The one who was captain of the *Enterprise,* aren't you?"

Glissa stared deep into Sam's eyes. "No," she whispered. "No, not you."

But his eyes held that one answer at least.

Glissa let the human's hands slip away from her hooves.

"Murderer!" the human woman said as she kicked another stone at the wounded man's side.

"Butcher!" The short human spat on the wounded man's boots.

Glissa stood up, torn, dismayed, but knowing that her job had to come first. "That's enough!" she growled at the rockriggers. "We've still got half a shift to put in and I want you back at work—*now!*"

They hesitated and Glissa gave them a snarl that needed no translation. Muttering among themselves, they left the lake bed.

The human she had known as Sam Jameson looked up at her as if to speak, but she raised a hoof to silence him, trying to suppress the shudder of revulsion that passed through her. This monster already had a world named after him. "There is nothing more to be said. I will have your account closed out and book your passage on the next outbound shuttle. You should . . . you should leave here as quickly as possible. Before too many others find out." She had to look away from him. "The company will not be able to guarantee your safety."

The human said nothing. Glissa left him to join the client workers and explain what had happened for those who didn't understand Standard. As if the name Kirk needed translation. As if the entire universe didn't know of his crimes.

While Glissa and the other Tellarites talked in low grunts and whispers, the two pups slowly approached the wounded human, watching with concern in their large black eyes as he stood up unsteadily and his blood dripped slowly to splatter on the ground.

One of the youngsters, braver than the other, stepped forward and solemnly untied his scarf. With tiny hooves, he held it out to the human, who stared at the scarf, as if uncertain about accepting it.

"Please," the young Tellarite said. "Let me help."

The human started, and as Glissa and the other Tellarites watched, he looked down into the pup's earnest eyes almost as if he were seeing someone else's face, hearing words that someone else might have said to him long ago. He spoke gently to the pup as he took the scarf and held it to his wounds. Then he turned and walked away, head upright, each step certain.

Glissa felt unexpected tears roll from her eyes as she watched him leave, for in all the worlds in all of space, she knew there was no place left for James T. Kirk to go.

TWO

☆

It had not been a clean death for his beauty. She had not, as he had sometimes imagined she might, been swallowed by a nova, or been lost by braving the unimaginable depths of a black hole. Nor, perhaps most noble of all, by giving her life so that others might live.

Instead, the *Enterprise* had been butchered—stripped of her power and her speed and cruelly deformed between the opposing infinities of normal space and the Cochrane subset. Much of the ship still remained, but her heart and her soul were lost.

Chief Engineer Montgomery Scott found himself thinking that it might have been better if the ship had died all at once. And he with her.

In the silence of the aft observation lounge, deserted in the ship's early morning cycle, Scott leaned his head against the cool smoothness of the viewport. He closed his eyes, thinking of another time when he might have touched any part of the ship and felt within her the hum of her generators, powered by the wedding song of matter and antimatter. But there were no vibrations now. That life had fled. The emergency lights strung haphazardly through the ship were powered by batteries beamed in from other vessels, and the occasional movement lags of the gravity generators fighting the inertial dampeners came from the rough handling of shuttle tugs and not the smooth pulse of the ship's own thrusters.

Scott opened his eyes again. His breath had fogged the viewport and the haze it made suddenly flared silver white as the *Enterprise*'s orbit took her over the terminator of the moon below, into the full reflected light of Talin's sun. Scott's torment at seeing the ship suddenly painted with the brilliant light reflected from the airless desert moving 500 kilometers beneath her was still as intense as the first time he had stared out and seen what had been done to her.

The bluewhite gleam of her hull metal was streaked with carbonized traceries from the energy arcs that had penetrated her overloaded shields. And the dark scarring was constantly being augmented by the thrusters of the workbee shuttles that hovered around her, carrying out emergency repairs so the ship could be safely towed back to the spacedock at Starbase 29—if and when the decision to fully repair her was finally made.

Scott's trained eye scanned the upper surface of the engineering hull, evaluating the inelegant arrangement of roughly bonded pressure plates and repair bands. He cringed at the imperfection of the work. No real crew member of the *Enterprise* would dare treat her that way, so inconsiderately, as if she were no more than metal and machinery. It was an attitude he might have had to remind new ensigns about in their first few weeks on board. But after a month or so, even the greenest recruits had needed no reminding about how to treat this ship. They felt it. They knew it. Not like those starbase mechanics who bounced from job to job and who were working on her now. Scott and a handful of others on board were all that remained of the *Enterprise*'s original crew.

The starboard support pylon was canted aft at least eight degrees from true, and Scott sighed as he watched the workbees' mechanical grippers attaching the large black panels of tractor-beam collectors to the surface of it. The mechanics planned to *force* the pylon back into position to restore warp balance to the ship's superstructure, so she could be towed at warp speed. But

Scott couldn't see the point. Not with the starboard warp-propulsion nacelle completely gone—the one that Spock had managed to jettison in time. Unlike the port nacelle.

The port nacelle was the reason why the *Enterprise* was still in orbit around Talin's moon—kept there so she could be studied in the same way Karunda coroner beetles swarmed to dissect the corpses of their prey. She was the first ship to have engaged warp drive while still within the Danylkiw Limit of a planet's gravity well and survive, even partially. Three and a half months earlier, Scott would have said that such a thing would not be possible. After all, until they had been properly tuned and balanced, it was still foolhardy to run tandem warp engines within the Danylkiw Limit of a solar system, let alone a class-M planet. And though the tuning procedures were improving each year as the technicians zeroed in on the theoretical upper limits of warp efficiency, Scott was certain that for at least the next ten years any ship attempting a tandem test run too close to a star would run the risk of falling into either an Einsteinian wormhole or a Danylkiw Singularity.

Certainly modern warp engines—properly tuned and broken-in, of course—could be engaged within gravity wells at depths corresponding to standard orbits, but it was almost unthinkable to imagine the day when a warp drive could be engaged so deep within a planet's gravity well as to be in atmosphere. At least, those had been Scott's thoughts at the time. But three and a half months ago, the *Enterprise* had done just that—engaged warp drive within the atmosphere of Talin IV. And the proof of it was the nightmarish remains of her port nacelle.

The forward section of the nacelle was still in perfect condition. At the time of the incident, the propulsion dome-disperser pylon had been deployed for routine discharge maintenance and the stubby projection was still in place, unbent and undisturbed. But thirty meters back from the lip of the dome, the first rippling deformations in the nacelle's cylindrical hull became apparent. Fifty meters back, and the hull took on the appearance of a piece of stretched taffy, just like the candy Sulu had once spent six months cooking and sculpting into birds and dragons on the ends of sticks. By sixty meters, the rest of the nacelle was completely gone, supposedly compressed to a point through the inconceivable multidimensional pathways that led out of four-dimensional spacetime and into the other realms in which warp speeds were possible.

Where the rest of the nacelle was actually located was still a matter of debate. Twelve experts from the Cochrane Institute on Centaurus had been brought in to study the wreckage, along with representatives from Starfleet Operations, its Science and Engineering Divisions, and the Space Safety Board. The first arguments among the twenty-being task force had apparently been settled when two weeks' worth of sensor readings convinced the experts that the nacelle continued to be drawn into warp space at the rate of about one atomic diameter a day. Scott had been outraged at the interpretation of the findings because any child knew that the secret of warp transition was that it was instantaneous. You were in or you were out, but you could never be halfway. He had tried to convince the experts that the phenomenon they were witnessing was somehow related to the fusion blasts the *Enterprise* had been subjected to, or the unfathomable subspace pulse that had burned out every centimeter of transtator circuitry in her, but the experts' only response had been to hold their subsequent meetings in private and continue to chart the slow disappearance of the ship, molecule by molecule.

As far as Scott could determine, cut off as he was from the experts and their planning sessions, the current debate raging through Starfleet Engineering was whether the remainder of the port nacelle could be detached from the *Enterprise* without triggering a slingshot reaction which would destroy the rest of her, or whether the ship should simply be decommissioned and serve out the rest of her days as a sacrificial experimental model, constantly monitored to see how far her gradual evaporation would proceed.

Scott rubbed his hands against his face, trying to bring order to his thoughts. Just thinking about the mad ideas of the know-nothing, planetbound, viewscreen jockeys who had the power to decide the *Enterprise*'s fate made his head swim. He had never felt such frustration, such helplessness. *At least,* he thought for the thousandth time, *at least if I had been on the bridge, then this would be over for me, too, and I'd be with the captain. Wherever the poor lad is.*

Scott put his hand to the viewport, only centimeters separating him from the emptiness of space. Somewhere James Kirk was out there. And somewhere, there were answers. Just beyond the reach of his hand.

Behind him, the observation lounge doors puffed open. Scott recognized the swagger in the steps of the officer who entered, and sighed.

"Good morning, Mr. Scott. The work is proceeding nicely, wouldn't you say?"

Scott took a breath to calm himself. In the viewport's reflection he saw the glowing lights of that damned swagger stick spin through the air as Lieutenant Styles flipped it under his arm. Scott didn't care if the insufferable, self-righteous ass *had* wrested the stick away from a Klingon in hand-to-hand combat. It was still a damned annoying affectation on a ship at least a hundred lightyears from the nearest equine creature.

"Aye, I suppose it is." Scott couldn't bring himself to look at the man. The lieutenant didn't belong in charge of the *Enterprise*. Only one person did. Only one person ever would.

Styles stood beside Scott at the viewport and bounced twice on his toes. He crossed his hands behind his back and waved the swagger stick around behind his back, as if scaring away flies. The chief engineer thought dark thoughts of a transporter beam set to maximum dispersion.

"You don't sound too pleased, Mr. Scott."

Scott stared at the lieutenant in the reflection, hating the smug smile that split the man's sharp features.

"There's only one way to treat this ship, Mr. Styles."

Styles rapped his stick against the viewport, indicating the swarm of workbees thrusting around the starboard pylon. "And you don't feel those chaps are treating this ship the right way?"

27

"I have already submitted my reports and my recommendations."

Styles turned to the engineer and Scott glanced at him. Then stared in shock as he saw that Styles no longer wore the stylized comet insignia of the USS *Monitor* on his gold command shirt. He wore the insignia of the *Enterprise*.

"Like it?" Styles asked, seeing the surprise in Scott's eyes.

"I . . . dinna understand."

"Now, Mr. Scott, how difficult can it be? Starfleet has reassigned me. I'm commanding the *Enterprise* now."

No, Scott thought. *Never.* "A ship needs a captain, Lieutenant."

Styles smiled again with far too many teeth. "An *operational* ship needs a captain, Mr. Scott. And the *Enterprise* is anything but."

"The 'experts' haven't made up their minds, then?"

Styles rocked his head back and forth. "In a manner of speaking. The decision has been made to detach what's remaining of the port nacelle. Of course, the tugs will take the ship out of the system first, just in case. . . ."

Scott had to look away. They were gambling with all that was left of the *Enterprise*. "In case she slingshots into warp? What do they think is going to happen to her then, that hasn't happened already?" He kept the remainder of what he wanted to say about the starbase mechanics to himself. No matter how badly he felt, he was still a Starfleet officer.

Styles tapped his swagger stick thoughtfully against the side of his neck, apparently oblivious to Scott's imperfectly concealed rage. "If the ship does slingshot, then it's apt to be an unfocused transition. The Cochrane people have calculated that the starbow effect could be quite . . . spectacular and the First Contact officials feel that every step should be taken to ensure that the event is not observable from the surface of Talin IV. The Prime Directive's taken enough of a beating down there as it is, wouldn't you say?" Styles chuckled. "Not that anyone thinks it's very likely that the Talin are putting much effort into astronomy these days."

"And if the ship doesn't slingshot?" Which she won't, Scott knew. There was more chance of her sprouting wings and flapping her way back to a starbase.

The lieutenant's cheeriness was intolerable. "Then there happen to be two Constitution-rated warp nacelles at Earth Spacedock—"

"Intended for the *Intrepid II*," Scott interrupted. He kept up with the production reports.

Styles shook his head. "Come now, Mr. Scott. It would take more than a year to finish a new ship from scratch. But with new nacelles and a full wiring team of construction drones, the *Enterprise* could be back in service in a tenth the time."

Scott stared at the man, suddenly seeing the real reason for his good spirits. "And then, of course, she'd be needing a new captain, wouldn't she?"

Styles reached out to pat Scott's shoulder. "Thank you for your vote of confidence, Mr. Scott, though I'm afraid I'd just be first officer to begin with. But in time . . . she would be mine. Oh, yes. And then we'd see how the *Enterprise* could perform with a real captain at her helm."

Scott had a difficult decision to make and, in the end, he decided not to deck Styles. There were more honorable ways to attempt to leave the service than by striking a superior officer. He was an engineer, after all, and not Dr. McCoy. "Lieutenant Styles, sir?"

"Yes?"

"When the time comes for the port nacelle to be detached . . ."

"Go on."

"With all respect, sir, I hope she slingshots ye all the way to hell."

As Styles sputtered, Scott squared his shoulders and marched unhurriedly from the observation lounge. He had to leave. Even if there were better ways to leave the service than by striking Styles, for the moment the engineer couldn't think of a single one.

Later, in the privacy of his quarters, Scott stared at his

personal viewscreen. A small yellow light flashed in the upper right corner telling him he had a message waiting, but he was damned if he was going to give any more of his time to the mechanics who were working to pass this ship into the insensitive hands of a sanctimonious prig like Styles.

Beside his viewscreen was a tall green glass bottle of single malt whisky from Earth, unopened and unsynthesized. Once, during the tense stationkeeping orbits around Sarpeidon, Uhura had decrypted Mr. Spock's birthday from his personnel records and had passed it on to other select members of the crew. Scott had planned to surprise the science officer with a gift from the Scottish heather when Spock's next birthday came around. He had had no doubt that on such an occasion Mr. Spock would take one of his rare drinks of alcohol—and that he would have no objection to Scott and McCoy and the captain, and the other select crew members, finishing the remainder of the bottle for him. But Talin IV had come around before that birthday, and those who were to share Spock's gift were never to be together again.

Scott hefted the bottle, imagining what it would be like to open it and have it all to himself, drinking enough that Styles and the *Enterprise*'s ruin would drop away from him. Perhaps enough that he could see his friends across the table from him again, the mission continuing, all as it should be, as it was supposed to be, forever. But he knew that wasn't an answer and never would be.

He studied the bottle's label, reading of the peat and the centuries-old traditions, remembering all the other times he had shared its like with the captain, thinking of all the other worlds they had traveled to, and all the other worlds there were still left for them to visit.

"Och, you're Mr. Spock's birthday present and I'll not be opening ye till we're all sitting together as we belong. In uniform or not." He laid the bottle on its side on his bunk, to protect it from any sudden lurches courtesy of the mechanics outside. He still had a few duties to attend to, even as chief engineer of a nonoperational ship. "Screen on."

30

Scott's viewscreen came to life, still displaying the final transmission feed he had requested the night before. The text caption running beneath the image identified the transmission source as sensor satellite two, one of eight the *Enterprise* had placed into orbit around Talin IV, half a million kilometers distant from its moon, on behalf of Starfleet's First Contact Office.

The satellite was in a fixed, geostationary position above the planet's main ocean, and three months earlier Scott had seen the images it had obtained of fission-powered sea vessels following diverse trade and transportation routes. The visual resolution from 38,000 kilometers had been crisp enough to show individual Talin on the decks of their vessels, enabling the FCO to distinguish between fishing factories, freighters, and passenger ships. In other wavelengths, electromagnetic and otherwise, the satellites could also pick up the heat trails of submersible vehicles, deep beneath the oceans' surface, and even identify the nation states to which they belonged from manufacturing and design differences, and the weaponry each carried.

But now, the oceans of Talin IV were devoid of vessels, submersible or otherwise, and the weaponry the nation states had stockpiled had all been expended. Where the planet's sun could still shine through the few gaps in the globe-encircling clouds created by that weaponry, the once blue ocean was stained deep purple. An as-yet-unidentified mutation in a single-celled algaelike organism had blossomed throughout the world's seas, swiftly overwhelming the radiation-devastated ecosystem. Undoubtedly other ecological outrages were unfolding as dramatically throughout the rest of the planet's biosphere as well.

"Change views," Scott said grimly and the screen flickered once, revealing a new image of the world from over the secondary temperate continent now, where the FCO had once concentrated their sampling runs. Scott recognized the distinctive southern coastline, but that was all. The major agricultural bands that stretched across the land mass were scorched and lifeless, as blackened as the battle damage that scarred the *Enterprise.* Once, the crops from that land had fed tens of millions.

Scott stared at the screen with grief and revulsion. At the Academy, all cadets were required to study the worlds that had been destroyed by their dominant species' wars and environmental mismanagement. Those harsh lessons were at the core of the Federation's underlying principles of respect for life in all forms. Even the Klingons knew how fortunate they were to have survived global warfare and ecological collapse to become spacefarers. So few self-aware, technological species had. The *Enterprise,* in her time, had visited enough of those barren worlds to engrave the lessons permanently in the hearts and minds of her crew: War was never an answer and life must be held sacred above all else. Only the Prime Directive came as close in importance in determining the goals and actions of the Federation.

And Scott still couldn't understand how such honorable ideals, in the hands of a captain who had dedicated his life to upholding them, could have possibly led to the horrifying obscenity of the dying world on the viewscreen.

But others could, it seemed. For the first time Scott noticed everything that was printed out on the screen to identify the feed: SENSOR SATELLITE FIVE / 310° LONG / 205° LAT / 00:91:24 / KIRK'S WORLD.

Scott slapped his hand against the base of the machine, hitting its manual power switch hard enough to make the screen shake. "Ye slimy sons o' . . ." His voice choked off in anger. He had heard the replacement crew using that hateful name for Talin IV, and now they had gone so far as to program it into the automated logs. Well, he'd program a worm to go through the computer and delete all references. He'd take Styles's name out of the duty roster as well, transfer him to kitchen operations. *I'll turn this ship upside down before I'll . . .*

"Och, what's the use?" Scott said to the silence of his room. He'd been thinking: *before I'll let them win.* But the truth was, they already had.

The message light kept blinking at him from the blank screen. *What could be left to tell me that would be worse than what I already know?* he thought.

"Computer: Present my messages, please."

"Working," the computer's familiar voice said. The ship's backup datastores had had enough shielding to escape the subspace pulse that had destroyed the computer system's main circuitry. Once the standard replacement components had been installed in the first stages of the *Enterprise's* emergency repairs, full computer functions and memory had been restored with only a 1.5 second gap in the sensor readings preceding the pulse, which was the length of time it took dynamic memory to be written to permanent backup. Even with mortal wounds, she was a fine ship.

The viewscreen presented the image of an unencrypted ComSys transmission screen—a common method by which Starfleet personnel could receive personal messages over subspace. Scott's name was clearly encoded at the top of the screen, overprinting the blue background shield of the United Federation of Planets. The stardate showed it had been received less than an hour ago. The message was tagged as one of one, but the sender's name was not listed.

Trying not to fool himself into hoping it was a message from the captain, Scott asked the computer to play back the recorded transmission. The screen cleared again, but not to an image of the message's sender—simply a screen of black text on a white background. Scott leaned forward to read it.

Command Bulletin: Effective this stardate, Spock, Ensign, S179-276SP, Science Specialist, Starfleet Technology Support Division, San Francisco, Earth, has resigned his commission in Starfleet. Resignation accepted, effective as received, Admiral Raycheba, Starfleet TechSupDiv.

Scott swore. "They broke him to a bloody *ensign?* What are they thinking of? How could—"

The viewscreen flashed the word 'more.'

"Continue," Scott said, and the message began to scroll.

Spock is the last of the so-called *Enterprise* Five to resign from Starfleet. Starfleet Command Information Office has issued related statements calling for all Starfleet personnel to learn from the tragic lessons of the incident at Talin IV, and to prove to the citizens of the Federation that the actions of a handful of renegade officers do not reflect upon the exemplary training and—

"Screen *off*, computer. Screen bloody off!"

The viewscreen darkened instantly.

"Computer: Who had the gall to send that message to me?" Scott's voice trembled so badly that he wondered if the computer would recognize him.

"Message unattributed."

Scott slowly and rhythmically pounded his fist on his work desk. "Aye, it would be, the cowards. It would be." He wanted to put his fist through a bulkhead. He wanted to shout loudly enough that they'd hear him back at Command. He wanted a stage to tell the worlds of the injustice of all that had transpired. But McCoy had been right.

The doctor had begged to be court-martialed. He had even punched Vice Admiral Hammersmith in front of witnesses at Starbase 29 when he and Spock had been transferred to Technology Support. That's when McCoy had sent word back to Scott that it was obvious that none of them was going to be put through any type of trial, secret or otherwise. As far as Command was concerned, the less said about Talin IV, the less damage would be done to Starfleet. "They have better ways to get us out of the damned service," McCoy had said to Scott in a subspace message.

And then the doctor had been the first to resign, without even going on report for striking an officer—proof as far as McCoy was concerned that Starfleet wasn't about to give any of them a public forum. Kirk followed McCoy's lead when Uhura had been jailed. Sulu and Chekov left together. Spock had been determined to fight from within the system, but it seemed that not even a Vulcan could stand up to the combined weight of Starfleet and the Federation Council. So, just as McCoy had said, the *Enterprise* Five had been banished from the service without incident, without trial, and without record. Starfleet had obtained almost everything that it had wanted.

I might as well give them the last of it, Scott thought, opening his fist into a useless hand. *There's nothing left to fight for. Not from here, at least.*

"Computer."

"Working."

"Prepare a hardcopy message to Lieutenant Styles, USS— no, make that to Vice Admiral Hammersmith, Starbase 29." Scott would be damned before he would acknowledge Styles as master of this ship. Since Starbase 29 was the closest Federation administrative outpost to the Talin system and had been given authority over the *Enterprise*'s disposition, Scott reasoned that the base's commander was the next logical choice to address his message to. He thought Mr. Spock would agree.

"From Scott, etc. Message goes: Effective immediately, I wish to tender my resignation from Star—"

"Clarification," the computer interrupted.

"Aye, what is it?"

"Starfleet Command Regulation 106, Paragraph 1, specifically identifies the role of the chief engineer and/or designated subsystem specialists as subject to preeminent exception to Term of Service Procedures as detailed in Starfleet Com—"

"Computer: Could ye digest that gobbledygook for me?"

"The chief engineer cannot resign while the *Enterprise* is undergoing a class-two refit."

Scott put his elbow on the desk and rested his head on his hand. It wasn't just personnel like Styles, even Starfleet equipment was out to get him. But Scott had picked up a few tricks in his years with Kirk. Especially when it came to Kirk's way with computers. "Computer, if I resign, effective *immediately,* then I will no longer be the chief engineer when Vice Admiral Hammersmith receives my message, therefore he will not be empowered to prevent my resignation."

But the computer didn't hesitate for a microsecond. "That is a circular argument."

"Well, then, let me put it to you this way: If you don't transmit my message to Hammersmith, then I shall rewire you into a food processor."

This time the computer remained silent.

"Well, computer? What are ye doing?"

"Scanning personnel records of Montgomery Scott to project hypothetical level of technical proficiency in the reconstruction of organic material synthesizers from duotronic components."

"And . . . ?"

The computer reset its audio circuits. It sounded like someone clearing her throat. "Message as dictated reads: 'Effective immediately, I wish to tender my resignation from Star—.' Please proceed."

Scott sighed. "Thank you, computer." It was a small victory, but these days Scott was grateful to take any that he could get. He felt it would be a long time before he would taste anything like it again, if ever. He glanced at the wall over his chest of drawers where his bagpipes hung. Twenty meters beyond them was open space. And the captain. And McCoy. And all the rest of those who rightfully belonged on the *Enterprise*. Perhaps by resigning, Spock was acknowledging that McCoy had shown them all the way. It was not logical to expect to uncover the real reasons behind what had happened at Talin IV by battling Starfleet. Perhaps Starfleet wasn't the enemy here. Perhaps there were other enemies, and other ways to find victory.

Scott turned back to the patient viewscreen which displayed the words he had dictated. Though it was difficult for the engineer to admit it, for the first time machinery wasn't enough. He no longer belonged on board the *Enterprise*. What had made this ship so special was her crew and her captain. The spirit of her would live just as well somewhere else, as long as they could be together.

And they would be together again, Scott suddenly realized. They had to be.

Scott smiled, the first time he had felt like it in months. Then he spoke the rest of the words that would free him from Starfleet, so like Spock and Kirk and McCoy and all the rest, he could do what duty demanded of him.

THREE

───────── ☆ ─────────

"They musta been sorta crazy, doncha think, mister?" the child asked, wrinkling her face in consternation. She was about eight standard years old, taller than most her age which meant she was probably from one of the smaller Martian cities where the citizens had voted against higher gravity. But the clothes she wore—a lacrosse jersey from one of the intersystem championship leagues sloppily pulled over balloon overalls and red Skorcher moccasins—could have come from child outfitters anywhere from the Venus highdomes to the Triton hollowcells. Sol system, which once had been such a grand adventure, had become one large city, less than one-millionth of a subspace-second across.

Leonard McCoy scratched at the six-week growth of whiskers that was slowly and itchily becoming a beard. It was one thing being back in his home system in a cabin in a nature reserve, but civilization was making him edgy. When had the Moon gotten this built up and civilized, anyway? It wasn't the same as he remembered it had been when he was a boy.

"Doncha think, mister? Huh, mister?"

McCoy looked down at the child standing beside him at the railing. "Don't you know you shouldn't talk to strangers?"

The child blinked at him. "You're not that strange, mister. I

38

38

talked to an Andorian once. They listen through these feeler things on their heads. They look sorta like they got two blue worms stickin' up from their heads or somethin'." The child shook her head knowingly. "Now that's strange."

"Well, young lady, Andorians think we're strange because our ears are squashed to the sides of our heads. In fact, they wonder how we can hear anything. And compared to them, we don't hear a lot." McCoy decided to spare the child a recitation of the standard frequencies of a typical Andorian's hearing range.

"Wow, do you know any Andorians, mister?"

McCoy was bothered that the child was impressed by the fact that he might have known an Andorian or two in his life. It was such a little thing. Especially considering that the child and McCoy were standing at the viewing railing of Tranquility Park. Fifty meters away beyond the transparent aluminum wall, the spindly-looking second stage of the first crewed vehicle to land on Earth's Moon sat beneath the brilliant, unfiltered sunshine as it had for more than two hundred years. Where McCoy and the child stood had once been an unimaginable frontier, the quest for which had shaped the dreams of an entire century of living, breathing, and hoping human beings.

Those pioneers had come to this dead world in fragile ships powered by chemical rockets and controlled by binary computers only one step removed from an abacus. They had come without the capability for remaining more than a handful of hours, and decades before the development of any technology that could be reasonably utilized here. Why? So they could hop around for a few minutes in constricting, multilayered environmental suits that had been needle-sewn together by hand, and scoop up an unrepresentative few kilos of surface rocks and soil. Now almost two and a half centuries later, the anonymous spot which Armstrong and Aldrin had reached by risking their lives as the final two humans in a chain of thousands who had toiled years toward that goal, had become a holiday resort—a favorite stop for honeymooners and students on day excursions from Earth.

Civilization, McCoy thought sourly. *The death of dreams.* He narrowed his eyes at the child. "Look, kid . . . what's your name?"

"Glynis," she said.

"Well, Glynis, do you know what that is out there by the old flag?"

The child gave an exaggerated nod. "The lower stage of the Lunar Excursion Module, *Eagle*," she recited. "Launched July 16, oldstyle one nine six nine C.E. The first of twelve successful landings on the Moon prior to the building of Base One. Launch authority was . . . um, the National Space and . . . no, the National Aeronautics and Space Administration. Uh, the United States of North . . . no, just of America." Glynis grinned happily up at McCoy. "Neil A. Armstrong, Commander. Edwin E. Aldrin, Lunar Excursion Module pilot. Michael Collins, Command Module Pilot. 'We came in peace for all mankind.'"

McCoy was impressed. He was never surprised when children could reel off the names of every lacrosse player in the system—along with their favorite colors and breakfast foods, or the complete lyrics and plot nuances of the latest holosaga, but he thought it rare to find a child who had turned her innate talents to the study of history. "That's very good," he said, and meant it. "Now how does a girl your age happen to know all that?"

The child became very solemn. "I have to."

McCoy raised an eyebrow. "And why's that?"

"You haveta know that stuff to get into the Academy."

"Starfleet Academy?"

Glynis nodded again, mouth set, very serious.

"How old are you?" McCoy asked.

"Almost nine."

"And you already know you want to join Starfleet?"

The child looked puzzled as if she didn't understand why McCoy had asked the question. "I have to," she said.

"You have to? Why?"

She drew herself up and looked proudly into McCoy's eyes. "I'm going to work on a . . . starship."

McCoy heard the slight hesitation in the child's voice as she said that final word, almost as if there was too much magic in it to ever speak the word lightly. He understood. But still . . .

"You want to work on a starship and you think the Moon pioneers were 'sorta crazy'?"

Glynis gazed out at the lunar landing stage in the middle of the stark graywhite landscape. "That's nothin' like a starship. It's kinda small, doncha think? And they didn't have enough radiation shielding. And no gravity. And they had to use electricity to run their systems. And—"

McCoy squatted down by the child to bring his eyes level to hers, and held up a finger to quiet her, just for a moment. "You know, a hundred years from now, if they ever build that transporter beam wave guide from the Earth to here and people can visit the Moon in two seconds instead of two hours, little children are going to be saying the same thing about us and how crazy we were because we had to get here in old-fashioned impulse shuttles."

The child looked skeptical. "Yeah?"

"Yeah," McCoy said. He pointed out to the *Eagle*'s landing stage. "What you have to remember when you look out there is that that machine isn't some flimsy, primitive, radiation-transparent antique."

"It's not?"

McCoy shook his head. "More than two hundred years ago, when children looked at the *Eagle,* that was *their* starship. And they dreamed about flying on it for all the same reasons that you want to fly on the starships we have today."

Glynis looked away from McCoy, squinting out through the double-story window overlooking Tranquility Base. "That was sorta all they had back then, wasn't it?"

"But when they launched it, it was the best."

"And there're going to be better starships a hundred years from now?"

McCoy nodded.

"But the ones we have now . . . they're the best, right?"

"Yes. They are." McCoy was hit with a sudden wave of sadness and he wasn't surprised.

The child thought about that answer for a moment, and McCoy could almost see her rearranging facts within her mind, pulling out pictures of old-fashioned spacecraft and sticking them beside state-of-the-art Constitution-class vessels.

"I wonder what it was like to live back then," she said.

McCoy straightened up again. "Just the same as it is to live now." He smiled at the child's look of surprise. "The spaceships change, but people don't. That's one of the things you'll learn in the Academy."

After he had spoken, McCoy realized that he had hesitated slightly when he had mentioned the Academy—as if it, too, like 'starship' to the child, was more than a word to him.

Glynis had heard it, as well. "Hey, mister. What do *you* do?"

McCoy scratched at his beard again. "Me? I'm retired."

"Yeah? From what?"

McCoy chewed on his lip for a moment. Five minutes with this child was turning out to be more enlightening than two weeks watching pine trees grow in Yosemite. "From Starfleet," he said.

Glynis's mouth dropped open and her eyes widened. "Why? Why would anyone retire from . . . Starfleet?" Such magic in the way she said that word.

McCoy stared out across the lunar vista. Beyond what had once been the final frontier, he could make out the domes of the civilian spaceport, glinting white against the black sky of the Moon, just like the stars beyond.

"Why, mister?" Glynis asked again. "That's like quitting, isn't it? How could you quit Starfleet? How, mister? Why?"

But McCoy had no answer for her. At least, not yet.

FOUR

☆

Beside his Starfleet Command gold star, the tribunal judge wore a small IDIC emblem on his black robe. That meant he had studied law on Vulcan. But Uhura didn't care where, when, or for how long anyone had studied anything. She was right and Starfleet was wrong and that's all there was to it.

"Ensign Uhura," the judge said, his voice echoing against the hard walls of the nondescript Starfleet Lunar Hall of Justice hearing room. "Please approach the bench."

Alise Chavez, Uhura's legal representative, nodded at her. Chavez was a harried-looking lieutenant junior grade in Starfleet's Justice Division, with long hair spraying out erratically from an improperly fastened clip at the back of her head and a red specialist's tunic that was at least two sizes too large. Uhura's case docket was one of twenty microtape wafers spilling out of the case on the lieutenant's table, so Uhura suspected that a nod of the head was about all the expert guidance she could expect today. She approached the bench, rustling in her one-size-fits-all. standard-issue, blue prison jumpsuit.

"Ensign Uhura," the judge intoned. "Do you know why you have been brought before the tribunal today?"

"Yes, sir." Because it was three standard months to the day

since the first time she had been brought before the tribunal. *Let's get on with it,* she thought.

"Then I won't have to go into a long speech about your oath as a Starfleet officer—"

I'm an ensign, now, you bald-headed, red-eyed—

". . . nor about your duty to uphold the laws of the Articles of the United Federation of Planets."

"I am aware of both my oath and my duty, sir."

The judge looked down at his screenpad and scrawled some notes. *Probably checking off his list,* Uhura thought, *just like every other time.*

The judge cleared his throat. "Ensign Uhura, I am required to ask you if, at this time, you have reconsidered your refusal to sign the document displayed before you." He pressed a control on his screenpad and the disputed document appeared on the viewscreen built into the front of his high desk, directly before Uhura's eyes.

"Yes, sir," Uhura said formally, "I have reconsidered my refusal to sign that document."

The judge's eyes blinked in surprise. "I beg your pardon?"

"I have reconsidered it most carefully."

"You have?" He leaned forward, hands on either side of his screenpad. In Uhura's last eleven appearances before the other judges who had rotated through this tribunal, all she had volunteered were variations on the word no. "And . . . ?" he prompted.

"And after due reconsideration, I once again refuse to sign it because it is a false and—"

The judge pushed down on his desk's gavel switch and a low rush of white noise sprang from hidden speakers, preventing anything else Uhura said from being recorded by the reporting computer. But it didn't prevent her from speaking until she was finished.

"Are you quite done, Ensign?" the judge asked when Uhura's mouth had finally closed.

"Well, that's up to you, isn't it, sir?"

The judge's thick eyebrows quivered in irritation but he touched his fingers to the IDIC symbol he wore and Uhura could see his lips forming silent Vulcan phonemes as he repeated a calming koan.

"Very well, Ensign. Since you have seen fit to abrogate your sworn oath and—"

Uhura wasn't going to let him get away with it. She wasn't going to let anyone get away with it. "Your honor! I object!"

The judge shook his head and looked over at the overworked lieutenant j.g. "Lieutenant Chavez, could you please remind your client, *once again,* that she is the prisoner and cannot object."

Chavez hastily began to get up from behind her table but Uhura stared her down, smiling tightly, until the lieutenant lost the will to speak and sank back into her chair. After three months of dealing with Uhura, she knew no one could win an argument with the communications specialist once her mind was made up. And right now it was most certainly made up.

The judge began again. "Ensign Uhura, this tribunal, duly empowered by the authority of Starfleet Command, has found that you have abrogated your sworn oath of allegiance. . . ." He paused, but Uhura said nothing, for now. "And have consistently displayed your contempt for this court and its authority."

You got that right, Uhura thought.

The judge tapped a finger against the side of his screenpad and Uhura wondered what the man's Vulcan instructors would say about the telltale sign indicating that not everything was under control.

"Ensign, for three months you have defied the authority of this tribunal. First, by your refusal to testify during the board of inquiry hearing into the events at Talin IV—"

"Their minds were made up from the beginning!"

The judge glared but didn't stop talking. *"And now,* by refusing to sign this statement confirming your actions as recorded by the *Enterprise*'s log tapes. For three months you have been held in detention as punishment for that show of contempt. And now, unfortunately, as we are not at war and the charges against you do not pertain to the regulations covering vital secrets or mutiny, this tribunal no longer has the authority to continue your imprisonment."

The judge looked steadily at Uhura. "You do realize that there will be no going back after this?"

"The document is false. The conclusions are wrong." The judge held his finger over the gavel button but Uhura said nothing more.

"Very well." He signed his name on the bottom of the screenpad and began speaking in a rapid monotone. "Ms. Uhura, acting under the authority of Starfleet Command general regulations in peacetime, this tribunal declares you discharged from the rights, duties, and privileges of a non-commissioned officer in Starfleet. Said discharge to be listed on your record with dishonor. Your accumulated pay, pension, and education credits are forfeit. You are prohibited from ever accepting civilian employment with Starfleet, and are likewise prohibited from accepting employment with any civil branch of the United Federation of Planets, its member governments and bodies, for a period of ten standard years. You are reminded that your oath pertaining to safeguarding the classified information which might or might not have been divulged to you during the period of your service is still in effect, along with all pertinent publication and other dissemination restrictions. Failure to abide by the conditions of that oath and those restrictions may render you liable for both civil and/or criminal charges." The judge signed his name one final time. "This tribunal stands adjourned."

The judge slipped his screenpad under his arm and left the hearing room without looking back. Uhura went to the desk where Lieutenant Chavez gathered up her stack of brightly colored microtapes.

"What's the next step?" Uhura asked.

Chavez shrugged as she quickly checked the time readout on her portable computer screen. "You go to the quartermaster and get your own clothes back. And past that, you tell me. You got what you wanted, didn't you? You're a civilian." Her words were hurried. She had places to go.

"If I had signed that piece of garbage I would have had no choice but to resign. And all a resignation gives me is a chance to reconsider my decision within a six-month grace period. As if they'd let me back. At least I'm able to appeal a dishonorable discharge."

Chavez sighed as she slipped her computer into her case and closed it. "Come on, Uhura. You already know how that's going to play out. You file your appeal and they're going to assign you someone with even less experience and training than I have." She stood up to leave.

But Uhura placed her hands on Chavez's case, to keep the lieutenant in place for a few moments longer. "Chavez, I *am* getting someone to represent me."

"A civilian attorney? To argue a case against a Starfleet tribunal? You know how much something like that's going to cost? And you heard the conditions of discharge: You're going to be lucky to get work within ten parsecs of here to pay for it."

"I mean, I'm getting someone else in Starfleet to represent me."

Chavez stared at her in dismay. "Uhura, haven't you listened to a word I've said in the past three months? As far as the Admiralty's concerned, you don't exist. The whole Talin incident, the *Enterprise* Five, it's all being beamed out to a dust cloud."

"I'm not letting them do that," Uhura stated stubbornly.

"You're still not facing the facts! You were a fast-track officer on the best damned ship in Starfleet. There are two admirals at Command who came up through communications just like you. You had pull, tradition, a career path, top brass in your camp, and it didn't help you!" Chavez held her fist to her chest. "Look at what the Justice Division has done to you! I'm a junior grade who's spent the last year here on the Moon defending red shirts for slamboxing in bars on shore leave. Don't you get it? There's no one left in Starfleet who wants to have anything at all to do with you. Your captain didn't order any of you to do what you did, so you have no excuse. And *you* were the one who pressed the button that helped destroy a world. An entire world." Chavez pulled her case away from Uhura. "It's over, Uhura. No one in Starfleet will appeal anything for you."

"Spock will," Uhura said.

"The Vulcan?"

"He's been assigned to Technology Support in San Francisco. He's going to represent me."

Chavez reached out to take Uhura's hand, some sympathy still in her eyes.

"Uhura, he resigned."

"What?"

"Yesterday. It was in the ComSys updates. The last of the Five to go. He can't appear before any Starfleet tribunal as a civilian. Unless he's got a law degree. *And* has Sol system accreditation."

"But . . ." Uhura was speechless. She and Spock had talked less than a tenday ago. He had helped her plan her entire strategy from the beginning. He had told her to force them to give her a dishonorable discharge so he could launch an appeal and bring the whole case to open court. "Spock wouldn't abandon me . . . he couldn't."

Chavez patted Uhura's hand. "All of you people from the *Enterprise* have to start your lives again. The Vulcan must have realized that. By getting out, and leaving you behind, he did . . . the logical thing."

Uhura pulled her hand away. She would not be patronized anymore than she'd be railgunned into accepting blame for what had happened at Talin IV. "He is not 'the Vulcan'! His name is Spock and he's one of the most honorable beings I know."

Chavez nodded her head wearily, not wanting to argue anymore. "Matters of honor are seldom logical, Uhura. After having worked with a Vulcan for so long, I would have thought you'd understand them better than most." She tucked her case under her arm.

48

"I understand everything that's gone on better than any of you blinder-wearing, rule-quoting, Starfleet drones do! Here *and* on Talin!"

Chavez stepped away, her sympathy turning to pity. "But except for a few student protest groups, no one wants to know about Talin anymore, Uhura. They just want to forget. It's over. Accept it. It'll make your life a lot easier."

Uhura's hands knotted into fists at her sides. "The only thing I'm prepared to accept is the truth."

Shaking her head, Chavez walked toward the hearing room's doors and they slid open before her. But before she left, she stopped and turned. "What I can't figure out, is how you could have spent so much time in Starfleet, seen the way it operates, and still believe that you might have a chance against the systems that make it work as well as it does. I mean, what makes you think you stand a chance? Why keep fighting the inevitable?"

Uhura's voice was solid and strong in the silent room. "Because I once served under Captain James T. Kirk on the best damned ship in Starfleet," she said. "And I *will* serve with him on that ship again. And God help anyone, or any admiral, who gets in my way."

"Ask a simple question," Chavez said softly, then stepped through the doorway, her work at an end.

But for Uhura, it was time to begin.

The Starfleet Lunar Hall of Justice in Oceanview was one of those peculiar government buildings that seemed to have no particular style, other than a quest for monumentalism. It was close to a century old and had been built in the twilight of Earth's cultural fascination with anything Centauran. Unfortunately, the fact that it had been built on the Moon under natural gravity—long since augmented to Earth normal throughout the city's business sections—had inspired the architects to alter the proportions of loadbearing arches whose original graceful dimensions had been dictated by a more massive planet. In addition, the building's airy roof gardens were situated five meters beneath the inner surface of a dingy green pressure dome instead of under spacious blue skies, further removing it from the Centauran ideals of open post-harmony defensism.

McCoy stood in the plaza before the ungainly structure, wondering how anyone could have become enamored of an architectural style that had arisen on a world where people spent most of their time burying things underground so they couldn't be detected by hypothetical enemies from space. That cultural paranoia, supported by fiber optic data transmission that prevented stray radiation from leaking out into space, had kept Earth's first expedition to another star from discovering there was an inhabited, technologically advanced civilization virtually next door until the first shuttles were almost ready to land. *The members of the Federation are all so eager to find new life and new civilizations,* McCoy thought, *but when we find it, none of us wants to go first.* Maybe that was the real reason for what had happened on Talin: not that Kirk had been engaged in brash adventurism, but that everyone else involved, including the First Contact Office, had been too cautious.

"Doctor McCoy?"

McCoy turned to see Uhura come up beside him, her eyes fixed on his beard. She looked somehow out of place in her civilian clothes—a rough textured brown and white caftan that floated above her ankles. No doubt he looked similarly odd to her out of his science blues and in a vat-cotton, multistriped shirt and hiking trousers.

"How long have you been here?" Uhura asked, not taking her eyes off the beard.

"Just arrived," McCoy said. He ran his fingers through his whiskers. "I don't blame you for staring. There *is* a lot of white in it, isn't there? Took me by surprise, too."

"It's not the white, Doctor. It's just the beard. I didn't recognize you at first and I was worried that I had left you standing here for the past half hour." Then she peered more closely at the beard. "But you're right, that *is* a lot of white."

McCoy laughed, held out his arms to her, and they hugged

each other tightly. "It's good to see you again, Uhura. Damned good."

"I know the feeling." Uhura took his hand in hers. She looked somber for a moment. "Is there anything to your being late?"

McCoy smiled. "Oh, no. Not a thing. I got in this morning and went down to Tranquility Park. Had a very interesting discussion with a young lady."

Uhura smiled. "I see."

"A young lady of eight on a school band trip," McCoy clarified. "And with any luck, she'll be running Starfleet in fifty years." He pointed over to a tunnelway a few hundred meters west of the justice building. "There's a restaurant over there in the Park Dome. Wasn't too bad a few years ago. Want to get some civilian food to go with the civilian clothes?"

Uhura nodded. "I'd like that. I . . . I can't get used to . . . any of this."

"Neither can I," McCoy said and they began to walk to the park together, arms linked. "So," McCoy began after a few steps in silence, "how did the hearing go this morning?"

"Just fine," Uhura said. "For a dishonorable discharge."

"I'm glad they let you out." McCoy glanced sideways at a group of three officers walking by in gold shirts with commanders' braids. They saw him and Uhura as well, but there was no flicker of recognition. McCoy was surprised, considering the coverage the *Enterprise* Five had been given.

"No choice, Doctor. They could only hold me on contempt charges for three months in peacetime. Anything longer is against the Articles."

McCoy squeezed her hand. "Well, now that you're out, you should know that there's a big fat loophole in that regulation. Technically, they could have dropped charges against you one day before the limit ran out, held you over for any one of a hundred different minor violations, and the very next day brought new contempt charges against you good for another three months."

"What?" Uhura stopped walking and other pedestrians scrambled to move around her and the doctor.

"It's not often done," McCoy said, "but if they had really wanted you, they could have kept you pretty much indefinitely."

"I suppose that means my so-called legal advisor was right. Starfleet does want to cover up what happened."

McCoy tugged on Uhura's arm to get her walking again. "Starfleet doesn't go in for cover-ups, Uhura. The preliminary board hearing was a public forum and the update services got the full story out. There's no sign that Starfleet's trying to hide anything, even after the fact."

"But, Doctor, they didn't want to court-martial you—"

"That's because they said I didn't do anything. But I was on the ship. I would have . . ." He broke off, feeling his blood pressure soar.

"But they didn't want to court-martial the captain, either—or anyone. They just forced us all to . . . resign. Except for me."

"Careful here," McCoy warned as they came to the edge of the civic dome and a large caution display warned that they were entering a zone of natural gravity. The sudden stomach dip into point one seven gee wasn't quite as bad as going into free fall, but it was close enough for McCoy. As far as he was concerned, even cycling down to point nine gee was one point variation too much.

He let go of Uhura's hand so they could both use the guide rails set up for tourists and, he was sorry to read on the signs, for seniors. Meanwhile, a flurry of youngsters went bounding back and forth through the brightly illuminated interdome tunnel like giant rabbits on cordrazine. The automatic safety system's voice droned on nonstop to tell the children they were moving at too high a velocity for public safety.

As he moved stodgily along, feeling the breeze created by the bouncing youngsters, McCoy found himself thinking of the old two-dees the first Moon explorers had taken on their brief visits here, and during the construction of Base One. What the doctor always found remarkable on those tapes was that almost within seconds of their first arrival, the explorers had all instinctively begun hopping like these children, and that this type of locomotion was still common in Moon-normal gee fields today. McCoy marveled that the human body was so adaptable, not just for the Moon but for a thousand other worlds as well. It was a body designed to be propelled wherever its mind pushed it. No matter what. He thought about the young girl again.

"Well, don't you think that seems suspicious, Doctor?" Uhura asked. "Getting us to resign like that?"

McCoy was momentarily startled and he glanced back as he pulled himself along the railing. "Uhura, if you were in their position, wouldn't *you* rather have avoided the publicity of court-martialing the entire bridge crew of one of your most prominent ships when there were easier, less noticeable, and less damaging ways of getting rid of them?" He stopped talking for a moment to catch his breath. Why did lower gravity fields always seem to take more effort to move around in? "What happened at Talin happened. It's a closed datafile. Starfleet doesn't want to cover it up. It just doesn't want to reopen old wounds."

Uhura pushed off against the tunnel floor and jumped to McCoy's side, then pulled down on his arm and forced him under the guide rail where they could stand face-to-face without impeding the flow of others moving through the tunnel. She dropped her voice to an angry whisper. "Doctor McCoy, if I didn't know you better, I'd say you were talking as if you believed what Starfleet says. You can't, can you?"

McCoy hooked his hand under the guide rail and pushed down, increasing the pressure of his feet on the tunnel floor to lessen the feeling that the turbolift his stomach was on was going to hit bottom any second. "Of course, I don't believe it. I was there, remember? All I'm saying is that I understand Starfleet's position on this. I'm not saying that I like it or that I'm not going to try and change it, but as somebody somewhere once said, 'It's logical.'" McCoy put his hand to his eyes as if to clear them. "Lord, I never thought I'd miss hearing those words as much as I do now."

Uhura waited for a few moments while McCoy collected himself. Then she spoke again. "Did you know that Mr. Spock had resigned?"

McCoy's shocked expression said that he hadn't.

"I just found out today myself. My legal advisor told me. Apparently it was in yesterday's updates."

"But he was supposed to help you with your appeal," McCoy said. "I mean, that was the whole point of you going through this, wasn't it?"

"That's what I thought."

"Has he contacted you at all? Sent a message through anyone?"

Uhura shook her head. "When I thought you were late in coming to meet me back there, I thought maybe . . . well, that you and he were . . . together."

"I haven't heard a thing from Spock since that . . . meeting with Hammersmith at Starbase 29."

Uhura laughed in spite of her mood. " 'Meeting' wouldn't be the word I'd use for it."

McCoy smiled, too. And then he frowned.

"What is it?" Uhura asked.

"Over the past few weeks, I've just started to realize how spoiled we all were on the *Enterprise*. We could talk to anyone virtually anywhere over subspace."

"We still can, Doctor McCoy."

"But have you seen how long it takes to get online just to send a text-only message to Centaurus? And that's a local transmission. Good Lord, on the ship we never had to wait to gain access to anything. And we had personal communicators. And shuttles. The computers always ready. Even the transporter." He groaned. "Listen to me, I'm missing the blasted transporter."

"All that technology is available right here. It's available almost any place."

"That's not my point. Here, we have to present our travel documents, we have to wait in line, go through channels. . . . On the *Enterprise*, why, we could just *do* something. Spock's missing? The sensors could do a sweep and you'd have locked

54

onto his communicator in five seconds flat." McCoy took his hand away from the guiderail, holding both hands empty before him. "We're powerless now. It's so much harder to do just about everything."

"Are . . . are you giving up?" Uhura's voice roughened.

McCoy watched as three children sped past, bouncing high through the tunnel and turning somersaults in midair, their laughter drowning out the staid warnings of the safety system. "On the shuttle here this morning, I thought about it, Uhura. I really did. But at Tranquility . . . they didn't have much. Hell, they didn't have anything any sane person would have taken into space. But they came here anyway, didn't they?"

Uhura nodded her head silently as children played around them on what had once been an airless, lifeless rock.

"It wasn't the equipment they built," McCoy continued, watching the stream of people, humans and otherwise, passing through the tunnel. "It wasn't the knowledge or the experience they had. It was"—he shook his head, out of words—". . . something else."

Uhura's eyes filled with relief. "I know," she said softly. "I know."

"So to answer your question, Lieutenant. No. I am—"

Uhura placed her hands on McCoy's shoulders. "Thank you, Doctor."

"For what?"

"You called me 'Lieutenant.' I've missed hearing that."

McCoy took a deep breath. The thoughts he had been struggling with these past months at last came together. All because of a child he had happened to meet.

He thought of being at the end of a chain of thousands, of millions who had worked so hard to push humans so far. *How could you quit?* the child had asked him, and McCoy had had no answer for her. Because there was no answer. Because he hadn't quit. He wouldn't quit.

"Well, listen carefully, Lieutenant. Because to answer your question: No, I am not giving up. It's just that . . . I'm not quite sure what to do next."

"Don't worry about it, Doctor. Because I do." Uhura ducked back under the guide rail.

"Are you going to tell me?"

Uhura flashed a brilliant smile, then leapt across the tunnel in two four-meter hops to the pedestrian pathways leading back into the civic administration dome.

McCoy grumbled, pushed himself over the guide rail, and joined her, barely missing being blasted out of the tunnel by runaway tumbling children. "So what do we do, Lieutenant?"

"We go back," Uhura said.

McCoy looked down the tunnel. Through the distant opening, he could still see a corner of the squat Hall of Justice. "To Starfleet?" he asked in puzzlement.

But Uhura shook her head. "Back to where it all began, Doctor. To where the answers are." She smiled in satisfaction at the look that came over his face. "That's right," she said. "To Talin."

"The last I heard, Uhura, there was no regular tourist service out to the frontier. How do you suggest we get there?"

Uhura patted McCoy's arm. "I told you not to worry. We can find someone who'll want to take us there."

"Talin is blockaded, my dear. And the only ones who will be trying to get past a Starfleet blockade are criminals and pirates."

Uhura nodded. "I know that."

McCoy glanced around, and lowered his voice. "Just what are you suggesting we *do*, Uhura?"

She smiled disarmingly. "Know where we can get a good spaceship cheap?"

FIVE

☆

There was only one Klingon ear nailed to the wall above the cash box, so it wasn't the toughest tavern Sulu had been in on Rigel VIII. But as he ducked beneath the swinging arc of a diburnium barstool, feinted to his right and kicked out to his left, he decided it probably ranked somewhere up in the top two. He didn't remember much about the other place, except spending the next two days in sickbay.

Sulu's kick clipped the charging Orion on the side of his black-maned head and sent the green-skinned alien flying into a flimsy table wisely abandoned by its occupants when the fight broke out. After the splintering crash of brittle Rigellian furniture alloy, there was a brief instant of peace in the tavern. The bartender stayed hidden behind a chrome-plated cabinet of imported liquors, unprotected customers scurried away to the back rooms, one solitary patron in a black cape poured another ale from a pitcher he hadn't paid for, and the combatants reevaluated each other.

Sulu crouched in a defensive *tesare* position. He felt a Vulcan form of self-defense seemed preferable at the moment because he knew there was not a hope in hell of him actually defeating three Orion males in hand-to-hand combat. But sometimes there were other things worth fighting for than immediate victory.

"No use, human," Krulmadden said matter-of-factly. The massive Orion shipmaster still sat at the end of the bar, hands folded together, one elbow resting by a slender flask of Ganymede Green. He laughed then, and the gemstones in his teeth flashed as brilliantly as the ones studding the eight rings he wore, lit by the near blinding light from a molecular fusion sunball floating near the rippled metal ceiling five meters above him. The light also gave a glimmering sheen to Krulmadden's deep green skin and the emerald *destin* scales of his tunic. "No win for you."

Sulu tipped his head at the Orion in a fencer's salute. "Then I shall lose." He glanced back at Lasslanlin, the mate who had crushed the table in his fall. He was slowly getting back to his feet, shaking his head, jeweled earrings making gentle chiming music in odd contrast to his 150-kilo bulk. Sulu took a breath and repositioned his foot to prepare for Lasslanlin's inevitable rush.

But Artinton raised his head from behind the bar where Sulu had flipped him a few seconds earlier. A string of thick orange blood hung from the second Orion mate's black beard and he smiled at Sulu, grunting like a Tellarite as he spat out more blood and at least two teeth.

Now that's not fair, Sulu thought. *I should be able to flatten at least one of these walking mountains.*

"Lasslanlin, stay." Artinton placed both gargantuan hands on the bar top. It had been cultured from a single cell of ironwood and Sulu swallowed as he heard it creak beneath the Orion's mass. "This one owes teeth."

Sulu's eyes widened as the second mate vaulted the bar as if he were strapped to antigravs, and landed less than two meters away.

Oh, great, he's been toying with me for the past five minutes. He could have had me any—

Artinton leapt and Sulu reflexively dropped to one knee, angling forward to catch and deflect the Orion's momentum with his own shoulders and back. But the Orion had expected the move and brought his knee up against Sulu's neck, jerking him from his planned direction and destroying his balance.

Sulu's breath left him with an explosive huff as the Orion drove him to the metal floor. Without being able to breathe under the Orion's crushing force, the outmatched human tried to flip around and crawl away. But Artinton's monstrous green hand grabbed the collar of Sulu's quilted, spun-down jacket and shoved him back against the iron plates of the floor.

Black stars flickered at the edges of Sulu's vision and the floor's rivets tore into his cheek. He struggled to ignore the giant above him and concentrate all he had on breathing again. Just one breath. Half a breath. Anything.

Sulu felt himself rise up from the floor and spin around under someone else's control. Artinton's hand was like a mechanical pincer against Sulu's neck, lifting him by a fistful of crushed fabric until the toes of his boots left the floor completely.

At the end of the bar, Krulmadden clapped two beefy hands together, applauding the fight's conclusion. Sulu edged his eyes to the side as Lasslanlin approached to stand beside his shipmate. The Orions began to laugh, deep and booming. Sulu could feel himself sway with the force of Artinton's murderous good humor. He tried to swallow again but nothing could get past the pressure of the huge fist against his throat. *So much for Vulcan self-defense tactics,* Sulu thought. *I guess they work better when you've had fifty years of practice.* As far as he could see, there was only one thing left to do.

Sulu closed his eyes, wincing as Artinton's foul breath flooded over him in even louder gales of laughter.

"Look at little insect!" the Orion howled. "He wants to sleep, forget bad dream!"

Eyes clenched shut, Sulu sensed the Orion bending closer to him, almost nose to nose. "But not dream, little insect. And not over!"

"You bet it's not," Sulu grunted then jerked his head forward at warp ten. In the next instant he had the triple pleasure of flattening Artinton's nose like a jellyfish, feeling himself slip from Artinton's suddenly limp hand, and hearing Artinton's earsplitting screech of shock.

Sulu kept his balance as the Orion stumbled backward to bounce against the bar and crumple like a five-atmosphere probe in a fifty-atmosphere pressure chamber.

But Lasslanlin grabbed Sulu's shoulder and spun him around. "That ship's friend, little insect hatchling zygote."

"If you're going to speak Standard then at least get it right!" Sulu shouted as he swung his fist. "I'm a *mammal!* Get it? A—"

Lasslanlin caught Sulu's fist in his black-gloved hand like a tractor beam stopping a meteoroid cold. His forearm didn't even travel back a centimeter as he absorbed the full force of the blow. *What a shame it will be to be taken apart by someone who knows so little about biology,* Sulu thought with regret. *But at least I got one of them.*

Lasslanlin raised his other hand and a dancerknife suddenly shimmered into view, its blade an indistinct blue humming form.

Sulu braced himself, but knew he had nothing more to draw on to resist. He wondered if the tavern keeper would let the Orions at least nail his ears *above* the Klingon's.

"First, ears," Lasslanlin promised. "Then, *mammal,* the little pair of—" The Orion suddenly jerked, mouth gaping in surprise. He shuddered again as if he had been hit from behind and let go of Sulu's fist.

Sulu staggered back, ready to run out from the tavern and disappear into the maze of the spaceport's back alleys. Lasslanlin didn't try to stop him. The Orion looked over his shoulder—just in time to catch a gleaming barstool with his face. The dancerknife spun from Lasslanlin's hand and its blade melted into air before it hit the floor.

"Stator rell . . . ?" Lasslanlin moaned, and then Sulu saw a flurry of five quick closed-hand chops pepper the Orion's face, ending with a final full roundhouse to his jaw.

Lasslanlin's eyes rolled back beneath his chartreuse lids, his knees wobbled once, then he fell to join his friend on the floor. The unexpected ally who had dropped the Orion stood above the unconscious body. He straightened his black cape, pulled back his cowl, and smiled disarmingly at Sulu. "Karate," he said, "originally inwented in Russia. Before being stolen by the Chinese."

Sulu dropped his hands to his side in relief. "You were supposed to be here an *hour* ago, Chekov."

Chekov pointed over to a small table with a now empty pitcher of ale. "I *have* been here. All ewening."

Sulu raised his hands again in sudden anger. "Then why weren't you helping me?"

"Up to now, you didn't need it."

Sulu shook his head, then reached out to hug his friend. Behind them, Krulmadden applauded once again.

Sulu and Chekov faced the Orion shipmaster together.

"How touching," Krulmadden growled. "Two *f'deraxt'la*, like slavegirls carrying on."

Chekov glanced at Sulu. "Does *f'deraxt'la* mean what I think it means?"

Sulu nodded. "Three parents, all related, and it rhymes with 'Federation' in the Trader's Tongue."

"We cannot let him get away with this."

"That's the point I've been trying to make, Chekov."

The two humans began to move apart. They had been friends long enough that no words were needed to establish their strategy. It wasn't the first time in a bar brawl for either of them.

Krulmadden smiled and slowly moved his hand to scratch his monstrously rounded belly. But when his hand came back to the bar, it held a jewel-encrusted disruptor in a platinum housing. "Suggest move back together, humans. Audition over."

"Audition?" Sulu asked.

Krulmadden waved his hands expansively and his gemstones flared so brightly Sulu saw multicolored afterimages. "This all play. With shipmaster's mates." He pursed his lips and shook his head at the unconscious bodies of Lasslanlin and Artinton.

"With shipmaster, me." Sulu cringed as Krulmadden nonchalantly pointed at himself with the barrel of his disruptor. "And two worldkillers in one bar. All play."

"Why do you call us worldkillers?" Chekov asked.

Krulmadden stuck out his lower lip and waved the disruptor again. "Why hands in cape, Chekov Mister?" He smiled at Sulu. "And you Sulu Mister. Both *Enterprise*, no? Krulmadden knows all. Fine shipmaster, Krulmadden."

"But in this case," Sulu said evenly, "the fine shipmaster is wrong."

Krulmadden used his free hand to pick at an emerald in an upper tooth for a moment, as if carefully considering what Sulu had said. Then he shrugged, thrust the disruptor forward, and a small patch of iron at Sulu's feet bubbled up in red hot blisters.

"Krulmadden not good with Standard Tongue," the Orion said. "Some things you not hear right. Some things you say . . ." He tapped the disruptor against his ear and stepped from his barstool.

"So again I say, Sulu and Chekov shipmates, but no ship." He walked closer to them, steel-soled boots clanking on the floor plates, the disruptor swinging back and forth with each waddling step. "True, you *f'deraxt'l* shipmates. But other *f'deraxt'la* not want you. So no ship, but . . ." He stood before them, grinning with a mouth like a backlit rainbow. ". . . *Krulmadden* ship!" He slipped the barrel of the disruptor into a wide burgundy sash that rested high across his stomach. "So audition over." He reached out and slapped two meaty hands on Sulu's and Chekov's shoulders. Sulu winced. "You ship again."

Chekov looked concerned. "I . . . I am not sure that I understand—"

Sulu felt another heavy hand hit his other shoulder, and smelled a familiar stench as Artinton leaned forward from behind. The Orion's voice was thick and nasal.

"Shipmaster say, little . . . mammals," Artinton said, digging fingers like daggers into Sulu's trapezius muscles, "you *hired.*"

SIX

Surprisingly, the naming of ships was not a universal habit. Scholars speculated that the root of the practice might lie within those ancient instincts, common to some species such as Klingon and human, from which sprang such strife-ridden concepts as territory and combat. However, even the Vulcans acknowledged the logic of giving ships names to honor individuals and places worthy of remembrance, or to remind all who served aboard the vessels of the qualities they should seek to master.

But there were those other races that had taken up the custom in *all* its detail, without really comprehending the finer points of the practice. They christened their ships not with names from their own history or culture, but from those of the alien races who had originated the practice.

Thus cobalt-blooded Andorians bravely piloted massive troop carriers named the *Robert E. Lee* and the *Surak;* Tellarites traveled from world to world aboard the *Rhode Island* and the *Claw of the Vindicator;* and even the Centaurans had called the first warp-powered craft launched from their planet the *Daedalus.*

Which is why Pavel Chekov was not surprised to read the name ornately emblazoned upon the hull of Krulmadden's ship, high in orbit above Rigel VIII. Despite all the alien influences of its mismatched components, and the fact that it was a Rigellian Registry Vessel, it made perfect sense to Chekov that the craft was proudly named the RRV *Queen Mary*. He had seen stranger.

"Holding at two hundred meters from the outer shields' perimeter," Sulu announced, making a final adjustment to the shuttle's attitude thrusters. Chekov had been impressed at how well his friend had performed at the controls of Krulmadden's stripped-down orbital shuttle. It had been a long time since either of them had flown in anything without its own gravity generator. He supposed that was yet another adjustment they would have to make now that they were no longer flying the cutting-edge craft of Starfleet.

"So, my helmsman, what do you think of my brightest jewel?" The shuttle's small flight cabin became even more cramped as Krulmadden floated into it from the aft cargo hold. Chekov couldn't help but notice that Krulmadden's command of Standard had improved substantially since they had left the tavern for the shuttle landing field.

Sulu studied the *Queen Mary*'s configuration from the pilot's window. The ship was a balanced but ungainly vessel, in the style of warp-capable craft not designed for atmospheric flight. Its main hull was a 30-meter, Mars-built disk slung beneath an elliptical Rigellian warp pod. The pod was joined to the disk's trailing edge by a short linking pylon, and was topped by a hard-edged, Andorian military surplus impulse drive which had clearly not been part of the ship's original design.

Beside Sulu, in the copilot's sling, Artinton unfastened his acceleration harness and pushed off. He slipped around Krulmadden, back toward the hold, grinning at Chekov who bobbed in the navigator's sling at the rear of the flight cabin.

"It looks trim enough," Sulu said appreciatively. "Though if you haven't got any upgrades under those impulse conduits, I don't see how she could hit anything higher than half cee in normal space."

"*Very* good, little mammal." Krulmadden beamed, though

his jeweled teeth did not sparkle in the dim shuttle cabin lighting as much as they had planetside. The blue-white infernos of the Rigellian twin giants and twin lessers were hidden behind the planet for now. In addition to cutting back on expenses by having a shuttle without artificial gravity, Krulmadden had explained that he didn't like to waste power on radiation shields when he could simply park his ship in geosynchronous orbit in the almost perpetual shadow of Rigel VIII's rings. The light reflected from the planet's major moon was more than enough to steer by. But watching the ease with which Krulmadden buoyed his bulk around in microgravity, Chekov thought that perhaps there was another reason for the absence of gravity generators.

The shipmaster pointed out Sulu's window. "That Andorian impulse shell is just that. A shell. A delusion."

"Uh, do you mean 'illusion'?" Sulu asked.

"Whatever. Beneath it is a dual tangent, full magnetopulse field coil with an artificial singularity." He said every word perfectly, a proud father naming his children. "Relative rest to half cee in less than one second. With full cargo, still reach nine-nine cee in less than thirty."

Sulu whistled. "I didn't think artificial singularities were licensed for use by anyone except Starfleet and some planetary defense units."

"They are not." Krulmadden gave as good an impression of a shrug as he could in microgee. "And for good reason. It would give unscrupulous types too much advantage over f'deraxt'l border patrols. Not good, no no no." The shipmaster slapped his own hand, then chuckled as his rhythmic exhalations began to spin him around.

Sulu glanced over at Chekov as Krulmadden steadied himself. Chekov nodded. He understood. The Orion's ship was obviously better equipped than they had hoped, which meant their plan was going to be much easier to bring off than they had anticipated.

"What procedures do we follow now?" Sulu asked.

At that, Krulmadden's face became unreadable. He was not a

being who was comfortable with questions. "Now, Artinton kindly asks my sweet jewel to drop her shields and not to blow my shuttle out of space. And then, I see how good you are at docking."

Chekov was troubled by that. It meant the *Queen Mary* had an automated defense system for the times it was left unattended. He and Sulu would have to devise some way of intercepting the recognition code Artinton was apparently going to transmit to inform the *Queen Mary's* computers that the shuttle was a friendly craft. If his and Sulu's plan was to succeed, they would need to be able to transmit that information themselves, eventually.

Krulmadden clamped his hand firmly on Sulu's arm to steady himself. "Hold this position relative to my ship precisely, helmsman. If you deviate by more than a half *sateen*, you will owe Artinton more than his teeth."

Chekov converted the Trader's Measure. *Three centimeters.* He wondered why the shuttle would have to maintain such an exact position simply to transmit a subspace code. Or even a radio signal. And why would not holding that position be dangerous to Artinton? The answer that came was both obvious and unexpected.

A yellow-orange flickering light suddenly filled the shuttle's cabin, originating from the aft hold and accompanied by a faint but distinctive musical chime. Artinton was *transporting* over to the *Queen Mary.* But how?

"Is that safe?" Sulu asked. "While the shields are up?"

Krulmadden didn't take his eyes from his ship. "As long as you hold this position, it is."

Must be a prearranged interference gap in the shield, Chekov decided. *Just wide enough for a transporter carrier wave from the ship to reach through. And the shields must be stacked deep around the gap so the wave can return only from a specific position.* He frowned in thought. There would be no security code to intercept. Artinton was going to shut down the automated defense systems physically from onboard the *Queen*

Mary herself. The task of stealing the Orion's ship had just become more difficult.

A strip of running lights suddenly flashed into life along the side of the *Queen Mary*'s warp pod and orientation lights began to blink on the main hull.

"Shields are down," Sulu announced, reading his control panel's tactical display.

"Shuttle berth is on the disk, on the opposite side of the warp pod pylon," Krulmadden said.

Sulu tapped a readiness code into the thrusting system. "That's not a standard configuration."

Krulmadden laughed again. "The entire ship is not standard configuration. You would be a clever mammal to always keep that in mind." He turned to make sure that Chekov was listening to his lesson as well. "It might help prevent needless . . . accidents."

Without looking at any control panel readings, Sulu brought the shuttle smoothly around the *Queen Mary*'s disk and guided it toward the lit circle that indicated the airlock berth. He docked the shuttle with so little vibration that Krulmadden had to study the board to make sure the airlocks had mated. "Very good, mammal. Smooth as a slave's . . . ah, but then you are *f'deraxt'la*, and would not know about such things . . . thus far."

Krulmadden pushed himself over to the copilot's controls and hovered by them, the orange tip of his tongue showing in concentration. "Your duties are finished. I shall take care of the remainder." He ran his fingers over the control panel and Chekov's ears popped as he heard the shuttle's airlock whoosh open into the *Queen Mary*.

A row of blue lights glowed on top of Krulmadden's board and he threw a locking switch, freezing the controls. Chekov surmised that a security code would have to be input before they would unlock again. That was another condition he and Sulu would have to get used to as civilians: the lack of trust that was reflected in the engineering of private spacecraft. Aboard a

Starfleet ship, when life or death could depend on a crew member's ability to initiate action within seconds, there were few built-in safeguards to restrict access to critical controls. It was simply accepted that Starfleet personnel who had earned the opportunity to serve on a starship were among the most loyal and balanced the system could produce, so why spend time and engineering effort preventing such people from misusing controls when they would never choose to do so in any case? The added risk that complex ships such as the *Enterprise* might be made more vulnerable to hostile takeover from within had many times been proven worth the increased efficiency and flexibility such an open system provided. But judging from its shuttle, the *Queen Mary* was organized along completely different routines—almost as if Krulmadden were expecting someone to steal it from him every day. *Well*, Chekov thought, *at least this time he is correct.*

Krulmadden spun away from the copilot's station and pointed at Chekov. "Now *you* must help take Lasslanlin to the medic booth." Chekov unclipped his harness and floated off to begin his first work assignment for the shipmaster. It seemed an appropriate task considering he was the one who had made Lasslanlin require the medic booth in the first place.

In the hold, Lasslanlin was still wrapped in a stretcher cocoon and lashed to the 'down' bulkhead, his sleep inducer strapped to his head. Back at the tavern, the bartender had used a black-market medical tricorder to diagnose the Orion as having a broken nose, broken jaw, and concussion. On the *Enterprise*, Chekov knew that Dr. McCoy could have dealt with those injuries in less than half an hour, but with only a computer-run medic booth on board the *Queen Mary*, Lasslanlin was looking at two or three days of uncomfortable recuperation. Chekov hoped the stories he had heard about Orion vengeance oaths had been exaggerated.

The airlock was set in the hold's 'up' bulkhead—a departure from normal configuration. It should have been in the aft wall. As Chekov unhooked the elastic cords holding Lasslanlin's stretcher in place, he tried to determine if any other modifications had been made in the shuttle. Estimating the interior volume of the hold, he realized that it was not as large as he had expected it should be, based on what he had seen of the shuttle on its landing pad at the spaceport. The interior storage area appeared to end about two meters short of the craft's outside dimensions, even allowing for upgraded shielding, and Chekov suspected that Krulmadden had additional customized equipment installed in the dead volume.

Since a gravity generator would have had to run behind the 'down' bulkhead, Chekov decided he would give even odds that the shipmaster had added a small warp unit—maybe factor 1.5 to 2—or extended life-support capability. Either choice would make sense for someone who might have to make a quick getaway or need a place to hide out for a few months. Chekov reminded himself to pay close attention to other dimensions onboard the *Queen Mary*, to establish if any more capabilities were being hidden from him. He was certain there would be.

Artinton appeared on the other side of the *Queen Mary*'s airlock, looking through at everyone in the shuttle's hold. He held his hands out. "Be cautious pushing Lasslanlin through the lock. Go very slowly so the transition will not jar him."

"Transition?" Chekov asked as he carefully rotated the stretcher into an orientation that would enable it to fit through the narrow airlock. "Is there grawity on the *Queen Mary?*"

Krulmadden stared at Chekov. "Would you care for acceleration to nine-nine cee in thirty seconds without it? Krulmadden has clients who would be happy to spread what's left of you on their biscuits."

Chekov angled Lasslanlin perfectly, braced his feet on the 'down' bulkhead, then pushed the stretcher toward Artinton. "I was just surprised that you left it turned on when no one was aboard."

Krulmadden shook his head at Chekov. "You jump to too many conclusions for navigator. Who told you there were no others on board?"

"Why, no one. I . . . just thought . . ."

"I am shipmaster. I do thinking for all my crew."

Silent now, Chekov guided the end of the stretcher through the lock. When the opening was clear, he launched himself toward it to grip its metal lip, still cold from space despite its insulation. Then he felt the soft rippling pressure of the *Queen Mary*'s gravity field.

As he crawled through the meter-long tunnel, he decided he was not happy about Krulmadden's intimation that there might be other beings on board. Overpowering three Orions would not be beyond him and Sulu working together, especially if they struck while Lasslanlin was confined to the medic booth. But if there were other crew on board, especially other Orions, then it was beginning to look as if he and Sulu had just made the worst mistake of their brief civilian careers.

When Chekov was fully within the gravity field, he was puzzled at the amount of muscle tone he must have lost during his months of civilian life. The sudden transition from microgee was a surprising shock, much more strenuous than he had anticipated. And then he realized that yet another obstacle had been placed in their way. The artificial gravity field on the *Queen Mary* was set to normal for Rigel VIII—almost two Earth gees.

Chekov paused for a moment in the airlock—now an opening in a corridor floor—to reposition his hands for better purchase. But before he could move again, Artinton grabbed him under the armpits and hauled him up the rest of the way without apparent effort. The Orion mate moved as easily in the heavy gravity as he had in the low-power 'tourist field' that operated through most of the spaceport's alien quarter.

When Sulu appeared in the airlock, Artinton hoisted him through as well, and he enjoyed the look of surprise on Sulu's face as his feet hit the corridor floor faster and harder than he had expected. Chekov saw the look of apprehension on the helmsman's face and knew why it was there. A few days in this gravity and neither one of them would be able to crawl, let alone take on Krulmadden and his crew.

Artinton squatted down to slap an antigrav to Lasslanlin's

stretcher, then stood, lifting the mass-neutral stretcher with one powerful hand. "You wait here for shipmaster. On big ship like this, you could get lost . . . forever." He grinned at Chekov, flicking his tongue to show the holes where several teeth used to be, then started the stretcher gliding down the corridor.

Sulu stood by the airlock and rocked experimentally from foot to foot. "That's got to be at least a one point eight."

"It feels like five," Chekov said and stepped back to lean against the corridor bulkhead. As he rested, he glanced up the corridor in the direction that Artinton had gone. It was obviously a main branch that ran along the disk's diameter. Its narrow and utilitarian appearance, thick with exposed conduits and service access panels, was similar to the old class-J ships that Academy cadets trained on.

"From the way she looks on the outside, I wasn't expecting her to be even this up-to-date," Sulu said.

"That is only the light." Chekov fought the high gee to lift his hand and shield his eyes from the dazzling bluewhite glare that came from the corridor's ceiling panels. Like the gravity, they were set to produce Rigel VIII normal. "We will have to wear eye filters."

Before Chekov could find something else to complain about, Krulmadden smoothly popped through the airlock under his own power. He tried a few kneebends, then pounded his fist against his chest so his rings clanked against his tunic's hard scales. "Ah, the invigoration of real resistance!" He clapped his hand enthusiastically against Sulu's side and the helmsman slammed into the corridor bulkhead.

Krulmadden scowled as Sulu fought to keep his balance. He turned to Chekov. "A few months in real gravity and you behave like true shipmates. But in meantime, what you need is . . . exercise! Ur'eon exercise!" He laughed at the uncomfortable expressions on his new shipmates' faces. "You may think of that as an order."

Following Krulmadden's doubletime march through the *Queen Mary's* corridors reminded Chekov of being a cadet again, and he had hated being a cadet. The only good thing about that status was that it had led to the day he had become an ensign. But he knew that was exactly what he and Sulu had become again—cadets in Krulmadden's private navy. The shipmaster was making a pointed show of the control he wielded over them.

But still, there had to be limits. "Excuse me, Shipmaster," Chekov said, puffing as he eyed the third set of steep, interlevel ladders Krulmadden intended to lead them up, "but are there no turbolifts?"

"No room for drive tubes! No power!" Krulmadden grasped the rung of the ladder inset in the corridor wall. "Has the f'deraxt bred the spine out of its mammals as well as the brain and heart?" He leapt up the ladder, hand over hand, singing boisterously in a language Chekov had never heard before.

Chekov stared at Sulu. "I think perhaps it is a form of torture we are unfamiliar with."

Sulu looked up the ladder. "I think we're going to need a new plan."

Krulmadden's voice thundered down from above. "Waaaaiting, little mammals!"

Sulu began to climb. Chekov waited for the way to clear so he wouldn't suddenly be crushed by Sulu falling at 19.5 meters per second, and then he followed, already feeling blisters form on his hands.

From the sloping angle of the ceiling on the next level, Chekov concluded they had reached the main hull's top deck. Surely Krulmadden wasn't intent on taking them up to the warp pod, but Chekov wasn't even sure what the shipmaster's motives were for bringing them this far.

Krulmadden slowed his pace as he directed them along a curving corridor leading to port. Chekov, inhaling deeply to catch his breath, could hear Sulu breathing hard behind him. But when Krulmadden stopped by a set of doors and turned back to see how his new shipmates were doing, the huge being had not even broken a sweat.

Krulmadden placed one hand on the doors and leaned against them, waiting for Sulu and Chekov to catch up with him. "So my little mammals, do you have any idea where we are on this jewel of mine?"

"Top deck, main hull," Chekov wheezed, putting his hands on his knees to ease the strain on his back.

"Port side," Sulu gasped. "And we went through one-and-a-half circuits of the deck below us."

"Good, you pay attention." Krulmadden looked at the door panels beneath his hand and when he returned his gaze to Sulu and Chekov, he wasn't smiling. "Have you noticed anything else . . . unusual about this ship?"

"Besides no turbolifts?" Chekov asked.

"Very few doors," Sulu said. "Is the hull hollow?"

Chekov carefully watched Krulmadden for a reaction. If the *Queen Mary* were less massive than its apparent volume indicated, then it would be capable of greater acceleration than a potential enemy might expect. But the subterfuge would only work once and a large enough sensor array could detect a significant mass/volume discrepancy.

"On contrary," the shipmaster answered. "Is quite full. But of what, you need not know for now. Is enough simply to know not everything here is as it seems. And so is much danger . . . and destructions." He paused, but neither human interrupted. "Thus, all that remains . . . is to know if *you* are as you seem."

It was a threat, Chekov knew, and whatever happened next, Krulmadden had ensured that both humans would be too exhausted to try and make their way back through the ship to the shuttle. There was no choice but to continue with whatever the shipmaster had in mind.

"I don't understand," Sulu said. "You said you recognized us in the tavern."

Krulmadden ran his tongue over the diamond set in his incisor, and said very carefully in his best Standard, "Don't you find it convenient that I, a shipmaster in need of crew, and you,

73

crew in need of a ship, found each other on such a large planet in such a big galaxy?" He scratched at the corner of his eye. "Why were you in the tavern? So far from home?"

Chekov and Sulu exchanged a look: The strategy was in Chekov's hands.

"We were . . . looking for a ship."

"Why?"

"We have none."

"Why?"

Chekov was in no mood for this. "Because we are no longer in Starfleet."

Krulmadden stared at Chekov without blinking. "Why?"

"Because they called us worldkillers," Chekov said angrily. "I thought the great Krulmadden was supposed to know everything."

"How else to know than by asking questions? And now, a final one: Are you the worldkillers they say you are?"

Chekov hesitated before answering. Which would an Orion shipmaster prefer to have serving on his ship? Two brutal, reckless criminals that Starfleet had condemned by innuendo if not by courts-martial, or two wrongly accused officers who felt their honor had been smeared? He didn't know the answer, so he told the truth.

"No. The charges are false."

Krulmadden raised his thick black eyebrows. "Famed Starfleet is wrong?" He bit his knuckle and growled softly.

"Not wrong," Chekov said. "They just do not understand what truly occurred."

The shipmaster drummed his fingertips against the doors he leaned against. "What do you intend to do about it?"

Now that Chekov had established the plan, Sulu joined the conversation. "There is nothing more we can do about it. We resigned when that became obwious."

"Surely, you have . . . feelings about the way Starfleet has treated you?"

Chekov grimaced. "That is why we were looking for a ship."

Sulu smiled tightly through clenched teeth.

"Any ship? Or one ship in particular?"

"The type of ship we could find in a tavern. On Rigel VIII."

Krulmadden took his hand from the doors. He had made his decision. "The thirst for revenge can be as invigorating as the resistance of true gravity. I welcome you as crew on the jewel of all the stars."

"I thought that's what you did after the fight in the tavern," Sulu said, still wary.

"All that fight told me was the seriousness of you. I didn't need to know your anger with Lasslanlin and Artinton. I needed to know your anger with Starfleet. Too many spies have tried to board this ship in past."

"And what would have happened if you had decided we were spies as well?" Chekov hated unanswered questions.

"Then, my little mammals, you would have gone through these doors." Krulmadden smoothed his beard. "But, instead we shall go through those." He pointed to a second set of closed doors farther along the corridor. "Come." Krulmadden put his hand to his chest and began to croon again as he led the way.

As Chekov passed the doors Krulmadden had leaned against, he looked at the marker on them. But he couldn't read the Trader's Script. Sulu could. "Recycling room," the helmsman said.

Krulmadden stopped by the second set of doors and punched in a security code, using his massive body to block his fingers from Chekov's eyes.

"What does this one say?" Chekov asked, pointing to the marker on the new doors.

Sulu shrugged. "Cargo storage, I think."

The doors slid open and a warm breeze filled with a heady scent of rich cinnamon and other less familiar spices spilled past them. The room beyond the doors seemed huge.

"You read the Trader's Script well," Krulmadden said as he stepped aside and motioned for Sulu and Chekov to enter. "Indeed, this is part of my jewel's greatest cargo. Which you are welcome to enjoy."

Sulu entered first and Chekov saw him suddenly freeze only a few steps inside. Beside Chekov, Krulmadden laughed. "Ah, yes, quite a sight, are they not?"

Chekov stepped forward, feeling the weight of Krulmadden's hand patting him on his back.

"We do things differently from Starfleet onboard *Queen Mary,*" the shipmaster said gleefully. "You will be paid first and work tomorrow!"

Chekov peered into the vast room over Sulu's shoulder. "What is this?"

"The exercise I promised you!" Krulmadden laughed. "True Ur'eon exercise! Come, come, you are *f'deraxt'la* no more."

Then Chekov saw what had stopped Sulu dead and he realized the true nature of the monster they were forced to deal with if they were ever to clear their names.

In a long row of small cubicles stretched against one wall of the immense cargo hold were more than twenty Orion females. Their green skin glistened and their long black hair shone in the blue glow from the repulsor fields that ringed each open doorway, keeping them in place as inhumanly as any chains or irons.

Krulmadden was more than just another Orion pirate. He was the worst kind: an outlaw whose hideous crime had been condemned on each world of the Federation and was believed to have been forced into extinction. But perhaps evil was more powerful than even the Federation had realized. Because Shipmaster Krulmadden was a slaver.

And now, Chekov thought in rage, *so are we.*

SEVEN

Kirk remembered the *Farragut*, the first real ship he had served on—a Constitution-class starship like the *Enterprise*. He had been a green lieutenant and the *Farragut* was to be his first deep-space mission. The endless week between receiving his orders and finally arriving aboard her had been filled with his dreams of the new life of exploration and excitement that awaited him: first contact with alien worlds, going eye-to-eye with the Klingons, saving colonies, securing the frontiers. Then Kirk had run straight into what his father disparagingly called the "new Starfleet" and had spent his first six months managing supply crates in the *Farragut*'s cargo bay. He found it somehow fitting that he had returned there now, in spirit, if not in fact.

Surprised that he had retained so much of an almost fifteen-year-old skill, Kirk deftly managed the controls of a Mark IV Tractor Web to receive, sort, and secure the rapid stream of cargo crates being loaded onto the freighter, SS *Ian Shelton*. It helped that the old Mark IV was virtually identical to the one he had operated on the *Farragut*. His familiarity with it was how he had managed to swing the job of stevedore in the first place, jockeying the transfer of cargo from Intrator II's commercial spacedock to the freighter which was stationkeeping 200 meters away.

As Kirk worked the controls, the voice of the Orbital Transfer Controller came over the communicator link on the Mark IV's console. "How are you doing in there, *Shelton?*"

"All conditions are nom—uh, everything's okay so far." Kirk still had to concentrate to keep from falling into the old patterns of speech. He wasn't looking forward to another unveiling as had happened with the rockriggers, even though, despite his beard and longer hair, he knew it was inevitable. He had been surprised to find out how small a universe it was within the boundaries of Federation space.

"Sure you don't need a break in the flow to sort things out?"

"Keep 'em coming," Kirk said.

He could hear the grin in the Controller's voice. "Okay, hotshot, let's see if we can go for a new record."

The crates began floating through the open cargo-bay doors of the *Ian Shelton* at ten-second intervals, almost twice their previous rate. They were standard, interstellar modular crates whose polyhedron-angled sides were designed to prevent shifting during transport and which were just as easy to handle in microgee or with tractor webs as the less stable, cube-shaped crates still used for strictly planetside shipment.

"Hey, *Shelton,*" the Controller asked jovially, "sure you don't want us to slow it down to give the computer a chance to take over?"

"Slow it down?" Kirk asked, trying to sound puzzled. "I'm still waiting for you to speed it up."

The Mark IV's main projectors were arranged around the cargo-bay opening and along one bulkhead to produce a three-dimensional grid of tractor beams through which the crates moved. An inertial feedback circuit told Kirk the mass of each crate as the web acquired it so he could spread the density of the cargo throughout the hold as the crates were stacked, to keep the freighter's lines of thrust balanced. If the cargo had been completely uniform, or each crate had been outfitted with a reliable transponder to identify its contents, or there had been enough time for a sensor system to evaluate the crates for a computer that could stack them a thousand different ways in

78

memory as it searched for the most stable order, then Kirk's job could have been automated. But the real world of interstellar trade was not so orderly, so the almost infinite flexibility of a living mind was required. Along with absolutely no distractions.

Kirk involuntarily tensed when he heard the cargo-bay control room doors slide open behind him. Keeping a mental picture of the positions and masses of almost sixty crates in his mind at once as he tried to stack old ones at a rate exceeding the arrival of new ones, he didn't dare turn around to see who it was. A split second of hesitation on his part could lead to crate collision, cargo loss, and even hull damage. *Why do I get myself into these situations?* Kirk asked himself. It was one thing to go all out when the safety of his crew or his ship had depended on it. But for a ten-credit-an-hour job?

"Don't look up," a voice behind Kirk said. It was Anne Gauvreau, the ship's captain and his employer of the day. From the corner of his eye, he saw her standing by the console to look through the cargo-bay viewport. Then he heard her whistle.

"When Control said we were taking on cargo at one per ten, I thought they were joking."

Kirk made a noncommittal noise. His board showed the rate was already up to one crate every eight seconds. As far as he could see, in less than a minute there were going to be only two ways out. The first was to start stacking the crates without worrying about their mass. There was a possibility that the stacking density might balance out by chance, but if it didn't, then he'd be personally responsible for keeping the freighter in orbit for hours while he reshuffled the cargo.

The board showed a shipping rate of one per seven and Kirk knew he had reached his limit. No matter how uncomfortable he found the decision, he had to choose the second way out. The bottom line was that it wasn't his ship. He had to admit defeat. *It's only a job,* he told himself. He wasn't convinced.

"Come in, Control," Kirk called out to the communicator.

"Give us a break, *Shelton*. You don't have to rub it in."

Kirk didn't answer. He hadn't expected that reply. And then

he saw that no new crates were floating into the bay, though the manifest screen indicated there were still several hundred to load.

Kirk took the chance. "Orbital Transfer Control: What seems to be the trouble out there?"

The Controller took his time answering. "Uh, seems we got a burned-out impeller coil at the transfer bay, *Shelton.*"

Because he wasn't on an image link, Kirk smiled. Now he remembered why he got himself into these situations.

Gauvreau leaned forward to the console's communicator. "Orbital Transfer Control, Captain Gauvreau here. Tell me, do you happen to know why the coil burned out . . . ?"

The Controller was surprisingly contrite. "Because we couldn't keep up with the rate at which you were receiving cargo."

Gauvreau tapped her fingers on the console. "If I'm not out of here in two and a half hours, the business office is going to owe me some hefty penalties."

"We'll get back to you when the repairs are finished," the Controller said glumly.

Kirk heard the channel click off. He forced the smile from his face and looked up at Gauvreau with earnest concern. For a moment the freighter's captain had an expression of stern concentration. "Offhand, Leonard, I'd say you were one lucky bastard." Then she laughed and Kirk joined her.

"So what do you figure?" Gauvreau asked once the tension of the near-disaster in the cargo bay had been dissipated. "I'd say you were about two more seconds away from a chain-reaction pile-up that would have sent crates through the wall of the ship."

"Well, not exactly two seconds," Kirk began.

"Let me rephrase that," Gauvreau interrupted. "Through the wall of *my* ship."

Kirk tried to keep the smile from his face but had little success. "When I called Control, that's when I was going to . . . admit defeat and have them shut down the stream."

"One per eight on a Mark IV," Gauvreau said, shaking her head. She looked back out through the viewport. "You know, with the penalties they're liable for if I don't break orbit on schedule, they're going to be rushing that impeller repair. So I'd take care of that holding pattern you've got in there while you've got the chance."

Kirk turned back to the console and without the confusion of new crates arriving every few seconds, the stacking procedure was simple. He kept a few unusually massive and unusually light crates floating in temporary stacks and assigned the rest to a final storage configuration.

When he had finished, Kirk kept his hands on the controls, fully expecting the Controller to inform him that the coil had been replaced about one second before the first crate came blasting through the bay doors. At least with the extra time Kirk had had to straighten out the hold, even at one crate every five seconds he could handle the rest of the flow simply by keeping everything in temporary stacks. There would be room enough according to the manifest.

Gauvreau read the mass display of the final stacked crates appreciatively. "Good arrangement," she told Kirk. "Don't know how you built that pattern so quickly."

"That's my job," Kirk said.

Gauvreau seemed about to say something, then thought better of it. "So how does a young guy like you know how to run a Mark IV, but still keep up with new loading strategies?"

Kirk smiled at being called young. He estimated Gauvreau was only a few years older than he was, with just a few telltale strands of white in otherwise sandy and curly short hair. She was young for a commercial freighter captain—the way he had been young for a starship captain.

"Actually, I'm not that young. I trained on the Mark IV a long time ago. And I don't know anything about new loading strategies." Kirk had not been inclined to keep up with the literature since the day Captain Garrovick had rotated him out of the *Farragut*'s cargo bay.

Gauvreau tapped the mass display. "I've never seen that distribution pattern before. And I do know all about new loading strategies. That's *my* job."

There was something to her tone that put Kirk on the defensive, almost as if she were testing him.

"Do you play three-dimensional chess?" Kirk asked.

"Love it."

"Look at the mass display again. Think about middle games."

Gauvreau peered down at the screen, studying the density map of the cargo crates stored in the hold. "The Siryk Variations . . . ?"

Kirk nodded. It was a conservative approach to 3-D chess favored by players who preferred to wait until their opponents made exploitable errors. The variations of defensive placement developed by the Vulcan Grand Master Siryk emphasized arranging pieces in an interwoven pattern of strong and weak that did not permit much leeway for sudden offense, but created a near impenetrable defense.

Gauvreau laughed now that the seemingly new stacking pattern had been revealed as a game strategy more than four hundred years old. "The low-mass crates are pawns, the heavy-mass crates the more powerful pieces."

"That's it," Kirk said. "And I kept track of each crate's position by picturing the hold as an expanded 3-D chess grid."

"Very inventive." Gauvreau sat on the edge of the console and folded her arms. Kirk could see she had territory patches from dozens of star systems on the sleeves of her flight jacket. The back of the jacket held even more. Quite an accomplishment for someone who served in the merchant fleet, where freighters rarely had the capability for exceeding warp 2 and most stars were long months apart.

"You must be quite a player," she said. "Any grand master points?"

"I've never been in any tournaments."

"But you know enough about the Siryk Variations to fill a hold with them." She was obviously skeptical.

"I have . . . had a good opponent. A full grand master." He knew he shouldn't be surprised at the sudden ache he felt. But it was one of the few things he seemed to have no control over. Almost as if he expected never to see his friends again. "He was very dedicated to the Vulcan modes of play."

"Ever beat him?"

Those memories brought a smile back to Kirk's face. "Enough to bother him. The, uh, relentlessly logical approach to the game doesn't hold up all that well to completely . . . unexpected changes in tactics."

Gauvreau stuck her tongue in her cheek for a moment, reading between the lines. "'Unexpected changes in tactics,' hmm? As in 'acts of complete desperation'?"

Kirk hated to give away his secrets but the freighter captain was sharp. "Not complete desperation, exactly." But desperate enough to totally disrupt Spock's carefully planned, long-range attacks and keep him in awe of his captain's skills, never quite realizing that Kirk's ability not to show his panic accounted for much of his perceived mastery of the game.

The mass acquisition alarm sounded and the first crate floated into the hold beyond the viewport. Gauvreau glanced at the rate display. "Ha! One per twenty. You broke their spirits today, Leonard. You might as well put the bay on automatic."

Damn, Kirk thought. It wasn't much but he needed that ten credits an hour. He had been stunned at the cost of transportation on the frontier. The things he had taken for granted.

Gauvreau put her hand on his shoulder as he guided the first crates around the hold. "Don't worry about the credits for this job." Kirk was surprised at how well she read him. "If you're interested, the *Shelton* needs a supercargo."

Kirk hesitated at the controls long enough for the computer to divert a crate to a holding pattern. "This ship's only a few years old, fully automated. I'm surprised she even needs a captain."

"Like I said, Leonard. She's my ship. I *own* her."

Kirk was impressed. For an individual to own and operate a warp-capable ship as large and as expensive as the *Shelton* was quite an accomplishment. Usually ships of this class were the property of interstellar consortiums who spread the cost and the risk through the financial networks of four or five worlds.

"But still," Kirk said, "with tractor webs to keep everything secure, you only need a supercargo when you're in port. And there are lots around to hire." He knew. He had spent five days waiting for employment in the dockworkers' pool at Intrator II's spacedock, suffering the indignity of paying for food, water, and oxygen.

"Look, Leonard, I'm not used to trying to talk anyone into a job on the *Shelton*. Usually I'm in the position of telling people like you why I *don't* want to sign them onboard."

Kirk could believe it. But still, there was something about her. Young for a freighter captain. Was familiar with the Siryk Variations. Knew that he had pushed too hard to handle the cargo. There were few places from which people that sharp could come. He was almost surprised that he had never heard of her before today. *Of course, she thinks my name is Leonard Scott. Who knows what her real name might be?*

"Leonard, the next stop is Hanover. Two and a half lightyears toward the Arms of Avalon. At warp four we can be there in just under fifteen days."

"The *Shelton* can do warp four?"

Gauvreau looked impatient. "Yeah, and in addition to choosing my own engines, I got to pick the color of the bulkheads, too. Hanover, Leonard. Do you know it?"

Kirk thought for a moment, easily keeping up with the flow of crates into the hold. Two and a half lightyears to Hanover would put him about a lightyear closer to Starbase 29, without having to pay for passage. But there were still formalities, even on the frontier. "I don't have any commercial fleet certificates or proficiency papers." Not ones without his real name, at least.

Gauvreau put her hands on her hips and stared at Kirk in amazement. "Did I ask to see papers?"

"No."

"Then why be such a Herbert? Look, do you want the job or not?"

She didn't need him for the job she said she wanted him to do. But maybe it was just for the companionship. And a few games of chess. Whatever the reason, it would get him closer to where he had to go.

"I don't bite, Leonard, if that's what you're worried about." Kirk glanced at her. *I bet you do,* he thought. *I bet you tear apart anyone and anything you think might get in the way of what you want.* He understood that attitude. He felt he knew her already.

"All right. I'll take the job."

"Well, all right."

"All right."

Gauvreau stalked to the control room doors and they opened before her. "Well, okay," she said, then left before Kirk could try again to get the last word. It was going to be an interesting two weeks.

The *Ian Shelton* was little more than an unadorned cylindrical hull with a central bridge tower stuck amidships as if it had been no more than an afterthought. A small portion of the hull contained the warp and impulse propulsion systems. The rest of it was pressurized cargo area. Five crew and passenger cabins, the life-support system, and sensor and flight computers were crammed into the tower along with a bridge that was about the same size as Kirk's cabin had been on the *Enterprise.* But, still, he preferred being on the freighter's bridge to being in any of its cabins, each of which seemed to be the same size as his storage closet had been. At least on the bridge, no matter how cramped, he could see the stars move past the viewscreen. Even if he did have to put up with the ship's cats.

At the moment, one day out from Intrator II, cruising steadily under automatic pilot at warp four, two of Captain Gauvreau's orange and black cats were sleeping together on the chair by the impulse station. The third cat was somewhere else in the ship, all levels connected by open ladderways angled enough for the cats to use them. Kirk enjoyed the cats' noninterference, however temporary it might be, and sat at the engineering station, drinking coffee, watching the stars slip past. Talin's sun was outside the sweep of the forward sensors, but Kirk knew he was drawing closer. To the planet, and the answers.

He heard clanking footsteps behind him on the ladder leading up to the bridge. Unless the missing cat was like the one he had seen on Pyris VII and had suddenly gained a great deal of mass, then it was Gauvreau coming up. She was the only other person on board.

"Thought you might be interested in a game of chess," she said as she walked onto the bridge, checking the readouts on the three crew stations. She was still wearing her flight jacket and comfortable tan and black fatigues. She also carried a small packet about the size of a book.

"We're coming up to the first course correction," Kirk said. "Thought I'd check it out, and then . . . certainly." Kirk swallowed the last of his coffee—something that had once been somewhere near a coffee bean, at least. It had come out of the galley dispenser as a small dry cube in a pressure skin and he had had to place it in a cup of hot water himself. He had never appreciated how good the synthesized blend on the *Enterprise* had been, either.

"Leonard, the computers have been making this run for the past year. If the course correction doesn't match the navigation computer's projection, then an alarm goes off. And out here, no matter which direction we go in, we're still at least a day away from hitting anything."

Kirk nodded but he didn't leave his chair. "It's my way of doing something to earn my keep."

Gauvreau shrugged, then crouched down by the chair with the cats to scratch their ears. One of the cats shifted its position to place a second ear beneath Gauvreau's fingers, but neither cat opened its eyes to acknowledge its benefactor.

Give me a dog any day, Kirk thought. But still, he knew that one of the secrets of getting along with others was to take an interest in their interests. What made the approach so easy for Kirk was that he genuinely was interested in just about everything. Even, on a slow day, cats. "They're Earth cats, aren't they?" he asked.

"That's right," Gauvreau answered, and Kirk could hear the enthusiasm in her voice. She must have clocked a lot of parsecs with her companions. "Used to be called housecats, or domestics."

Kirk had heard of barn cats on Earth. There had been a couple on the farm in Iowa. But a housecat was something else again, he thought. "Aren't housecats those creatures on Meridian that, well . . ."

"No, no, the Meridian housecats got that name because that's how big they are. And because of the, uh, unusual symbiotic relationship they have with the smaller creatures who live inside them and are necessary . . . for their . . . reproduction." One of the cats wrapped its paws around Gauvreau's hand and gave it an experimental chew. "But anyway, that's why the boys here are called Earth cats these days, to distinguish them from all the other catlike creatures everywhere else."

"Are they any particular breed or clone branch?" As a child, Kirk and his brother, Sam, had had a Golden Lab named Lady and he had always told himself that someday, when he retired, he was going to get another. Though, now, even after resigning he still woke up mornings not feeling as if he had actually left Starfleet. He wondered if he would ever feel that he had.

"No," Gauvreau said. "That's the nice part. They're an old-fashioned, natural mix. Fairly hard to get these days."

Kirk checked the navigation board. The course correction was three minutes away. "They look so much alike. That's why I thought they might have been clones."

When Lady had become too old and the vet had been called, Kirk and Sam had pleaded with their parents to clone the dog so they could have another just like her. But George Kirk had refused. Cloning was fine for livestock cultures and transplant parts, he had told his sons, but an individual couldn't be treated like property. Their pet must be respected, and mourning her death would show that respect. The vet had eased Lady's discomfort and let her slip peacefully beyond all pain. Both boys had cried off and on for days.

It had been years before Kirk had realized what his father had been trying to teach him that day—how the fact that each person's life will end in death made life so precious. Since there could be no ultimate victory, Kirk had finally understood that what gave life meaning was the struggle. What few victories might come along the way could only be brief respites.

Fifteen years ago, on the *Farragut*, Captain Garrovick and more than two hundred crew had died horribly, red blood cells drained from their bodies, because of what Kirk had believed to have been a mistake on his part. It was remembering what his father had said the night Lady had died that had, in part, given him the strength he had needed not to leave Starfleet then, overcome by personal failure. The past must be accepted, the dead remembered, but the mission must always continue.

More than a decade later, on the *Enterprise*, Kirk had finally realized that he had not contributed to the *Farragut*'s tragedy. His only regret about the incident now was that his understanding of his father's lesson had come too late for him to thank George Kirk. But he could accept that situation, with sadness certainly, but without guilt or regret, because it was in the past. It was the present he was at war with, and always would be.

Gauvreau hit a spot on one of the cat's sides which made him roll onto his back, paws kneading the air. "You can't clone a pet," she said, and her voice was wistful, almost as if she also shared a moment like Kirk's in her past.

"What are their names?" Kirk asked, trying to break the solemn mood they had both succumbed to.

"Ah, this is Komack, this is Fitzpatrick, and Nogura is below decks sleeping on the mass converter."

Kirk stopped to play the names back for himself again, to be certain he had heard them correctly. "Komack, Fitzpatrick . . . and Nogura?"

Gauvreau smiled, one of her secrets revealed.

Kirk realized that one of his secrets had been revealed as well because of the way he had reacted to the names. "How long were you in Starfleet?" The cats were each named after an admiral.

"Twenty-one years," Gauvreau said, a hint of sadness returning to her voice.

"Twenty-*one?*" Kirk asked. Full retirement benefits were available after twenty years of service. Personnel generally retired then or not at all.

"Took me an extra year to figure out that I wasn't going to get what I wanted."

Kirk looked into Gauvreau's eyes. He didn't have to ask the next question. He knew the answer.

"One of these," she said, tapping her fist against the impulse control console. "Of my own."

"So you bought one."

Gauvreau nodded. "Not quite what I had in mind back when I was eight years old and decided what I wanted to do with my life. But at least she's mine. And Komack, Fitzpatrick, and Nogura can't say a thing about it."

"What was your rank?" Kirk asked. He found it surprising that a person with Gauvreau's qualities hadn't made it to command rank. He realized that's why he found her so familiar. She reminded him of himself.

"Commander."

Kirk was puzzled. She *had* made it to command rank. "There are more than a thousand ships in Starfleet." Why wasn't she given one?

Gauvreau stood up beside the cats. "At the time I left, there were only thirteen that mattered."

"Ahh," Kirk said. She was *exactly* like him.

"I exec-ed on the *Yorktown* for Decker. That gave me a taste of it. When he transferred to the *Constellation*, I was certain I'd get his chair. I knew the ship, had the ratings, the recs, and the experience. But they brought in von Holtzbrinck. They offered me the *Hawking*, instead."

Kirk nodded in understanding. The *Hawking* was a science vessel with a crew of just over one hundred and, as such, its mission was restricted to worlds without intelligent life, or which had already been exposed to the Federation. Science vessels either withdrew from critical situations so a starship could take over, or came in to complete follow-up studies of what a starship had already discovered. For a scientist or technical specialist, it was a near-perfect posting, offering the chance for lengthy and detailed analysis. But for an explorer, it was equivalent to being condemned to perpetual second place.

"I protested," Gauvreau went on, watching the stars on the viewscreen.

Gutsy, thought Kirk.

"I sent subspace memos to every starbase, and to Command, demanding a review."

Bordering on madness.

"And, 'after due consideration, blah, blah, blah,' nothing changed." She turned back to Kirk. "Decker said he'd take me with him to the *Constellation.* But being second . . . again. And as things turned out, maybe I did do the right thing by not going with him. Decker was a good officer. A good man."

The *Constellation's* entire crew had been lost. Decker had destroyed both himself and his ship to avenge them. He had been Kirk's friend. "I know," Kirk said. And then added, "I was, uh, in Starfleet, too," to cover his slip.

Gauvreau stared at him, as if making a decision. "I know you were, Captain Kirk."

Kirk sat rigid, prepared for another angry confrontation. They were a day out from anywhere, two weeks still to go to Hanover. If Gauvreau was another like those he had encountered among the rockriggers, if she not only accepted what had been said about him but believed he had not been punished enough. . . . "How long have you known?" No sense in denying it. He had to come up with a strategy for overpowering her without hurting her. If it came to that.

"Since I saw you in the dockworkers' pool. There was some subspace chatter about you being caught rockrigging for

Interworld, so there was a good chance you were still in the neighborhood."

Kirk had the sudden terrible feeling that she had been looking for him, and had brought him onboard the *Shelton* for a reason. He stared at his empty coffee cup. It had tasted so bad. So wrong. What did she want with him? What were her motives?

"So what happens now?" Kirk asked.

"First of all, you relax. I'm not a one-person recycler mob."

"Then what are you? Why 'hire' me?"

"To get you closer to Talin."

Kirk showed his surprise.

"That is where you're going." She made it a statement.

"Why do you say that?"

"Because that's what I'd do." She didn't wait for him to ask more questions. "Look, I know you, Kirk. At least, I know your type. You're like me—the kind of officer that gives the Admiralty their gray hairs. You've got to be resourceful and inventive enough to run the show when you're weeks away from getting advice and orders from Starfleet Command. But when you get those orders, you have to be the kind of person who'll follow them, even if you don't agree. It's an almost impossible mix. Like matter and antimatter. Starfleet has to be the magnetic bottle and you know how tricky those can be to keep properly aligned."

"What's your point, Captain?" Kirk was getting edgy. He hated not knowing what her motives were.

"My point is, whatever else you might be—maverick, impetuous, stubborn—and all those other things starship captains have to be, you're not a worldkiller. I know what you had to go through to get the *Enterprise.*" She held up two fingers, a centimeter apart. "I know what I went through to get even this close to a starship of my own. And I know the system doesn't let maniacs get that close, or go so far. For all that I have my reservations about Starfleet, even I have to admit the system works."

"It didn't give you your ship." Kirk wondered how much of what she said was the truth as she believed it, and how much was her trying to set him up for some other purpose.

"Thirteen starships, Captain Kirk, fifteen, maybe sixteen now, and how many thousands of would-be captains in Starfleet? I had my chance. I got close. And the same system that funnels us all through to one of those fifteen or sixteen chairs doesn't tend to produce officers who'd be happy to settle with second best, or with command of the *Hawking*."

"I still don't understand." On the viewscreen, the stars shifted slightly to port as the navigation system carried out the planned course correction. The change in heading was smooth, the inertial dampeners kept the ship feeling motionless. "If the system works as well as you say, then why don't you accept what the hearing on Talin concluded?"

Gauvreau sat at the navigation station to check the new course. As her fingers worked the controls, swiftly, almost instinctively—the legacy of her Starfleet training—she kept talking. "I accept most of the hearing's conclusions. Talin IV was a living, civilized world, a few decades at most from First Contact. The *Enterprise* went to the Talin system and . . . within five days Talin IV was a graveyard for an entire civilization."

"But you don't accept that it was my fault?"

Gauvreau looked over from the board. "Do you?"

"No." The word hung in the silence of the small bridge like a proclamation from the heavens. There was no equivocation in it, no hesitation or hint of qualification.

Gauvreau smiled at him. "Then why be surprised that I think the same thing?"

"Because Starfleet Command thinks otherwise."

"And you know what I think about Command. I said the system works. It's the current Admiralty I have trouble with." She turned in her chair and leaned forward. "Look, Kirk, don't be so defensive. I'm on your side. That's why I brought you onboard, all right? I figured you might need a couple of days of not feeling that the whole galaxy was trying to track you down. I figured if you were already out so far in this sector, then you'd probably appreciate getting another parsec or two closer to Talin."

Kirk watched the stars. He asked himself what he would have done if, after the Battle of Ghioghe, Starfleet had reassigned him to another patrol ship instead of giving him the *Enterprise*. Would he have stuck it out in a second-place command, hoping for another chance, knowing that once Command had made up its collective mind, an officer's career path might as well be etched in dichronium? Or would he have done what Gauvreau had done? Left Starfleet and taken command another way? He chuckled suddenly, surprised by the answer that came to mind.

"You changed the rules," he said.

"I beg your pardon?"

"The scenario Command laid out for you didn't suit you, so you changed the conditions of the game." He looked around the bridge. "And you won."

Gauvreau grimaced. "In a manner of speaking. This isn't the *Yorktown*."

"But it isn't the *Hawking*, either." Kirk took a closer look at the bridge, suddenly becoming aware of the subtle thrum of the Cochrane generator far below decks, and the gentle airflow of the life-support circulators. If the cards Starfleet had dealt him had not included command of a starship when he felt the time was right, instead of lose their game, he would have refused to play it. And he would have ended up here on the *Ian Shelton*, or a ship just like her. A winner by the only rules that counted—his own.

"We *are* alike," Kirk admitted. Because he knew if their roles had been reversed and Gauvreau had been cast out and he had been a commercial captain who could offer her a few days of rest, then he would. Not to gloat over Starfleet's failure or another person's misfortune. But because he and Gauvreau were . . . family. Two members of an exceedingly small family in an extremely large galaxy.

"Good," Gauvreau said. She tossed over the small packet she had carried up to the bridge. Kirk opened it. It was a manual grooming kit. "Thought you might like to wide beam the beard. Subspace visual's carrying tape from the Interworld rock so it's not much of a disguise anymore. I don't have a grooming booth on board but I can handle your hair, if you want."

Kirk scratched at his beard. There was no point in hiding behind it any longer. Not this close to his destination. "Thank you," he said.

"But . . . ?" Gauvreau asked, detecting the question building in him.

"How can you be so sure about me? You don't have the slightest idea about what really happened on Talin IV."

Gauvreau turned back to the navigation board. "But I will, won't I? If I were you, I'd want someone else to know the whole story. And I tell you, Kirk, fourteen days in space on an automated ship is a long, long time."

Not as long as my five days at Talin IV, Kirk thought. But Gauvreau was right.

It was time to tell his story.

Part Two

---- ☆ ----

THE LAST MISSION

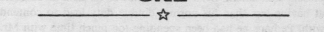

ONE

☆

Captain's Log, Supplemental. We are in the third day of our approach to Starfleet's First Contact Office outpost on the moon of Talin IV. Our slow travel toward the Talin system has been mandated by the FCO because of the planet's old-style radio astronomy capability. Though Talin astronomers could not visually detect the *Enterprise* at this distance from their planet, Starfleet does not want to risk the possibility that they might observe the radiation effects of dust and debris being swept from our path by our deflector shields at high-impulse velocities. Such anomalous signals might alert the Talin to the fact that an alien spacecraft is moving through their system at an appreciable percentage of lightspeed, which would, of course, be a violation of the Prime Directive. Thus we must travel at a velocity slow enough that our deflectors are not needed.

Sulu has done an admirable job of piloting the ship at speeds far less than those any of us are used to. For some of the crew, the past three days of standby duty and communications blackout have been a welcome break. However, other crew members are . . .

In the privacy of his cabin, Kirk tapped his desk screen to shut off the log recording. Somehow, the phrase 'crawling the walls' was not one he wished to consign to the permanence of an official log. Besides, as far as he could tell, he was the only crew member having trouble coping with the forced inactivity of this present assignment. Even Chekov showed no signs of edginess at having less than his normal double duty load to contend with. Perhaps he had been spending too much time with Mr. Spock and was acquiring a most uncharacteristic patience. Or maybe the old Academy legends were true and the ship's doctor *was* putting something into the water supply to keep everyone . . . tranquil.

Kirk told the computer to get him sickbay and Christine Chapel appeared on the captain's screen.

"Yes, Captain?"

"Put McCoy on." *What a starship needs is a bar,* Kirk thought. *A nice lounge somewhere, maybe forward where there'd be a good view, a few tables, a place to go and relax off duty.* Perhaps he'd suggest it in his next report. Starfleet Command was always looking for new ways to extend the mission time of their ships and a social gathering place might be a welcome addition to the ship's recreation facilities.

"The doctor's not in, Captain. Is there something—"

"Not in?" Even when he was off duty, McCoy was generally in his office, reviewing files, or reading the journals.

"He's at the A and A briefing, sir. Shall I get him for you?"

"No, that's fine, Nurse. It wasn't important." Kirk reached out to shut down the screen again.

"Excuse me, Captain. Just while I have you on the screen, according to our records, you're still overdue for that physical and perhaps—"

"Not now, Nurse Chapel. Try me later."

"But, Captain . . ."

"Thank you, Nurse." Kirk signed off and sighed. He drummed his fingers against his desk. Two more days of this. He told the computer to get him the bridge.

This time, Ensign Leslie appeared on the screen. "Bridge here."

"Where's Uhura?" Not the most pleasant way to greet a crew member, Kirk knew, but after all, this *was* Uhura's duty cycle.

Leslie looked nervous. "Uh, with the communications blackout, sir, she said . . . she said that there was no point in staying at her station, so she assigned me to monitor for emergency signals."

Kirk was surprised but decided he couldn't take Mr. Leslie to task for Uhura's actions. He knew he himself had set the precedent that allowed most bridge specialists on his ship to choose for themselves when their work could be better performed at other locations in the ship. But that flexibility really couldn't extend to essential personnel such as helm and navigation—and he had never thought of communications as anything other than equally essential. *Except, perhaps, during a communications blackout.*

"Tell me, Mr. Leslie, where *is* Lieutenant Uhura?"

"Uh, I believe she's at the A and A briefing, sir. I could call her—"

"That's all right, mister. I'll . . . have a talk with her later. Get me Spock, please."

"Um, Mr. Spock is not on the bridge either, sir."

This time, Kirk was more than surprised. "We're traveling into a system we've never visited before and Spock isn't at the science station?" *Has everyone decided to take the day off?*

"Sir, the FCO has spent eight years surveying the Talin system in considerable detail and since we can't use our main sensors because of the blackout . . . well, almost all the science departments are shut down for maintenance."

Kirk sighed again. "I see. And would you happen to know where Mr. Spock is?"

"Yes, sir. He's attending the A—"

"—And A briefing. Why not? Everyone else is. Tell me, is there *anyone* on the bridge other than you?"

The ensign looked puzzled for a moment. "Well, uh, Dr. M'Benga is here, and—"

Kirk felt a welcome rush of adrenaline. "What's the doctor doing on the bridge? Has there been an accident?" Kirk jumped up by his desk, ready to run for the turbolift.

"No, sir," Leslie answered calmly. "Nothing like that. It's just that . . ." He looked away from the screen for a moment. "Well, since we're not traveling that fast, Mr. Sulu is sort of letting everyone try—"

Kirk held up his hands. "Don't tell me. I don't want to know." One of his worst nightmares had come true: The *Enterprise* had turned into a cruise ship.

The viewscreen flashed over to the helm station. Sulu was just sitting down. M'Benga stood behind him, looking sheepish. "Sulu here, Captain. Everything's under control, sir."

"I'm glad you think so."

"Really, sir. Helm and navigation are supposed to be part of the emergency preparedness program, but it's not too often that we get the conditions where regulations allow EPP trainees on the controls. And at this speed and heading, sir, believe me, we've got those conditions."

It's not going to be one of those days, Kirk thought. *It's going to be one of those months.* "I have the utmost faith in you, Mr. Sulu."

"Thank you, Captain."

"Just one question."

"Go ahead, sir."

"Why aren't *you* at the A and A briefing?"

Sulu smiled. "I lost the toss to Chekov, sir."

"I see. Well, carry on, Mr. Sulu—or should I say, Dr. M'Benga. Just try not to hit anything . . . like a planet."

M'Benga leaned down to bring himself within range of the helm communication scanner. He adopted his best, serious-physician demeanor and spoke gravely. "I'll *try,* Captain." Then he and Sulu broke into wide grins.

Kirk waved his hand at the screen, searching for the words, any words, to show that he could go along with their joke. He knew his crew already suspected that the past three days had turned their captain into a high-strung worrier and there was no need to give them additional ammunition. But he couldn't think of anything to add that they wouldn't take the wrong way. "Kirk out," he said in defeat, and the screen shut off. *At least morale is high,* Kirk thought. *Everyone else's that is.*

He spent a minute or two staring at the walls of his cabin until they seemed to be moving in on him and that's when he knew he had had enough. "When on Centaurus," he muttered, and then left his cabin to attend the A & A briefing.

Lieutenant Carolyn Palamas had been the ship's A & A officer from the start of the five-year mission. In that time, Kirk could remember her accompanying him on a handful of landing parties, most notably the near-disastrous return mission to Avalon and the run-in with million-year-old warrior robots at the Asteroid Tessel excavations. She had also been present on Pollux IV when the *Enterprise* had encountered an alien who might well have been known to ancient humans as the Greek god, Apollo. In short, she had served competently during a wide range of experiences typical for a starship crew member. She was also an attractive, blond-haired and blue-eyed human, and well-liked by her staff and crew. Especially by Scotty a few years back, Kirk recalled, though nothing had come of it.

But even so, Kirk was hard pressed to understand why almost one hundred other crew members had turned up in the ship's theater for the lieutenant's briefing on Talin IV. It seemed rather unusual that so many of the *Enterprise's* crew shared a passion for Palama's specialty: anthropology and archaeology.

When Kirk entered the theater, he had to silently refuse a dozen crew members who offered to give him their seats. He preferred to lean against one of the back walls. At least there he could sneak out again if the presentation wasn't interesting. He noticed Spock sitting off to the side in the second row, close to the podium in the center of the stage. Surprisingly, McCoy was sitting beside him. Every few seconds, Kirk could see the two officers whispering back and forth. McCoy was even looking pleased with himself. Kirk reminded himself to get in on whatever was going on between the two later, then settled back to listen to the lieutenant.

"Coming up on the screen right now is a computer composite of a typical set of Talin IV's dominant intelligent species." Palamas touched a control on her podium and a detailed, political and cartographic display of Talin IV was replaced by an image of two reddish-skinned adults and one green-skinned child. Lying beside them was what appeared to be an incompletely formed larval version of a Talin. However, according to the scale grid, the softly rounded, pale white form was the same size as the two adults on the screen—about two and a half meters high.

The adults' faces were each the shape of a smoothly curving, forward sloping egg, sliced through the bottom third by a wide, lipless mouth which opened and shut, revealing an upper and lower row of small, sharp teeth. Kirk could see no nostrils as such, unless they were somehow incorporated into the asymmetrical hearing membranes on either side of the head, near where the jaw pivoted. Each adult's face was dominated by a pair of large, yellow eyes, perhaps twice the size of a human's and dotted by small black central pupils. The child's face had less slope, no teeth, and much larger eyes.

Palamas then rotated the computer composites through a full four hundred degrees. The images moved to show the mobility and gait of the Talins' long arms and legs. As he studied the images, Kirk noticed that each adult wore a biblike covering that hung from a loop of fabric around its neck, continuing down to another loop that slipped between the legs to hook over a small protuberance at the end of the spine. He guessed it was a vestigial tail.

"As you can see," Palamas explained to her attentive audience, "the Talin are saurian bipeds, though completely different in body structure from the Gornaran archosaurs. Instead, the Talin share some of the characteristics of Earth lizards and birds, notably in the loose folds of pebbly-textured skin and the

102

thin and delicate skeletal structure. As is typical on more than ninety percent of class-M planets, there are two sexes on Talin IV and the female parent carries the live young to term. Preliminary fauna sampling runs indicate that the evolutionary predecessors of the Talin were egg-laying."

An ensign wearing a red support-services shirt raised her hand and Palamas nodded at her. "Is that what the fourth figure on the screen shows? An egg casing? It looks so large."

"No, but that's a good question. What we're looking at here is an adult hibernation cocoon. Apparently, it's an evolutionary artifact from the Talin's predecessor species. Many equatorial lifeforms on the planet continue to exude a moisture-impervious substance which hardens into a protective shell. The creatures undergo this type of sealed-in hibernation during the extreme seasonal variations when water virtually disappears from the planet's equatorial deserts. The Talin themselves still retain this capability, though because of their relatively advanced technology—including extensive irrigation projects, climate-controlled housing, and efficient agriculture—a hibernation cocoon like this one is rarely seen among the Talin except in cases of extreme trauma or illness. Indeed, in most of the major nation states, there is a cultural prejudice against it—almost as if it's a reminder of their bestial past. We have noticed that in their popular entertainment, references to the hibernation cocoon and the distinctive odor of the skin secretion which forms it are usually at the level of what we would call crude humor."

"How can you tell male from female?" another crew member asked. Kirk looked again at the image on the screen and though both adult figures were virtually identical, he decided the male was probably the adult with the more pronounced cranial crest—it seemed to be composed of thick tufts of hair about ten centimeters high which ran in a stripe from the center of the head along the extended neck, getting shorter until it vanished about halfway down the creature's back. The other adult's crest was only half as high and disappeared on the neck, not the back

Of course, Kirk had seen enough different lifeforms in his career that he wouldn't be surprised if the male turned out to be the small, green, childlike figure.

"Another good question," Palamas said. "There are few obvious body structure differences and, among Talin themselves, the chief distinction seems to involve odor. The FCO suspects that pheromones are also involved, though Talin biologists have not yet formalized the concept of hormones that act outside the body, so there is no real literature or transmissions Starfleet can study." Palamas continued, looking back at the screen. "Other sex-related differences are the range of colors through which the skin can change, similar to that of the Vulcan askor or the Earth chameleon. Males can color change further into the red spectrum; females change further into the blue. Again, color changing might be far more complex than it appears to be in just the visible spectrum, but the Talin haven't investigated this so we can't know for sure, ourselves.

"Now, as you can see here, Talin children start out green and, as they mature, slowly acquire the ability to change skin color. We believe the whole phenomenon involves a mixture of conscious and autonomic control, somewhat similar to our own breathing process. The FCO doesn't claim to have a great understanding of the importance of skin-color changing— timing, setting, taboos, and so on—because it is somehow closely related to pair bonding and mating. As I've said, the Talin are very similar to humans circa 1975 to 2000 C.E., and that extends to their cultural reluctance to discuss or depict the details of their mating habits in broadcast transmissions or any publications intended for wide release. Unfortunately, those are the only data sources the FCO has been able to study in detail thus far."

"That's only because the *Enterprise* hasn't gotten there yet!" someone called out and the audience cheered and broke into applause. Kirk smiled at their enthusiasm. According to the report he had received along with his orders, one of the *Enterprise*'s functions on this mission would be to place FCO intrusive-collection specialists into important data-collection sites to extract more detailed information than was currently available.

Palamas glanced at the screenpad on her podium as the applause died down, then said, "Well, that's about all the time we have for today, so—yes, Dr. McCoy?"

McCoy stood up beside Spock. "Just one last question, Lieutenant. You say the Talin are similar to humans in the last quarter of the twentieth century?"

"That's right."

Kirk saw Spock whisper something to McCoy, but McCoy ignored him. "In other words, they're showing great promise in technology, they're on the brink of stepping out into space, they've achieved global communications, and have made a start at conquering most major diseases."

Palamas thought the doctor's words over for a moment. "Well, yes, in general, I'd say that is the case."

McCoy raised a finger and Kirk could see that he was winding up for the kill. "And, just to clarify things, these creatures do have emotions, don't they? I mean, they don't try to hide them or anything?"

Kirk could see Palamas take a quick look at Spock. "They're not Andorians, Dr. McCoy, but the Talin do have a complex range of emotions, of which most are incorporated into their culture in an open and accepted manner."

McCoy smiled at Spock. "Thank you, Lieutenant. Great achievements. Openly emotional. I just wanted to make sure I was clear on that."

As McCoy sat back down, Spock stood up.

"Yes, Mister Spock?" Palamas asked. Kirk could see she knew she was not going to be able to get away easily. After almost five years onboard the *Enterprise*, most of the original crew knew that when McCoy and Spock were involved in one of their 'discussions,' the best place to be was on another ship. Or in another sector.

"A further point of clarification, if you please, Lieutenant. Is not one of the main points of comparison between the contemporary Talin and late-twentieth-century humans the fact that

Talin is currently poised on the brink of a devastating thermo-nuclear war between several of its most advanced nation states?"

Kirk knew he wouldn't have to ask what Spock and McCoy had been discussing during the briefing. Their questions were making it all too obvious.

"That's correct, sir," Palamas acknowledged. The fragile stability of Talin was one of the chief reasons for the urgency of the *Enterprise's* current assignment.

"And furthermore," Spock continued, "is it not true that the root cause of the conflict between the Talin nations is based not on need but on ideological differences?"

"As far as we can ascertain, that's also correct, yes, sir."

"Ideological differences that could best be described as . . . emotional in nature?"

But McCoy wasn't going down without a fight. "You're joking, Spock. You can't honestly believe that a debate that's been going on for a century between all the different sides on Talin is an *emotional* conflict?"

Vulcans had emotions, they just didn't permit those emotions to show in public or allow them to control their actions. But Kirk suspected that the bland expression on Spock's face as he looked down at McCoy was really an unbridled display of Vulcan superiority. "Dr. McCoy, the histories of a thousand worlds offer ample proof that, at root, virtually all political conflicts are emotional in nature, no matter how well-disguised they are by ideological rhetoric."

"Good Lord, Spock, the Talin are arguing over who has the right to educate their children, who controls the water resources, at what regional level government responsibilities should be—"

"Doctor, the Talin are arguing over who is bigger and better. Everything else is beside the point."

McCoy folded his arms against his chest. "Well, at least you're the right one to be discussing *points.*"

"Doctor, I fail to see—"

Palamas leaned closer to the sound pickup on the podium so

106

her amplified voice overpowered Spock's. "We're out of time for now, so I'd like to thank you all for your attendance today. Tomorrow, I'll continue with an overview of a few of the unique characteristics of the Talin and their planet which has made applying the Richter Scale of Culture so simple. For a change." The large viewscreen above Palamas shut down and the audience broke into appreciative applause, drowning out McCoy's reply to Spock's unheard statement.

Kirk moved against the flow of people leaving the theater so he could join Spock and McCoy. Both officers were now in a private discussion with Palamas at the podium as she gathered up her screenpad and microtapes. As Kirk approached, he heard her saying something about 'the MAD deterrence.'

"MAD?" Kirk asked as he stepped up behind McCoy and Spock.

"Mutual assured destruction," Palamas said. "Each of the belligerent nation states on Talin possesses enough fusion weapons and appropriate delivery systems to totally annihilate its adversary, no matter which side attacks first. The MAD theory, as it was called when it was developed on Earth, presumed that since there was no advantage to striking first, then peace would be maintained. Or at least, conflict would not escalate past the point of no return."

"A typically human theory," Spock commented.

McCoy leaned past Kirk to glower at the science officer. "It worked on Earth, Spock."

Spock raised an eyebrow. "For approximately sixty years, Doctor. Until your Colonel Green decided quite emotionally, and quite illogically, that there *would* be an advantage—"

Kirk held up his hand. "Gentlemen, I don't think we have to give the A and A officer a rundown on Earth history." He smiled at Palamas. He had forgotten how brilliantly blue-gray her eyes were.

"Thank you, Captain," the lieutenant said. "And actually, both Dr. McCoy and Mr. Spock are correct."

McCoy bowed his head. "Why, thank you, Lieutenant."

"She said we were *both* correct," Spock emphasized.

"How so?" Kirk asked.

"Historical records from the time do show that at particular times of tension, the leaders of Earth's nation states made the decision not to commit fusion weapons to a conflict because they feared the resultant escalation of hostilities would lead to a conflict in which both sides would be destroyed. Therefore, when both sides are perceived by each other to be evenly matched, then the MAD deterrence can be said to be effective."

"The key word being 'perceived,'" Kirk put in.

Spock nodded. "As soon as one side in a conflict determines that it has an advantage over the other—at the time of Colonel Green, it was Hanson Smith's surprise development of the particle curtain ten years earlier than the scientific community thought possible—then there is a benefit to be had in striking first, before the sides can be equalized again."

McCoy put his hand on Kirk's shoulder to prevent the captain from interrupting. "But Spock, even the Third World War didn't involve the use of fusion weapons. Surely that means that *something* was working."

"Doctor, the Eugenics Wars of the 1990s were not called such by historians until three decades after the fact. There was so much upheaval in your world at the time, that few, if any, of the general population were aware that the struggle between the so-called genetic supermen was actually going on behind the scenes. Only with the revelations made possible by the passage of years did Earth historians decide to reclassify key events. Because of those reclassifications, your Second World War was deemed to finally end in the early 1990s with the events immediately following arbitrarily being called the Third World War. But you are quite right in that it was not an open conflict of munitions and armies. It was a hidden and secretive conflict of science and politics. And, I need not add, of emotions."

Palamas smiled in conciliation at McCoy. "I'm afraid he has you there, Doctor. But who knows? In another hundred years, we could have new interpretations."

"History is history," McCoy grumbled.

"And it's written by the winner," Kirk said. Then, before

either Spock or McCoy could continue, "But tell me, Lieutenant, is the situation on Talin actually that precarious? I know that what I saw in the FCO report was alarming, but we've seen dozens of worlds successfully pass through tense political situations. And the Talin cultures do appear to be stable."

Palamas frowned. "We have also seen dozens of worlds fail to survive situations similar to what Talin is experiencing, Captain. I think that's why the crew has become so caught up in our mission to Talin IV."

"Please, let me get those." Kirk reached out to take the screenpad and collection of microtape wafers from Palamas. He ignored the look that McCoy and Spock thought they exchanged without him seeing. If he was being obvious, then at least his actions wouldn't be misinterpreted. "And perhaps, Lieutenant, you'd like to continue this conversation over a drink in Dr. McCoy's cabin." With Scott still working overtime to get the sensor satellites adjusted to the FCO's specifications, that's where the best liquid refreshments aboard were to be found.

"Thank you, Captain, Doctor. I'd enjoy that." But she didn't relinquish any of the items she was carrying. "And I can carry my own books home from school, thanks anyway."

Kirk ignored her words and focused instead on the smile she had given him. Two more days without too much to do might be pleasant after all, provided he had someone to share them with. As he led Palamas, Spock, and McCoy from the theater, he said, "You were explaining to us why you thought the crew was so involved with our mission, Lieutenant."

"There are a number of factors, Captain. I think we're all hoping that the Talin will survive their present difficulties, the way Earth did. And since the majority of the crew is from Earth and Earth colonies, there is definitely a sense of personal involvement."

Kirk walked toward the theater doors without breaking stride and they swept open before him. "To be fair, Lieutenant, I've yet to see a mission that this crew didn't get personally involved with."

"Well, yes, sir. The crew is an extremely committed group. But . . . "

"Go on, please," Kirk said as they moved through the corridors toward the turbolift.

"I think some of the crew are hoping that this might turn into a first contact mission, sir."

Spock stopped almost as quickly as Kirk. McCoy took a few more steps before he realized he was walking by himself.

Kirk frowned. "Why would anyone think we're on a first contact mission?" The *Enterprise* had seen her share of first contacts with other civilizations, but most had been the inevitable meetings between spacefaring explorers. The Talin had barely left the orbit of their own planet and were firmly under the jurisdiction of the FCO.

Palamas shrugged. "Reading between the lines of the FCO report on the political situation on Talin, sir, there is a better than fifty percent chance that they will become involved in an all-out fusion war within the next six months."

"Sixty-four point five percent," Spock said.

"What does that have to do with anything?" Kirk asked.

Palamas looked embarrassed. "Well, sir. Membership in the Federation has been shown to have a . . . calming influence on a planet's regional disputes. Some of the crew feel, that . . . perhaps to save the Talin—"

"We'd reveal ourselves?" Kirk was astounded.

"Well, yes, sir. Something like that."

Kirk turned to Spock. "Spock, according to the FCO projections, when might the Talin be expected to be able to learn that there are several spacefaring cultures in their vicinity?"

"Apparently, Talin IV does have some unique characteristics which make a precise time difficult to calculate, Captain, but at the minimum estimation, the Talin are at least twenty to thirty standard years from achieving the required technological breakthroughs."

Kirk looked back at Palamas. "Twenty to thirty years, Lieutenant. Whoever makes first contact with the Talin, it won't be us. And I'm surprised the crew isn't more aware of General Order Number One."

"Oh, they're aware, Captain Kirk. A lot of them just can't see the point of noninterference if it means an entire race might die."

McCoy stepped closer. "You can't blame them for hoping, Jim. It's not easy for any one of us to just stand back and watch a disaster unfolding. And I'd guess that you know that as much as anyone onboard."

"Captain," Palamas said, "I know that there is no member of this crew who is planning on doing anything other than his or her duty on this mission. It's just that given the severity of the situation, they think that Starfleet and the Federation Council might make an exception to the Prime Directive."

Spock placed his hands behind his back. "As soon as an exception is made, Lieutenant, it is no longer the Prime Directive. As a historian, you should be aware of the tragedies that inevitably result when a more powerful culture attempts to set standards for those that cannot stand against it. The Federation flourishes because it is founded on the principles of informed choice and cooperation among equals. We cannot presume to have either the moral or ethical right to proclaim what other cultures should do until they have achieved a level of development sufficient enough to consider what we have to offer as equals. They must be free to turn us down, without feeling forced to capitulate in order to gain our advanced technology and knowledge. For those reasons, among many others, it is a most logical and necessary position."

Kirk could see the fire building in the lieutenant's eyes as she listened to Spock's lecture. "But as a historian, Mr. Spock, I am also aware that it was an uncrewed Vulcan robot probe that prevented a cometary fragment from wiping out half of central Europe in the early 1900s, by diverting the body to explode over an uninhabited region of Siberia. That changed the future history of the entire planet."

"That incident," said Spock, "was a preventable natural

disaster, not in any way caused by the humans of the time. The Prime Directive explicitly directs us to protect emerging cultures from similar disasters, provided we do not reveal ourselves. Indeed, the *Enterprise* herself has done so many times in the past."

Palamas was not up to debating Spock. In fact, Kirk decided, there was no one onboard who was. The only reason McCoy kept trying was because he didn't know any better. Upset now, but trying not to let it show, the lieutenant conceded the argument. "I do think a case could be made for treating an unthinkable war as a natural disaster of the worst kind, but a Starfleet lieutenant is not the person to do it, Mr. Spock. It's just that I shall be very sad if we are forced to do nothing as we witness an entire race commit suicide."

"As shall I, Lieutenant," Spock said, and Kirk knew it was a rare admission for him to make to someone he did not know well.

Palamas watched Spock for a moment, as if realizing what it took for the Vulcan half of him to comment on his feelings, then nodded at Kirk. "I think I'll pass on that drink for now, Captain. I . . . have to prepare for tomorrow's briefing."

It was Kirk's turn to concede. It was apparent he would not be spending the next few hours in her company and he would not dream of trying to change her mind. "I'll look forward to hearing it," he said graciously.

Palamas said her good-byes, then headed back down the corridor, away from the lift.

McCoy watched her go, unconsciously duplicating Spock's pose by placing his hands behind his back as well. "Well, at least someone on this ship has feelings about our job."

Spock's face rested in his habitual, neutral expression. "And at least she does not allow those feelings to interfere with the proper performance of it."

Kirk saw McCoy and Spock narrow their eyes at each other, preparing to launch into yet another round. "Gentlemen, I believe we were headed to the doctor's cabin," he said to interrupt them. "Perhaps we can continue our discussion of ancient history there." He began walking toward the turbolift and heard McCoy and Spock fall into step behind him in silence. For the moment, peace had returned to his ship, even though he knew it wouldn't last. Because Lieutenant Palamas wouldn't be the only crew member who would be upset if the *Enterprise* were forced to do nothing but watch as a world destroyed itself.

But it won't come to that, Kirk told himself. *It can't come to that.*

He was a starship captain.

He would not allow it.

TWO

☆

Of all the strange and miraculous discoveries humans had made in their expansion into space, perhaps none had been as initially unexpected as the revelation that life was literally everywhere.

That knowledge had grown slowly with each step outward that humans had taken: life on Earth; fossils on Mars; space-borne organisms blowing in the solar wind; plant analogues on Titan; and then the *Icarus's* surprising first contact with the Centaurans and the subsequent discovery of all the other spacefaring civilizations.

At first, the realization that the *absence* of life was the exception to the rule was greeted with doubt and disbelief. There was maddeningly inconclusive evidence to suggest that perhaps some planets had been deliberately seeded by an ancient and more advanced race, unofficially known as the Preservers, and that, as a result, the natural incidence of independently arisen life could never be known. But, more often than not, detailed bioanalyses demonstrated that life was an almost inevitable by-product of planetary development throughout the galaxy. And since planets themselves had been shown to be a virtually inevitable by-product of stellar forma-

114

tion, contemporary scientists were more surprised *not* to find life than to find new forms around any given star.

The other startling discovery about life, which was also accepted as an inevitable by-product of universal principles throughout the galaxy, was the degree of evolutionary congruence it exhibited. If a planet had a thick enough atmosphere, then it had creatures that could fly. If it had free water, then it had creatures that could swim and extract oxygen through gill-like structures. And if a planet had existed peacefully for enough millennia without major extinctions or drastic ecological upheavals, then as surely as dilithium crystals extended into the fourth dimension, that planet would give rise to intelligent life. According to the latest Federation estimates, there were millions of such planets existing in the galaxy, and to contemplate the hundreds of millions of other galaxies wheeling beyond the great barrier surrounding the Milky Way was to experience a sense of wonder about life which could overwhelm even the orderly minds of Vulcans.

But there was more than wonder and new scientific knowledge accompanying the Federation's realization of the universality of intelligent life, there was also the burden of great responsibility. Because, for every civilization which was more advanced than those making up the Federation, there were a hundred which were less so. And every one of those less-advanced worlds would, in time, have been overwhelmed by the Federation's superior technological culture and well-intentioned aid and enlightenment—unless drastic measures were taken.

Thus, for the good of intergalactic peace, to acknowledge the uniqueness of each culture without prejudice, and in recognition that each intelligent lifeform must be free to choose its own future, the Federation created its most severe, most troublesome, yet most honorable and sacred commandment: Starfleet's General Order Number One.

The principle was this: The Federation would never allow itself to act as judge and jury to a developing alien culture. Only when cultures had developed to an appropriate point where they could withstand exposure to an interstellar community would they be informed of the Federation's existence.

To set conditions of development, to monitor emerging civilizations, and, when conditions were right, to break the conspiracy of silence, the worlds of the Federation authorized Starfleet to form one of its most important branches. It was called Starfleet's First Contact Office, and the beings who ran it, above all else, were the keepers of the Prime Directive.

With more relief than Kirk thought he had ever before heard in his helmsman's voice, Sulu announced that the *Enterprise* had achieved standard orbit around the moon of Talin IV. Evidently, Kirk wasn't the only one who sensed what Sulu felt, because the entire bridge crew, with the exception of Spock, applauded.

"Well done, Mr. Sulu." Kirk spun around in his chair. "Lieutenant Uhura, when will we be able to raise the FCO?"

"Coming up on the horizon in three minutes, Captain. Subspace tightbeam standing by to send and receive."

"Very good." Kirk swung back to face the main screen, enjoying the feeling of having the ship come alive around him again. This trip had been the longest five days he had ever spent on her. "Let's have some scenery on the screen, Mr. Chekov."

"Aye-aye, Keptin." The viewscreen image changed to show the sunlit surface of Talin's moon moving eight hundred kilometers beneath the ship. It was a typical, airless planet— heavily cratered, studded with sharp, unweathered mountains and swept with dark seas of ancient lava flows. It reminded Kirk of Earth's Moon, back in the old days, before it had been spoiled by overdevelopment. At least Earth's Moon was one of the last worlds to have been treated in such a way. It might take a long time, but the success of the Federation had shown that humans were capable of learning how to change their behavior, as individuals and as groups.

Chekov abruptly turned away from his board. "Keptin, there

is a space wessel approaching. Three thousand kilometers, sir. And we are closing fast."

"Spock? An FCO shuttle?"

Spock peered into his science station scope where complex data from the ship's sensor networks were holographically presented without interference from the bridge's main lighting. "Difficult to say, Captain. With the blackout conditions, we are forced to rely on passive sensor systems only. No indication of impulse propulsion." He looked up. "No indication of any kind of propulsion."

"Could it be a meteoroid?" Kirk asked.

"No, sir," Chekov answered. "Light-reflection profile indicates a regular shape. Definitely artificial."

"Then is it a Talin lunar satellite?" Kirk tapped his hand on the arm of his chair.

"It is not in lunar orbit," Spock said. He turned back to his scope. "However, the trajectory does indicate Talin IV as its likely launch point."

Kirk stepped from his chair to look over Chekov's shoulder at the deviation plotter. "We know the Talin have sent three missions to their moon. Is there any way we can determine if there's a crew on board the approaching ship, without using our sensors?"

"Not with certainty at this distance," Spock said. "However, I am running a comparison of the vessel with known schematics of Talin lunar satellites and crewed vessels."

Kirk turned to the communications station. "How are we doing with that tightbeam to the FCO, Uhura?"

"One minute to horizon, Captain. But, sir, if that *is* a Talin lunar mission, the FCO would have warned us about it with an emergency pulse."

"Assuming they knew about it, Lieutenant. Spock? How about a guess?"

"I have computer confirmation. It is definitely a Talin spacecraft, Captain."

"Is there a crew?"

"I am endeavoring to determine that. However, the ship is

not a standard configuration. I am running a thermal profile and—"

"Keptin! I am detecting a radiation signature."

Kirk rapped his fist against the top of Chekov's chair. If it was an uncrewed vessel, then there was no need to be concerned. However, if there was a chance of a Talin space explorer seeing the *Enterprise*, he would have to break orbit. Unfortunately, that would mean contacting the FCO by unshielded transmissions which they had been warned might be detected, if not understood, by Talin-based receivers. Kirk still wanted to get all the details about that unlikely technological possibility. "Is it radiation from an energy generator, Chekov?"

"It is not radiating strongly enough for the amount of fissionable material on board, sir."

"Spock?"

"The spacecraft is pressurized with a sizable percentage of empty volume. Seventy percent chance that there is a Talin crew on—"

"Sulu! Take us out of orbit now. As much impulse as you can manage without using deflectors."

The helmsman's fingers flew over his board and the image on the viewscreen suddenly showed stars as Talin's moon dropped away. At the low speed at which Sulu had changed the ship's trajectory, the inertial dampeners didn't even have to compensate. The ship turned without a vibration.

"No change in the Talin wessel's course, sir. Thirty-five hundred kilometers and increasing."

Kirk went back to his chair. "Uhura, how soon before we'll be in tightbeam range of the FCO outpost again?"

Uhura looked up from her controls, one hand holding her earpiece in place. "Sir, I did get a few seconds of transmission from the outpost before we broke orbit."

"And . . . ?" Kirk didn't like the look on Uhura's face.

"I'll run it through again, sir." She hit the playback control.

There was a burst of static, then a rough and angry male voice said, ". . . *Enterprise*. Pull away! Pull away! That is a crewed

Talin vessel! Damn you, *Enterprise!* Why aren't you listening on the emergency channels? Get out of there! Get . . ." It ended in another rush of static.

"And that's all we managed to get, sir."

Kirk gripped the arm of his chair. "Why *haven't* we been listening on the emergency channels, Lieutenant?"

"Sir, we have been listening. But we have received absolutely no emergency broadcasts—or any other kind—for the past five days."

Kirk joined Uhura at her station. "Then how do you account for what that transmission just said?"

"I don't know, sir."

"Scan the channels now."

Uhura punched a command sequence into her main board. Nothing.

Kirk read the status displays. "All the equipment checks out."

Uhura froze. "Are you questioning my ability, Captain?"

"No, Lieutenant," Kirk said diplomatically. "But you did assign your post to less experienced officers several times in the past few days. Perhaps . . . something was missed."

Uhura was not going to accept that explanation. "I programmed this system myself, Captain Kirk. If any emergency transmission had been received, then automatic recordings would have been made and the computer would have alerted whoever had the conn, as well as me, regardless of who was at this post."

Spock came up behind Kirk. "Uhura's system was quite foolproof, Captain. She had me review the program code before assigning junior officers to the station. If the communications log does not indicate the reception of an emergency broadcast, it is because none reached us."

"It might be equipment trouble at the FCO outpost, Captain," Uhura suggested. "They wouldn't be able to use it very often, so they might not be aware of any deficiencies."

"That is a possibility," Spock concurred.

Kirk accepted their judgment. He was not inclined to argue with specialists—at least not his own. "All right. But we know their line-of-sight tightbeam transmission works." He left the communications station. "Mr. Sulu, how soon can you get us back within tightbeam range of the outpost?"

Sulu looked at Spock. "Mr. Spock, may I use full impulse once the *Enterprise* is on the farside of Talin's moon?"

"I shall have to perform the calculations to determine the length of time residual-ionization effects from the deflectors would be detectable versus the rotational period of the moon itself." Spock remained silent for three seconds. "Yes, provided you resume slow impulse within seven hundred and eighty-three kilometers of the farside cut-off and remain at least five thousand kilometers distant from the Talin lunar craft."

Sulu turned back to his board. "That's fifteen minutes to reach the farside . . . twenty seconds to cross it . . . another six minutes, then . . . we'll be in range within twenty-three minutes, Captain, taking up a polar orbit to avoid the other ship if it does come around."

Kirk looked with admiration at both Spock and Sulu. "Lay it in, Mr. Sulu. And Uhura, keep monitoring the emergency channels. In case they correct their equipment problem," he added.

Uhura smiled at the apology. "Aye-aye, Captain."

Precisely twenty-three minutes later, the subspace tightbeam broadcast from the FCO outpost came through again, and whoever was on the other side was still angry.

"*Enterprise*. Come in, *Enterprise*. This is FCO Outpost 47 on scrambled tightbeam at—"

"Outpost 47, this is Captain Kirk of the *Enterprise*. You apparently are having some equipment prob—"

But the FCO was interested in only one thing. The angry voice cut Kirk off in mid-sentence. *"Did they see you, Kirk?"*

"The Talin lunar vessel?" Kirk asked.

"Of course the Talin vessel! Put your science officer on. I want a full log download of the encounter. And so help me, if you've compromised this outpost by your incompetence, I'll see that—"

Kirk glared at the moon's surface on the main screen. No one talked to him that way. "Who is this? Identify yourself."

"There's no time for any more stalling, *Enterprise,*" the man snapped. "We need that download now so we can tell how much damage you've done. *Stator rel!*"

Kirk was surprised to hear the FCO contact swear in the Orion Trader's Tongue. He held up his hand to signal Uhura to cut his next words from the commlink. "Spock, could the Talin crew have seen us before we changed orbits?"

"Almost impossible that they achieved a naked-eye sighting. They would have to have been looking directly at us, and tracking us with optical magnifying devices. However, given the state of Talin technology, there is at least a two percent chance that some automated navigational camera recorded an image of us. If that is the case, then at worst they will not know they have photographed an alien vessel until the images are processed on their return to their homeworld. At best, we could be dismissed as a chromatic aberration."

"That's something we can handle," Kirk said. He signaled Uhura again. "Outpost 47, identify yourself."

The voice at the other end knew that the commlink had been severed on the *Enterprise*'s end and his irate tone had risen sharply. "Download your encounter log—now!"

But instead of responding in kind, Kirk sat back calmly in his chair. "Outpost 47, regulations require that you identify yourself, to enable us to know that you have not been compromised or taken over by an alien force."

"There's no—"

This time Kirk had Uhura cut the FCO off. "If you do not identify yourself, then to avoid further contamination of the alien culture, we are authorized to abandon this outpost."

Uhura opened the channel again. *"I'm going to report you, you—"*

Uhura closed the channel. "And I am going to report *you,*" Kirk said. "*Enterprise* out."

When Uhura toggled the channel open again, there was only dead air. Then, the unidentified man came online again, much more subdued. "Very well, Captain Kirk of the *Enterprise*." Kirk heard the man pause in an attempt to prevent an angry edge from building in his voice again. "For the record, Captain, I am Dr. Alonzo Richter, Special Advisor to the FCO." He paused, to let the name sink in. And it did.

Kirk turned to Spock. Spock raised both eyebrows.

Silently, Kirk mouthed the words, "Did you know?" Spock shook his head.

Richter continued. "And now, Captain Kirk, would you be so kind as to have your science officer download your *karskat* encounter log?"

"Downloading," Spock announced, ignoring Richter's use of the Andorian word for 'misbegotten.'

"Very good," Richter said flatly. "And I'll expect to see you here within the hour, Captain. Within the hour! Depending on the analysis of your log, we will either discuss your mission on behalf of the FCO, or why I should not report you to Command for a violation of the Prime Directive. Richter out."

Kirk sat back in his chair and put a hand to his face. This was about as good as the time when he and Gary Mitchell were both cadets and had rigged a bridge simulator at the Academy so it would respond to requests for spacedocking drills by recreating unexpected high-gee combat maneuvers. How could they have known that Rear Admiral Chan was going to tour the simulator that day? Fortunately, the rear admiral, despite being one hundred and ten, had risen through the ranks during the Romulan Wars. He had performed well on the combat maneuvers and hadn't pressed for a full computer investigation to learn who had reprogrammed the equipment. Though the tactics instructors had known there were only two plausible suspects and had started them both on a month-long, highly personalized calisthenics program.

However, Alonzo Richter's reputation was not at all like Rear Admiral Chan's. Kirk briefly considered wearing phaser armor for their meeting—though if Richter were really as bad as the stories about him said he was, Kirk knew that no amount of protection would help.

It was the most extensive communications blackout Kirk had ever operated under. The *Enterprise* was even prevented from using her transporters while on the side of the moon visible to Talin IV—and there was still no explanation why. That meant that for the next ten days at least, all travel between the ship and the lunar outpost would be by shuttle. Thus, in the interest of saving as much transit time as possible, Kirk brought a full landing party down to the outpost in two shuttles. That way, there would be extra room for FCO personnel to return to the ship when it was time for the mission to Talin IV to begin.

Sulu piloted the shuttle *Galileo* with Uhura, Chekov, and Carolyn Palamas. Kirk himself sat at the controls of a second shuttle, the *John Burke,* accompanied by Spock and McCoy.

As Kirk explained to McCoy what had transpired when communications had finally been established with the FCO outpost, the doctor also expressed his surprise that Richter was stationed on Talin's moon, but for a completely different reason.

"Isn't he dead, Jim?"

"Given the fact that the captain stated that he and Dr. Richter have just spoken with each other, that is a most illogical question, Doctor."

"I stand willing to be corrected, Spock."

"That has not been my experience."

"Let me rephrase that: I stand willing to be corrected by those who know better than I do."

It was going to take Kirk thirty minutes to reach the outpost by traveling in a long course that would put the shuttles' final approach within the shadows of the mountain range under which the outpost had been constructed. It would be an unbearable thirty minutes if he had to listen to Spock and McCoy trying to outdo each other the whole way.

"Dead, Bones? What made you think that?" Kirk asked to break the rhythm of his officers' conversation.

"Back in med school I took an elective course in the history of theoretical cultural dynamics. We had to study the Richter Scale of Culture and, as I recall, Richter was an old man even back then. He'd have to be well over a hundred years old by now."

"One hundred and seven," Spock said. "I continue to study Dr. Richter's work, and he has remained quite productive and formidable, despite his advanced years."

"So tell me, Spock," McCoy began, and Kirk could hear the playful challenge in the doctor's voice, "after your years of continued study, do *you* understand the Richter Scale of Culture?"

"The basic underlying structure of the Scale which identifies and quantifies similar organizational principles of disparate cultures through a systematic series of—"

"Yes or no, Spock," McCoy interrupted.

"The Richter Scale of Culture is not a 'yes or no' system, Doctor, which accounts for—"

From the corner of his eye, Kirk saw McCoy lean forward in his seat. "What he means, Jim, is that he doesn't understand it, either."

"Who does?" Kirk returned the doctor's smile. The Richter Scale of Culture was considerably more art than science, though in the absence of any other objective means of assessing the development of alien civilizations so they could be compared to each other, it was the best system the combined sciences of history, anthropology, comparative techtronistics, exopsychology, sociology, and nonhuman ethnology had yet created.

Since its original publication more than sixty years earlier, the Scale had been continually revised and refined by Dr. Richter to become the Federation's most important tool for determining at which point in a civilization's development the Prime Directive need no longer apply. Unfortunately, over the same number of years, the Richter Scale had become so complex that only a handful of specialists could apply it to any civilization much advanced past first-level Bronze Age, or

A.345-34019-1 dr.1, as the current revised Richter Scale would describe it.

For the majority of nonspecialists, it was a simple matter to interpret gross Richter Scale ratings by memorizing the basic forty-three preface-letter descriptors which ranged from AA— to indicate no tool use—to the last meaningful letter rating of Q, which was generally taken to mean no technology advanced beyond the current theories upon which Federation science was based. A forty-fourth category, the one with which the general lay public was most fascinated and Starfleet most concerned, was XX, which indicated an *apparent* culture with *apparent* technology that *apparently* was absolutely beyond any explanation based on *any* current understanding and/or theory of science.

Qualified personnel who had studied theoretical cultural dynamics for a minimum of two years could interpret more detailed Richter Scale listings which ran, in some cases, to three preface letters, combined with twenty-one explanatory qualification digits, followed by five exception letters and twelve philosophical-comparison pointers. However, to actually analyze a new technological civilization and create a Richter Scale of Culture Rating for it was something that perhaps only a thousand beings in the entire Federation were capable of doing with consistent results. Since most of them worked for Starfleet's FCO, given that there were almost a thousand to choose from, it was all the more surprising that someone as old as Alonzo Richter himself would have been required to make the long trip to Talin and live in a notoriously spartan FCO outpost.

"The Richter Scale of Culture is not that difficult to comprehend, Captain," Spock said.

Kirk nodded. "Agreed." A good library computer could give the textbook definitions of a complete Richter rating in perfect detail. "But I think what Bones is referring to is how difficult it is to create an original Richter rating to begin with."

"That is true, Captain," Spock agreed, though Kirk knew he would not have, if McCoy had just stated the same thing.

Kirk enjoyed the silence for a moment. But he was still concerned about the trouble he might have inadvertently caused himself. Alonzo Richter's influence within the Council and Starfleet Command was legendary. "Spock, since you've been keeping up with Dr. Richter's work, do you have any idea what he's doing at the outpost?"

"I have no obvious answer, Captain. And because I have no obvious answer, then I must conclude that Dr. Richter's presence here has been intentionally kept secret by Starfleet."

"But that makes no sense," McCoy protested. "This is hundreds of lightyears away from any disputed territory with the Klingons or the Romulans. And the Talin present no new military threat to the Federation. Why keep the FCO's operation here secret?"

"Not the entire operation, Doctor. Just Dr. Richter's presence has been kept unreported."

"But why?" Kirk asked, smoothly changing the shuttle's heading. He checked Sulu's position on his board. The *Galileo* was perfectly on course exactly two kilometers astern.

"Since his presence was unreported, obviously I cannot give an exact answer. However, I can suggest possible reasons for his presence under these circumstances."

Kirk heard McCoy shift position in his seat. "Just answer the damned question, Spock."

"I can think of several possible answers." As Spock qualified his statement McCoy snorted noisily. "But I would conclude that the most likely explanation is that some questions have arisen concerning Talin IV's placement on the Richter Scale of Culture and that Richter himself has been brought in to settle the dispute."

"But differing interpretations of Richter ratings is extremely common, isn't it?" Kirk asked. "Especially the more technologically advanced a given civilization is."

"Correct, Captain. Some debates have continued for decades, all to do with minute differences in the philosophical-comparison pointers or a one-digit shift in an explanatory qualification rank. But whatever debate there is that concerns

Talin IV's Richter rating, it cannot be allowed to continue over a long period of time."

"Because the threat of all-out war might mean there soon could be no more Talin civilization to rate?" McCoy asked.

"Not exactly, Doctor. Richter ratings can and have been made from studies of dead civilizations. After the number of years the FCO has observed the Talin, I have no doubt that in time a thorough rating could be evolved from existing data, even if the planet were to disappear tomorrow."

Kirk swung the shuttle into a straightline run through the shadows of the lunar mountain range and locked navigation onto automatic. He wouldn't need to return to the controls until the final landing descent began. Even then, the onboard computers could complete the flight automatically; it was just that Kirk savored the experience of bringing a craft in under his own control. But for now, he turned around to pay more attention to what Spock was saying.

"But since Dr. Richter could just as easily reevaluate someone else's rating assignation from the Richter Institute offices on Mars, it appears that there is indeed a time constraint in operation. And the most logical time constraint is the threat of hostilities on Talin IV."

"Just a minute," Kirk suddenly said. "Remember what Carolyn—Lieutenant Palamas—was saying a few days ago? About how some of the crew were hoping that this might turn into a first contact mission?"

McCoy grinned. "Yes, I remember *Carolyn* mentioning that."

"Suppose the FCO is also thinking along those lines?"

"That would be most improper, Captain. According to the Richter rating of Talin IV—"

"But that's just it, Spock! That original rating which said that the Talin are still several decades from being contacted by the Federation is apparently under review. For a civilization that is this far along, a change in its Richter rating could open the door to a Federation first contact message."

Spock shook his head, unconvinced. "I will admit that I

understand why the idea of preventing a world war is appealing, but the technological-threshold boundaries that would allow the Federation to open communication channels to the Talin are stringent and the Talin have not achieved them."

"But what if they're *about* to, Spock?"

Spock eyed Kirk thoughtfully. "I take it you mean: What if the Talin are about to exceed the contact thresholds within the immediate future, perhaps over the next few months, instead of over the next few decades?"

"Exactly." Kirk's speech became more rapid as he realized he had found the explanation for Richter's presence and all the other peculiar conditions surrounding the mission to Talin. "Think of the blackout conditions. It's completely standard procedures not to use deflectors when entering an uncontacted system in which radio-astronomy technology exists. But how often have we been told to also shut down intrusive sensors and subspace communications other than tightbeam?"

Spock answered instantly. "Except under battle-ready conditions, never in my tour of duty under Captain Pike or yourself."

"And how often have we been ordered not to use transporters within line of sight of an uncontacted planet?"

Spock took a few moments to think about that. "I am not aware of any ship in Starfleet ever receiving similar orders except, again, under battle-ready conditions."

"So what does that tell us?" Kirk asked, already knowing the answer.

So did McCoy. "That along with the technology to detect ordinary radiation signals in the electromagnetic spectrum, the Talin have the ability to detect subspace signals."

"Impossible," Spock said. "There is absolutely no indication in any of the technological briefs I have read that the Talin have progressed to the point of building transtators, let alone applying the multidimensional mathematics which describe their function. And without transtator technology, the subspace spectrum of energies we use in faster-than-light communications, *and* sensing, *and* matter transmission, is unequivocally impossible."

For a few seconds, the only sound in the shuttle was the soft hum of the impulse engine running at less than two percent of its rated output. "Impossible or not, Spock, I submit that in light of the unprecedented blackout conditions and Alonzo Richter's presence, that somewhere on Talin IV right now is a device that is capable of detecting subspace frequencies. It might be the first of its kind. It might be a single crude transtator the size of this shuttle, but it's down there. It's the only logical explanation."

Spock looked uncomfortable. "It is indeed logical, Captain, but it also remains impossible."

"Is there anything worse than a stubborn Vulcan," McCoy said to the shuttle's roof.

"Several things, Doctor, including a physician who—"

But Kirk held his hand out. "Really, Spock. What other explanation could there be?"

"I cannot think of one at the moment, but my inability to suggest a second reason in no way implies that no other exists."

"But if my conclusion is correct," Kirk said, "and there is a working transtator-based receiver somewhere down on that planet, then you know what that means, don't you?"

Spock nodded his head, admitting the inevitability of Kirk's argument, if not its accuracy. "If such a device exists, then it is only a matter of days before the Talin will use it to detect stray subspace transmissions which, by their regularity and coding, will be easily identified as components of a vast interstellar communications network."

"And . . . ?" Kirk prodded.

Spock's words were a slight rephrasing of the preamble to the charter of the First Contact Office, as if he did not wish to take personal responsibility for adding more weight to Kirk's argument. "And, since the Talin will then become aware of the existence of an interstellar community of planets because of the results of their own efforts without extraplanetary interference, then according to the conditions set out in the Prime Directive, the initial first contact technological threshold will have been passed and Starfleet, through the First Contact Office, will be empowered to transmit to the Talin a message of greeting, and so begin an official, open, and nondirective dialogue between that planet and the Federation."

Kirk sat back with a look of satisfaction. "And that could all happen within the next few days."

Spock's expression did not change. "As could the Talin's self-destruction as a race."

Before Kirk could respond, the navigation computer sounded the landing-alert chime and Kirk took over the controls of the *John Burke.*

The time for talk is past, he thought, *and now it's time to test the two competing theories—Spock's and mine.* Surprisingly, he found that for all he liked the challenge of competition and the thrill of winning, Spock was the only being to whom he never minded losing.

Thus, as Kirk brought the shuttle down toward the FCO outpost, he knew that he was in a no-lose scenario, since whatever they found out next would bring victory to either Spock or himself. He smiled to himself at the controls. It was a rare and not unwelcome feeling.

As the landing-pad acquisition signal flashed, Kirk expertly guided the shuttle directly at a jagged outcropping of heavily shadowed lunar rock and, ignoring McCoy's sudden surprised protest, he flew straight into it.

THREE

☆

"I hate holograms," McCoy groused as the *John Burke* settled gently to the landing pad. "They're getting too damn real. Whatever happened to the days when you could see them flicker from the corner of your eye?"

Spock stood up in the now motionless shuttle and began to unstow the two carry cases of computer files that he had brought for the FCO's databanks. The communications blackout made extensive subspace downloading of data impossible. "Dr. McCoy, if the holographic projection of a mountain wall did exhibit a detectable flicker, then it would serve no useful purpose as a camouflage technique to hide the outpost's presence."

"I didn't say I didn't understand why it was there, Spock. I simply said I don't like them." McCoy squeezed pass Spock in the narrow aisle between the shuttle's two rows of seats to gather together his medical supplies. As standard procedure, he would be making medical checks of as many outpost personnel as time allowed and, because he could not have any required supplies beamed down on demand, he had been forced to bring a broad general assortment and hope for the best.

Kirk watched through the shuttle's forward viewports as the

Galileo under Sulu's skilled guidance silently glided through the holographic mountain wall to join the first shuttle on the pad. As soon as the craft had come to rest, Kirk saw two large pressure doors begin to slide together. The outpost's landing pad chamber was just slightly larger than the *Enterprise*'s hangar bay.

Within seconds of the towering metal doors sealing, Kirk heard the whistle of air outside as the chamber was pressurized. At the same time, now that all transmissions would be kept safely within the bounds of the lunar mountain, the communications speaker came to life. "Full atmosphere will be achieved in twenty-two seconds. Stand by." It was a woman's voice, not Alonzo Richter's.

Kirk stood up and stretched. "Not the most cordial greeting we've ever received."

McCoy shrugged. "If your guess about what's going on is right, then I wouldn't be surprised if all personnel were standing on their heads trying to—" McCoy broke off and stared at Spock. "Don't say it."

"What, Doctor?" Spock asked innocently.

Before McCoy could say anything more, the pressure equalization light came on above the shuttle's door.

"Time to go, gentlemen," Kirk said. He reached out to the shuttle's control board and slowly turned down the artificial gravity field until all he felt was the moon's point two natural field, slightly more powerful than that of the Earth's moon. McCoy moaned as Kirk felt his own stomach rise into the new, lighter field. Then he popped the shuttle's door.

As Kirk stepped out of the *John Burke*, Sulu, Chekov, Uhura, and Palamas were leaving the *Galileo*. Like Spock and McCoy, each carried one or two cases containing supplies or microtapes which they might or might not need over the next few hours. Kirk was suddenly conscious of his empty hands and even though he knew Uhura had no trouble handling them in the low gravity, he took one of her equipment diagnostics packs. It was not the time to offer to help carry Palamas's gear again, after that awkwardness in the corridor following her first A & A presentation.

As the landing party waited for an FCO official to greet them and direct them to wherever their briefings would begin, Sulu looked around the landing bay chamber appreciatively. Except for the main pressure door seals and the personnel and supply airlocks leading into the outpost itself, the chamber's walls were bare black rock. Lighting rings on an exposed current conduit provided a soft, shadowless illumination. "How did they manage to build an outpost this big without the Talin knowing about it?"

Surprisingly, Palamas beat Spock to the answer. "Talin visual astronomy is limited to ground-based optical instruments. They can't resolve any detail here much smaller than about a half kilometer."

"And unlike the Earth's moon," Spock added, "this body rotates so that during each cycle, the outpost is out of view from the planet for approximately thirteen days. Usually, most traffic to and from the outpost is scheduled during those periods."

McCoy was intrigued by Spock's statement. "Then the fact that we've been brought in during the outpost's exposed cycle could be another indication of the time pressure they're under."

Kirk nodded. Palamas looked puzzled. But before she could ask what McCoy had meant, Sulu whistled and began walking over to another section of the chamber.

"Now that's what I call 'traffic,'" the helmsman said enthusiastically.

Five Wraith-class atmospheric shuttles were parked against the chamber's far wall. Kirk had seen spec reports on similar vehicles, but so far the *Enterprise* had never carried one. Each was a stubby winged vehicle, smoothly rounded as if partially melted, which could carry about half the cargo and crew of the *Enterprise*'s blocky Mark 12s. The finely ribbed, spaceblack skin of the craft made them virtually undetectable to anything less than advanced mass sensing technology. But it was the unique dual propulsion systems of the Wraith which gave it its reputation of being one of the most difficult—and exhilarating —atmospheric flying machines ever built.

"Like it?" a voice asked from nowhere as the rest of the landing party joined Sulu in admiring the Wraiths.

Kirk turned to see a young, red-haired woman in a pilot's flightsuit approaching. Her eyes went to the stripes on Kirk's sleeves. "You must be Captain Kirk. I'm Carole Mallett, manager of sampling operations." Her warm smile was an unexpected surprise given the type of reception Kirk had anticipated.

Kirk automatically looked for the rank markings on Mallett's uniform before reminding himself that Starfleet ran the FCO as a completely independent operation, without ranks, answerable directly to the Admiralty and the Council. He shook her hand and introduced her to the rest of his party.

"Do you fly one of these?" Sulu asked, running his hand along the rough-finished leading edge of one of the Wraith's wings.

"I wouldn't exactly call it flying," Mallett said. "When the anti-gravity drive is engaged, it's more like choreographing a series of freefalls onto a trampoline."

"I've heard they're pretty hard to handle."

"Understatement of the millennium," Mallett said. "If it weren't for the FCO's unique requirements for covert sampling craft, I don't think there'd be any reason to build them at all."

"What's so special about them?" McCoy asked.

Mallett led the doctor to the tail of the vehicle. There were no propulsion exhaust vents, just impulse baffles. "In space, not much. We run on a small impulse unit that can give us point oh oh one cee, which is good enough to get us to Talin in about half an hour. But once we hit the outer atmosphere, we switch to antigrav. The advantage is that there's no engine noise, no exhaust trail, no radiation signature, no chemical emissions. It's just the thing for exploration and sampling runs where the Prime Directive is in force and where there's a moderately high level of native technology."

"And what are the disadvantages?" McCoy asked, hearing the pilot build up to them.

"If you've ever felt momentum lag effects in your starship during violent maneuvers, then you know how painfully sluggish artificial gee fields are. When you fly one of these things, you have to think about five seconds into the future. Basically, what you're doing is gliding through a partially controlled fall, then hitting the antigrav to bounce back up before you hit the ground. And if you want to land, you have to time the antigrav reaction perfectly, otherwise you smash in at full speed or rebound like a bouncing ball. It's terrible, trust me."

"That doesn't sound terrible," Sulu said earnestly. "That sounds exciting."

Mallett smiled at Sulu and shook her head. "They all say that. Until they fly them. If you've got time, we have a Wraith simulator you can try out. If you bring your own white bags."

Sulu beamed and looked at Kirk. Kirk shrugged. For once, it wasn't up to the captain. From the moment the *Enterprise* had entered orbit, her time and crew belonged to the FCO.

"Ms. Mallett," Kirk said, "I think the first order of business will be to meet with Dr. Richter and begin finalizing your mission requirements. It is our estimate that you are operating under a severe time constraint."

Mallett nodded, abruptly appearing inexplicably upset. "They're waiting for you in the ready room off the main monitoring lab. I, uh, I'll have to let the director fill you in, past what you've already been told in the formal reports."

"And is the situation as bad as we've been led to believe?" Lieutenant Palamas asked.

"No matter what you've been told," Mallett said sadly, "it's worse. Far, far worse."

The main monitoring lab was at the heart of the FCO outpost, five levels down from the landing chamber. To Kirk, it resembled a starship's bridge enlarged ten times—a circular layout, ringed by at least fifty subsystem stations, with a central command desk instead of a conn. Five technicians, outfitted with audio inputs, sat at the command desk constantly adjusting controls while observing a master viewscreen twice as tall and four times as wide as the bridge screen on the *Enterprise*. But instead of showing a single scene, the screen presented well over a hundred identically small, rectangular displays along with ten expanded ones. Kirk couldn't make out what was being shown on most of the displays, but he did recognize adult Talin on some of the large ones. One display showed a close-up of a Talin's face and, in the background drone of noise in the monitoring lab, Kirk heard a whispery and unfamiliar alien language that appeared to be in synch with the Talin's mouth movements.

"What's all that?" Kirk asked. The overall effect was overwhelming. There was far more information than could be assimilated at once.

Beside him, Mallett smiled. "How's your knowledge of old technology? That's what they used to call television."

"Oh, of course," Kirk said. He had read about it, even seen it on Planet 892-IV. "Two-dimensional image transmission by . . . analog signals of electromagnetic energy."

"That's the technical end of it," Mallett said. "But just like late-twentieth-century Earth, there's an incredible cultural component to it as well, which is still surprising considering that there is almost no capability for interaction."

Kirk blinked. "You mean the Talin just *watch* those transmissions without the ability to alter them as they proceed?"

Mallett nodded.

Kirk wanted to ask why, but he had seen too many alien customs during his years of explorations to be truly surprised by any culture's odd habits.

Mallett continued. "We have camouflaged electromagnetic reception antennae over three two-hundred-square-kilometer areas of this moon so that one is always pointing at Talin IV. It lets us pick up about three hundred of these television public transmission channels, and more than five thousand audio-only channels—what used to be called radio, if you've heard of it"—Kirk nodded to answer her question—"as well as a few hundred thousand private communication channels every day," she concluded.

Uhura's eyes flashed with interest. "Every day? Can you process all those signals in realtime?"

Mallett could see a kindred spirit in the communications officer. "The staff here can personally handle less than one percent of all data channels, but our monitoring equipment tracks everything, checking for key words, phrases, and images, then flags transmissions we should analyze in more detail."

"Listens to everything," Uhura said, staring at the hundreds of flickering images on the main screen. "What systems are you using? What protocols? Are you on full duotronics?"

Mallett held up her hand. "I'll have to get you together with Mario. He runs the entire communications system here and he can give you all the technical specs."

As Mallett and Uhura continued their discussion of the outpost's signal-intercept capabilities, Kirk looked at each system station in turn, testing himself to identify each one's function from the layout of its controls and the type of data displays it had. He was surprised at the number of military monitors he saw. Then he was aware of Spock at his side.

"Captain, I believe you should look at the third large display from the right on the main screen."

Kirk turned to it, along with everyone else in the landing party, and Mallett.

"Is that a pickup from a security sensor in the outpost?" Kirk asked as he stared at the image on the screen, not wanting to believe what the alternative was.

"No," Mallett said, and all excitement had vanished from her voice. "That is what is called a news broadcast. It's like a one-way update channel."

It was then that Kirk understood the reason for the tension in his dealings with this outpost, and the reason for the unprecedented communications blackout—and they weren't the reasons he had deduced. There on the screen, from a Talin news transmission, was a blurry but all-too-recognizable image of

137

what was unquestionably a Federation Wraith-class atmospheric shuttle in flight. It could only mean that the FCO itself was on the brink of compromising the Prime Directive, however inadvertently.

"I think we've done enough sightseeing for now," Kirk said. "It's time to meet Dr. Richter."

The first thing Kirk thought when he saw Alonzo Richter was: *No wonder he's so old. He looks too mean to die.*

The man was skeletally thin and his upper back and shoulders were hunched over, pugnaciously forcing his neck and head forward. He had a full head of white hair, but it was cut more severely short than a cadet's first trim, giving him a harsh, militaristic look. And the folds of ancient flesh on his face had fallen to form a deep and perpetual scowl.

In centuries past, when normal aging had changed people's appearances in this way, there was nothing that could be done. But the fact that Richter shuffled into the ready room supporting his low-gravity weight on a cane of black, gleaming wood, indicated that he was past the point where modern rejuvenation procedures would work, or that he had declined them.

Kirk and the others rose in respect for the man as the ready room doors slid shut behind him. Mallett went to help him to his chair at the head of the briefing table. But Richter pulled his arm away from her grasp and thumped his cane on the floor.

"You!" he snapped, and his voice sounded just as rough and as angry as when he had fought with Kirk over the tightbeam transmission. "You're not fooling anyone!"

All heads followed the old man's gaze to Dr. McCoy.

"Put that contraption away. All it'll tell you is that I'm dying, but they tell me I've been doing that for the past twenty years."

McCoy folded in the top of his medical tricorder. He had been trying to run it from where it hung at his side to take surreptitious readings of Richter.

"And sit down, all of you. I'm not some *patak* admiral."

Kirk saw Uhura blink at the Klingon curse, then try to hide her amusement. Richter muttered a few more barely audible

Klingon epithets as he slowly made his way to his chair under his own power. He sat down with great difficulty, but with extreme satisfaction when he was finally in place. Then he sucked on his teeth, took his time looking at everyone around the table, and finally settled on Kirk.

"So you're the young troublemaker who's trying to announce his presence to the whole *kreldan* planet."

Kirk glanced at Uhura but her only reaction was one of puzzlement. Obviously, "kreldan" was an alien curse which even she had never heard.

"As I explained when we talked before," Kirk said patiently, "we were unaware of the Talin lunar mission because we had not received any emergency transmissions from this outpost."

"Of course not," Richter said. "Of course not. We were just beaming them at you nonstop for five days. Why would we expect you to pick them up?"

Kirk held his hands calmly together. "I have brought my communications officer down to run a full diagnostics on your equipment. It might have a malfunction."

Richter sneered at Uhura. "There's nothing wrong with our equipment down here. Go back to that ship of yours. Go back."

Kirk shifted forward. "Dr. Richter, I suggest that in the interest of time, we let our respective technical specialists track down the reason for the communications failure. I believe we have more important matters to discuss."

"We certainly do. We certainly do." He held up his hand to his mouth and coughed deeply. Kirk saw McCoy quickly glance down to something he held beneath the table—probably still trying to take some medical readings.

Then they all sat in silence for a few moments.

"Well," Kirk said, uncertainly, "perhaps I should begin with—"

"You'll do nothing of the sort," Richter said testily. "This is a First Contact Office outpost. A Prime Directive operation. Everything goes by the book. No exceptions. Too important."

Spock folded his hands on the tabletop before him. "We are all aware of the gravity of the situation, Dr. Richter."

139

Richter strained his head forward and peered at Spock as if seeing him for the first time. "Yes, *you* would be. But for these other *sal'tasnii* . . ." He shook his head and waved his hand, dismissing them all but Spock. "At least you know enough to wait for the outpost director and the communications manager to arrive."

"Of course," Spock said.

So that's what we're waiting for, Kirk thought.

"They'll be here any moment," Mallett explained. "They're preparing some datafiles for you."

A few more moments of silence passed by, broken only by the dry whistle of Richter's breathing. Then the doors slid open again and two men entered.

Mallett stood. "Captain Kirk, may I introduce you and your crew to Zalan Wilforth, the outpost's director, and Mario Cardinali, manager of communications."

Kirk stood to greet the men. Wilforth was a young pale-skinned human and, going by his name, Kirk guessed he was of combined Earth and Centauran heritage. The Centauran part was confirmed when they shook hands and Kirk felt the extra joint in the director's little finger.

Cardinali was a large human, powerfully built, probably from a high-gravity colony world. His sideburns were trimmed to an Academy point. *Just on temporary assignment,* Kirk thought. Mallett had the crispness of an Academy graduate about her, too. He was beginning to see a series of special conditions having being set at this outpost.

"So," Wilforth began without preamble, "I understand you've seen the Talin television news broadcast." He sat down to the right of Richter. Cardinali sat beside Mallett at the table's other end.

"With the television images of the Wraith," Kirk agreed. Wilforth frowned and nodded. "How much do the Talin know?"

"It's not what you think, Captain Kirk," Cardinali said.

Kirk didn't know how it could be otherwise. "As far as the

Talin are concerned, they have an image of an alien spacecraft, don't they?"

"Some think so," Cardinali said. "Many Talin are forward thinking and their successes in orbital and lunar missions have awakened the . . ." Cardinali shrugged. *"Le rêve d'étoiles,"* he finished, using the Academy phrase. Without question he had come up through Starfleet, Kirk decided.

"And, as on most spacefaring, pre-contact worlds," Cardinali continued, "there is considerable public debate going on concerning the likelihood that other civilizations might exist around other stars."

Even McCoy smiled at that. Kirk knew that there would be no one at the table who wouldn't feel a special connection to a world in Talin's position. Under ordinary circumstances, and with luck, some of the Talin alive today might see the day that the dream of stars was proven to be real. But Kirk knew that he and his people were there to discuss matters of a more practical, immediate nature.

Spock joined the conversation. "I take it, then, that also as on most spacefaring, pre-contact worlds, there is considerable intellectual resistance to the idea that other civilizations might exist?"

"Most definitely," Director Wilforth said. "We have seen news transmissions indicating that sometimes there have been violent altercations between supporters of both groups. And the Talin are not a particularly violent race."

"Yet they are poised on the brink of global war," Spock observed.

"Yes," Wilforth agreed. "And frankly, that's one of the problems we're facing."

"One of the problems?" Kirk said.

Wilforth gestured to Dr. Richter. The old man's eyes were bright and alive beneath his scraggly eyebrows and wrinkled forehead. "That's why we asked Alonzo to come to this outpost. From most viewpoints, the Talin are a textbook example of a simple Richter F culture: broadly speaking—Earth circa 1975 to 2000 C.E. Eight years ago, when the initial surveys were completed, there was every indication that they would pass through Richter FF to Richter G without major incident—unlike Earth—and from there it would be just a decade or two until they hit Richter H and Starfleet would initiate communications with them. An open-and-shut first contact. There're at least twenty other worlds under FCO jurisdiction in the same predictable circumstances."

"So what's causing their problems?" McCoy asked. He still had one hand beneath the table.

"Well, if we knew," Wilforth sighed, "we wouldn't have had to ask Alonzo, or you, to help us."

"Basically," Mallett added, "the Talin are on the brink of global thermonuclear war, but there is nothing in their cultural history to suggest that they would ever be capable of reaching such a position. The FCO has never seen a culture progress so rapidly toward self-destruction."

Chekov cleared his throat. "But in the same relative time period on Earth, Russia and the United States were in a similar position."

"Yes, yes," Richter said with irritation, "but there was a long chain of historical and cultural events which made that period of confrontation inevitable as a prelude to their reconciliation and eventual cooperation to create a true unified planetary government. The Talin do not share that same historical and cultural background."

Kirk began to suspect that the FCO officials were somehow afraid to go past a certain point in describing the details of whatever problems they were facing. *But why?* Kirk thought. *What do they have to hide? They're just observers here.* And then he realized what the link was and why he detected fear in the officials. He looked across the table at Spock and silently formed the words, "the Wraith?" He saw the flash of sudden knowledge in Spock's eyes as the science officer instantly came to the same conclusion. Kirk nodded to him and Spock took control of the conversation.

"Since you maintain that the Talin themselves do not possess the cultural and historical precedents to account for their current world situation, it is logical to assume that their normal development has then, in some way, been altered."

Kirk saw Director Wilforth frown even more, but no one from the FCO said anything to interrupt Spock.

"It is therefore also logical to assume that the First Contact Office is in some way responsible for that interruption in normal development and that the disturbing Talin news image of a Wraith-class shuttle might be one of the ways in which that interruption has been caused."

"By God, the FCO could use a few more Vulcans like you, boy," Richter cackled. "Just saved us half a day of sitting around listening to these so-called experts overqualify their findings till Talin's a cinder. By God, more Vulcans."

"That's very close, sir," Wilforth admitted. "Very close, indeed."

"How long ago was the Wraith detected?" Kirk asked.

Mallett answered. As manager of sampling operations, she was responsible for all atmospheric and landing sorties to Talin IV. "We believe the image that has been released through the public channels was obtained during an ocean sampling run six months ago. There's a chance that the Talin have obtained other images but not released them."

"Why?" Kirk asked.

"The imaging technology used to detect the Wraith is at the leading edge of the Talin's technology. That would—"

"Of course," Kirk interrupted. "Given the state of the planet's political situation, all of its advanced technology would be coming out of the military. One side might not want to release the images, to prevent the other side from gaining information about the state of its advanced imaging technology."

"If I may," Lieutenant Palamas asked, *"are* there only two sides involved in the potential conflict? The reports we received weren't conclusive."

Cardinali answered. "Except in the case of their world's name, and a few other rare exceptions, the phonemes of the Talin language are difficult for humans to reproduce, so we call the opposing sides the Browns and the Greens. The Browns are the most powerful nation state on the primary continent, which is mostly equatorial desert. The Greens are a union of five nation states on the secondary continent—mostly temperate forest and grasslands. The two cultures have slightly different organizational and political procedures, but, from a purely objective standpoint, the main reason for the dispute between them appears to be . . . emotional."

Spock turned his head to look impassively at McCoy. McCoy rolled his eyes.

But Kirk pressed on. "What other indications do you have that the Talin have detected your observation of them?"

"That's just it," Wilforth said. "Absolutely nothing. Yet they're behaving as if they're aware of us. Both the Browns and the Greens have gone through an unprecedented upgrading of their sensor systems—mostly EM bounceback systems."

"Radar?" Chekov asked.

"Yes, that's an old name for it," Wilforth confirmed. "Plus, they've added visual tracking systems—which is what we believe caught our Wraith. But quite honestly, Captain Kirk, until they did get that image of the Wraith, we could not have possibly done anything at all to attract their attention."

"Director Wilforth," Spock began, "I do not understand why you ordered a complete communications blackout, including matter transmissions, if you are convinced the Talin's sensors are limited to the electromagnetic spectrum. Do they or do they not have transtator capability?"

Kirk suddenly felt his stomach tighten. If the Talin were still years away from developing transtators, yet they had transtator capability, there could be only one possible explanation—one hideous explanation.

"Director Wilforth," Kirk said, forcing himself to keep his voice calm and controlled, "has the FCO lost or abandoned advanced technology on Talin?"

Richter laughed at Wilforth's sudden look of discomfort. "Absolutely not, Captain Kirk. And I am most insulted that you would even think to ask that question."

"It is most logical," Spock observed.

"I don't care. As director of this outpost, I assure you that every piece of equipment is counted before, during, and after any planetary sampling run."

"Then why are you afraid the Talin will pick up subspace radiation without transtator technology?" Kirk demanded. What other explanation could there be?

Wilforth glanced at Richter, asking a question with his eyes. Richter shrugged. "If you can't trust Starfleet . . ." he said. Then he glared at McCoy again. "Just don't trust that quack. I know what you're trying to do under there with that thing."

McCoy sighed and brought both hands above the table. Kirk heard a tricorder click off.

"What information are you withholding, Director?" Spock asked.

"The Talin do not have transtator capability that we know of. However, they have what appears to be a solid foundation in the multidimensional mathematics required for the development of multiphysics—though for now they think it has no practical application. And, on the quaternary continent, which virtually all nation states had access to during the planet's age of sea exploration, there is a large, and quite anomalous deposit of . . . rubindium." Wilforth looked embarrassed.

Spock's eyebrow shot up. "Natural rubindium crystals?"

"Damn right!" Richter snorted. "How about that?"

"How extraordinary," Spock said quietly in a reserved tone which Kirk knew meant the science officer was thoroughly surprised.

But Lieutenant Palamas was not. "I don't understand the significance of rubindium crystals," she said. "Why are they important?"

"They are wery crucial to the dewelopment of subspace technology," Chekov explained. "They contain a four-dimensional molecular lattice structure on the same order as dilithium and so are able to conwert subspace radiation into transtator current—in much the same way ordinary quartz crystals conwert electromagnetic waves into piezoelectricity.

We still use rubindium in transporter transponders just like the ones in our communicators. And they can be cut so small that we can ewen inject tiny crystals under our skin for—"

"I think she understands now, thank you, Chekov." Kirk turned to Wilforth. "Do the Talin know what rubindium crystals are capable of?"

"They are aware that rubindium is not normal matter. They have furthermore recognized the same temporal irregularities in approximately two to three percent of their planet's naturally occurring quartz."

Kirk was impressed. After the discovery that a second level to the periodic table of elements existed and the confirmation that dilithium was indeed a second-level crystal, subsequent investigation revealed that between two to three percent of the quartz on Earth was actually dilithium. Visually, dilithium had a dozen different three-dimensional physical configurations which could make it resemble several varieties of ordinary crystal. It was the portion of dilithium's molecular lattice that extended into the fourth dimension which made it so unique and so valuable—and that could not be determined by ordinary physical inspection or testing. In the mad dilithium rush almost two centuries earlier, Kirk remembered reading that many Earth museums became incredibly well-funded overnight simply by tearing apart their geology exhibits to find dilithium crystals which had been misidentified as quartz for generations.

"I see," Spock said. "If the Talin are at present conducting tests of rubindium or dilithium, then any strong subspace activity in their system could produce transtator current effects in the crystals being observed. And, with the theoretical mathematical foundation for multiphysics already in existence, they could conceivably come to the logical conclusion that they had detected an interstellar communications network in operation, even though they would not have developed the technology to intercept, generate, or receive messages of their own." Spock paused for a moment. "I am aware of no other culture that has ever been in a similar situation."

"Exactly, by *flaxt'a*," Richter said happily, slapping his hand on the tabletop. "A whole new category for the Richter Scale. At least five more years of work to rejig the whole thing. It's wonderful. Wonderful."

"Has the FCO made a ruling on how these special circumstances might affect the application of the Prime Directive?" Kirk asked Wilforth.

"No, Captain. The Prime Directive is perhaps the most rigorously enforced regulation in the Federation, and one of the most complex. Best-guess estimates won't do. Any special ruling would have to be made solely on the basis of precise, unquestionable data."

"And you don't have that." Kirk finally saw where the conversation was going.

"No, sir, we do not."

"And that's why you asked for the *Enterprise:* to help you get it."

"That is correct."

Kirk pushed back in his chair. Normally, he would have no difficulty in performing any mission for a First Contact outpost. His general orders clearly covered total cooperation with the FCO as a sister branch within Starfleet. But the more he found out about the situation on Talin, the more he realized that it did not fall within the range of general orders.

"Director Wilforth," Kirk said at last, "what precise and unquestionable data do you have at your disposal now?"

Wilforth pushed a stack of microtapes across the table. "These are specialist datafiles and go into considerable detail, but basically, it comes down to this. First, circumstantial evidence which we have obtained through the monitoring lab facilities leads us to believe that the Talin are aware that they are under our covert observation—though we do not know precisely how that is possible. The discovery of our Wraith shuttle came only after their sensor systems were upgraded. It's an effect, not a cause.

"Second, the majority of Talin—especially those in positions of leadership—do not accept that the covert observation they are under could be the activity of non-Talin aliens. Instead, the

Browns believe the Greens have advanced surveillance and transportation technology, while the Greens believe the same of the Browns."

Kirk looked over at Spock. They both understood the nightmarish situation the FCO was in. "Therefore," Kirk said, "there is a chance that FCO operations have intensified the feelings of distrust between the two sides and that the increased potential for war which now exists on Talin is the result of . . . interference."

"Exactly," Wilforth said. He didn't appear to have the strength to say anything more.

"How do you propose to prove or disprove your hypothesis?" Spock asked.

"That's where the *Enterprise* comes in," Mallett said. "Obviously, we need access to information that is not being released publicly."

"Information from military sources?"

"Precisely, Mr. Spock. We need to know all the details of the Wraith sighting. We have to know what phenomena spurred the Browns and the Greens to upgrade their sensor systems. And, most importantly, we have to know how far along their study of rubindium and dilithium crystals has progressed."

Kirk's mind filled with the logistics of what the FCO wanted his ship to accomplish. "The initial report said that four key installations had been identified for intrusive data collection. I take it those are military installations?"

"That is correct."

Kirk looked at the rest of his landing party. "And the results of intrusive data collection could determine if the FCO is responsible for the hostilities on Talin and, if so, determine what could be done to correct the situation?"

"Yes, sir."

"Well, Director Wilforth, you've got our work cut out for us." Kirk started to stand.

The director looked expectantly at him.

"So you'll be able to get our people to Talin immediately? We've got our collectors standing—"

"No," Kirk said plainly. "Not immediately. I'm sure you understand that in a situation like this, I have to report back to Starfleet Command for specific orders. To take the *Enterprise* into a mission that might compromise the Prime Directive is beyond my authority as a starship commander."

"But you can't report back to Starfleet," Wilforth said plaintively.

"I have to," Kirk said. "And I will."

"Captain Kirk, because of the blackout, it will take you five days to leave the Talin system. It will take you four days to hear back from Starfleet after you transmit your report—assuming they can answer immediately without the need to hold a board of inquiry—and then it will take you five more days to return."

"I'm quite aware of the time frame, Director Wilforth."

"No, Captain, you're not." The director looked down at the tabletop, afraid to meet Kirk's eyes. "You see, the situation on Talin is impossible. It cannot hold for another fourteen days. There's a very good chance it won't last even three more days. No matter what your orders say, general or specific, you don't have time to contact Starfleet."

Kirk was shocked. *Three days?* The situation was far worse than the reports had stated. Or else it had changed dramatically in the three weeks since the reports had reached the ship.

"I'm sorry to do this to you, Captain Kirk," Wilforth continued, "but I do know that when a starship commander must act within a time period which prevents communication with a higher command, that starship commander is authorized to act independently in a manner which he or she believes is in keeping with the best interests of Starfleet and the Federation."

Kirk sat back down. The director was right.

"There is no more time, Captain Kirk. And under the circumstances, as a starship commander, you are the highest authority in charge of what happens next." Wilforth looked up and finally met Kirk's eyes. "The fate of an entire civilized world and the lives of more than two billion beings rest in your hands, sir.

"What will you do?"

FOUR

☆

In the deserted landing chamber, Kirk sat in the *John Burke* considering his choices. When he had been forced to operate without Command guidance in the past, the situations he had usually faced were so critical that he had had only minutes or seconds to make his decisions. But in the matter of Talin IV, Kirk had the unusual option of having hours to decide upon a reasoned course of action. The fact that he had those hours would definitely be taken into consideration by the inevitable Starfleet board of inquiry. Also definitely, in the event of error, Kirk knew the board members would not be as forgiving as they had been in the past when he had been forced to commit himself and the *Enterprise* on little more than a split-second hunch.

He heard a rapping on the shuttle's hull and turned to the open door to see McCoy.

"House call," the doctor said. "Mind if I come in?"

Kirk greeted McCoy and gestured for him to enter.

"It isn't an easy one, is it?" McCoy said as he sat down across from Kirk. "But then, they never are when we're cut off from Command."

Kirk smiled at McCoy. "Though usually that's when I like this job best."

150

McCoy shifted sideways in his chair so he could face Kirk. "I know it's not strictly in my line of duty, Jim, but have you come up with what you're going to do about this mess?"

Kirk opened his mouth to answer just as a second rapping sounded on the hull.

"Request permission to come aboard," Spock said formally.

"The door is open, Mr. Spock," Kirk answered.

"Pardon me for interrupting, Captain, but I was curious to know if you had determined your course of action." Spock sat behind McCoy, and also turned to face the captain.

"Partially, Spock. I was just about to go over it."

"Please continue."

McCoy's eyes flashed at Spock. "Oh, yes, Captain, please do," he said facetiously.

Kirk stretched out his legs and hooked an arm over the back of the pilot's chair. "My main concern is to keep all our options open until the last possible second. The less I commit the *Enterprise* to do, the less likely the chance of inadvertently compromising the Prime Directive."

"Leaving command decisions to the last second sounds pretty risky, Jim."

"But striving to maintain the Prime Directive is most logical."

Kirk had the sudden feeling that if he ever decided on a course of action that both Spock and McCoy supported, then he would be sure to be making a mistake. "I admit that it's a compromise. But in the meantime, I'll be gathering as much new information as possible about current conditions before deciding additional actions." Kirk watched as Spock nodded and McCoy's lips tightened. *Good,* he thought, *they're still not agreeing. Maybe this plan has some merit after all.*

"The first thing that concerns me," Kirk continued, "is what that Talin lunar mission is up to. Given the state of their world's economy and the war footing the nation states are on, I don't think it's reasonable at this time to expect them to commit such considerable resources to a purely exploratory lunar mission."

"It is a troubling development," Spock said.

"So, I've sent Scotty his orders by tightbeam. He's to lock sensors on the lunar vessel the next time it passes out of line of sight from Talin. Then the first thing he's to do is to send out a quarter-second sensor pulse to see if the vessel is carrying rubindium or dilithium."

"If it is," McCoy cautioned, "then subspace resonance is going to light up those crystals like the dickens."

"But only for a quarter second, Bones. And if the sensor return indicates that crystals are on board, then the scan will not be repeated. That's well within the bounds of the Directive."

"However," Spock interjected, "if the sensor scan reveals no such crystals are present, then the Talin aboard will not be able to detect further investigation by sensor."

"Exactly," Kirk agreed. "In that case, Mr. Scott is instructed to conduct a full sensor survey of the Talin vessel. At the same time, any stray subspace signals will be blocked from ground-based stations on Talin by the moon's mass. And from those radiation signatures Chekov picked up, I'm betting that we find fusion warheads on that ship."

"Why the hell would the Talin send warheads here?" McCoy asked. "They have no bases on the moon."

"But the FCO says some Talin suspect extraplanetary surveillance. This moon is a logical place to conduct such surveillance. The early Vulcan observer missions to Earth used our moon as a base from time to time, correct, Spock?"

"That is true," Spock admitted.

"So you think the lunar mission's part of the war effort," McCoy asked, "come to wipe out the alien invaders?"

"Remember what Wilforth's data files told us, Bones: The Talin leaders don't believe in aliens. That ship's more likely to have been launched by one Talin nation state to seek out and destroy a base believed to belong to another. Which is why we have to have a complete scan of it. If the vessel *is* on a war mission, *and* it has warheads, *and* it's carrying instruments which might locate this outpost, then everyone stationed here is at risk."

McCoy looked grim. "There're more than a hundred personnel here, Jim, and their evacuation plan depends on a ship with the *Enterprise*'s capabilities. There's no way the outpost could be evacuated quickly without revealing our presence."

"Believe me, Bones, if we have to evacuate the outpost because the Talin have launched warheads at it, they'll already know we're here."

"The *Enterprise*'s sensors do have the ability to selectively disable the old style electronic components used for detonating such warheads, Captain."

"I know, Spock. I'm already having Scotty run simulations to prepare for that possibility. Though if it ever did come to us taking that action, once again they'd know we were here—and that we're technologically superior to them. And if that happens, the whole mission has failed. Ours and the FCO's."

"So much for Talin's moon," McCoy said. "What are you going to do about the Talin planet?"

Kirk frowned, showing he had still not completely made up his mind. "So far, I've told Director Wilforth that I'll take his people into orbit over the key military installations he's interested in. I'll decide then whether or not to beam down his intrusive-collection teams."

"What will determine your decision at that time?" Spock asked.

"A lot will depend on how well Scott can keep the *Enterprise* hidden from the Talin's sensors. She's not a Wraith, gentlemen. And she won't be passive. While we're in such low orbit, we'll have to use our deflectors plus full electronic and subspace countermeasures to remain invisible to the Talin sensor stations."

McCoy didn't look pleased. "How low is 'low'?"

Kirk shrugged. "Scotty's working on it. He says it's likely going to be somewhere between sixty and eighty kilometers above the planet."

"A very good estimate," Spock commented.

But McCoy scowled. "Damn it, Jim, the *Enterprise* is a

starship, not a glider! What the blazes are we going to be doing literally in the planet's atmosphere?"

"Endeavoring to keep stray transporter radiation to a minimum," Spock said, "by cutting the transporter beam to the lowest gain which will still allow for the safe transmission of intelligent lifeforms."

"Exactly, Spock. We'll do a preliminary test run at a higher altitude for the orbital insertions of the passive sensor satellites the FCO wants launched. If everything checks out and we've not been detected, then I'll authorize a low-orbit pass over the key installations. Then, and only if we're still undetected, I'll authorize the collection teams to beam down."

"I tell you, Jim," McCoy said, "if something starts coming at us while we're at that altitude, even I know we're not going to be able to warp out of orbit. Not that close to a gravity well."

"I understand, Bones. And so does Scotty. But the only way to eliminate all risk is to do nothing. And if I do nothing, then I have just about the same chance of breaking the Prime Directive as I would if I did the wrong thing."

McCoy turned to look at Spock, eyes wide. "I don't believe it. You're not going to quote the odds?"

"Doctor, I regret that in this situation I am incapable of quantifying all possible scenarios."

"Really?" Kirk asked in true surprise. "I was hoping for some input from you."

"I am still at your disposal."

McCoy shifted in his chair. "Well, what would logic dictate that the captain do, Spock?"

"Exactly what he has outlined. Uphold the Prime Directive while minimizing risk and maximizing knowledge. At this stage, there is no more that can be done."

Kirk bowed his head. "Thank you, Mr. Spock. I'm satisfied with that input."

"That's it?" McCoy asked. "That's as far as logic takes you?"

"Because of the unusual situation that exists on Talin, there are too many variables to prepare additional strategies without additional information."

McCoy leaned back against the shuttle's bulkhead and smirked.

"Bones, from the look on your face, I'd say you had some input of your own for me."

"Damn right I do," McCoy said smugly. "I know why the Talin are convinced they're under extraplanetary observation even though the FCO has done nothing to alert them."

"Is that so?" Kirk asked.

"Indeed," Spock said dryly.

"Because someone else is observing them!" McCoy stated proudly.

Kirk looked at Spock.

"There is no one else in the system, Doctor. Except for ourselves, there are no alien lifeforms and no alien probes. Because this is a system under FCO jurisdiction, everything that enters or leaves Talin space is monitored by the automated sensor stations in place at the edge of the system, and they have detected nothing in eight years."

"Klingons with Romulan cloaking devices," McCoy said, though less smugly. Then his smile disappeared in stages as Spock offered another explanation.

"We are so far removed from the Klingon Empire that even they would realize that the Organian Peace Treaty would give them no right of claim over this system. Likewise, the Romulans are too far away. Furthermore, the Talin system offers nothing of unusual value which would entice distant invaders to risk penetrating this far into Federation space. There are hundreds of uninhabited systems with natural resources of far greater value than Talin's in many disputed territories much closer to our frontiers. Not only is there no one else in this system, no others would travel to this system for what it has to offer."

"Well, Spock, at least you've got to admit it was a good suggestion. Logical even."

Spock turned back to Kirk. "If your definition of logic includes ignoring established facts, then it was indeed quite logical, Doctor."

"Thanks, Bones," Kirk said, trying to soften the blow. "It was one of the first things I thought of, too. But not even a cloaking device could fool the sensor stations surrounding the system long enough to get a ship to Talin IV."

"So that's it?" McCoy asked. "The whole plan?"

Kirk nodded.

"But it's not enough, Jim."

"Best I can do under the circumstances, and I know it's not much. To be honest, I'm not holding out too much hope that I actually will allow Wilforth's people to beam down because the last thing a war-ready nation state needs is to catch aliens materializing inside a military installation. And that means, if the Talin do have their war, that we might never recover the data we'd need to determine—even in hindsight—exactly what the best course of action should have been for me to follow."

"And we'll never know how things went so terribly wrong down there," McCoy said. He sounded stricken.

"You don't have to tell me, Bones. I can't see a way out of this one no matter what happens. I'm going to be happy just to get the *Enterprise* out of orbit in one piece and let Command and the Council work it out. The last thing I need is a run-in with a board of inquiry over the Prime Directive."

Spock nodded. "You are in a classic no-win situation, Captain."

Kirk tried to keep the look of pain from his face but without success.

McCoy turned to the science officer. "Mr. Spock, you could have talked all day and not said that."

"But he's right, Bones," Kirk said. "If things on Talin really are as bad as the FCO's updates indicate, then there are not going to be any winners in the next few days. Either here or on Talin."

McCoy stood up and put his hand on Kirk's shoulder. "I know it doesn't happen very often, Jim, but you have been known to be wrong before. And I hope this is one of those times when you're wrong again."

"So do I," Kirk said. But he knew he wasn't, and from the

guarded look in Spock's eyes, his friend and science officer knew it, too.

For the first time in almost five years, Kirk was preparing to take his ship and his crew into a mission he knew he could not possibly complete with success. But to fulfill his duty to Starfleet, to defend the Articles of Federation, and to uphold the Prime Directive, he had no choice but to seek out and accept defeat.

It was the one thing he had never been taught at Starfleet Academy—and the one thing he had never learned to do on his own.

FIVE

☆

No matter what Kirk thought he might face in the next forty-eight hours, he had no doubt that the best place to face it would be the bridge of the *Enterprise*. Returning there, as always, he felt renewed.

The instant the turbolift door opened onto the somehow soothing noise and activity of the bridge, Kirk saw Scotty step out of the central chair.

"It's good to have ye back, Captain," Scott said.

"Good to be back, Mr. Scott." Kirk stood by his chair, one hand on the arm, surveying his domain. Behind him, Uhura and Spock took up their stations. In front of him, Chekov and Sulu took up theirs.

"Satellite status, Mr. Scott?" Kirk asked.

"All eight ready to go when ye give the word, sir."

Kirk turned to Uhura. "Has the hangar bay reported yet?"

Uhura wheeled in her chair, one hand to her earpiece. "Three Wraiths have landed and are being stowed, Captain. All assigned FCO personnel are onboard."

"Status of Talin lunar craft, Mr. Spock?"

"Approaching farside cut-off in seven minutes, Captain."

"ETA on intercept orbit, Mr. Sulu?"

"Seven minutes, ten seconds to arrival, sir."

"Talin warhead status, Mr. Chekov?"

"No change, Keptin. Two armed, four on standby."

Kirk paused in silence. Each person on the bridge was poised, waiting for his words, his commands.

He took his chair.

"Helm, take us to Talin vessel intercept."

"Aye-aye, sir."

The *Enterprise* effortlessly slipped from her station-keeping orbit, dropping lower and faster to the moon of Talin, heading for the primitive vessel thousands of kilometers ahead. The mission had begun.

Seven minutes later, the Talin lunar vessel filled the main screen. It consisted of a main eight-meter metallic sphere ringed by six bell-shaped thruster skirts. The main sphere was connected by a ten-meter-long open grillwork tube to two six-meter spheres, one of which had folded-up landing legs. The overall structure was heavily textured with wiring conduits, three small antenna dishes, and a variety of asymmetrical bulges which could be anything from attitude thrusters to instrument bays.

"What are they throwing at us, Mr. Chekov?" Kirk asked.

"Sweeping with standard radar signals only, Keptin. Our sensors are creating perfect inwerse phase delays to show there is nothing in the immediate wicinity."

"Orbit intercept," Sulu announced. "Holding back ten kilometers, running lights out." At their angle to the Talin craft, the *Enterprise* was safely hidden within the glare from the lunar surface.

Scott stood beside the captain's chair and made soft tsk tsk noises.

Kirk smiled. "What do you make of her, Scotty?"

The chief engineer cocked his head skeptically. "They deserve an A for effort, but I don't know how they're managing to keep an atmosphere in her. My preliminary scans showed absolutely no magnatomic adhesion bonds in the whole craft."

Spock stepped up to the railing by his station. "I believe you'll find the entire pressurized crew compartment is sealed by welding and rivets."

Scott shook his head. "Och, then she might just as well be carved of wood for all the structural strength she'll be having."

Chekov turned away from the screen for a moment. "Is it supposed to be a one-way trip for them, Mr. Spock? I don't see any part of the craft which could surwive an atmospheric re-entry."

"The Talin strategy at this time is to leave their re-entry vehicle in orbit around their homeworld rather than expend the extra fuel required to send it to their moon and back," Spock explained.

"But they'll be using up far more fuel trying to slow down enough to dock with it on the return," Scott said.

"The Talin have a great deal of patience, Mr. Scott. In the past, their lunar mission profiles included a week's worth of high-orbit deceleration loops to match orbits with their reentry vessel."

Scott frowned. "Then they'll be spending extra fuel for carrying their increased life-support consumables. I don't understand their reasoning."

"Life-support consumables are minimal owing to their ability to cocoon themselves when conditions are less than optimal. There is a complete report—"

Kirk interrupted. "We are due in Talin orbit within the hour, gentlemen. Perhaps we might proceed to the next phase?"

"Aye, Captain" Scott said, going to join Spock at the science station. "The sensors are all set for ye, Mr. Spock."

But Spock stayed at the railing. "I believe you are more qualified than I at what must be done, Mr. Scott. I do not claim to have your level of engineering expertise."

Scott appeared to be surprised by Spock's compliment, and pleased by it as well. "I'd be happy to handle the procedure."

"Then please do," Spock said, offering Scott his station.

Scott peered into the hooded science scope and blue light

flooded his face. "Mr. Chekov, would ye please transfer tractor beam controls to the science station."

"Transferring now, Mr. Scott."

"That's a fine lad . . . now . . . now . . . scanning for the detonators . . . easy . . . easy . . ." Scott kept a quiet conversation going with himself as he simultaneously manipulated controls for the ship's finest resolution sensor probes, as well as for the tractor beams. But Kirk tuned him out. It was just a sign that Scott was completely absorbed in what he was doing. And what he was doing demanded no less than total concentration.

Earlier, as Scott had followed Kirk's tightbeamed orders from the FCO outpost, the initial quarter-second sensor pulse had revealed that the Talin lunar craft was not carrying rubindium or dilithium. That meant its crew would be completely oblivious to further sensor scans, provided they were done on the side of the moon opposite any detectors on Talin. Subspace radiation from the ship's sensors could easily travel through the moon's solid matter. But with the sensor's focus controls tuned to line-of-sight nearspace, the radiation that emerged would be virtually undetectable by any but the most sophisticated sensing systems. And no matter how unusually advanced the Talin might be with their discovery of second-stage matter's subspace resonance effects, they were still decades away from building the transtator technology that could fully exploit that class of natural phenomena.

Scott's subsequent sensor study of the Talin vessel had confirmed Kirk's suspicions: It carried six fusion warheads mounted on missiles capable of independent launch. That information, combined with a series of methodical orbit changes that eventually would bring most of the moon's surface within scanning range of the vessel, confirmed beyond a doubt that the two Talin onboard the ship had been sent on a mission to locate and destroy what their commanders must have assumed was a hostile lunar base.

Scott's sensor study had also shown that the lunar vessel was equipped with simple mass-detector instruments sensitive enough to reveal the presence of the FCO outpost's machinery and extensive metal shielding. Judging from the way the vessel shifted orbits, those detectors would be in position to locate the outpost within two days. Kirk could no more allow the outpost to come to harm from nuclear bombardment than he could blow the Talin vessel out of space. But fortunately, in this situation at least, there had been a middle ground which even Spock admitted would not conflict with the Prime Directive. Provided Scotty's hands were steady for the next few minutes.

As Scott continued talking softly to himself, Kirk heard the lift doors slide open, followed by a familiar, shuffling walk.

"Dr. Richter," Kirk said, leaving his chair to greet the man, "welcome aboard . . ."

Accompanying the old scientist were Director Wilforth and his two managers, Mallett and Cardinali.

". . . everyone," Kirk concluded.

Richter gestured aimlessly with his cane. "Is that it?"

"The Talin vessel?" Kirk asked.

Richter sneered. "No, a *razfelsin* white whale." He stepped slowly down to the central level of the bridge, eyes fixed on the viewscreen. His almost permanent sour expression softened as did his tone of voice. "Odd that there are no markings. And how fragile it is."

"And how lethal," Spock amended.

Zalan Wilforth clasped his hands together. "Does that mean the procedure did not work?"

Kirk pointed to Scotty. "My chief engineer is taking care of the warheads now. How's it going, Mr. Scott?"

Scott didn't look away from the science scope. "'Tis delicate work . . . delicate . . ." His hands moved almost imperceptibly over the station's controls.

Carole Mallett stood beside Spock. "What exactly is he doing?"

Spock watched Scott's actions carefully. "He is attempting to link our sensors with our tractor beam in order to physically alter the circuitry of the warhead detonators."

"From here?" Mallett asked in astonishment.

162

"It is an exceedingly sensitive operation."

Scott abruptly stood up from the scope and took a deep breath. Sweat beaded his forehead.

"Scotty . . . ?" Kirk began.

"That's the four on standby, Captain," Scott said. "They'll still be able to respond properly when they're armed, but the detonators will misfire for certain."

"And the other two that are already armed?" Kirk asked.

"Aye, I'm coming to those. But they are the trickier ones. Full of malfunction alarms and failsafe backups. Och, but the Talin are clever beasties." He bent back to the scope.

Mallett's face filled with concern. "When the Talin launch the warheads and see they don't go off, won't they know they've been interfered with?" she asked.

Spock shook his head. "Dr. Richter informs us that Talin nuclear weaponry has an accurate function rate of approximately sixty percent. The Talin who launch the warheads—if they do—should be expecting at least two to three of them to malfunction in any event. And if all six warheads are launched and fail, at least the Talin will not have any evidence of tampering remaining onboard."

Cardinali joined Mallett and Spock. "If you're rearranging electronic circuitry by tractor beam and sensors, isn't there a chance you could trigger one of the detonators?"

Scott spoke to the science scope. "Triggering them is the easy part. If it weren't for the two Talin on board, we could set the whole contraption off from half a million kilometers. But the detonators are well protected, so there's little chance of them going off on their own, even with us fiddling near them. The trick, mind you, is not to fiddle with them directly." He sighed. "There's one. Any response from the ship, Mr. Chekov?"

"Nothing showing, Mr. Scott. No alarms, no sudden computer use."

"Here goes for armed warhead number two, then," Scott said.

"I didn't think tractor beams could be so finely controlled," Cardinali said.

"Mr. Scott has made extensive modifications in virtually all systems of this ship," Spock explained. "He has—"

"Increased computer activity on the Talin wessel," Chekov announced.

"A weapons system alert?" Kirk asked.

"Can't be sure, Keptin." Chekov's hands flew over his controls. "Mechanical systems coming on line. Fuel pumps opera—"

Kirk spun. *"Scotty! Cut the tractor beam now!"*

On the screen, the Talin vessel rushed toward the *Enterprise* as four thrusters vented shimmering exhaust. Suddenly the craft could be seen to shudder violently.

"Beam off!" Scott cried, jumping back from the scope. But he was too late. An arc of transtator current crackled from the control panels as the tractor beam circuits fed back into the sensor system.

"They felt that, Keptin," Chekov announced. "The tractor beam was engaged when they changed orbit."

"How badly?" Kirk asked.

"Thrusters firing again," Chekov said, reading his board. "Their reserve fuel is adequate for orbital correction. Pressure holding."

Kirk saw that Scott was uninjured and that the fire-abatement systems had extinguished all sparks from the overloaded equipment. He turned back to the viewscreen. The Talin ship was gone.

"Where'd she go?" Kirk asked.

"Astern," Sulu said grimly. "Shot right past us. We're forty kilometers ahead of her now, leaving her orbit."

Kirk slumped back in his chair. "Did they get within visual range?"

"If they were looking through the portals, they might have seen us for a second," Sulu said.

Wilforth came forward. "Don't worry, Captain Kirk. These things happen in first contact situations."

"What things?"

"Mistakes."

Kirk's eyes flashed at the word. "Not on my ship they don't. Mr. Chekov, why weren't we prepared for their orbit change?"

"This was not one of their regular changes, Keptin. According to the pattern they were following until now, they should not have changed orbit for another two hours."

"Did they detect Mr. Scott's activity?"

"No indication of that, sir. The wessel simply changed orbit . . . at random."

"And experienced a momentum lag because of our tractor-beam attachment," Kirk said in disgust. "Well, Mr. Wilforth, what's the FCO's procedure on this type of situation?"

Wilforth looked sheepish. "Unofficially, we hope they didn't see us."

"And if they did see us?"

"Then we hope they didn't record an image of us."

"And if they did record an image?"

Wilforth shrugged. "Between 1955 and 2018 on Earth, there were at least eighteen legitimate, two-dimensional photographs taken of Vulcan probe ships. They were, without exception, dismissed as frauds and hoaxes." Wilforth shrugged again. "The Talin are as skeptical as humans were back then, Captain. A single image of the *Enterprise,* even in the unlikely event that it is accepted as genuine, is not the same as regular observation of Wraith shuttles. It will not compromise the FCO."

"Pardon me for being skeptical as well, Mr. Wilforth," Kirk said, "but a single image of the *Enterprise* would reveal a great deal about the structural engineering required for warp balance. And that's advanced technology."

Then Kirk felt Richter's hand patting his arm. "Don't worry about it, Captain. Most technology is developed according to a strict, almost evolutionary pattern. If the Talin survive their present political situation, they'll be in contact with us long before they get around to figuring out efficient warp configurations. Most contacted races end up learning that type of thing during exchange programs at Starfleet Academy."

Kirk was uncomfortable with a mistake being dismissed so lightly, no matter how inadvertently it had been made. He was especially surprised by Richter's calm acceptance of the event. "Mr. Chekov, what's the Talin vessel's status now?"

"Settled in its new orbit, Keptin. All systems back to normal operation."

"See?" Wilforth said.

Kirk turned back to Scott, already busy replacing the science station's controls with new modules from the bridge storage compartments. "Ready to go after that last warhead, Scotty?"

"I think I might have already got it, sir. When I get the sensors back on line, I'll be able to confirm its status." Scott took his circuitplaser away from the open control panel for a moment. "Is there something wrong, Captain?"

"A few too many coincidences, Mr. Scott." Kirk swung back to Wilforth. "That Talin ship approached this moon just as we were arriving. It changed orbit just as our tractor beam was locked on to it. And it's looking for the FCO outpost after only one image of a single Wraith shuttle was recorded."

Wilforth looked around the bridge but saw that Kirk was speaking only to him. "What . . . what are you suggesting?"

"I'm not sure," Kirk said threateningly. "What *am* I suggesting, Spock?"

"That the Talin are in possession of more information than the FCO would have us believe, through means which the FCO has not revealed to us."

Wilforth stammered.

"Thank you, Mr. Spock," Kirk said.

"This is outrageous," Wilforth finally managed to get out.

"Isn't it," Kirk answered.

"First of all, Captain Kirk, both the *Enterprise* and the Talin vessel arrived at this moon for the same reason—because of the escalating tensions on Talin IV. Why is it so hard to accept that you both arrived at the same time while responding to the same conditions? Second, the Talin vessel is searching for a hostile base belonging to the other side—not an alien outpost. Third, since the Talin ship is on a military mission, why is it difficult to believe that it might engage in sudden maneuvers to confuse any hostile vessels that might be in pursuit? I mean, really."

Kirk pursed his lips. "Spock?"

"Each statement is logical, Captain, though for them all to be true requires a fragile chain of coincidence. Also, there is as yet no explanation for why the outpost's emergency broadcasts to the *Enterprise* were not received. Both Lieutenant Uhura and Communications Manager Cardinali were unable to find any reason for equipment malfunction either here or at the outpost."

Kirk watched the FCO director carefully. *"Could* there be another reason for the communications failure, Mr. Wilforth? Other than equipment malfunction?"

The director's face turned red with a pattern of roughly hexagonal shapes—a peculiarity of the Centauran circulation system. "Are you . . . are you daring to imply that the FCO has compromised its mission here?"

"As I said, Mr. Wilforth. There appear to be too many odd occurrences here. Should I explain them away as a 'fragile chain of coincidence,' or should I look for a single explanation?"

"Which would be . . . ?" Wilforth said, shaking with anger.

"That the Talin know that you are here and they're coming looking for your outpost—not another side in their political conflict, but for an alien base on their moon."

"Captain Kirk, really," Carole Mallett interrupted, "that would be impossible. Other than possibly observing the Wraiths, the Talin know nothing about us or our operations here."

Cardinali joined her. "And our communication intercepts have revealed no indication that the Talin leaders seriously consider the existence of alien lifeforms. Captain Kirk, what we're seeing played out on this planet is a classic case of war jitters—lunar mission and all."

Kirk assessed Cardinali and Mallett carefully. They seemed sincere. But Wilforth was too hard to read through his rage. Was he really incensed at what Kirk was implying, or was he terrified that some secret was about to be exposed? Kirk decided it was time to test Richter, who had been uncharacteristically quiet for too long.

"Well, Doctor? Haven't you anything to add to the FCO's defense?"

Richter snorted. "The whole FCO's a naive bunch of *tarfel-licking rostonagons*. Should have done away with the whole thing years ago. The Prime Directive's an impossible piece of work so why even bother to try to uphold it?" He shook his head. "But Wilforth's telling you the truth. He's not smart enough to lie about anything like this."

The last clear spaces on Wilforth's face filled in bright red. "Alonzo! How could—"

"When you're my age, Zalan, it's easy. The last thing you feel like doing is wasting time with social niceties. Now shut up." Richter tapped his cane against the back of Chekov's chair. "So can you get that ship back up on the screen or what?"

Chekov looked to Kirk for confirmation, got it, and the Talin vessel reappeared on the screen. This time it was a view from the front.

"Are you looking for something in particular, Dr. Richter?" Kirk asked. For the moment he was satisfied that if anything improper was going on within the FCO outpost, its director, at least, was unaware of it. Richter, though, was another matter. His assessment of the Prime Directive as not being worth upholding was disturbing. Clearly, his loyalties were not firmly entrenched with Starfleet.

"Here's another mystery for you," Richter said, then coughed loudly. Sulu sat forward uncomfortably, apparently in the man's line of fire. "Take a good look at that ship, Carole. See how it's different from the others they've sent here?"

Mallett studied the screen carefully. "It's assembled from standard components, Dr. Richter. The only difference I see is that it has two lunar-landing supply spheres instead of the usual one. I presume that means the warheads are in the second sphere."

"Aye," Scott said, back at work on the repaired science controls. "That's exactly where they are."

"I don't mean the engineering," Richter snapped. "Look at it! Look at it! Where are its colors? Where are its markings?"

Cardinali shrugged. "Why does it need them? It's clearly a ship from the Brown nation. The Greens use a completely different cylindrical module design."

"Pah! If it's on a war mission, it should have the Browns' battle colors on its side," Richter insisted. "It should have a registration code on the main sphere, too. But it's blank. The whole *nyeem* thing."

"It's carrying six fusion warheads," Kirk said. "Trust me. It's on a war mission. Scotty, how's the second warhead coming?"

"It's disarmed, Captain, I got it the first time." He leaned back to stretch his back after hunching over the scope. "How d'ye manage that all day, Mr. Spock?"

"I have never done it for an entire day," Spock answered. "Dr. Richter, if the Talin lunar mission was rushed because of the so-called war jitters on the planet, it would be logical to assume that certain nonessential elements were left out of the mission's preparations, including the painting on of decorative nomenclature and colors."

Richter scratched at his cheek. "Colors are very important to these creatures, Mr. Spock. But I'll accept what you say as a theory. For the moment. Though I think you might be wrong."

"Do you have another explanation?" Kirk asked.

Richter shook his head. "Colors are so important to them that it's hard to imagine anything urgent enough to make them embark on a military mission without those colors."

"Are you suggesting that their mission is other than military?" Spock asked.

"As the captain said, Mr. Spock, they're carrying fusion warheads. That's not your typical first contact methodology in this part of the galaxy." The old scientist began to cough again.

Kirk checked the chronometer mounted between Chekov and Sulu. The *Enterprise* would be coming out of the farside protection of the moon in a few minutes. "Mr. Scott, can you guarantee that those warheads no longer threaten the FCO outpost?"

"Aye, sir. They'll hit like a ton of bricks, but only a ton of bricks. The outpost's structure could withstand all six of them impacting at once. No fear of detonation, though the fissionables will require some cleaning up. Plutonium it is, not too pure, but nothing a good environmental suit can't keep out."

"Good work, Scotty," Kirk said. "Mr. Sulu, take us to Talin IV, sensor satellite insertion orbit."

For the next few minutes, the bridge was the focus of intense activity. Scott left for the hangar bay with Cardinali and Mallett to prepare for satellite deployment. Chekov took up his position at the defense subsystems monitor to bring the *Enterprise*'s antidetection countermeasures on line. Ensign Fisher took over navigation. Three sensor technicians tested the repairs to Spock's science console. Spock set up Wilforth and Richter at the engineering subsystems monitor where they could follow the satellite deployment, and Uhura established a fully automatic communications scanning network to track all Talin military channels for any reference to a sighting of an unidentified space vehicle. Kirk sat quietly in the midst of the hurried preparations, the calm at the eye of the storm.

When Talin's surface filled the entire screen, Spock came to stand at Kirk's side. "All systems and personnel are ready, sir."

Kirk nodded. He knew. On the *Enterprise*, the systems and personnel were always ready. Any errors or mistakes belonged only to one person.

Spock dropped his voice, not quite to a whisper, but to something which only Kirk could hear. "If I may, you seem preoccupied."

Kirk glanced at his science officer. He hadn't spoken as a member of the crew. "Just reviewing my options."

"You expect complications?"

"Spock, we had complications dealing with a primitive spaceship that had only two crew members. And now we're facing an entire planet. Complications isn't the word for what I'm expecting."

"You have prepared for every foreseeable eventuality," Spock said.

"It's the unforeseeable ones I'm worried about."

"It is not logical to worry about that which you cannot know. Rather, you should have faith in your ability to respond to the unexpected, as you have demonstrated so ably in the past."

Kirk knew that Spock was making a touching attempt to give a pep talk to his captain, but as usual, the science officer was far too serious in his delivery of it. "Faith, Spock? Doesn't that smack of . . . emotions?"

Spock's face became completely blank, a reaction which Kirk had long since recognized as the half-human, half-Vulcan's response to minor embarrassment.

"Perhaps I have used a colloquialism where it was not necessary. I was simply trying to suggest that you have strong reason to have confidence in your skills as you have used them in the past." Spock glanced away for a moment. "I was speaking as a friend, not as a semanticist."

"Why, Mr. Spock, you're sounding more like Dr. McCoy each day."

Only someone who knew Spock well could see the subtle look of alarm that came to his face. "I most certainly hope not," he said, then returned to his post.

"We are within groundbased detection range, Keptin," Chekov announced. "Talin active sensors consist only of low-level radar. Talin passive sensors are confirmed as optical tracking networks."

"Full countermeasures, Mr. Chekov," Kirk said.

"Aye, sir. No surprises."

Kirk scanned the substations ringing the bridge, looking for alarm signals. But there were none. The *Enterprise* was undetectable to the Talin's current level of technology because her sensors could completely manipulate any electromagnetic signal sent in her direction. And with her running lights extinguished and all ports shuttered, there was virtually no chance of an optical scanning system spotting the *Enterprise* in the high orbit necessary for deploying fixed-position sensor satellites.

A paging whistle sounded from the bridge speakers. "Scott to Captain. We're ready to deploy the first satellite, sir."

"Mr. Chekov?" Kirk asked.

"All boards clear, sir."

"Lieutenant Uhura?"

"All military communication channels are being monitored. No change in readiness levels."

Kirk knew he had to make a decision. The sensor satellites were small and radar transparent. But they would orbit in altitudes accessible to the Talin and transmit data in tightbeam bursts. It didn't matter that the First Contact Office had requested their deployment and took full responsibility. *I'm the one giving the final order,* Kirk thought. He made a fist, certain that there was more to Talin than anyone yet suspected. But the bottom line was that he had no good reason for refusing to proceed. Only a hunch. And that wasn't good enough.

"Away satellite," Kirk ordered.

A few seconds passed. Kirk watched the lights on the control panel as they told the story of what was happening in the secondary hull. The hangar bay doors opened. The satellite boom deployed. The tractor beam pushed. The umbilical detached.

Scott's voice came back on the speaker. "Satellite one away, Captain."

"Shall I run a systems check?" Spock asked.

But Kirk waved the question aside. "We've got a whole planet on alert down there, Spock. Let's not do anything until all the satellites are in position. That way, if we do have to hightail it out of here, at least we'll be able to collect some data from a distance."

"'Hightail,' Captain?"

"Strategic withdrawal, Mr. Spock."

Sulu turned around. "Coming up on second insertion point in five minutes, Captain."

Kirk nodded. "As long as the boards are clear, we proceed." But the boards only responded to active sensors like radar, and

Spock had said the Talin were extremely patient. For Kirk, that meant one of the options he had to consider was that the *Enterprise* was already under optical surveillance, and that the Talin were biding their time. He didn't like that option at all.

Minutes from the deployment of the eighth and final satellite, Lieutenant Carolyn Palamas came to the bridge. She wore a communications earpiece and carried a small device, about twice the size of a screenpad stylus, which Kirk had never seen before.

Palamas took up position by Kirk's chair. The *Enterprise* was on the planet's nightside and the screen was filled with the constellations of glittering cities, tracing the rough shorelines of the primary continent.

"More than two billion of them . . ." Palamas said softly.

Kirk knew what was in her mind. There was something godlike in traveling unseen and unknown over such a planet, knowing that the power of the *Enterprise* would be enough to forever alter the planet's history and development. But in this case, the *Enterprise* was restrained by an even greater power: the words of the Prime Directive.

"For what it's worth," Kirk said, "Talin's military leaders appear to be responsible beings. They know what all-out warfare would mean and are in constant negotiations to prevent it."

"I know," Palamas said. She held up the small metal cylinder she carried. "I've been listening in."

"What is that?" Kirk took the cylinder from her. It had an FCO serial number stamped on its side and a familiar though surprisingly small computer display. "Not a universal translator?" If Starfleet engineering had begun another round of downsizing, they were going to have to start issuing new smaller fingers as well.

"Not a full translator," Palamas explained. "This is programmed just with the Talin languages. Eighteen major families and two hundred and twenty-seven dialects." She offered Kirk a second earpiece. "The crew is extremely interested in knowing what's going on on Talin. I've been preparing update digests for them."

Kirk slipped the earpiece into position and heard a computer voice re-enacting both sides of a conversation concerning a violation of airspace. One side claimed that an illegal overflight had taken place. The other side denied that any aircraft had been in the area at the time. Kirk felt his stomach tighten.

"They're not talking about us by any chance, are they?" Though he knew that Uhura would have informed him of that situation, he wanted to take no chances.

Palamas shook her head. "The incident took place about two hours ago near one of the Greens' polar airbases, long before the *Enterprise* took up orbit. Mr. Cardinali suspects a Brown highspeed surveillance aircraft was detected executing an unauthorized flyby."

Kirk pointed to the earpiece. "Who are we listening to here?"

"Regional military commanders talking over a diplomatic radio frequency. It sounds as if they're both trying to defuse the situation. It would be a lot better if the Browns simply admitted that one of their aircraft had strayed too close to the Greens' base, though."

Once again Kirk was caught by the lieutenant's clear eyes and the hope that shone so brightly in them. "Things are seldom that simple, Lieutenant. Especially in a military confrontation."

Palamas seemed not to hear. She moved closer to Kirk's chair. "I like it when you look at me that way."

Kirk smiled, but only for an instant. They had shared important time together in the past few days and he was glad of it. But the bridge of the *Enterprise* was not the proper forum for such memories. He handed back the earpiece and the translator. "You have me looking forward to the long voyage out of this system," he said softly, and it was all the acknowledgment he would make to her.

"Let me know how the situation plays itself out, Lieutenant." Kirk was referring to the airspace dispute.

"I'm anxious to know how it turns out myself," Palamas said, referring to something else. She took her translator unit over to show Uhura.

"Coming up on final satellite insertion point," Sulu announced.

Chekov followed the routine that had been established. "All boards still clear."

Uhura was next. "No change in military alert levels."

Kirk gave the order to deploy the last satellite. All went smoothly.

"Shall I begin the systems check now, Captain?" Spock asked.

"Mr. Sulu, set in an automatic warp-out-of-orbit maneuver to engage at the first indication we've been detected." Kirk turned to Spock. "When Sulu's finished programming our escape hatch, you may proceed, Spock."

Wilforth stood up from his chair beside Dr. Richter at the engineering subsystems monitor. "May I go prepare the intrusive-collection team, Captain Kirk?"

Kirk had known there was a good reason for the way Richter and Wilforth had conducted themselves so conscientiously during the last orbit. They knew he still hadn't committed to allowing an FCO team to be beamed down from low orbit.

"You may *prepare* the team, Mr. Wilforth, but the final decision to send them remains with me."

"We've already agreed to that, Captain." Wilforth offered his hand to Richter to help the old man from his chair, but Richter waved his cane to force the FCO director back. Wilforth shrugged and headed for the turbolift.

"Mr. Wilforth," Kirk said suddenly, "are you intending to beam down with the team? If I give the word?"

Wilforth seemed surprised by the question. "Why, of course, Captain. It's my operation. I must take full responsibility."

Kirk shook his head. "That's not quite correct, sir. As of now, it's my operation. And I'm the one who must take full responsibility."

It took a moment for Wilforth to realize what Kirk had said. "Surely you don't intend to . . . beam down with us? Do you?"

Kirk enjoyed seeing the look of discomfort on Wilforth's face. "Come now, Director, it won't be the first intrusive-collection landing party I've been on."

"Oh, I realize that," Wilforth said, eyes wide and round. "I just hope it won't be your last."

SIX

☆

Lieutenant Kyle leaned over the transporter console and punched in a final string of setting commands. "And that's the lowest I dare go to guarantee brain function, Mr. Spock. Even then, an unexpected solar flare or energy burst could disrupt the signal so badly that . . ." He shrugged.

Spock was unperturbed. "At an altitude of sixty-three kilometers the transporter beam will be effectively shielded from solar flares by the planet's atmosphere. Energy bursts might arise from nuclear weapons detonation, but if war does break out on Talin, then we shall be under no constraints to maintain low-level power settings for the transporter. This setting should be safe."

McCoy groaned. "'Should be safe'? Would *you* use the blasted thing at those settings to beam down there?"

Spock didn't bother to look up. "Your question is moot, Doctor. It would be foolish to expose Captain Kirk and myself to the same risk at the same time. And since Captain Kirk has invoked his command privilege to lead the landing party, I, of course, will not use these settings to beam down."

McCoy held a hand to his eyes and shook his head. "Jim, you can't be serious about this."

Kirk stepped down from the transporter platform where he

had been doublechecking the two tall cylinders of collection gear that would be beaming down with the landing party—*if* the landing party beamed down. "I've transported under worse conditions, Bones. And so have you."

"Don't remind me. 'Guarantee brain function'? Good Lord," he muttered.

Kirk rolled up his sleeve and held his arm out to the doctor. "Time for the transponder."

McCoy took a spray hypo from his kit and adjusted the setting on it. "You know, someday Starfleet's going to wake up and change the regulations so that the captain will be the *last* crew member to be authorized to lead a landing party."

Kirk grimaced as the centimeter-long transporter transponder was forced under the skin on his forearm. The FCO communicators that the landing party would carry, along with all their other equipment, were rigged to self-destruct in the event of capture or loss. But with the team's subcutaneous transponders in place, the *Enterprise* would always be able to lock on to each individual.

"The captain has ultimate responsibility over each mission, Bones. And ultimate authority. How can I exercise that authority or take that responsibility if I'm not on top of the situation?"

"Well, it's too damn risky."

Kirk rolled his sleeve back into position. "The system's worked so far."

McCoy frowned. "And that's the problem. The day the system doesn't work is the day you're not going to know about it because your brain will have been permanently scrambled by this damn machine."

Kirk clasped his hand to the doctor's shoulder. "As long as I know that you're waiting up here to put me back together, I won't worry."

"Oh, for—"

The doors to the corridor slipped open and the rest of the landing party entered—Wilforth, Cardinali, and two FCO technicians Kirk hadn't met. Richter and Mallett accompanied them.

"Do you require transponders?" McCoy asked.

Wilforth shook his head. "They're permanently implanted in all FCO personnel. Sudden extractions are standard operations, I'm afraid. How are things on the bridge, Captain?"

"The dispute over the polar airspace seems to be growing—though at a controlled rate. Other than that, no disturbances. And no indication that the Talin have detected us or our satellites."

"So we're approved for beaming down?"

"Not yet," Kirk said. "Sulu's going to take us down for a quick run past the main defense installation on the primary continent, just to check the effectiveness of the Talin scanners at close range. If we get by them the first time, then we'll beam down at the secondary site."

"Impossible," Richter said, leaning on his cane, and for once he didn't sound angry or provocative, just tired. "It's all so complicated—judging the development of cultures and technologies. So much room for mistakes to be made, so little chance to help."

"But that's precisely why we need the Directive," Kirk said. "Because there *is* so much opportunity for causing damage, even accidentally. It's better to let each world choose its own way."

An expression of sadness passed over Richter's face. "You only say that because those are your orders."

"Yes, they are my orders," Kirk agreed. "But I do believe in them."

"But think of all the time and effort that's wasted, because we do not help."

"Perhaps, someday, we'll know how to help other worlds without the possibility of causing harm, but for now, we do the best we can with what we know."

"Even if a world should die, Captain Kirk?"

Kirk shook his head. "This world won't die, Dr. Richter. I've been using the FCO translator to listen in on their negotiators. Talin patience is serving them well. They know what they're facing if they dare break off talking with each other." He stepped up on the transporter platform. "While we're down there, you listen in on those talks yourself. The Talin have got what it takes to survive this, and fifty years from now, maybe fewer, there's going to be another Federation starship in orbit around this world . . . and that starship won't be trying to hide."

Wilforth, Cardinali, and the two technicians joined Kirk on the platform.

"Why wait fifty years, Captain? Why not do it now?" Richter asked.

"If the Federation revealed itself to the Talin now, we don't know what would happen." Kirk felt the ship shudder around him and reached out a hand to steady himself against one of the equipment cylinders. The transporter-room communications panel whistled.

"Sulu here, Captain. We have entered the Talin thermosphere. Altitude one hundred and five kilometers. The inertial dampeners are absorbing our kinetic energy in an even curve."

Richter balanced himself with his cane. "If the Federation contacts Talin fifty years from now, we still don't know what will happen."

The vibration of the ship became rhythmic. Kirk could hear the whine of the impulse generators as they absorbed more energy from the inertial dampeners than they put out. "But at least fifty years from now, what happens will be the *joint* responsibility of the Talin and the Federation. We will not be in control, we will be partners."

Richter's sadness became almost overpowering. His voice was barely audible over the growing whine of the impulse system. "But fifty years from now, Captain Kirk, I shall be dead and not know anything."

It was then that Kirk finally understood Richter's impatience, but it was too late to respond. Sulu's voice spoke rapidly from the bridge.

"Altitude eighty-five kilometers, Captain. Entering the mesosphere. Thirty seconds from acquisition of primary target."

Uhura's report followed. "No military traffic, Captain."

"All boards clear," Chekov added. "We're absorbing all signals perfectly."

The vibration evened out as the atmosphere thickened and the ship's speed dropped to avoid creating an incandescent trail in the Talin sky. The energy expenditure was enormous, but the *Enterprise* could manage atmospheric flight for a brief time, though Scott would be complaining for weeks to come about the pounding the ship was taking.

"Over primary target," Sulu said. Kirk could hear the excitement in his voice.

The same excitement was in Chekov. "They do not see us, sir. We are still clear."

"Secondary-target acquisition in forty seconds," Sulu said. "Altitude seventy-five kilometers. Passing through the mesopause."

Kirk felt all eyes on him.

"This is it, Captain Kirk," Wilforth said. "Do we go or not?"

Kirk ignored McCoy shaking his head. "Mr. Kyle, lock on to secondary target. Do not energize without my signal."

Kyle set the controls to standby.

"Mr. Spock, I want a complete retrieval after one orbit."

Spock nodded in agreement.

"But that gives us less than an hour," Wilforth protested.

"If everything works out, we can return," Kirk said.

"Altitude sixty-eight kilometers," Sulu said. "Secondary-target acquisition in ten seconds."

Kirk held his hand up by his shoulder. "How are those boards, Mr. Chekov?" he called out.

"All clear, Keptin."

"Five seconds to target. Altitude sixty-four kilometers."

Kirk made his decision. He pointed at Kyle. "Energize."

The shuddering of the ship was instantly muffled by the sudden wash of the transporter effect. Kirk watched as Kyle and Richter and Spock and McCoy dissolved into the random sparkles of a quantum mist. And then the movement of the ship was gone along with the bright lights of the transporter room. Kirk felt a solid floor materialize beneath his feet, felt the sudden heat of the desert and the sensory shock of air that carried a hundred unknown scents. He was on another world. For a moment, he felt a brief thrill of triumph. Then the transporter effect was gone completely and he heard the others of the landing party shift around him, altering their stance in the slightly higher gravity of Talin IV.

Kirk looked around. They were in a long, high-ceilinged room, dimly lit by wall-mounted panels.

Good work, Kyle, he thought. *A perfect touchdown.*

A sudden swath of light cut through the room and Kirk heard Cardinali swear. He turned to the communications expert wondering what had gone wrong. And then he saw what Cardinali saw and knew exactly what had gone wrong.

Everything.

Two Talin stood in an open doorway, mouths open. And they screamed.

SEVEN

☆

Kirk felt himself slip into a state of intensely accelerated consciousness. Even as his hand instinctively reached for his communicator to request a beam out, he knew that the *Enterprise* had already moved beyond the range of her stepped-down transporter system.

Those Talin are not supposed to be here, he thought simply. The only reason he had agreed to even consider the possibility of an intrusive-collection landing party was because Director Wilforth had assured him that each selected site would be deserted. *Or did Wilforth know? Did he bring us down here on purpose, knowing what would happen?*

Suddenly, the two Talin in the open doorway were engulfed in a shimmering blue aurora and collapsed to the roughly textured floor. The technicians whom Kirk had yet to meet rushed forward to pull the motionless bodies forward. Kirk turned to Wilforth. The FCO director held a small weapon in an unsteady hand—an egg-shaped area disruptor with a gleaming diamond emitter cone. Kirk's hand lashed out and knocked the weapon from Wilforth's grip.

"What did you hit them with?" Kirk demanded. He kept his voice to a harsh whisper. *How far did those screams carry? How many others are nearby?*

"A mild electrical charge," Wilforth stammered, terrified by the rage in Kirk's eyes. "We ... we couldn't risk phasers because we don't know how the Talin metabolism would react to them. But a neural stun causes no long-term damage."

Kirk froze. "'No long-term damage'? You *know* that? You've done this before?"

Wilforth couldn't speak, but he jerked his head up and down.

Then Kirk felt Cardinali's hand on his shoulder. It wasn't a fighting grip but Kirk still twisted away.

"It's all right," the communications manager said, trying to calm Kirk. "Inadvertent contact happens all the time in these conditions."

"The Prime Directive expressly forbids it!"

"But we're not *interfering* here, Captain Kirk," Wilforth said, his voice still trembling. "No harm is done. No information has been passed. Our existence is still a secret."

Kirk pointed to the unconscious Talin. The technicians attended to them with what appeared to be modified medical tricorders. "Except to them. What happens to them when they wake up? Or do you take them back with you to the moon?"

"Captain Kirk, slow down," Cardinali said. "What did they see? They opened a door, saw a few strange shapes in the shadows, then, as far as they know, they fainted. To the Talin, the effect of getting a neural shock is a bit like what happens when a human gets a violent blow to the head. There are a few seconds' worth of short-term memory that don't get laid down in the neural pathways. They'll remember nothing of us."

Kirk fought to control his anger. He had jeopardized the mission—and a planet—by trusting everything that Wilforth had told him. But as was so painfully obvious from the weapon Wilforth had carried, and the modified medical tricorders his technicians used, and even Cardinali's knowledge of Talin neurochemistry, he had not told Kirk all that he knew. And unfortunately, now was not the time to find out just how far the deception had gone.

"Who else has weapons?" Kirk asked.

Cardinali knew what the question meant. He unhooked a

disruptor from his belt and handed it to Kirk. "We each have one. There's only one setting. Nonfatal. And by holding the green stud while twisting the emitter cone, you can fuse the interior circuitry so it can't be studied."

Kirk held the disruptor in his hand. "You, too," he said to the technicians who had finished with the Talin.

Wilforth nodded his head. "Do as he says," he told them. "We don't have much time."

Kirk took the technicians' disruptors and slapped them to his belt. "How long will they be out?"

"No less than twenty minutes, no more than an hour," Cardinali answered.

Kirk held out his hand. "Give me your tricorder."

The instrument was standard issue and Kirk quickly swept a half-kilometer circle for lifeform readings. "Are these signals Talin normal?" he asked as the display showed five individual readings three hundred meters distant.

Cardinali checked the readings and nodded. "But they're at rest," he said. "Or sleeping."

"That's why we expected this facility to be safe, Captain," Wilforth added. "It's late at night here. And this is just a records storage warehouse."

Kirk held the tricorder in one hand, the weapon in the other. The *Enterprise* was still more than half an hour away from returning overhead to beam them up. "How many Talin have seen a member of the FCO?" How badly had this world been disrupted?

Wilforth sighed. "As far as we know, nine." He looked at the floor. "Not counting those who might have seen one of the Wraiths on a sampling run."

"Nine," Kirk repeated. Out of two and a half billion. Perhaps the situation wasn't as bad as it might have been.

"Though according to their public broadcasts," Cardinali volunteered, "there are at least four or five thousand more who *claim* to have seen us."

"What?"

"The Talin are on the brink of leaving their planet, Captain

Kirk. They *want* to believe that other lifeforms exist. The same wish-fulfillment phenomena of spacecraft sighting and alien contact has occurred in the past on virtually every other spacefaring planet, including Earth."

"Earth was being observed by the Vulcans," Kirk said grimly.

"But until official contact was made, those few brief sightings and encounters did not interfere with the development of Earth," Cardinali argued. "Just as the inevitable sightings of us by the Talin will have no appreciable effect on them. The Prime Directive is safe, Captain Kirk. We have done nothing here to circumvent it."

Kirk decided not to pursue the discussion. His problem wasn't with Cardinali. It was with Wilforth, who had a convenient way of withholding information, and with Richter, who had no love for the Directive. There was nothing more he could do until they had all safely returned to the *Enterprise*.

"All right, Director Wilforth, have your people go to work. I'll watch the Talin. And the door."

Wilforth, Cardinali, and the two technicians moved quickly to the equipment cylinders which had been beamed down with them. At their touch, the storage tubes split open like metal blossoms, displaying a complex range of miniaturized sensing devices. One technician took a large, white wand which reminded Kirk of Richter's cane and began to slowly walk along a wall covered with rows of thick tubes, each the size of a human forearm.

"Those are Talin datadisks," Cardinali explained as he set up another piece of equipment on the floor. It looked like a type of primitive data terminal, almost as large as a chair. "The technician is taking micromass readings so we'll be able to reconstruct the written words and pictures stored in them."

"From only one pass?" Kirk asked.

"We're not miracle workers," Cardinali said with a smile. "It'll take three passes at least."

Kirk kept his eyes on the Talin. They breathed more rapidly than humans, but both breathed evenly, gently fluttering the membranes at the sides of their heads. He took that to be a good sign. "What equipment are you setting up?" he asked Cardinali.

"We've constructed a model of a Talin computer interface. The facility we're in maintains historical records for some of the nation states associated with the Greens. Much of the information is what we would call classified, so it is never transmitted outside the computer network that's in use here— which means we have never been able to tap into it." Cardinali patted the top of the device as a display screen came to life with Talin script, resembling rows of paint splatters. "Until now."

Beside him, Cardinali had several boxes of thick round objects, about five centimeters wide. "These are our own Talin-style datadisks. We made them at the outpost according to Talin specs to make downloading easier." He began slipping the disks into various slots on the side of the terminal.

Kirk did not interrupt any of the FCO personnel again and they worked swiftly and with a minimum of talking. Obviously they had rehearsed their routines many times. The readings on the five sleeping Talin three hundred meters away never varied and the stunned Talin on the warehouse floor didn't stir. Ten minutes before the *Enterprise* was due back, Kirk found himself thinking that there was a chance the landing party would be successful after all.

Then he heard a far-off explosive sound, followed by a drawnout rumble. He went immediately to Cardinali. "Where exactly are we in this facility?"

"A basement storage area, Captain. Five meters underground. Three or four levels built above us."

"Then that was definitely a loud noise out there," Kirk said. "Thunderstorm?"

"Not here. Not in this season."

There was a second noise, louder than the first. Kirk watched as the lifeform readings of the sleeping Talin began to change: temperatures rising, increased respiration, minor movement. "The ones that were sleeping heard that. They're starting to wake up."

Wilforth came over from an equipment cylinder he had been packing up. "It wasn't a weapons detonation, was it?" He sounded nervous.

Kirk flipped the tricorder from lifeforms to energy settings. "There are a couple of generating sources nearby . . . electrical . . . but everything's controlled. Nonexplosive." A sudden flurry of peak numbers rushed across the tricorder's screen. A third explosion echoed around the storeroom.

"That was something flying above us," Kirk said, fine tuning the controls. "Too small for the *Enterprise* . . . an aircraft of some sort . . ." Then he realized what they had heard. "Those were sonic booms."

Cardinali took his tricorder back from Kirk. "Zalan, pack up my terminal while I check this out."

"What is it?" Kirk asked, reading the screen upside down. He couldn't tell what Cardinali was scanning for.

"I'm trying to see if those are missiles or airplanes. Could be bombers . . . could be fighters."

"An attack?" Kirk asked, feeling shock. The negotiators he had listened to had seemed to be so reasonable, so eager for peace.

More rumbles.

"That's it," Cardinali announced tensely. "Lifeforms on board. They're piloted aircraft. And with so many of them at that speed . . . they have to be military."

Kirk felt sick. The *Enterprise* was still five minutes away. But what did the landing party matter compared with a world that was going to destroy itself? "Is this facility a target?" he asked, already suspecting the answer—it held classified information.

Cardinali nodded slowly. "As far as we know, yes. An important one."

Kirk stepped over to the cylinders. "Then, let's stand ready." Wilforth, Cardinali, and the technicians moved to join him.

They waited.

They heard footsteps in the hallway outside the door. Kirk gestured rapidly to everyone to move the equipment cylinders to the edge of a bookshelf and then crouch down behind them. The *Enterprise* was less than two minutes away. *If she's still there*, Kirk thought. He knew Spock wouldn't risk coming in over a squadron of attacking warplanes.

"Give us the disruptors, Captain," Wilforth whispered urgently.

But Kirk shook his head. "If the Talin here are under attack and we stun any of them . . . they won't have a chance to go to a shelter. I won't let that happen to them."

The door to the hallway opened and bright light fell in again. Kirk peered through the crack between the two cylinders. Two Talin stood backlit in the doorway, a male and female, delicate saurians, two and a half meters tall, and impressive. Their large yellow eyes moved quickly across the storeroom as their cranial crests rippled like seaweed. The larger Talin's gaze came to rest on the cylinders and Kirk saw the quick flicker of blue inner eyelids. The creature's wide and lipless mouth opened to reveal a serrated ridge of fine, sharp teeth. His exposed skin flushed deep red.

Then the other Talin called out with a high-pitched whistle. She had found the two Talin Wilforth had stunned.

Kirk was amazed at how quickly and gracefully the creatures moved as they knelt down to examine the unconscious pair.

The *Enterprise* was one minute away.

Be there, Kirk thought. It was an order.

Then one of the stunned Talin began to make a sound that sounded like coughing and the male beside him helped him sit up. Kirk watched as the awakening Talin shook his head, stared up at his benefactor, then turned to look farther into the storeroom, at the cylinders.

The creature's taloned hand shot out toward them and he began to shriek again.

"The disruptors!" Wilforth begged.

The floor shook with another cluster of sonic booms.

Kirk clutched the cylinders. *Enterprise!* he called out in his mind. *Come to me now.*

189

The male Talin stood. His hand went to a long pouch strapped to his bibcloth covering his chest and withdrew what could only be a chemical projectile weapon.

The ground shook again.

The Talin raised his weapon.

And the storeroom filled with the light of the ship who had come to claim her master.

190

EIGHT

☆

The transporter room formed around Kirk and he felt the familiar transition back to the *Enterprise*'s gravity. The faces of Spock and McCoy as they waited by Kyle's console were also welcome.

Kirk jumped down from the platform. He saw Spock's eyes drop to the cluster of disruptors he had strung around him.

"Who's attacking the university? What's the situation below?" Kirk asked. He was puzzled by the way McCoy suddenly burst into a brilliant smile. "Good to see you, too, Bones."

"The university's not under attack," McCoy said.

"The situation is quite remarkable," Spock added.

Kirk looked from one to the other. Behind him, the FCO personnel broke open their equipment to retrieve the Talin datadisks. "We heard warplanes," Kirk said, still confused.

"Yes," Spock agreed. "There are hundreds in flight even now."

Kirk didn't understand. A world was at war and yet no one seemed to care.

"They are being recalled," Spock said simply.

"What happened?" Kirk asked.

McCoy's grin was blinding. "Peace, Jim. The Greens and

Browns are withdrawing their forward troops. All over the planet."

"Wh-what?" Wilforth stuttered. Beside him, Cardinali and the technicians stopped their work.

As Kirk paused, wondering if he was going to have to ask more questions or whether some member of his crew might decide to fill him in, the transporter room doors slipped open and Carole Mallett ran in. Her smile was as broad as McCoy's and she went straight to Cardinali to hug him.

"They're going to make it!" she told them all. "They're really going to make it."

Before the doors closed again, Kirk had time to hear what sounded like a party in the corridor. He actually heard a noisemaker blow.

"Spock . . . ?"

"It has been a most fascinating sequence of events, Captain. The Talin had brought themselves to the brink of complete disaster."

"But that's what saved them!" McCoy's voice broke in. "They went straight to the brink—right to the edge, Jim, and they stepped back." The doctor spoke so quickly, so excitedly, that his Georgia drawl surfaced and his words ran together. "We were all listening to it on the bridge. Hell, we were all listening to it through the whole ship. Carolyn put it on the intercom.

"They *knew* they were minutes from destroying themselves, and they *chose* not to." McCoy shook his head at the wonder of it. "They chose not to."

Kirk was elated. It was the last thing he had expected to hear. "Bones, that's wonderful. It's more than wonderful."

"It's unbelievable," Wilforth said quietly.

"But most logical on the part of the Talin," Spock concluded.

McCoy shook his head in dismissal. "Oh, spare us the logic of it, Spock. Those beings down there were scared. Cold, senseless, *emotional* fear. It was their feelings that saved the day. Not logical thinking. Emotions!"

"It was their emotions that brought them to this point in the—"

"Please, Spock, Bones, before we have to ask the Talin negotiators to come up here next." Kirk put a hand on the console to reassure himself that he was back and that all he was learning was real. "What brought them to the brink so quickly? Things weren't that bad when we beamed down, were they?"

"It was the dispute over polar airspace," Spock said. "Because of the difficulties in monitoring the area through the interference of the planet's magnetosphere, they—"

"The Greens thought the Browns were exploiting gaps in the continent's defenses," McCoy said, to cut through Spock's detailed explanation. "But the Browns kept denying it. So the Greens thought that the Browns were really up to something and started to escalate their war readiness. And that made the Browns convinced that the Greens were making up the whole thing as an excuse to go to war, so *they* started escalating. It was like one of your bloody chess games with Spock. No one knew when to call it off."

McCoy and Spock stared at each other.

"And . . . ?" Kirk said, not wanting the story to be cut off there. "What happened?"

"The Talin negotiators intervened," Spock said. "Each side realized that there was no advantage to the other for doing what each was accused of doing."

"They blamed the whole thing on communications failure," McCoy said, "to save face. Hardly logical but it sure worked."

"And they were able to have their armies stand down so quickly?" Kirk asked.

"The Talin have an elaborate system of oaths," Spock said. "Invoking some of them carries a great deal of authority. And some of those oaths were invoked between the Browns and the Greens for the first time."

Wilforth's mouth dropped open in a way which reminded Kirk of the Talin who had seen the cylinders. "The Browns and Greens invoked oaths of common kinship?"

"Yes," Spock said. "That was the term used by the translator."

Kirk thought Wilforth was going to faint.

"An hour ago," the FCO director said, "I would have sworn that would have been impossible." He looked at Kirk and frowned. "I told you we should have stunned that second pair. They didn't need to go to a shelter."

Kirk deflected Spock's question by speaking first. "We were detected by one pair of Talin and stunned them. A second pair saw us—or at least saw the cylinders beam out."

"A not uncommon occurrence during FCO operations," Spock observed.

"So I've been told," Kirk said dryly.

Cardinali came up beside him, one arm around Mallett. "Captain Kirk, this is an unprecedented moment in Talin history. Perhaps one of the greatest gifts we could give them when contact is finally established is a complete record of what transpired during this incident. I'd like permission to have the sensor satellites go to full scan under the *Enterprise's* control for at least the next week."

Kirk began to say no. He didn't want to extend his stay in this system any longer than he had to.

But Cardinali's exhilaration was infectious. "Remember how much Earth appreciated the communication logs made by the Vulcans during the last decade of the twentieth century? So many questions were answered."

Kirk turned to Spock. "If we keep to tightbeam, can we stay in an orbit beyond the range of their sensors?"

"Most efficiently," Spock said.

"Very well," Kirk said to Cardinali. "Coordinate your communication requirements with Lieutenant Uhura."

Cardinali thanked Kirk excitedly, then left with Mallett. The party sounds from the corridor sounded even louder when the doors opened a second time.

"No problem on the close orbit while I was gone?" Kirk asked Spock.

"The Talin had other matters with which to occupy themselves."

For the first time since his initial meeting with Wilforth, Kirk felt himself begin to relax. He had gone into this mission expecting the worst, yet it had unexpectedly ended with the best possible result. He knew he'd have to be careful or he'd begin to start expecting this to happen all the time. He smiled at his friends. He had won again, even though this time he hadn't known all the rules of the game.

"I guess you know that that leaves us with only one thing to do," McCoy said.

"Absolutely," Kirk agreed.

Now it was Spock's turn to be puzzled. "I do not understand. I am aware of nothing more that needs to be done at this time."

"Of course you don't understand," McCoy said as he headed for the doors. "Because *you* don't have anything left to do."

Spock looked at Kirk. Kirk smiled. "What Bones means is that since it's going to be at least fifty years before we can celebrate with the Talin, right now we have to celebrate *for* them."

Spock thought that over. "An entire planet has been saved today. A race has been preserved and someday will have a chance to spread among the stars. Yes, I believe a celebration is in order."

McCoy stared at Spock in amazement. "Well, I'll be . . . Maybe there is hope for you after all, Spock."

Kirk patted the doctor on the back. "If the Talin can make it, Bones, anyone can. Come on, Mr. Spock, we've got some logical celebrating to do."

Kirk kept reading the quartermaster's report and reached out for the coffee cup on the yeoman's tray without paying attention. The QM subprogram warned that alcohol consumption had shown an alarming increase among the crew but Kirk signed off on it. Yesterday's Talin celebration party had been the first real blowout his crew had had since the last Nobel and

Z. Magnees Prize ceremonies. They were entitled. Then he became aware that he had closed his hand around empty space. He glanced up from his screenpad to see what had happened to the coffee.

The tray was out of reach. Slowly he realized that his yeoman had pulled it away from him.

"Yeoman Frietas, what are—oh."

"Hello, Captain," Carolyn Palamas said smoothly. "Did you want some coffee?" She brought the tray back within reach.

Kirk took the cup. Being fifty thousand kilometers out from Talin and monitoring the ongoing peace developments had given the bridge of the *Enterprise* a different feel. He was glad to see her there.

"Why, Lieutenant, I don't recall approving your transfer to yeoman."

Palamas moved a fraction closer. "I didn't request a transfer. It's just that someone ran off without his breakfast this morning and I thought you could use some . . . coffee."

Kirk smiled. It had been a wonderful celebration and he was happy to have someone to share it with. "What I could use," Kirk said, "is the five-day slow voyage out of this system."

"I thought you didn't like slow voyages."

"Depends on whom I'm voyaging with," Kirk said. Their eyes met and held.

"Excuse me, Captain," Spock said from his station.

Kirk turned instantly.

"Sensor satellite five does not respond to its scheduled tightbeam data upload," Spock reported.

Kirk stepped from his chair and had time to nod good-bye to Palamas as she headed for the turbolift. She nodded in return, understanding in her eyes. The mission and ship came first, always.

Kirk checked Spock's readouts. "The satellite's still in orbit. Is its power supply functional, Mr. Spock?"

"Without a tightbeam upload, the only way to be sure is with a sensor scan, Captain. But at this distance, the sensor probe would spread enough so that residual radiation would reach Talin's surface and might be detected."

"Get Scotty up here to go over the controls. He rigged the satellites. He can fix them."

"Very good, Captain. But if we are unable to regain contact with the satellite?"

Kirk looked at the image of Talin IV on the main screen—a world at peace. "Then we'll go in for a look. Nothing to worry about down there now."

The crisis abated, Kirk returned to his chair and the quartermaster's report. He looked toward the turbolift as he stepped down to the central area, but the doors were closed and Palamas was gone. *Oh, well,* he thought, *at least we've got the voyage out.*

Chief Engineer Scott appeared on the bridge within two minutes of Spock's call. "I don't understand," he said as he went to work at the engineering station, "those satellites were perfect. They'll still be working fifty years on."

"But one is not working now, Mr. Scott," Spock said.

"I can see that, Mr. Spock, but there's no reason for it. Look at these readings for yourself. It's perfectly clear. The dual-looped power units were fully coiled on the two-fifty bypasses and the L-37s were securely crosslinked to all duotronics."

Kirk leaned against the railing and listened to Spock and Scott trade technical jargon. He knew what almost everything they mentioned was but he wasn't sure how any of it should go together. It had been a long time since some of his Academy classes.

After a few minutes of increasingly incomprehensible specifications had been cited and all controls had been adjusted and readjusted, the science officer and the chief engineer appeared to have hit an impasse.

"Should we go down and take a look?" Kirk asked.

"No need," Scott said. "It's the software."

"We should," Spock said. "The hardware appears to be at fault."

Both men turned to look at Kirk. *Now this* is *a classic no-win situation,* Kirk thought. "Sorry, Scotty, but if there's the slightest chance that the satellite has been damaged somehow, we can't risk it re-entering by accident. We'll go in close enough so that we can scan for damage without flooding the Talin with sensor radiation, and once the equipment's checked out we can come back here to work on the software at leisure." Kirk hoped he had talked fast enough.

"Aye, Captain," Scott said and smiled at Spock. "And I'd be more than willin' to give you a hand with your reprogramming, Mr. Spock."

"Thank you, Mr. Scott, but I believe that will not be necessary once the satellite has been repaired."

Kirk left them to it and went to Sulu to request a change in orbit. But Sulu had overheard and the orbit was already plotted.

"Very good, Mr. Sulu, take us in."

Chekov jumped up to take his place at the defense subsystems monitor and prepare countermeasures. Ensign Leslie left his environmental station to take over Chekov's navigation post. Kirk sat back in his chair. All operations were smooth and routine as Talin grew in the viewscreen.

Kirk turned back to his screenpad and the QM's report. The program warned that if current consumption was maintained, the ship's stores of real chocolate would be exhausted within two months. It recommended encouraging a switch to consumption of synthesized chocolate. Kirk shuddered at the thought and vetoed that suggestion with a quick flick of his stylus.

"Coming up on satellite five," Sulu announced.

Kirk glanced up. The curve of Talin filled the lower half of the screen. The satellite was too small to register though he could see its sensor echo on the astrogator screen. He signed off on the QM report and the week's medical log synopsis appeared on the pad.

"Within focused sensor range, Mr. Spock," Leslie announced.

"Scanning," Spock said.

Kirk vetoed the medical log as well. All that was in it were ten requests for Kirk, James T., to report to sickbay for a scheduled checkup or risk being put on the captain's disciplinary list.

"All equipment checks out," Spock said.

Kirk looked up. It had been subtle but there had been surprise in Spock's tone.

Scotty smiled. "You're sure I can't be giving ye some help with the software, Mr. Spock?"

Spock shook his head. "The software does not seem to be the problem either, Mr. Scott. It is no longer resident in the satellite's control circuits."

Kirk put the screenpad down on the arm of his chair.

"I beg your pardon, Mr. Spock?" Scott said.

"The control programs have been erased?" Kirk asked.

Spock nodded. "It is quite impossible, but all memory storage on the satellite is empty."

"Explanation, Mr. Scott?"

"I . . . have none at the moment, Captain. I don't know how such a thing could be possible without . . ."

"Without what, Mr. Scott?"

"Well, the password authorization . . . the encryption codes . . . the scrambling mechanisms. . . . The satellites were prepared according to FCO specifications. They're near impossible to program or extract information from by brute force."

"Mr. Spock, any theories?"

"Absolutely none. A violent subspace pulse could have burned out the transtator circuitry but we have not detected any phenomena of the required intensity. I shall have to—"

"Keptin! I have detected an energy burst on the planet's surface."

"What kind of energy?" Kirk scanned the screen. Just beyond the terminator on Talin's nightside, he saw a brilliant white flare. "Helm, magnify. Is that it, Chekov?"

Chekov looked over at the screen. "Y—yes, sir."

The viewscreen swam, then fixed on an enlarged image of the flare. Kirk could see pinpricks of red fire spring up around it. "What is it, Ensign?"

"N—nuclear, Keptin. It is a forty megaton nuclear detonation."

Kirk felt as if the ship had jumped to warp nine without warning. "Where?" he asked. On the screen, from the pattern of city lights along the coastline, the detonation appeared to be in the center of the Greens' continent—their agricultural heartland, Palamas had called it.

Chekov read off the coordinates. "The Green nation state," he said, voice choking. "Eastern administrative district. Subregion five."

Kirk stared at the glowing spark of hellfire on the screen. An entire city might already be ashes.

"Those are the coordinates of a missile silo facility," Spock said.

Kirk tensed. It was a military target. It could only mean one thing. "Why would the Browns launch a first strike now?" he asked.

"And why would they launch a first strike with only one warhead?" Spock said. He bent to his scope.

"Keptin! I have missiles launching! I have missiles launching!"

"Dear God," Kirk whispered. A regular pattern of red dots had appeared across the Green continent. Hundreds of missiles were in flight.

"Go to red alert," Kirk said. It was standard procedure, but he knew the missiles were not meant for his ship. He had Uhura kill the warning sirens on the bridge, but the red alert lights still flashed.

"Captain," Spock said. "My sensors show that detonation occurred deep underground."

"Depth, Spock? What was the depth?"

"Consistent with underground missile emplacement."

"No!" Kirk said. He turned to the screen. More red dots. A thousand missiles in flight. "It was a *mistake!*"

Uhura cut in. "Communications intercept from the planet's surface, Captain. Brown forces have detected the Green launch." There were tears in her eyes. "Captain, they're retaliating."

"Brown missiles are launching!" Chekov called out. "Brown missiles are launching!"

"It's a mistake, you fools!" Kirk shouted at the viewscreen, at the dying planet. "Spock! It has to be! The Talin warheads are faulty. Only a sixty percent accuracy rate! The Greens were dismantling their missiles and accidentally set off one of their own damn warheads!"

Spock's face was rigid. His eyes were fixed on the screen. "That would be . . . the most logical explanation."

"A mistake!" Kirk slammed his fist against the side of his chair. "No!"

"Captain?" Spock asked.

"I will not allow a mistake to destroy this planet." He burned with anger. This planet was going to survive. Any other fate for it was a personal insult.

"Captain, we can do nothing," Spock said. But his words and his tone conveyed two different meanings. "The Prime Directive forbids us from interfering."

"No!" Kirk snapped. "The Prime Directive forbids us from interfering in a planet's normal development. Look what's going on down there. Spock, that's not the planet's normal development. That's an accident. An accidental detonation has triggered off an aberrant chain of events. The Talin are not doing this to themselves on purpose."

Spock's face flickered with an expression of pain, quickly hidden. "Captain, I agree you can make a case for this being a . . . natural disaster . . . an event similar to a runaway asteroid about to impact . . . but still we cannot be seen to interfere."

"But we won't be seen, Spock." Kirk's mind raced. There had to be a way out. There always was a way out. Change the rules, change the goals, do anything. But find that way out. "We can do it. The *Enterprise* can do it. And the Talin won't know what happened any more than they'll ever know what set off that first missile in its silo. We won't be interfering, Spock. We'll only be giving them some time. Some time to sort things out on their own. That's all."

The bridge crew froze at their stations. They would do anything their captain told them to do, but they knew their captain would tell them nothing if Spock did not agree.

Spock leaned on the railing.

Kirk held his hands out before him, imploring. "Spock . . . think it through. It works. The Prime Directive is upheld. They won't know what has happened."

Spock spoke slowly. "Yes . . . the Directive . . . is upheld." He squared his shoulders. "I shall prepare coordinates." He turned to his scope.

Kirk gave orders in an endless stream. There was no time to stop to think or consider his actions. There was time only to do, to take action, to save a world.

The *Enterprise* flooded Talin IV with sensor radiation. Within seconds, her computers established the location and trajectory of each missile arcing through the skies below.

Scott was the one who knew how the warheads worked. He took over five percent of the *Enterprise*'s computing capacity to decode and transmit self-destruct signals to the missiles in flight. They vanished from the screen by the hundreds.

Uhura knew the radio codes. Another eight percent of the *Enterprise*'s computers went to decoding and translating radio voice callback signals to bomber wings and fighters and submersible weapons platforms. Most Talin who received those messages did not turn back immediately, but they held in failsafe positions and requested verification, unsure of their commanders' commitment.

Chekov moved back to his station and took over the main phaser banks. Four hundred and twenty-seven missiles refused to respond to Scott's signals. Chekov took them from the skies with pinpoint precision.

In forty minutes, Sulu had taken the *Enterprise* around the planet twice. The Browns' missiles were gone. The Greens' missiles were gone. The bombers were returning. The submersibles were silent and still. The skies of Talin were clear.

Kirk's shirt was drenched with sweat. His voice was hoarse. The red alert signal still flashed.

Uhura cleared her throat. "Captain . . . I am on the diplomatic frequency. The negotiators are back on line. They are . . . apologizing, sir . . . they are . . . sir, they are praying to their gods together to thank them for salvation from . . . from a terrible . . . accident." Uhura wiped the tears from her eyes. "They know it was an accident, sir." Scotty went to her and put an arm around her. His hair was plastered to his forehead.

Kirk didn't turn from the screen. The nightside of the planet was scattered with thousands of small fires from the flaming debris of the destroyed missiles, but the planet was still there. A world still existed. A race still survived.

"Lieutenant Uhura," Kirk said, "download all bridge records of the past hour, unedited audio and visual, to the FCO main computer on Talin's moon. Then download duplicates of all records into two separate message buoys for Starfleet Command and launch immediately."

"Aye-aye, sir," Uhura said hoarsely.

The turbolift doors slid open and McCoy stormed onto the bridge. "What the hell is going on around here?" He stopped when he saw the small fires blazing across the face of Talin IV. "Good Lord, what're those?" He looked at Kirk, saw his exhaustion, brought out his medical scanners. "What have you done?"

It was Spock who answered, perfectly calm, perfectly controlled.

"Dr. McCoy, we have done our job."

NINE

Kirk wore his formal tunic. He knew that technically there was no need for it, but when the board of inquiry replayed the tapes of these proceedings, he wanted them to know that he took his actions and his duty as seriously as they took theirs.

Spock, Scott, and McCoy sat with Kirk on one side of the table in the conference room. Zalan Wilforth, Alonzo Richter, and Yeoman Jorge Frietas sat on the other. The yeoman operated the recording computer as if it were an extension of himself.

"Recording, Mr. Spock," Frietas said as the verification lights flickered across the computer terminal, constantly encoding all that it registered with elaborately sequenced security codes which could not be duplicated, thus ensuring that the original tapes could not be altered in any way. It was a new system designed to prevent abuses such as had occurred in the past.

Spock folded his hands on the table and began his formal recitation for the record. "The third session of the preliminary hearing into actions taken by Captain James T. Kirk at Talin IV is now in session. This hearing has been called by Captain Kirk himself because of his concern that some or all of his actions at Talin IV might be considered to have contravened the noninterference directive of Starfleet General Order One. This hearing's purpose is to gather preliminary information which may or may not support the captain's claim that all his actions were performed without such contravention. Any or all preliminary information gathered by this hearing is subject to further review and verification by Starfleet Command, if and when so desired."

Spock waited patiently for a few moments. "Director Wilforth," he said at last, "you may speak now."

Wilforth squirmed in his seat. "Oh, ah, Zalan Ko'askla Wilforth, Director, Starfleet First Contact Office, Outpost 47, Talin IV." He looked at Spock for approval.

"Please continue, Director."

"Ah, I wish to present a report prepared by the communications section of FCO Outpost 47 concerning communications intercepts carried out in the three Talin days following the accidental detonation of a native nuclear warhead on Talin IV." He held up a yellow microtape. "W—what do I do with it?"

Kirk sat calmly. This was an official procedure and, as a show of his respect for Starfleet, for once he was not impatient. Wilforth could take all day as far as he was concerned.

"Place it in the recording computer," Spock said, "and then present your summary."

Wilforth offered the microtape to Yeoman Frietas, but the young man shook his head. "You have to place it in the reader, sir. I can't touch it."

"Oh, of course," Wilforth said. He fumbled at the side of the terminal with the tape, then slipped it into place with a click. "And, ah, to summarize. Ahem." He coughed into his fist. "The hours following the accidental detonation of the warhead on Talin are being referred to as the Blue Season Miracle. Ah, Blue Season is the native calendar designation for the current . . . ah . . . calendar period on Talin. Um, anyway, the use of the term 'miracle' is important in the FCO's interpretation of events because it establishes that the Talin have clearly assigned an almost supernatural significance to what has happened on their planet. That is, they do not ascribe those events to the actions of an indigenous or extraplanetary agency.

"Briefly, the FCO intercepts show that the Talin are aware that the detonation of a missile in the Green nation state was, without question, an accident. Though, owing to the destruction it caused, the reason for that accident will likely never be determined. The Talin are also aware that the resulting launch of approximately one quarter of the Green nuclear arsenal was triggered solely by automated alert systems which were scheduled for dismantling over the next few Talin . . . ah . . . months, I suppose you'd call them.

"Likewise, the retaliatory launch of approximately one third of the Brown nuclear arsenal was also a programmed response, again not initiated by deliberate orders."

Wilforth looked around the table. His nervousness finally seemed to be under control.

"It is my expert opinion, as an FCO director, that the Talin as a race believe that an unimaginable accident nearly came to pass three days ago and that an almost equally unimaginable sequence of equipment malfunctions, programming conflicts, and even weather conditions, contributed to the failure of the warheads being exchanged.

"To support Captain Kirk's claim that what he did was not in contravention of General Order One, I should like to emphasize that because his actions preserved the Talin global communications system, the military and political leaders of the various nation states on the planet were able to enter into immediate, joint discussions which enabled them to prevent any further commitment of their remaining forces.

"It is the FCO's opinion that Captain Kirk's actions served only to give the Talin approximately fifteen to thirty minutes of extra time during which they were able to reaffirm the strong commitment to world peace that the Talin have demonstrated so often during our observation of them. The FCO believes the Talin have been saved from an unpredictable and uncontrollable disaster, not of their own making, and are now able to continue their normal and expected development as a race and a culture.

"Most importantly, according to all communication intercepts available to the FCO, Captain Kirk has accomplished this humanitarian deed without revealing in any way to the Talin that an extraplanetary agency was involved." Wilforth cleared his throat a final time. "Our conclusion is that the Prime Directive has not been contravened and Captain Kirk deserves the Federation's highest commendation for the preservation of life and peace."

Kirk didn't smile or otherwise acknowledge Wilforth's summary. As a career officer, he was used to listening to others praise him, and he knew how quickly that praise could turn to censure. He appreciated Wilforth's contribution because Kirk believed it to be true, but he also knew that the final authority to decide whether or not General Order One had been obeyed rested with Starfleet Command. However, he realized that for once he wasn't worried about second-guessing Command—he had saved an entire world, and given the politics of the Federation and the Admiralty, no one was going to go after a winner.

"Does anyone have anything more to add?" Spock asked.

No one replied.

"This hearing is adjourned."

We pulled it off, Kirk suddenly thought. *The* Enterprise *saved a world without revealing herself.* He felt a welcome rush of accomplishment. Then it was checked by one last realization. *If I didn't trust Wilforth's judgment two days ago, why should I trust him now?*

"I have this idea for a bar," Kirk said. He took a bite of his sandwich and gazed out through the herbarium's viewport. Talin was full and alive fifty thousand kilometers distant. The air around him was filled with the scent of blooming roses. The *Enterprise's* greenhouse facility was his favorite room on the ship. Especially during ship's night.

"Funny, you don't look like the bartender type," Palamas said teasingly. On the park bench reproduction they sat on, she finished spreading out the picnic Kirk had packed.

"No, no," Kirk said, talking around a mouthful of chicken salad. "On the ship. Or a ship, anyway."

"A bar on a Starfleet vessel?" She was skeptical now.

"For times like these." Kirk turned to her and smiled. "The mission is accomplished. We're in friendly waters. It would be nice to have a place to go to enjoy these moments. Something with a bit more . . . atmosphere than the rec facilities or the mess hall. Could take the edge off waiting for shore leave, too." He took another bite of his sandwich. "Just a thought."

"Well, it sounds like a nice one. These ships can get pretty sterile sometimes." Palamas began to peel an orange, staring at it thoughtfully. "Jim . . . how do you feel about what you've done?" She sounded flustered. "Have I asked that the right way? Do you know . . . ?"

Kirk nodded. He inhaled the scent of the flowers. He remembered his mother's garden back on the farm. Just a small patch with a few rose bushes, some petunias, a rhododendron which never seemed to bloom. His father had always said flowers were nonsense on a farm. You couldn't eat them. But he was always out there with her, weeding and pruning. And smiling, Kirk remembered. They were always smiling when they were out in their nonsense garden together.

"I know what you're asking," Kirk said. "But to tell the truth, Carolyn, I don't think about it that way." He saw the confusion in her eyes. "I did what I had to do at the time I did it. And now, it's done, so . . . it's time to do something else."

But Palamas shook her head. "You saved an entire civilization, Jim. Two and a half billion beings . . . their history . . . their hopes. . . . "

Kirk put his sandwich down and took Palamas's hand in his. "I didn't save a world, Carolyn. This *crew* saved a world. This *ship* saved a world. I was just the one in the center seat, and there are lots of others who could sit there just as well."

Palamas stared into Kirk's eyes, questioning him with more than words. "You really believe that, don't you? This isn't false modesty . . . or conceited humility . . . you honestly believe that you did nothing extraordinary on your own . . . ?"

Kirk put a hand to her face, tracing the soft contours of her cheek and her lips. They were in friendly waters. There was room for just a few moments to themselves. "There are one or two extraordinary things I can do on my own," he whispered.

"I know." She touched his face in return.

Surrounded by the scent of flowers and life and precious memories, they kissed.

The red alert sounded two seconds later.

The paging whistle was like a knife.

Chekov's voice thundered from the intercom. *"Bridge to Keptin! Bridge to Keptin! We have missiles launched on Talin IV! We have detonations!"*

Kirk pushed his way through the turbolift doors and arrived on the bridge out of breath.

The viewscreen showed the terrible truth in full magnification. The dayside of Talin glittered with the brilliant flares of fusion fireballs. Dozens. Hundreds. More sparkling into hellish life with each second.

"Why?" Kirk said. He whirled to Uhura. "What happened?"

Uhura looked desperate. "Unknown, Captain. There has been no mention of any war preparations on any of the comm channels we've been monitoring."

"Sulu! Take us in there! Full impulse."

Even as the helmsman acknowledged the order, the image of Talin swelled on the screen. The ship was in geostationary orbit in seconds, poised over the terminator.

"Chekov! Evaluation!"

The ensign's hands trembled over his controls. "It's insane, Keptin. All weapons have been launched. All weapons. There is no strategy. No plan. Just . . . they are firing *everything.*"

Kirk saw his straw and grasped at it. "Are you saying

209

malfunction, mister? Is that it? Is that a malfunction down there?"

Chekov shook his head in confusion. "They can't want to do this. Not like that. It must be something else that caused it."

The turbolift doors burst open again. Spock rushed onto the bridge still adjusting his uniform. His mouth opened as he saw what was on the screen, but he said nothing.

"Everything's been launched, Spock," Kirk said urgently. "No plan, no strategy."

"That is senseless," Spock said.

"Exactly, Spock. Senseless. Another accident. Something to do with disarming the automated alert systems. That's the only explanation."

"Yes," Spock said. Even he was shaken by the destruction spreading on the screen. "The Talin are not capable of such . . . insanity. But without more information, we can't be sure what triggered it. We can't be certain what to do."

Kirk turned to his crew. "Bring those missiles down."

"No, Captain," Spock said. "Without data, without communication logs . . . you cannot."

"I know, Spock, I know." He thrust out his arm to point at the screen. "But look what they're doing to themselves down there." He made his decision. "Everyone: I cannot order you to do what we did before—when the situation was clearer. But I believe that something else beyond the Talin's control has caused this. And I believe we are justified in stopping it."

Kirk looked at each of his bridge crew in turn. "But I cannot order you to act against the Prime Directive."

Chekov spoke first. "Sir, I wolunteer to bring down the missiles."

"Transmitting self-destruct and call-back codes," Uhura said.

Sulu brought the ship about. "Moving in on main missile flights."

"Processing targeting data." Spock was at his station.

McCoy and Wilforth ran from the turbolift. Richter shuffled

out with Cardinali and Mallett, then stopped in horror at what he saw. "My God."

McCoy was more forthright. "Those ignorant fools."

"It's not their fault, Bones," Kirk said. "It's a massive equipment malfunction. They trusted too much to their computers. Or maybe—"

"Captain Kirk, all radio frequencies are jammed, sir." Uhura jabbed at her controls in frustration. "Nothing can get through. Not even the Talin's own messages."

"Can you broadcast on subspace and phase down to radio frequencies once you're past the jamming boundary?" Kirk asked.

Uhura looked at Spock. "Mr. Spock, I'll need your help to—"

"I will begin the proper sensor alignment," Spock said.

Kirk stared at the screen, willing the miniature suns that grew silently on it to disappear. On the planet's nightside, the arc of atmosphere already glowed red from the firestorms that had erupted.

"Where are those phasers, Mr. Chekov?"

"Sir, targeting modes are not working. I can't lock on to anything."

Kirk was out of his chair. "What do you mean not working?"

"I am not getting a target-acquisition return signal. Perhaps it is the jamming. . . . " Chekov kept trying to reset his weapons systems, over and over.

"But those signals go over subspace," Kirk protested, going to Chekov's station. "Uhura said the jamming was in the electromagnetic spectrum."

Then Spock called for the captain. "Subspace frequencies are jammed as well."

"What? That's impossible! The Talin don't have the technology."

Spock looked up from his scope. "Nevertheless, subspace is jammed, sir."

"Could it be an effect of all the fusion explosions?" There

were still more of them. The planet looked as if its core had exploded and was bursting through its shell.

"Perhaps, Captain, but our sensors are useless."

"What if we went in closer? Boosted power to all subspace systems and punched through the interference."

"That could work," Spock decided.

"Sulu! Take us in past the jamming layer."

Sulu hesitated for an instant. "Sir, that will take us through the ionosphere and into the atmosphere proper."

"Won't be the first time," Kirk said, fists clenched. "Take us in."

The *Enterprise* fell for the planet.

Within seconds, the rough buffeting of atmospheric flight shook the bridge.

"Chekov, try those phasers again."

The whine of the phaser capacitors echoed through the bridge.

"They're working!" Chekov cried triumphantly. "Limited range but they're working!"

"Uhura, try the self-destruct signals again."

"Yes, sir. Getting some response, sir."

Then Chekov screamed and flew from his chair as his navigation board erupted in sparks and flame. McCoy ran to him. Richter kept muttering to himself.

"Subspace feedback through phaser targeting system," Spock said.

Cardinali and Mallett broke out oxygen eaters from the emergency lockers and began spraying the sputtering console to help the automatic damage-control systems. Sulu stayed at his post, blackened with soot, breathing smoke. The ship bucked wildly.

"Shock waves from multiple explosions," he said, hands moving feverishly over the controls. "It's like flying through water, sir."

Uhura gasped and pulled her earpiece from her ear.

"Subspace feedback on all comm channels," Spock said.

"This is not a natural phenomenon. This is a deliberate attempt to—"

"Incoming missiles!" Sulu shouted.

"Impossible!" Kirk answered.

"We have been targeted," Spock confirmed. "Missiles are locked."

"They can't do this!" Kirk said. "They don't have the capability."

The comm page sounded. Scott's voice came over the line. "Scott to bridge. If ye don't mind me asking, what the hell's going on up there?"

"Five seconds to impact," Spock announced.

"Full power to shields, Scotty! Now! Now! Sulu, get us out of—"

The viewscreen flared brilliant white until the visual compensators cut in. The ship shuddered as if it had smashed into solid rock. Uhura fell from her chair. Spock slammed over the railing. Richter cried out. And all Kirk could hear was every bridge alarm screaming at him in betrayal.

"Captain!" Sulu cried. "Impulse is gone. We're in free fall. Impact on planet's surface in one minute."

The rush of air outside the hull rose in a frantic wail.

Kirk felt his heart stop. There was only one way out. But it was madness. Madness.

"Warp us out, Sulu. Warp us out!"

Scotty shouted over the intercom. "Captain! We're within the Danylkiw Limit. Too deep in the gravity well. We won't survive the transition."

"Now, Sulu! There's no other—"

The hull metal shrieked and the ship twisted as another flight of missiles detonated against her shields. Spock pulled himself back to his feet. Green blood flooded his eyes from a gash on his forehead. Mallett sat beside Sulu, trying desperately to bring any of Chekov's nav controls back on line.

"Thirty seconds to impact!" Sulu cried. "Going to warp . . . now!"

It was like death.

The viewscreen went to black. The lights cut out. Gravity failed and there was only a long endless fall into utter darkness. Then the emergency lights flickered back on and Kirk saw everything before him blur in a highspeed vibration.

"Emergency systems on line," Spock said, voice distorted. Partial gravity returned. Color trails flickered from every object as local time slowed down.

Scott's voice was plaintive, slow, and warbling over the commlink. "Warp generators are runaway. Linked to singularity on runaway."

"Jettison nacelles!" Kirk felt trapped in thick liquid. The *Enterprise* had to cut her warp space link to Talin IV's gravity well or they would become trapped in an endless moment of time.

"Crew evacuation complete!" Spock rumbled. "Starboard nacelle away!"

Kirk felt stretched like rubber. The viewscreen flickered to show the infinite fractal nightmare of the gravitational wormhole that loomed hungrily before them. He felt a part of him wrenched away as the long white graceful form of the starboard warp nacelle flew down the maw of the beast—distorted in dizzying eddies of higher dimensional realities.

Gravity failed and they fell again. His hands gripped the sides of his chair. His feet hooked under the seat to hold him in place. Someone flew through the air beside him. Equipment consoles flared and sparked.

No! Kirk thought. *I won't let you go. I won't let you go alone.*

"Port nacelle locked in position!" Spock said. "Cannot jettison!"

Only one more chance, Kirk thought. *Worse than the last.*

He ordered Spock to eject all matter and antimatter into the wormhole. Spock didn't argue. If the singularity won, they would not even know death—only the torment of being forever trapped in the instant just before the end.

Kirk saw the twin ionized jets of matter and antimatter stream down the wormhole with agonizing slowness. Then at last they met and interacted.

The screen went blank. Time stopped.

Kirk fell into oblivion.

TEN

He awoke to the sound of a spray hypo. McCoy stared down at him. The doctor's face was haggard and bloodsmeared. "Good," he said. Then he moved on.

Kirk pushed himself from the floor of the bridge. He did it on a lean because the gravity field was out of alignment, placing the floor on a relative five-degree angle. Smoke filled the air. He heard moans. Half the station displays were out. The other half flickered with gibberish. Only a few battery lights were working, making the whole area dark and murky.

Spock staggered to Kirk's side, a greensoaked bandage covering a gash on his forehead. "It worked," he said hoarsely. "The matter-antimatter explosion pushed us past the Danylkiw Limit into normal space."

"But what else did it do?" Kirk asked. His ship was dying around him. "How long have I been out?"

"Three minutes, eighteen seconds," Spock said. He seemed weak, distracted. "Every transtator circuit in the ship appears to be fused. The subspace energy pulse directed at us was . . . incredible."

"But from where?"

"Unknown, Captain." He coughed roughly. "Unknown."

Kirk saw a shape move onto the viewscreen. It was Talin. The

216

planet was on fire. The entire planet. It floated across the screen, then disappeared. The *Enterprise* spun slowly, adrift in space.

"We are quite powerless," Spock said before Kirk could ask.

Kirk heard a dull thudding noise and then one of the kick-in panels by the turbolift popped out of position. Scott appeared holding a hand light that sent a solid shaft of light through the smoke. He was followed by two medical technicians. Oddly, the kick-in panel on the other side of the lift was also open.

"Ah, thank heavens you're all right, Captain. I couldn't know that any of you had survived. The comm system's out. The turbolift's . . ." He saw Talin pass by the viewscreen again. "Och, no . . . how did it happen? And what happened to the ship?"

"We were attacked by Talin missiles," Spock said flatly.

Kirk watched Scott's reaction to that. The fact that the Talin had attacked the *Enterprise* meant that without a doubt they had known the ship was in orbit around their planet—in direct and flagrant violation of the Prime Directive. Scott was a good officer. He'd know what he would have to do next under those circumstances.

McCoy came up beside Kirk. "Everyone here will be all right, Jim. But I can't find Mallett or Cardinali."

Wilforth limped up the rise of the deck. "But they were here," he coughed. "They were here when . . ."

"It's all right, sir," Scott said. "We passed them in the ladderways heading down to check on their equipment. But Mr. Spock, are ye sure that the Talin missiles were directed at the *Enterprise* herself?"

Kirk put his hand on Scott's shoulder. "They were, Scotty. The Talin knew we were here. They came after us."

Scott looked at the screen. He looked at Talin dying in the heat of a thousand killing suns. Already more than half the planet was enshrouded in brown and black clouds.

"Och, Captain Kirk," he said weakly. Kirk saw the knowledge in the engineer's eyes. Scott had not been on the bridge. That made him untainted, and the next in line.

"It's all right, Scotty," Kirk said gently. "You know what you have to do."

"But, Captain, I . . ."

Kirk couldn't look at his chief engineer. "Damn it, Scotty. You're a Starfleet officer. You *know* what you have to do."

Scott nodded. The funeral fires of Talin filled the bridge with their hideous glow. "Aye," he said. "That I do."

Chief Engineer Montgomery Scott faced his captain.

"James Kirk, as per Starfleet Command Regulation 7, Paragraph 4, you must now consider yourself under arrest, unless in the presence of these fellow officers you give satisfactory answer to the charge which I now bring." Scott faltered, but only for an instant. "Sir, I charge you with knowingly and willfully contravening Starfleet's Prime Directive as set forth in General Order One. Can you answer that charge, sir?"

Kirk shook his head. There was nothing more that could be done. He had destroyed his ship.

He had destroyed a world.

"James Kirk, you are relieved of your command." Scott looked toward the viewscreen.

Talin burned.

"And whatever gods there are," he whispered, "may they have mercy on your soul."

Part Three

TALIN

ONE

☆

The subtle incense that lingered in the air of the embassy's waiting hall reminded Spock of his childhood. The scent had been one of his mother's favorites at the time and he was surprised at the memories that were so suddenly unlocked without effort. He realized then that he did not know when he would see Vulcan again and that the thought of never returning troubled him. He knew that reaction was not logical and decided that he would meditate on it later that evening to understand whatever had brought that feeling to him, and to control it. But in the meantime, he smelled the fragrance of kevas and trillium and in his mind he saw his mother's smile.

Beside him, Marita's baby snuffled sleepily. Spock wondered if the child, when grown, would have any recollection of his visit to the Vulcan Embassy on this day. Perhaps when the child smelled the incense again, Spock decided. The ancient structures of the Vulcan and human brain were almost identical, and scent was a key to the deepest of their memories. Spock found the linkage between scent and memory to be an interesting problem. Mentally, he began to manipulate three-dimensional images of airborne molecules to picture how they would fit within Vulcan and human olfactory nerve receptors. At the same time, he reviewed his arguments for the discussion that would follow in the next few minutes. Behind him, past the doors of the harshly lit, black granite-tiled chamber, he heard footsteps approaching, perfectly measured.

"He is coming," Spock said.

Sitting beside him on the carved rock bench, Marita looked up, puzzled. She had heard nothing but, refreshingly for a human, she did not question him. Spock had concluded it was because she was younger than most other humans he usually dealt with—only twenty-two. And despite her involvement in politics, she was still in college, still learning about her world and open to new experiences—including having a Vulcan staying with her and her partner in their small student flat.

Marita brushed a lock of long brown hair from her face and adjusted the position of her child as he snuggled into her arm. Alexander Llorente was five months old and thus far had observed proper decorum for his surroundings.

"I don't know if this is correct in the circumstances," the young woman said, "but good luck, Mr. Spock."

If she had been another person, and this had been another time, Spock might have tried to correct Marita. But he understood the cultural conventions which made her offer the superstitious wish and he accepted it as the gesture of support it was meant to be.

"Thank you. But in the affairs of Vulcan diplomacy, luck is seldom a factor."

"Then for the Talin," Marita said, not wishing to give offense.

"Yes," Spock agreed. "For the Talin."

The chamber doors swung open on perfectly balanced hinges constructed without metal. Spock rose and Marita followed. She smoothed her long skirt where her blanket-wrapped child had caused it to bunch up.

Spock held his hand up in the ritual salute. "Live long and prosper, Ambassador Sytok."

Vulcan's ambassador to Earth was magisterial in his poise and the elegant simplicity of the black robes he wore were matched in tone by Spock's own somber brown tunic and leggings. Though he did not react, Spock was disappointed that Sytok was not garbed in his ambassador's robe and jewels of office. This discussion would have had more of a chance to forward his cause if the ambassador had chosen to treat it as a formal meeting.

Sytok raised his own hand to return the salute. His face was perfectly expressionless and the short fringe of graying hair which lay across his forehead was crisply trimmed. "'Live long and prosper,' Spock? Have you so forgotten the ways of your home that you must speak in this alien tongue?"

Spock hadn't expected to be insulted and quickly reformulated a new and more forthright strategy for the meeting. "My associate is not experienced in the subtleties of the diplomatic dialects," Spock explained, nodding toward Marita. In truth, she barely could manage to say hello in the primary Vulcan language.

"I am pleased to meet you, your Excellency," Marita said.

Sytok glanced at her as if seeing her for the first time. He said nothing and Marita was uncomfortable with the intensity of his gaze.

The ambassador turned back to Spock without acknowledging the young woman. "What is the purpose of your request for this audience?"

"I had thought it would be apparent," Spock said innocuously, returning his own insult to Sytok.

"Your actions and motives have passed beyond the bounds of logic, Spock."

"Logic can be subtle. Patterns can be difficult to see if one's own vision is clouded," Spock countered. He watched as Sytok calculated the time remaining until his next appointment. How long was the ambassador willing to spend in the exchange of purposeless barbs? However long it was, Spock knew Sytok would not be able to wait him out. The ambassador was busy and Spock had nothing but time.

"Debates are best left to students," Sytok said. "I presume you wish aid in returning to Vulcan. Therefore, the embassy will provide—"

"No," Spock said. He hid his surprise completely. Could it be that Sytok had not deduced the reason for his visit, even with Marita at his side? But then, Sytok had not deigned to be introduced to the woman. Perhaps he hadn't recognized her.

"There was a fifty-five percent chance you would be seeking financial aid for a return ticket to Vulcan," Sytok said impassively. "There is a further thirty percent chance that you are, instead, seeking passage to a Vulcan colony world."

Spock could not resist. "What is the calculated chance that I do not wish to leave Earth at this time?"

Sytok hesitated, but only for an instant. "One point five percent."

Spock angled his head condescendingly. "I do not wish to leave Earth at this time."

Sytok was silent. Spock deduced that the ambassador or his staff had not bothered to devise a response for something that had seemed so improbable.

"I require the help of the Vulcan embassy," Spock began.

"You are still a citizen of the Federation. You require no consular help to stay on Earth."

Spock was astounded that Sytok still hadn't realized what it was he planned. The ambassador was one of Vulcan's finest.

"There is a meeting of the Federation General Council in five days," Spock continued.

Sytok remained impassive, even though Spock knew there was no doubt that he had at last surmised what Spock wanted.

"I wish to address it," Spock said.

"That is quite impossible."

"No, it is not."

Marita looked from the ambassador to Spock and back again. Neither Vulcan moved nor blinked as each stared into the other's eyes. Alexander opened his eyes as if he, too, were aware of the intense argument that raged in the subdued fashion of the Vulcans.

"This embassy will not help you," Sytok finally said.

"You do not have a choice," Spock stated. "You must."

"Spock, you have been trained as a scientist. I cannot expect you to know the intricate legal restrictions involving interstellar law and—"

"I know the law," Spock interrupted. "We had the same teacher." Spock's father, Sarek, was Vulcan's most senior ambassador and in an earlier time, before their bitter estrangement and eventual reconciliation, he had hoped his son would follow in his career path.

For the first time, Sytok allowed an expression to come to his face. He frowned, the corners of his mouth moving down a fraction of a centimeter, and spoke stiffly to Spock.

"I acknowledge that I came up through the corps with your father's guidance and instruction. I was his assistant at three Babel conferences. I both respect him and I honor him. It is because of that respect and that honor that I agreed to this unorthodox meeting."

"By law, I am a Vulcan," Spock pressed on. "By law, you are required to grant my request for an audience. Respect and honor have little to do with it."

"The waiting list for such audiences is more than seven Earth months long, Spock. It has been only three days since your request to see me."

"I thank you for your speed in complying."

Sytok frowned again. "But this is all the time I can allocate to you. I—"

"Ambassador Sytok, I wish to address the Federation General Council," Spock repeated formally. "And you have the authority and the obligation to allow me to do so."

Sytok said nothing. To Spock, it was acknowledgment that his argument was correct.

"I will also require the assistance of a junior member of your staff in order to file the proper briefs with the Council recorders," Spock added. "Of course, temporary civilian accreditation will also be necessary, for myself and my associate."

Sytok looked at the woman again, as if he had suddenly recollected the presence of the young human at Spock's side. Her baby blinked back at him.

"And which of these humans is your associate, Spock?" The

ambassador's sarcasm was uncharacteristic and Spock took it to be a reflection of the deep anger that Sytok must be controlling.

"Ambassador Sytok, may I introduce Marita Llorente."

Though Sytok had not recognized her face, he did know her name. Once again, his mouth drew down almost imperceptibly.

"Spock, I cannot allow this. The organization which this woman heads has a long history of attempting to disrupt Council meetings and the legitimate work of the Federation. She cannot be admitted to a Council meeting. Even I cannot authorize that."

Marita looked calmly at the ambassador, unruffled by his rejection of her.

"But you can authorize me," Spock said. "Whom I chose to have accompany me is my own right and responsibility."

Sytok adjusted the collar of his robe and stared past Spock and the woman. Alexander burbled into the silence and Marita gently bounced him in her arms.

"What is the nature of the address you wish to make to the Council?" Sytok asked with reluctance.

"It has to do with certain legal implications of the events at Talin IV which I believe have not been satisfactorily addressed by Starfleet or the Federation."

"The events at Talin were dealt with completely within Starfleet, Spock. You of all people should know that. The Federation was never involved."

Alexander gave a small shriek, which both Vulcans ignored. Marita began rocking from foot to foot, whispering softly to the child.

"Which is precisely why I desire to address the Council, Ambassador. I wish to point out to them that there are other legal concerns at stake than simply Starfleet's jurisdictional liability for its personnel failing to uphold the Prime Directive."

Sytok shook his head decisively. "There are no other legal concerns, Spock."

"Ambassador, if you are not aware of them, then it is all the more compelling that the members of the Council who do not share your expertise in the law also are informed of those concerns."

Sytok seemed to grow impatient as Marita paced back and forth across the hard granite slabs that lined the floor of the chamber, talking to her baby. "Are you going to tell me what those mysterious, other legal concerns are?" he asked.

Spock slipped his hand into his tunic and withdrew a folded-over sheaf of printed notes. "I prefer to keep the details confidential. If I revealed the core of my argument now, then I fear I might risk insulting the Council by taking up their time in reciting information which they could already have received second hand."

"It might be faster," Sytok suggested.

"But not as accurate," Spock said. "However, these notes should enable the staff member you assign to help me in preparing the proper preliminary documents."

Sytok accepted the papers Spock held out but didn't look at them. "Why should I upset the business of this embassy by rushing through your request to speak in five days, rather than allowing it to go through normal channels?"

"If you process my request through normal channels, then I will not be able to address the Council for more than a standard year. I am aware of the usual waiting periods."

"Have you also forgotten patience, Spock? It is one of the most important lessons your father taught me."

"For myself, and my career, I have no need to rush. 'For life is long and there is much to be learned in unhurried contemplation,'" Spock quoted. "However, my concern for speed is on behalf of others."

Sytok glanced at the woman. She held her baby up and blew kisses at the child. Sytok closed his eyes and sighed. "Humans are always so agitated and in too much of a hurry."

"Indeed, the life of a human is short compared to ours," Spock observed. "But the others I refer to are those survivors who still live on Talin IV."

Sytok allowed a private, ritual expression of shared remorse to appear on his face, though none but a Vulcan could recognize the difference between it and a face of repose. "Nothing can be done for them, Spock."

"On the contrary, I believe something can be done. Please, Ambassador, read my notes."

Sytok unfolded the sheaf of papers and rifled through them in seconds. "There is nothing in here that the human woman's organization has not said before. It is merely another attempt to introduce a radical and ill-thought plan to circumvent the Prime Directive. They would force the Federation to offer aid to every known world, contacted or not, which is not as developed as the existing member worlds. Such a policy would clearly lead to tragedy and chaos."

Marita came back to the two Vulcans as Sytok spoke. Her eyes flashed with anger. "You're wrong, Ambassador. The Federation has more than enough resources to share with less developed worlds. The Prime Directive is a morally indefensible attempt to keep the wealth of a thousand worlds safely within the hands of a few powerful planetary governments."

Sytok turned frostily to Spock. "I do not have time to debate this with a child," the ambassador said. "Spock, since it appears you have more time than I, please explain to . . . your associate that the Prime Directive is the foundation upon which the Federation is built."

"Marita Llorente is correct," Spock said.

Ambassador Sytok blinked once in the Vulcan equivalent of a gasp of shock. "What?"

"A case can be made to support the proposition that the Prime Directive is morally indefensible and must be stricken from the laws of the Federation," Spock said.

Sytok blinked twice. "Spock . . . that statement goes against every principle of peace and equality the Federation is sworn to uphold . . . that statement is a complete abandonment of the ideals in which Vulcan joined with other worlds to form the Federation. It denies history. It—it is not logical, Spock."

"Nevertheless, I believe it to have merit."

Sytok looked long and hard into Spock's eyes and Spock

found himself readying his mental defenses against a sudden attempt at melding. The ambassador seemed that unsettled by Spock's position.

"Do you hate Starfleet that much, Spock? Do you have such bitterness for what they've done to you that you would strike out against the Federation so senselessly?"

"I do not hate the Federation, nor do I hate Starfleet. I simply wish to improve them."

Sytok crushed the papers in his hands. "I will not allow you to dishonor the Council with such general and ill-conceived charges."

"They are not general. I intend to bring specific civil charges against Starfleet and those of its personnel who destroyed Talin by attempting to uphold the Prime Directive."

Sytok's lips actually trembled. "Is this your idea of a human joke? You intend to bring charges *against yourself?*"

Spock nodded. "Logically, I have no other choice."

"Logic?" Sytok almost sputtered. "You dare to speak of logic in connection with this absurdity? If you do this, Spock, you will be announcing to all the worlds that you have forsaken your Vulcan heritage. Don't you remember the controversy that arose at home when you decided to join Starfleet? Don't you remember how the elders said you would become less than Vulcan by being in such close proximity to humans. If you go through with this senselessness, you will prove them right." Sytok held the papers out to Spock, asking him to take them back. "As a friend of your father's, I request you reconsider. Think what will be said of you."

Spock kept his true thoughts and feelings well shielded. "I did not care what others thought when I applied to Starfleet. I do not care now." He placed his hands behind his back, refusing the papers. "Ambassador Sytok, will you or will you not prepare my credentials to address the Council as a citizen of Vulcan and the Federation, as is my right?"

Spock saw Marita smile triumphantly at Sytok. She knew so little. But her unbridled display of emotionalism helped Sytok compose himself.

"Yes, Spock," the ambassador said blandly, no trace of the hidden passion which had threatened to surface moments ago. "I shall authorize your credentials, as a citizen, to address the Council in five days' time. I must warn you though, if I place Marita Llorente's name on the forms as your associate, the Council will be likely to postpone its meeting in order to prevent her from disrupting it."

Perfect, Spock thought. The plan had worked. Sytok had become distracted by his emotions and ignored the logic of what Spock was maneuvering him to do.

"Ambassador," Spock said, "may I suggest then that you have your staff simply prepare the forms without naming Ms. Llorente directly. I believe you are able to issue a blanket credential for myself and 'others to be named later.'"

"Yes," Sytok said. "I can do that because no Vulcan has ever misused the system in the way in which you intend."

"Please believe me, Ambassador, I have no wish to misuse the system."

Sytok held the papers up in his fist. "And yet you give me this."

Spock stepped back and held up his hand to offer the salute of leaving. "Live long and prosper, Ambassador Sytok. I shall return in four days to receive my credentials."

Sytok did not offer a salute in return. "I warn you, Spock, after what happened at Talin IV, if you disrupt a Council meeting they will deport you as an undesirable."

Spock shrugged. "I will have had my say in the proper forum." He turned to go.

"And Vulcan will not take you back," Sytok said.

Spock shrugged again as if he didn't care.

And Sytok saw something in that. Spock knew it instantly. The ambassador had detected a telltale hint of deception.

Sytok glanced thoughtfully at the papers again. "This is not like you, Spock. This is not like Sarek's son at all." He looked up. "You have planned something else."

Spock knew he had to act quickly. The ambassador must be

diverted again. He held out his hand to Marita, index and middle finger extended, the rest folded back.

"Marita," Spock said, "attend me."

The woman smiled seductively and matched Spock's gesture, touching her two fingers to his in the intimacy of the Vulcan ritual embrace.

Spock heard the paper rustle in Sytok's fist as he crushed it even more. The ambassador was speechless in his outrage. Spock's tactic had worked.

Still joined with Marita, Spock walked toward the chamber's exit. The carved granite doors swung open silently.

"Spock!" Sytok's voice echoed in the hall.

Spock stopped to look back at the ambassador.

Sytok shook his head. "What would your father say?"

Spock raised an eyebrow. "I believe he would wish me good luck."

TWO

☆

Lieutenant Kyle stuck his head out from beneath the control console in transporter room four. His blond hair and pale skin were smudged with insulation dust and blue coolant.

"I think that's got it, Mr. Scott."

Scott stood to the side of the console, using a transtator tester on the wiring circuits exposed beneath the flipped-up surface panel. He hadn't expected to hear from Kyle for at least another hour. "That's fast work, lad." He was afraid he knew why.

Kyle wiped at his face, then pulled himself out from the access opening under the console. "It was just the main node, Mr. Scott. The secondary circuits weren't touched."

Scott swung the panel down until it clicked into place. "Just like the phaser banks," he said, and he didn't like it.

"And the torpedo couplings," Kyle added. "And the main sensor sequencers."

Scott stared at the coils of power-harness cables that hung down from the openings in the room's ceiling. The starbase mechanics had done long baseline scans of the *Enterprise* and determined that every centimeter of transtator circuitry in her had been hopelessly burned out. But by actually poking and prodding their way through her, Scott and Kyle had discovered that less than twenty percent of her circuitry had actually been destroyed. Normally, that would be good news because, if the repair order were ever given, the wiring drones would only require a fifth the time to install replacement circuits throughout the *Enterprise*. But what worried Scott was that virtually all of that twenty percent of destroyed circuitry had been master control nodes. He knew that powerful subspace pulses could inflict erratic damage on a ship, but he had never heard of the damage being confined just to the most important circuits.

"I tell ye, lad," Scott said, "I don't like it. I don't like it one bit."

Kyle brushed the dust from his blue technician's jumpsuit. He looked as if he shared Scott's concern. They had had this conversation many times in the two weeks since the shipwright drones had been installed onboard to salvage damaged equipment. The drones' controllers had been surprised to find how little equipment there had actually been to salvage. But while the damage had been far less than expected, it was specific enough to render the ship useless.

"I still don't know how anything could focus a subspace pulse so precisely that it would only affect the main nodes," Kyle said. "I think it really does have to be a coincidence, sir. Or something about the way the pulse traveled through the circuitry. Maybe destructive interference built up at the main nodes because that's where the pulse signals met each other . . . maybe." His voice trailed off into uncertainty.

Scott shook his head. "Mr. Kyle, remember who you're talking to. And I'll not be swallowing any of that first-year engineering student yammer. Whatever kind of pulse hit this ship was *aimed* at us. And whoever aimed it knew exactly what it was they were doing."

Kyle looked pained. "Are you going to try to explain that to Lieutenant Styles? Again?"

"I know what I'd like to explain to that sli—" A discordant paging whistle shrieked from the companel and Scott cringed. "What the devil have they done to the power settings on that blasted—"

"Bridge Communications Center to Chief Engineer Montgomery Scott." It was Styles. It could only be Styles.

Scott leaned against the transporter console and rolled his eyes at Kyle. "Aye, Lieutenant Styles, Scott here."

"Vice Admiral Hammersmith's shuttle is arriving, Mr. Scott. Is that transporter working yet?"

"All the circuitry is back in place, Lieutenant, but we haven't had a chance to test it yet."

"Well hop to it, man. I told the vice admiral that I would have him *beamed* aboard. You've got ten minutes. Bridge Communications Center out."

The companel crackled with static, then went dead.

Kyle went over to the storage locker and broke out a box filled with various transporter test modules. They were essentially empty boxes made from metal only a few molecules thick. Any alignment or focus problems in a transporter would cause the intricately etched, reflective surfaces of the boxes to change to a dull and mottled appearance when they reformed. They were usually the first objects to be sent through any transporter that had been subjected to repairs.

Kyle examined the test modules carefully. "You know, Mr. Scott, these look to have been banged up pretty badly. We've got some dents and bends here that could affect the diffraction patterns. Make them look perfect when they're not. I don't think they'll do."

Scott thought for a moment. There was no possible way he would authorize human transmission in a transporter that hadn't been properly tested. Then he held up his hand. "Just a minute, Mr. Kyle. I think I've got it." Scott left the room through the doors he had jammed open with an old circuitplaser. The few sliding pocket doors which had been brought back online throughout the ship were behaving about as well as the companels. Everyone on board could be seen hesitating by closed doors and rushing through open ones to avoid being sandwiched by them. Scott had taken the easy way out by simply disabling the doors to any room he happened to be working in. He found it odd that none of the starbase mechanics had figured out the same thing, and so far he had noticed three of them with eyes blackened from walking into doors. Seeing them like that was one of the few things that made getting up in the morning easier these days. Especially because of what Hammersmith had done to him.

When Scott came back to the transporter room, he carried a small mechanical scavenger drone under one arm. The device's treads whirred uselessly and its manipulator stalks waved wildly. It and two hundred and twenty-two other shipwright drones on board were controlled by a portable repair computer installed in engineering. They had spent the past two weeks crawling through the ship, beeping and bumping and getting on Scott's nerves. He was going to enjoy this.

Scott carried the drone over to the transporter platform and plopped the machine down on the center pad. It rocked back and forth for a moment, then spread its manipulators all around itself, tracing the circumference of the transmission crystal.

Scott stood back. "All right, Mr. Kyle, before its control computer figures out where it is, would ye energize the wee thing."

The small machine squealed once, then faded away in a sparkling mist.

"Holding the pattern," Kyle said as he studied the board. "Carrier storage is one hundred percent. Power consumption following normal curves." He looked up at Scott and smiled. "Seems to be perfect, Mr. Scott."

"If ye say so yourself." Scott watched the platform. "All right then, bring the little beastie back."

The transporter chime grew louder, but then was overpowered by the metallic tinkle of small machine parts raining down on the pad.

"Aww," Scott said happily.

"Um, there appears to be a realignment problem," Kyle offered.

"You think so?" Scott walked over to the companel. "Myself, I don't think it's ready for a vice admiral, but I think it should work just fine for a certain lieutenant." He toggled the paging switch. "Chief Engineer Montgomery Scott to Bridge Communications Center. I'm afraid the transporter is going to be needing a wee bit more work. You better tell the vice admiral that he should park his shuttle in the hangar bay." Scott winked at Kyle.

When Styles responded, his voice was tight with officious rage, just as Scott had expected. "Chief Engineer Scott! I told the vice admiral that we would beam him aboard and by thunder we *will* beam him aboard."

"Lieutenant Styles, sir, the only way anyone's going to be coming out of this transporter is in buckets, if you know what I mean, sir." Scott grinned at Kyle as the transporter technician put a hand to his mouth to stifle a laugh.

The companel transmission picked up a rhythmic tapping interference signal that puzzled Scott until he realized that it was that damned swagger stick hitting the side of the center chair.

"Mr. Scott," Styles said like a petulant child. "I am holding you personally responsible and I shall tell the vice admiral exactly why he was forced to experience the inconvenience of a hangar landing." Tap tap tap tap. "Bridge Communications Center out."

"Good," Scott said, "then maybe Hammersmith will come to his senses and let me go."

Kyle popped open the control console again. "Are you certain that's what you still want to do, Mr. Scott?"

Scott clenched his teeth and the muscles in his jaw tensed and relaxed, tensed and relaxed. "If Hammersmith approves detaching what's left of the port nacelle, and the ship survives the separation, she'll be someone else's worry."

Kyle concentrated on the machinery in the console. Without looking up, he said, "But the *Enterprise* needs you, sir."

"I know that, Mr. Kyle. But the *Enterprise* is more than a

ship, and right now I could do a lot more for her by being away from her."

Kyle didn't move. "Do you think the captain's all right?"

"Of course he is, lad," Scott said, wondering if he could believe it as much as he wanted Kyle to. "But if I could get off this ship, I could find out for sure."

Kyle nodded. The blue glow of his circuitplaser flared from the console as he readjusted the reassembly timing delays. This was another conversation they had had many times.

Scott decided he had better report to the hangar deck to make sure the pressure doors were working properly. He still couldn't forgive Carole Mallett and Mario Cardinali for what they had done to the doors after the *Enterprise* had been set adrift. But before Scott could leave, in walked a young female ensign in services red and a Starbase 29 insignia, waving a simple, unicorder tracker in front of her.

"Pardon me, sir," the woman said seriously. "But have you seen a scavenger drone in this area? We appear to have lost one nearby."

"Aye, certainly," Scott said cheerfully. "We did see one of the little fellas around here. Seemed to have a small malfunction or somesuch."

The woman nodded with a knowing frown. "Ah, a small malfunction. That does happen from time to time." She kept her gaze on Scott, though the engineer said nothing. "And excuse me one more time if I may, sir. But can you tell me where the . . . little fella is?"

"Why, he's right over there, lass." Scott pointed toward the transporter pad. "And I hope ye brought a broom." Scott watched the ensign stare in disbelief at the tiny mound of drone components, no doubt wondering how the chief engineer would define a *major* malfunction. Then Scott left for the hangar and his next attempt to convince Vice Admiral Hammersmith that there was no place in Starfleet for such a willfully disobedient chief engineer as Montgomery Scott.

* * *

The huge curved doors of the ship's hangar bay only opened halfway now. Their elegantly engineered folding segments had been deformed by the shuttle that had smashed through them, then further degraded by the thick sealant baffles that the starbase mechanics had roughly attached to repair the damage until the doors could be replaced.

Scott still couldn't understand what had driven the two FCO managers to do what they had done. Approximately thirty minutes after the *Enterprise* had been blasted out of the timeslowing grip of Talin IV's gravity-well wormhole, she was powerless and adrift. But even when Scott had taken command of the ship, he had not been concerned about the crew's eventual rescue. After all, the hull was secure. Local battery networks could easily keep the air circulating and the gravity functioning for weeks. And once the FCO outpost picked up the *Enterprise*'s emergency beacon, the rescue shuttles from Starbase 29 were only four days away at maximum warp. So why had Mallett and Cardinali risked their careers in Starfleet —and the safe evacuation of the *Enterprise*'s crew—by virtually destroying the hangar deck?

Scott remembered passing Mallett and Cardinali in the ladderways as he and the medical technicians climbed their way to the bridge. The FCO pilot and communications manager had told Scott that everyone on the bridge was alive with no serious injuries, and then had said that they had to salvage their equipment. In the confusion of dealing with the crippled vessel, Scott had thought nothing of their apparent panic. He certainly had not suspected that they were both determined to abandon ship. But that was exactly what the two managers had done.

The three Wraith shuttles which had been stowed on the hangar deck were specifically designed to provide as few clues as possible about advanced technology should any of them crash, so except for their heavily armored antigrav generators and a subminiature subspace radio, there wasn't a transtator in them. Whatever had rendered the *Enterprise* a drifting hulk had left the Wraiths' major components untouched.

As far as Scott had been able to determine, Cardinali and Mallett had donned environmental suits, then rigged one Wraith to fly on autopilot straight through the inoperative hangar bay doors. Without deflector shields in place, the middle segments of the doors had shattered, explosively decompressing the bay. Cardinali and Mallett had then taken a second Wraith through the gaping hole and flown back to the FCO outpost on Talin's moon. A few weeks later, after the outpost had been sealed and all personnel transferred back to Earth, Scott had heard that the two FCO managers had claimed they had been trying to get word back to the outpost to send for rescue ships as quickly as possible. That explanation just didn't seem reasonable to Scott.

In the end, after his anger had cooled, he decided that they had just been frightened. But because of the damage they had caused to the hangar bay, shuttle evacuation had been impossible and it had taken more than a day for the rescue ships to beam the *Enterprise*'s crew to safety. Fear was one thing, but endangering lives was another. Scott hoped to one day tell them just what he thought of them and their cowardice. But in the meantime, he prepared himself to tell Vice Admiral Hammersmith exactly what he thought of a certain Starfleet vice admiral who wouldn't accept resignations.

Scott watched from the hangar bay's upper observation gallery as the vice admiral's shuttle eased slowly through the partially opened doors and settled gently on a section of the deck where most of the debris had been cleared away. As the doors jerkily slid shut again, Lieutenant Styles joined him.

"What are you doing here when you should be repairing the transporter?" Styles snapped.

Scott no longer even made a pretense of being civil to Styles. He obeyed the man's orders because the vice admiral had given Styles temporary command of the ship, he did his job as best as he was able; but he would be damned if he would pretend to respect the fool.

"I'm just making sure that the vice admiral isn't sucked

screaming out into space because the trained chimps ye have working the pressurization controls have confused the colors on the all-clear board."

Styles slapped his swagger stick against his open palm a few times. "Mr. Scott, I am at a loss to understand why you continue to address me in this insubordinate manner. What have I ever done to you to deserve such insolence?"

It's not what you've done to me, ye bandy-legged, spineless excuse for a starship captain, it's what you've done to my ship. "I'm afraid I don't know what it is you're referring to, Lieutenant. Perhaps we veterans of a long space voyage are just a wee bit crustier than you've come to expect after your three short months on the *Monitor.*"

"I'll have you know I've spent many years in space, Mr. Scott, and I have yet to hear highly trained Starfleet engineers refer to other highly trained Starfleet engineers as 'trained chimps.'"

"Well, it just goes to show ye, sir . . . even the likes of you can learn something new every day."

Styles slapped his stick into his hand and held it there. "Mr. Scott, I have tried to be patient with you. I understand what you must have gone through, serving on this ship for so many years, only to watch her nearly destroyed by some madman's delusions of grandeur. But I—"

"Don't you ever—I mean ever—talk about my captain like that again." It was all Scott could do not to throttle Styles. "Lieutenant Styles, sir, I am a Starfleet officer and you are my commander, and I am sworn to obey you to the best of my ability. But a man has his limits, sir, and I canna stand by any longer and listen to you insult a man who is my friend. As one officer to another, sir, I ask that ye please keep your opinions to yourself so I can continue to do my job."

As soon as Scott had said the words he knew they had been a mistake. Styles wasn't a complete buffoon. Incompetents would never survive to his rank in Starfleet. He had just been remarkably insensitive. But now Scott had let him know exactly what it was that upset him so—he had revealed his weakness and Styles jumped on it instantly.

"Mr. Scott, while your misplaced admiration for a man who used to be your captain might be considered honorable by some, I want you to understand once and for all that James Kirk is a traitor to Starfleet and the Federation. And we will not honor traitors aboard *my* ship."

Scott gave up. There was no sense in continuing the fight against someone so closeminded. *Let it be his ship,* he thought. *And welcome to her. One more drone to crawl around beeping and bumping with the others.*

"I apologize for speaking out of turn, sir," Scott muttered through gritted teeth. But even he knew the words meant nothing.

"That's better, Mr. Scott." Styles flipped his stick jauntily under his arm. "Now don't you think you should be getting back to that transporter?"

"With all respect, sir, I do have business with the vice admiral."

Styles rubbed the side of his face with the large end of the stick. The ready lights glowed green and red against his skin. "What business is that, Mr. Scott?"

"He has repeatedly turned down my resignation and I would like to discuss his reasons with him."

"Resignation?" Styles said. "Why would you want to resign? You had nothing to do with what happened on Talin."

I am a Starfleet officer, Scott told himself. *I am a Starfleet officer.* "And neither did James Kirk, sir. Nor Mr. Spock, nor Uhura, nor Chekov, nor Sulu, nor Dr. McCoy."

"If you leave Starfleet, mister," Styles said, punctuating every word by tapping Scott's chest with his stick, "you'll be saying that you're no different from any of the *Enterprise* Five."

Scott felt a wave of sudden inspiration hit him. "Aye, sir," he said with a terrible smile, "that's exactly what I'm saying." And then he reached out and grabbed Style's swagger stick and snapped it over his knee.

Styles's eyes bulged and his mouth opened and closed in shocked silence as he stared at the two pieces of his treasured memento on the deck.

But Scott felt free for the first time in months. He wondered if this was how McCoy had felt when he had swung on Hammersmith—filled with the certain knowledge that an irrevocable decision had been made. "And now if you'll excuse me, sir, I have business with the vice admiral who's been standing around on the deck for the past five minutes wondering where his welcoming committee is."

Scott smiled fiercely again as he saw the ready lights wink out on the stick, then left. He was sure he heard Styles sob behind him.

Vice Admiral Hammersmith was a powerfully built human with skin darker than Uhura's. His gold shirt was pulled tightly over bunched muscles and Scott was impressed that McCoy had actually gone so far as to hit him. But perhaps that was why the doctor had chosen Hammersmith and not some other officer. It wasn't as if McCoy could ever have hoped to actually hurt the man.

The vice admiral smiled as Scott approached him on the hangar deck. "Ah, Lieutenant Commander Montgomery Scott, I presume." His voice was deep and he held out a massive hand.

"Vice Admiral Hammersmith," Scott said, pumping hands vigorously with him. "Welcome aboard the *Enterprise.*"

Hammersmith stepped away from his shuttle as three of his staff began offloading equipment cases and supplies. He motioned for the chief engineer to follow him and glanced around the cavernous hangar bay, assessing the damage still unrepaired. "Mostly superficial," he said. "Pocket ruptures from the explosive decompression, but serviceable."

Scott was impressed. "Aye, that's true."

"See?" Hammersmith said. "I read everything you send me. Not just your resignation requests." He looked around again. "Where is Lieutenant Styles?"

"I have just broken a piece of the lieutenant's personal property," Scott said matter-of-factly. "And I believe he is too upset to make an appearance at this time."

Hammersmith shook his head. "What is it about you *Enterprise* people?" He held up his hand. "No, don't answer. Believe it or not, engineer, I do understand why you want to submit your resignation. And I am prepared to accept it."

Scott had expected anything but that. "Why, thank you, sir."

"But not quite yet."

Naturally, Scott thought in frustration. "Then could you tell me when, sir?"

"Well, that's up to you, engineer. How soon can you get this ship operational again?"

If Hammersmith were about to commission another feasibility study, Scott thought he would scream. He was supposed to work with machines, not paper. "Have you made your decision about her repair, then, sir?"

Scott was surprised again when Hammersmith nodded. "That's why I'm here. We're going to tow her out of system tomorrow and detach the port nacelle."

"And what if the warp reaction is still linked to the planet's gravity well?" Scott asked. "What if she slingshots?"

Hammersmith's eyes sparkled. "The experts who have been studying what they call the dimensional evaporation of the nacelle tell me that there is an eighty-five-percent chance that that is exactly what will happen. The instant the port nacelle is detached, they say that it will be drawn completely into the Cochrane subset at about warp eight point seven. At the same time, the remainder of the ship will also be accelerated to the same velocity in the opposite vector, but in normal, three-dimensional space where such velocities are against all the laws of nature." Hammersmith chuckled. "The experts tell me that the *Enterprise* will spread herself out over a spectacular starbow effect about a light minute long, then explosively transform herself into . . . well, neutrinos or tachyons, depending on which day of the week it is and which expert's name comes first."

Scott was tired of this nonsense. "And do you believe them?"

"I believe in specialists doing the work they specialize in, engineer. And I also believe in being prepared."

"Sir?"

"At this moment, the *Exeter* is en route from Earth at warp six. She is rigged with a cargo sling and carries the two Constitution-rated warp nacelles that were intended for the *Intrepid II.*"

Despite himself, Scott felt a rush of excitement. Those nacelles could make this ship whole again. "That's quite a trip for the sake of a ship that might be a handful of neutrinos by the time the *Exeter* gets here."

"In addition to the experts' reports, engineer, I've also read yours. I forget the technical details, but there was something about it being a cold day in Hades the day there would ever be a *partial* warp transition."

"Aye, that it would, sir."

Hammersmith's expression became intent. "I will confess that committing the *Exeter* to this run—and completely disrupting the construction schedule for the *Intrepid II*—is a gamble. Because I really don't know what's going to happen tomorrow when we blow that nacelle."

"That's all right, sir, I do. And it's not a gamble."

"That's one of the things I've been looking forward to discussing with you. Why do you have the presumption to think *you* know something that twenty of Starfleet's best scientists refuse to consider?"

Scott shrugged. "Because they're scientists, sir, and I'm an engineer. I've worked with this ship every day for almost the past five years, sir. I can tell what's going on inside her generators just by listening to them. And I was onboard the *Enterprise* when she was attacked."

"Now *that* I do know something about, engineer. Nuclear detonations—even in an atmosphere—don't do this to a ship." Hammersmith waved his hand at the debris and exposed coils of power harness poking through ruptured wall plates.

"The *Enterprise* was attacked by more than just nuclear warheads, sir." *Why not tell him the rest?* Scott asked himself. It was probably the first and last time he'd be able to discuss his theory with an intelligent superior officer who had no vested interest in personally commanding the *Enterprise*.

Hammersmith chewed on his lower lip. "More than nuclear

weapons? You haven't put that in any of your reports, have you?"

"No, sir."

"Good, because I don't recall having heard that before. What else was the *Enterprise* attacked by?"

Scott took a breath. "An extremely powerful—and precisely focused—series of subspace energy pulses that selectively burned out every major control node in the entire ship."

Hammersmith closed his eyes and rubbed at the bridge of his nose. "As I understand it, such an attack would be completely beyond the technological capabilities of the Talin. Is that correct?"

"Aye, sir, it is."

"And furthermore, such an attack would be completely beyond *our* technological capabilities. Is that also correct?"

"Aye, sir. I believe that is true."

Hammersmith walked back to his shuttle. His three staff members had finished stacking the cases they had offloaded. Now they were talking to a group of starbase mechanics who were supposed to be working on repairs to the shuttle elevator and turntable so that the undamaged shuttles in the maintenance shops below the hangar deck could be returned to active duty. But as was typical, Scott saw, the temporary workers had none of the urgency of the *Enterprise*'s real crew.

Hammersmith waved to his staff to let them know that he didn't require them at the moment, then opened a small case on the top of the stack to bring out a portable terminal. "Why wasn't this subspace 'attack' mentioned at the board of inquiry hearings?" the vice admiral asked.

"Because no one knew back then," Scott explained. "With the master nodes fused, the general scans of the ship gave the same results as if every circuit had gone. It was only when the shipwright drones came aboard and started trying to remove damaged equipment that we realized that the damage wasn't as extensive as we thought—just precisely selective."

"We?" Hammersmith asked. "Does Styles know about this?"

245

"No, sir. He doesn't seem to care too much about what has happened in the past. He's only interested in taking command of this ship sometime in the future."

"Nothing wrong with ambition, Mr. Scott. Now who's this 'we'?"

"Lieutenant Kyle, sir. Chief transporter technician. One of the original crew."

Hammersmith punched in something on his terminal keypad. "And he confirms your suspicions about an attack by selective subspace pulse?"

Scott wondered what the best way to describe the situation was. "To tell the truth, sir. He has seen the damage the ship has suffered, and knows it's peculiar, but he thinks it might possibly be the result of coincidence or a previously unknown destructive interference effect."

Hammersmith read whatever was displayed on his screen. He turned to Scott. "And what do *you* think it might possibly be, engineer?"

"Deliberate, sir. The result of an unknown weapon."

Hammersmith fixed Scott with an intense gaze. "If you're right in your theory about the ship's damage, you know what that might mean, don't you?"

Scott felt the thrill of sudden hope run through him. Could it be possible? Was Hammersmith going to be someone who would finally pay attention to all that had happened at Talin? "Aye, sir, I know exactly what that might mean."

"Good," Hammersmith said. "Good. Then given your past actions and your outspoken desire to defend Kirk at any cost, you'll understand why I must remain skeptical of any new facts you present which might serve to exonerate him."

No, Scott cried to himself. *Why did it always have t' be this way? Why couldn't there be just one person in Starfleet who was willing to give the captain the benefit of the doubt for just one second?*

Hammersmith tapped at the display screen on his terminal. "And because this Lieutenant Kyle has been with the *Enterprise* since the beginning of her five-year mission, I'm afraid that I'll also have to be skeptical of any claims he might make. However, if you could get someone like Styles to back you on this . . . well, it might even be possible to reconvene the board of inquiry."

Scott felt overcome with despair. *Someone like Styles*, he thought. Typical. The lieutenant was probably getting ready to phaser him in his sleep at this point.

"Is there nothing else that might do it, sir?" Scott asked, wondering why the fates were punishing him so.

"I'd say that's up to you, engineer."

"How so, sir?"

Hammersmith switched off his terminal. "If you can get this ship through the nacelle separation tomorrow, you'll have one week before the *Exeter* arrives. The deal I'll make with you is that if you give me your word that you will stick it out through the rest of the *Enterprise*'s repairs, with your full cooperation, I'll give you that week to take this ship apart and prove your theory."

Scott shook his head. "I'm afraid Lieutenant Styles would never allow it, sir. He's got too much for me to do as it is."

"Then for that week, Styles will be out of the picture. You'll report directly to me. And I will give you full run over the ship." Hammersmith held out his hand. "Is it a deal?"

Scott held back. "It's a big ship, sir."

"I'll request Kyle as well." He kept his hand extended.

"A week won't be enough time. Not for only two of us."

Hammersmith stared up at the hangar bay roof in thought, then said, "You drive a hard bargain, engineer, but I'm going to make my final offer. I can't do anything about the one-week time limit, but whoever else you want here to help—provided we can get them here on time—I'll get them for you."

"Whoever else I want?" Scott asked.

"Starfleet personnel only," Hammersmith clarified.

Scott reached out and shook the vice admiral's hand. "Vice Admiral, sir, ye've got yourself a deal."

"Then if the *Enterprise* is still in one piece tomorrow, you've got yourself a week."

THREE

─────────── ☆ ───────────

Sulu stepped from the airlock and the sudden plunge into microgee was like drifting off into a warm bath, every muscle instantly relaxing. Without thinking, he moaned with relief.

"Are you all right?" Chekov asked over the helmet commlink.

Sulu touched a control on the thruster extension and made a half turn. Chekov was still in the *Queen Mary*'s open airlock, one gloved hand on either side, ready to push himself out to his friend's rescue.

"Come on in," Sulu said, "the water's fine." He waved his thickly padded arm slowly. Krulmadden might have a state-of-the-art impulse drive, but his ship's environmental suits were overstuffed antiques.

Chekov leaned out from the airlock, then floated free of it, arms extended. Sulu heard him have the same reaction to leaving the *Queen Mary*'s oppressive two-gee gravity.

"That is much better," Chekov sighed as he swung down the control arm by his side and used the controls on it to maneuver closer to Sulu, about ten meters out from the ship.

Then Krulmadden's voice boomed over the helmet speakers. "You mammals sound like you enjoy vacuum more than enjoy slavegirls. What has *f'deraxtl* training done to you?"

"Like we keep telling you, Shipmaster," Sulu said, "your normal gravity is too strong for us."

The shipmaster snorted. "You mean you are too weak. Need more *Ur'eon* exercise you do."

In the dull light of the red giant star they orbited, Sulu saw Chekov's pained expression through the unfiltered faceplate of his helmet.

"What we need is Earth-normal gravity in our quarters," Chekov said.

"Too much power. Too expensive," Krulmadden snapped at them. "Always wanting to spend my credits. You make credits, you can spend them. Leave mine alone. Now go do your work or I leave you here."

Sulu heard the click of the commlink being broken. "Let's go," he said to Chekov.

Chekov made a thumbs-up sign, and Sulu placed his own hand on his thruster control. With three quick taps, he had rotated again, then propelled himself toward the *Queen Mary's* relative upper surface where the impulse engine was housed.

The hullmetal of the Orion pirate's ship glowed deep pink in the light of the red giant, two AUs distance. Though Krulmadden had refused to identify the star, Sulu had recognized its coordinates. It was TNC-5527 in the Minotaur Cluster, the last remnant of an ancient system which had long since lost all of its planets. The very fact that it had nothing of value to offer was why, Sulu presumed, Krulmadden felt safe in hiding out around it. Because that was exactly what he was doing now, hiding out, and with good reason.

Sulu triggered the visual sensor mounted to his helmet to begin recording images of the damage to the *Queen Mary's* impulse engine housing. Black streaks of rippled metal showed where the border patrol's phasers had hit. Whoever the frigate's weaponry officer had been, he or she had been good. That was one smuggling route that Krulmadden would not be able to use again, and the sale of his living cargo had been indefinitely postponed.

Sulu heard Chekov's whistle, rough and full of static over the old commlink system. "Wery precise control," he said. "Another half-second of contact and we would have been blown apart."

Sulu felt a sudden chill in his suit. He had known their run-in with the border patrol had been close. He just hadn't known it had been *that* close.

"Shipmaster Krulmadden," he said, then waited for the suit's computer to reopen the commlink with the *Queen Mary*'s bridge.

"Yes, little mammal?"

"There's a five-meter secondary gash on the upper impulse housing, port forward quadrant. I know you don't want to tell us too many details about your engine configuration, but we could do a better repair job if you told us what systems are beneath the damaged area."

Sulu floated peacefully by the ship, unconcerned that Krulmadden was taking so much time to decide how much he could tell his human crewmen. For all of the shipmaster's boisterous good humor when it came to maintaining the spirits of his crew, Sulu had realized early on in his three weeks on the ship that Krulmadden didn't even trust Artinton and Lasslanlin—and they were his cousins who had worked for him for more than twenty years.

"Use sensor probe, setting three twenty," Krulmadden said finally, sounding as if he were giving the combination to the safe in his stateroom.

Sulu rotated to Chekov and watched as he slowly pulled a sensor wand from the equipment bag strapped to his leg. It took Chekov a full five minutes to align the wand and change the setting on its control handle. The suits Krulmadden had given them had to be at least a hundred years old and more unwieldy than even the ones the Academy made cadets train in.

When Chekov at last seemed to have the sensor probe properly aligned, he aimed it toward the battle damage on the engine housing. Then Sulu heard him cry out in shock.

"What is it, Chekov?" Sulu thrust himself closer.

"Ionizing radiation! All around us!" Chekov turned his head

awkwardly in his helmet to catch a glimpse of Sulu. "Back away!"

Chekov suddenly spun off from the ship, cartwheeling slowly as he tried to stabilize his emergency withdrawal. Sulu took a moment longer to plan his own trajectory, then moved off after his friend. He caught up with him two hundred meters off the *Queen Mary,* where Chekov finally halted his wobbling rotations.

"We could have gone over to the other side of the ship, Chekov."

"I am not used to these thruster controls."

Suddenly, Krulmadden's voice blared at them again. "What do you do? Where do you go? What damage have you done to my jewel?"

Sulu rotated to face the ship, now small enough that he could blot it out with his hand. He swallowed as he realized how easy it would be for Krulmadden to pop into warp right now and leave him and Chekov as permanent satellites of TNC-5527. He decided he wouldn't let himself sound as angry as he felt.

"Sorry about that, Shipmaster. We were surprised by the amount of ionizing radiation venting from the hull breech." He tried to sound light-hearted. "We thought that maybe a matter-antimatter reaction might be starting."

Sulu was surprised when he heard Krulmadden laugh. "Where you think Krulmadden keeps antimatter on his jewel, stupid mammals?"

Sulu glanced at Chekov but couldn't see his friend's face through the red reflection flaring from his faceplate. However, he could hear him say, "In a magnetic bottle?"

"Ha!" Krulmadden shouted. Sulu could picture the way the green-skinned Orion's stomach would be quivering with laughter about now. "You know how much the cost of magnetic bottles? Big coils! Superconductors! Maintenance required every hundred lightyears!"

Sulu was confused, and excited. Given Krulmadden's tendency to acquire illegal technology, was there a chance that he had somehow obtained a method for storing antimatter that didn't require the complexities of magnetic storage?

"Excuse me, Shipmaster, but what *do* you keep your antimatter in?"

"What antimatter?" Krulmadden thundered. "What kind of fool do you take me for?"

Sulu saw Chekov spin around beside him and motion with open palms. He didn't know what the shipmaster was talking about, either.

"Then, how do you power your warp drive?" Chekov asked.

"Time-honored methods of my parents, and my parents' parents, and my so-ons and so-forths," Krulmadden said sagely. "First-stage matter! Fissionables!"

Of course, Sulu thought, *no wonder Krulmadden was always concerned about power expenditures and the cost of fuel.* Old-fashioned nuclear generators were only a hundredth as efficient as matter-antimatter reactors. *And that probably accounts for all the extra mass and hidden areas of his ship—denselead shielding to protect his 'cargo' and fuel supplies. He'd have to keep hundreds of tons of fissionables on board to give the* Queen Mary *even a minimal hundred-lightyear range.*

And then it hit home—shielding.

"Shipmaster?" Sulu said, trying to remain calm. "Did you send us out to inspect the damage knowing that your fissionable fuel supply might be venting?"

"Of course," Krulmadden replied in the most reasonable voice in the galaxy. He did not sound as if he had anything to hide.

"But," Chekov added, and he wasn't trying to remain calm, "why did you not send out remotes? Why did you send us to be exposed to first-stage radiation?"

Krulmadden responded as if he had no idea why Chekov was upset. "Little mammal, if I had sent my remotes to examine the damage caused by the *stator* border patrol, my precious little drones might have been damaged by the leaking radiation. So, Krulmadden sent his newest crew! Smart thinking, yes, you must think so, too?"

As best he could, Sulu gestured to his throat with a desperate cutting motion, telling Chekov to say nothing more. Two hundred meters out from their only way back to Federation space, he did not want to make Krulmadden angry with them.

"But Shipmaster," Sulu said placatingly, "did you not know that Chekov and I could also be damaged by first-stage radiation?" Who knew? Maybe Orions were naturally stabilized.

"Of course, Krulmadden know. Krulmadden fine shipmaster!" Sulu pictured the Orion leaning closer to the commlink because his voice suddenly became louder and raspier. "But if little mammals are damaged by radiation, Krulmadden will lock them into medic booth that will make them better, no charge, no cost. If remotes get damaged by radiation, Krulmadden must go back to Rigel VIII and pay evil, very bad Andorian criminals exorbitant payments for repairs." Krulmadden wheezed with laughter. "Mammals are cheaper."

Expendable, you mean, Sulu thought, but said nothing.

"Uh, Shipmaster?" Chekov began politely, "are you certain that your medic booth works on humans?"

"If I were you, I would hope so!" Sulu could hear Artinton and Lasslanlin join in Krulmadden's merry laughter. "Please communicate again when breech is sealed. Perhaps airlock will work then, too."

The commlink clicked off again.

Sulu maneuvered so he floated directly in front of Chekov. The shadow he cast cut the glare on Chekov's faceplate and they could see each other. "What kind of exposure did we get?" Sulu asked.

Chekov shook his head in his helmet. "The sensor wand is not calibrated for humans. But whatever it was, it was off the dial. What do you suppose we should do now?"

"Fix the breech," Sulu said in resignation. "You heard what he said. If we don't, he's not going to let us back in."

Sulu saw Chekov blink as Krulmadden's voice whispered over the commlink again. "Righty right you are. And the more time you take, the longer it might take me to decide not to change my mind."

Great, Sulu thought, *even out here he can hear everything we say.* Given the pirates' paranoia—something which neither he nor Chekov had anticipated—they had not felt safe enough to risk talking about a plan to take over the ship for the past three weeks. Not that the two-gee field had left them the strength to act on any plan.

"We're returning to the breech," Sulu said. There was no other choice.

But as he glanced down to check the positioning of his fat, gloved fingers on the thruster controls, he felt Chekov tapping the side of his helmet. "What?" he mouthed through his faceplate.

Chekov smiled and nodded his head enthusiastically. Sulu saw his lips move silently to form something that looked like, "exactly." Then Chekov flipped open the protective cover on his own chest plate and switched off his suit's main power. Sulu did a quick calculation and decided that they'd have about ten minutes before they'd need the oxygen recirculators turned back on, then he shut down his own suit, feeling nervous as the status lights above his faceplate on the inside of his helmet flickered out. *It's an old, old suit,* he thought. *Sure hope it doesn't lock up when I try to restart it.*

Then Chekov grabbed Sulu by the shoulders and brought their helmets together with a bang. Sulu froze, listening intently for the sound of leaking air. But all he heard was Chekov's voice, muffled and tinny. It was one of the lowest-tech tricks they taught at the Academy, but it worked. Sound vibrations passed easily from one helmet to the other as long as they touched.

"Yes . . . I . . . can . . . hear . . . you," Sulu shouted in response to Chekov's question, making each word separate and distinct.

"Everything . . . is . . . going . . . to . . . be . . . perfect!" Chekov said excitedly.

"That's . . . what . . . you . . . said . . . last . . . time . . . Chekov! This . . . was . . . your . . . idea . . . in . . . the . . . first . . . place . . . remember?"

Chekov nodded vigorously, shaking both of them in their suits. But he kept his same bright grin in place. "And . . . now . . . I've . . . got . . . another!"

Shipmaster Krulmadden used a sonic pick to clean the remnants of his dinner from his jeweled teeth, and every time he held the madly vibrating needle to his teeth, the high-pitched grating sound of it made Chekov cringe. Unfortunately, Krulmadden had seen his reaction and apparently enjoyed it. His teeth were long since sparkling—in more ways than one—but he kept tapping the sonic pick to them in order to see Chekov jump. Except for that annoying noise, the *Queen Mary*'s crew lounge was silent as everyone waited for Krulmadden's reply.

But he wasn't ready to give one. "You were not *f'deraxt'l* admiral in *stator*fleet," Krulmadden said skeptically.

Lasslanlin and Artinton laughed at the new pun on Starfleet their cousin had made.

"So you could not have big secrets like the one you tell me." Krulmadden placed the sonic pick against his teeth until his lips blurred with vibration. "Should I kill you for liars being?"

Chekov shook his head and prepared himself to tell the story again. He couldn't understand how a being whose brain worked as slowly as Krulmadden's had ever managed to stay in control of his own vessel for so long.

"I did not make myself clear," Chekov said wearily. The combination of four hours of EVA to repair the *Queen Mary*'s hull breech, the return to double gravity, and now the added discomfort of having a medic-booth intravenous cuff strapped to his arm was rapidly becoming more than he could bear. Beside him at the brilliantly gleaming steel mess table, he saw Sulu slumped in his chair, dark circles under his eyes, struggling against anti-radiation drugs and exhaustion to stay awake. A long glistening tube trailed from his arm as well, snaking across the floor to the humming and vibrating medic booth.

"We have time, time, time," Krulmadden said expansively. "Make yourself clear, little mammal."

"First of all, what I have told you is not a secret," Chekov said.

Krulmadden spit on the floor. "A million tons of fissionables which lie around for the taking—and they have not been taken? If they have not been taken, then they must be a secret."

"No," Chekov protested. "It's just that fissionables are not considered that important. Starfleet has complete jurisdiction over the planet and it is forbidden to take anything from it."

"Besides," Sulu said weakly, "almost all Starfleet vessels are powered by matter and antimatter. Starfleet doesn't need fissionables."

Krulmadden looked over at Lasslanlin and Artinton.

"They lie," Lasslanlin said.

"So kill them," Artinton concluded happily.

Chekov tried to wave his hands in frustration but he couldn't lift them from the tabletop. "How can you say that I'm lying if you won't even go to the planet to see for yourself?"

Lasslanlin had another suggestion. "If they not lying, then can we go ourselves to the planet?"

Artinton smiled with another idea of his own. "So we can kill them now still!"

Sulu shook his head back and forth. "No, Artinton. If you kill us before you go, then you won't be able to get past the Starfleet blockade. We're the ones who know the codes and the patrol patterns, remember? You need us to get in and to get out."

"Kill them afterward?" Artinton asked hopefully. "Just one?"

Krulmadden placed his hands on the table and the metal of his rings scraped like fingernails on slate. Chekov didn't know how much more of this his ears could take.

"This is Krulmadden's problem," he said. "You wish to steal from *stator*fleet. All right, Krulmadden understands this. You wish to shame them, hurt them, all fine and good, good, good as far as Krulmadden knows. But Talin IV is Kirk's World, yes, no?"

"Talin IV is Talin IV," Sulu said grimly.

"Whatever. The planet of many names was destroyed by

nuclear warheads. Updates say *all* weapons. All weapons launched when the *Enterprise* goes there and scares everyone. All weapons explode. Kill that world. Foof. No more nothing."

"That's right," Chekov said. "So what is your problem?"

"Exploding all weapons means consuming all fissionables. Krulmadden knows uniphysics. There are no fissionables on Talin IV. You lie to bring me dishonor. So I must kill you, nothing personal. Artinton, give me a dancerknife with a very slow blade."

Krulmadden held out his hand like a surgeon waiting for a protoplaser. Artinton pulled open his vest and began looking inside. Chekov heard the clink of fine metal.

"Wait! Listen to me for once!" Chekov tried to stand but only managed to get halfway up.

Krulmadden shrugged and brought his hand back. "Okay," he agreed.

Chekov stared at the pirate's new change of mood in disbelief. How could he keep reversing himself this way? The navigator couldn't stand it any longer. He didn't care what Sulu said about trying to stay calm. He had had enough. "Listen to me, you owerstuffed, jiggling mound of flame jelly. I have told you cossacks this a thousand times and I will only tell you once more before I rip those ridiculous rocks out of your mouth with your own belt buckles!" Chekov ignored Sulu's plaintive groan. "Not all the Talin warheads exploded. They have a failure rate of forty percent. Forty percent of the entire world's arsenal is still there—refined, weapons-grade fissionables. And no one on the planet can do a thing to stop you."

Krulmadden nodded wisely. "When you say it that way, you make it sound like an appealing business dealing."

Chekov wanted to put his head on the table and go to sleep for a year. "Say it what way? I didn't say anything that I haven't said before!"

"Ah," Krulmadden said approvingly, "but this time you said it with such passion." He made a fist and tapped his knuckles on the table. "Very well, the illustrious jewel of the stars shall go to Talin IV to show our *flars* to the *stator*fleet onions!"

"I think you mean 'minions,'" Sulu said weakly.

"Whatever. We shall show them, and then we shall retrieve a cargo of fissionables that shall make Krulmadden the richest trader in all the veils of heaven's harem." He beamed at Chekov with a jeweled smile. "And if you and your *tislin* survive the medic booth's treatment, you share two percent." He held up a thick finger before Chekov could say anything. "Nonnegotiable —unless you have your own medic booth you would like to use?"

"Two percent," Chekov said, hoping that he looked convincingly beaten.

"What a good little mammal." Krulmadden reached across the table and squeezed Chekov's cheek teasingly between thumb and forefinger.

Chekov pulled away and his head thudded against the back of his chair. *But Talin has almost Earth normal gravity,* he thought. *Sulu and I can recover there.* He tried to straighten his head as he spoke. "Shall I begin to plot in the approaches necessary to awoid Starfleet's patrols around Talin?" he asked.

"No hurry," Krulmadden said.

"But we're only about five days out from Talin," Sulu said.

Krulmadden's eyes glinted. "Ah, so you do know where we are. Even without charts. Krulmadden is impressed. But Krulmadden also has other concerns for the moment. And Talin IV is going nowhere but around its lonely little sun. We will go there soon enough. A month, a year, or once upon a time."

It worked before, Chekov thought. *Might as well try it again.* "How stupid does a shipmaster have to be to decide not to pick up a fortune in refined fissionables while he has the chance?"

Krulmadden looked at Artinton. The Orion mate pulled back his vest again and began searching for a dancerknife.

"How stupid does a mammal have to be to know that there is no sense picking up one cargo until the shipmaster has unloaded his first? Or do you and your *tislin* hate the slavegirls so much you would have me offload them in empty space without profit?"

Chekov pointed weakly to the intravenous cuff on his arm. "It's the medication," he said apologetically, trying to shrug despite the cruel gravity.

"Hope that it continues to flow," Krulmadden said in what was quite clearly a threat. "And in the meantime, I am shipmaster and say where the ship goes. And right now, this ship goes to trade with Black Ire."

"What is Black Ire?" Chekov asked, trying to keep Krulmadden distracted, but dismayed that it appeared it might still be several months before they could reach Talin.

"Black Ire a who, little mammal. A trader in greenskins and, unlike your dear, sweet, understanding Shipmaster Krulmadden, Black Ire a most fearsome and dangerous *pirate*."

"I thought that's what you were supposed to be," Sulu sighed.

"Me?" Krulmadden crowed. "Fearsome and dangerous?" He leaned forward, crinkling his pudgy nose and eyebrows at Chekov and Sulu. "How much you have still to learn, little mammals. And how much I shall enjoy teaching you."

FOUR

"What happened to the astronauts?"

"The what?" Kirk said. He watched as Nogura stepped carefully across the environmental control board, tail lashing. Kirk had quickly learned why the most critical controls of the *Ian Shelton* were protected with clear covers.

Anne Gauvreau caught up with the cat and scooped it under her arm. "Isn't that what they used to call space explorers? Astronauts or cosmonauts or something? You know, the two Talin in the lunar orbiter. Were they still in orbit when it happened?"

When it *happened,* Kirk noted. Not 'the disaster,' not 'the mistake,' Gauvreau just referred to what he had told her had happened at Talin IV as 'it.'

"I don't think anyone knows for certain," Kirk said. He stretched out in the crew chair, watching the stars slip past on the viewscreen at a steady warp four. The ship was two days out from Hanover and there wasn't a lot that Gauvreau didn't know about him or Talin. Two weeks on an automated freighter *was* a long time. "I wasn't kept informed about most of what happened over the next few days. I know that the rescue shuttles from Starbase 29 went looking for the Talin ship but I don't think anything was ever found."

Gauvreau chucked Nogura under the chin as she watched a consumables breakdown scroll past on a computer display. Kirk respected her ability to be able to keep up with several different sources of information at once. Good officers had to be able to do that in a bridge environment. The human resource specialists in Starfleet called it 'human multitasking.'

"Do you think they crashed?" she asked. "I mean, on purpose, seeing their world destroyed like that."

Kirk watched as Komack stuck his head up above the impulse board, ears flattened. Kirk had learned how to read the creatures' minds in the past two weeks: The cat was looking for a lap.

"I don't think anyone had the resources to scan the entire moon for such a small crashed vehicle. Maybe they even landed. But there was no sign that they tried to get back to Talin." Komack stepped precisely between the impulse controls and stood across from Kirk, staring intently at him. "I suppose we can't blame them for not wanting to."

Gauvreau came over to the impulse station and pushed Komack off the board so she could lean against it. She kept her hand busy on Nogura's ears. The stars swam behind her.

"It's not your fault, you know."

"Thank you," Kirk said. Now that she had heard the whole story, he didn't question her decision to accept his innocence.

"Too bad I wasn't on the board of inquiry, hmm?" She smiled at him, trying to get him to respond in kind. Kirk knew he hadn't been doing a lot of that on board the *Shelton*. But he decided that he couldn't be blamed for not wanting to, either.

"You still haven't told me everything that went on then," Gauvreau said.

"Not much to tell. The board members had full bridge log tapes up to the point we went into warp in the atmosphere—" Kirk saw that Gauvreau still shuddered at the concept. "—so they could see exactly what had happened. They reviewed the tapes. Asked a few questions for the record to determine what the state of our minds were at various times, then made their ruling."

"One ruling or two?" she asked.

"Five actually," Kirk said. "One for each of us who had willfully—"

"No, I don't mean how many crew members they ruled against. I remember the *Enterprise* Five. I mean, did they only make a ruling to cover the second time you tried to stop the exchange of weapons, or did they rule on the first time, too? After the accidental detonation in the missile silo."

"As far as the board was concerned, they weren't separate events. The core of their decision was that if I had not interfered the first time, then the second exchange would not have occurred."

Gauvreau stopped scratching her cat's ears and let him slip out of her hands to the deck. Nogura made a soft squeaking sound as he hit, then stalked off to the ladderway. Gauvreau sat in the navigation chair across from Kirk and leaned forward, putting her elbow on her knee and resting her chin on her hand.

"Now, how did they come to that conclusion?" she asked.

For once Kirk smiled of his own accord. "For what it's worth, my science officer said their reasoning was quite logical."

"Enlighten me," Gauvreau said.

Kirk kept his eyes on the screen and the stars. He could not deny that these were painful memories Gauvreau had been coaxing from him. Yet he knew he had to face them sooner or later, so he did not resist.

"They brought in three cultural specialists from the Richter Institute. And they maintained that, from the data assembled by Starfleet's own FCO, the Talin were clearly dedicated to global peace in their world."

"Despite the fact that they were armed to the teeth?"

"Many worlds have been in similar situations and survived. The specialists said that Talin IV had had an excellent chance of being one of them."

Gauvreau sat up, plainly upset. "The accidental detonation had nothing at all to do with whatever the Talin hoped for in the long run. And it could have led them to a full exchange even earlier."

"I'm not the board of inquiry," Kirk said defensively. "I'm only telling you what they ruled. And they ruled that had the Talin experienced a small example of the effects of a full-scale war because of the accidental detonation, it would have propelled them into serious arms and peace negotiations."

"Ah," Gauvreau said, "so the board decided that you spared them that particular lesson."

"Exactly," Kirk agreed. "If I had allowed a minor exchange of weapons to take place, then the major exchange would not have followed."

Gauvreau frowned in disbelief. "Were there any Vulcans on this board?"

"Two actually. The civilian members. And no dissenting opinions."

"I don't understand how they could come to that conclusion."

Kirk closed his eyes for a moment and saw himself standing before the board. He remembered each word they had said, because each word had taken away another small part of his dream.

"The board concluded that I had denied the Talin the opportunity to learn from their own mistakes. Because they did not have to deal with the consequences of an accidental nuclear detonation, some of them were recklessly encouraged to proceed with a more dangerous action. By interfering with their normal development, I made it possible for them to engage in an activity which led to the destruction of their world. A textbook example of what happens when the Prime Directive is not upheld." Kirk opened his eyes. Gauvreau looked away from him.

"Was there no defense you could give?" she asked.

"If I had refused to resign, they would have held a court-martial for each of us who took action on the bridge. We could have presented a defense then, but if the defense weren't accepted, then each of my bridge team might have faced twenty years' imprisonment. I couldn't do that to them."

"What about what you did to yourself, Kirk?"

"That's not important."

"What is?"

"The Talin."

"But if you don't believe you contravened the Prime Directive, then why be concerned with them?"

Kirk swung around to face her. It didn't seem like her to be so cold or so callous. "Let's get this straight, Captain. At the time I made my decision to act, to the best of my knowledge and ability, I believed I was following my orders and doing my duty. In hindsight, perhaps I did not uphold the Prime Directive, despite my best intentions. But no matter what actually happened on Talin IV—whether I'm technically or legally right or wrong—I do not intend to deny that I share some responsibility for what happened." He studied her, wondering if she understood what he was saying, if she understood the concept of duty as he did. "If I caused harm to the Talin, then somehow, some way, I will attempt to right it, no matter how little I can do, and no matter how long it might take."

Gauvreau stood up and slid her hands into the pockets of her multipatched flight jacket. "You can say that despite what Starfleet did to you?"

"All Starfleet personnel involved with the Talin inquiry did their duty as they saw fit. I have no quarrel with them. The answer lies elsewhere."

Gauvreau thrust her head forward, squinting in exasperation. "Then who do you have a quarrel with? You've been tighter than a cadet's bedsheet. I keep thinking you're going to haul off and kick one of my cats. If you're not angry at Starfleet and you're not angry at yourself and you're not angry at the damned board of inquiry, then who the hell are you mad at?"

"Captain Gauvreau," Kirk said seriously, "I'll let you know when I get back to Talin. Because whoever I'm mad at, that's where I'm going to find them."

Two days later, Kirk stood in the empty cargo hold of the *Ian Shelton* and tucked his kit bag under his arm. When Gauvreau came back and paid him for his tour as supercargo, he'd be able to beam over to Hanover's spacedock, then catch a shuttle down to the colony world's freighter yards. There he could try his luck again at getting a cargo handler's job, or even pay for freighter passage to another system closer still to Talin. Eventually, he'd get back there, he knew. And even if he didn't, he knew he would never stop trying.

He heard his name echo in the vast hold of the ship and turned to see Gauvreau standing on an observation platform near the control booth. She waved to him.

About time, thought Kirk, *now we can get this over with.* Two weeks in deep space with her and he still had no idea how to read her. He couldn't make up his mind whether or not he thought Starfleet had made a mistake in letting go an officer of her wide-ranging abilities, or had been wise in refusing to promote such an uncaring and emotionless perfectionist. At least her cats liked her.

Kirk arrived at the ladder leading up to the observation platform. He was pleased when he saw that among the packages and cases Gauvreau carried was the *Shelton*'s paymaster terminal. Liquid credits were slowly being phased out throughout much of the Federation as virtually unlimited power and manufacturing technologies became automated to the point where they were self-reproducing and maintaining. When the necessities of life had no value and interplanetary resources were prodigious enough to ensure that people could have almost anything they could imagine, a simple, cashless system of barter naturally arose. But out on the frontier, Kirk knew, there would always have to be some system of portable wealth so that credits could be taken from place to place in search of scarce commodities. Then again, who knew what the future would bring?

Gauvreau stepped back and Kirk climbed the ladder to join her. He saw her three cats in the cargo control room, staring through the window at her. She would not let them out into the hold, no matter how much they cried and rubbed at the airlock.

"Sorry to take so long," Gauvreau said. "You'll be pleased to know that the whole transfer of cargo was accomplished without damage. I get a bonus for that and you're going to share in it."

"Thank you," Kirk said. Whatever else Anne Gauvreau might be, she was fair. "Did you get a chance to find out about their public transporter facilities?"

"That's what I came back on," she said. "I even got you a rate card. But . . . why not come back inside for a few minutes?" She pointed toward the airlock leading to the control room.

Kirk was in a hurry and it showed.

But Gauvreau was determined. She held up a small brown package and Kirk smelled what was in it instantly. "Real coffee," she said triumphantly. "Stasis beans from Earth. Roasted locally. You can't say no."

Kirk couldn't. He followed her back into the crew areas of her ship.

As the scent of fresh coffee filled the tiny lounge, Gauvreau unpacked another small case on the games table. "One of the reasons I was held up was because I tried to get online with the Starfleet update channels." She glanced at him. "It's completely legal. They're a public channel."

They were, technically, Kirk knew. But to intercept them, civilians usually needed a Starfleet-licensed receiver, which the *Shelton* didn't have.

"So, I still have friends in Starfleet," Gauvreau said. "And a few of them at the Starfleet office over on the spacedock let me download update files."

Kirk watched the coffee bubble up from the osmosis inverter. He was surprised at how the prospect of reading Starfleet updates didn't seem to affect him either way—he was neither interested nor disinterested, as if he no longer cared. Instead he wondered why Gauvreau was going to such lengths to let him know she had some.

"Is there something special going on out in the galaxy you think I should know about?" he asked.

"Don't give me that," Gauvreau said. "You know there is."

Kirk listened to and read the main updates whenever he got

the chance. He knew that nothing had happened in the Talin system since Starfleet had blockaded it to keep out scavengers and exploiters. It had been estimated that the blockade would have to stay in place for at least five hundred years before the Talin came anywhere near their previous level of technological development. In the last two months, the only mention of Talin in the public updates had been in relation to the long-term resource allocations that the Federation was requesting for blockade maintenance. Starfleet had succeeded in doing what it had set out to do—close the datafile on the entire incident without withholding anything.

But now Gauvreau acted as if something had changed.

"Is it something you think I should know?" Kirk prompted.

"'A good commander learns all that she can,'" Gauvreau quoted, "'then uses all that she has.'"

"What's in the updates?" Kirk didn't want to recap Academy lectures. He wanted off this ship.

"It seems you're not the only one who wants to go back to Talin." Gauvreau slipped a microtape into a screenpad. "Recognize these names? Palamas, Carolyn. Frietas, Jorge. Let's see . . . M'Benga, Chapel, Fisher . . . about a hundred others?"

Kirk took the screenpad from her hand and scanned the list of names. There was no Starfleet imprimatur on the display but all the names were of Starfleet personnel. All the names were of *Enterprise* crewmembers.

"What is this?" Kirk said, feeling the anger build in him again as he realized something was developing of which he was unaware. "This isn't an update sheet from a public channel."

"It's a recall list, Kirk. Those officers and specialists are being reassigned to their previous posting."

Kirk felt gooseflesh crawl up his arms and neck. "The *Enterprise*?" he whispered. But his ship was dead. He had destroyed her himself.

Gauvreau nodded.

"Who authorized the recall? Where's the *Enterprise*?"

Gauvreau passed over another tape wafer for Kirk to read.

"Authorization source is Vice Admiral Hammersmith, Starbase 29. And the originating source is given as Lieutenant Commander Scott, USS *Enterprise*, on station, Talin System."

Kirk read the second tape and confirmed the code designations. His hands shook. "They told me she was dead," he said. "They told me . . . she'd never be operational again." And why was Scott still on her, almost four months later, unless . . .

"Where did you get these? How recent are they?"

"No more than a few days old, Kirk. And I'm afraid I'm going to keep my source at Starfleet communications a secret. They never pass on classified or military information, but sometimes it helps to know where the big ships are going to be—especially if I've got a hold full of real coffee."

Kirk looked at the tapes Gauvreau still hadn't passed over. As a civilian, it was a violation for her to have them. But perhaps some good could come of it. "No harm done?" he asked her, indicating the tapes. "Never," Gauvreau said. "Little more than the gossip I'd hear in a bar."

Kirk took the rest of the update wafers. Obviously, Gauvreau and her sources had gone to a great deal of trouble to pull out all recent transmissions which had contained the words "*Enterprise*" or "Talin." There were dozens of them and the story they told was staggering.

"They detached the port nacelle," Kirk read. "They told me it couldn't be done." He scrolled through the reports. "And nothing happened, per the reports submitted by Scott. Replacement warp nacelles are in transit . . . crew is being recalled. . . ." For a moment, he felt as if he couldn't breathe. "My ship . . ." he said. "The *Enterprise* . . . she's . . ."

Gauvreau reached out and took Kirk's hand. "I know," she said gently. "She's going to be given to someone else."

Kirk sat back and pulled his hand away. It was one thing for him to have lost his career *and* the *Enterprise* together. Without one, what could the other be worth? But to think of someone else taking out his ship, and his crew—he was wracked with terrible jealousy.

"They told me every circuit in her was fused. They told me

the nacelle was still drawing her into warp space and she could never be released."

"Here's a weapons-damage analysis report from Scott," Gauvreau said, handing the appropriate tape to Kirk. "Read it."

Kirk's eyes sped over the display. "Only twenty percent damage . . . precisely focused subspace pulse . . . ." He looked up, eyes blazing. "It was a deliberate attack. An attack beyond the Talin's capabilities." He looked back at the analysis. It wasn't signed off by Hammersmith and it was tagged as a preliminary report, but it meant there was a chance that another reason existed for what had happened to the *Enterprise.* And to Talin IV. "But how did anyone figure the damage pattern out?" Kirk asked. "To break it down like this someone would have to crawl through the whole ship on his hands and—"

And then he knew what Scotty was still doing on the ship. *Bless you, Scotty,* he thought, *You never gave up.*

He scrolled through the rest of the tapes, scanning supply requisitions and personnel transfers until he had an idea of the schedule Hammersmith was on in getting the *Enterprise* back into space under her own power. He clenched his jaw. He had less than a week to get back to Talin before they'd be starting warp trials with her to bring her new nacelles into balance. A week.

"Thank you, Captain," Kirk said, standing suddenly with the screenpad in his hand. "I can't tell you what this means to me."

"I saw the look on your face when you realized someone else was going to get her, Kirk. I know exactly what it means to you."

"That's not important," Kirk said. "It's this report from Scotty. If the *Enterprise* was hit with a precisely focused subspace pulse, then there's another factor which hasn't been included in the equation." He swung his kit bag over his shoulder. "May I use the bridge to place a call to the spacedock transporter?"

Gauvreau went to the coffee osmoser and poured two cups

from the flask. "Sit down, Kirk, you don't have to go anywhere, yet." She handed him a steaming mug.

"You don't understand, I have less than a week to get to the Talin system."

"The *Shelton* can make it in five days."

"I'm going to have to—what?"

"Don't look at me like that, Kirk. You heard what I said. I'm the captain and this ship's next port is Talin IV."

Kirk put the coffee mug on the table, but he no longer felt the need to rush away. Not until he found out what Gauvreau was up to. "The Talin system is blockaded," he said.

Gauvreau opened a small, soft-sided bag and pulled out two more pale yellow microtapes. "Now this one is from the public update services." She held it close to her, not letting Kirk have it yet. "You see, at the Starfleet office, I was able to request a search for everything to do with the *Enterprise* and Talin IV, because they're both within Starfleet jurisdiction. But for the rest of the *Enterprise* Five, I had to go to the public update bureaus."

Gauvreau glanced down at the tapes. Kirk didn't grab for them. He'd give her another minute to play her game. He knew what it was like to have another person hanging on every word.

"Now," Gauvreau said, "for Chekov, I found nothing. He resigned. Was last seen heading out on a pleasure cruiser to Eisner's World . . . in the company of Sulu. Same thing. No other mentions of him, either. The communications officer, Uhura, well, she was released from detention on the Moon. Was met there by . . . Leonard McCoy . . . the one who took a swing at Hammersmith . . . then they both went back to Earth, then to Mars, then to . . . Rigel II of all places . . . and then no more references, just like the others."

"That just leaves Spock," Kirk said.

"And you," Gauvreau countered. "But for what it's worth, you've been spotted on just about every seedy frontier world, doing everything *except* rockrigging and handling cargo. As for Spock, well, he's one of the reasons why the Talin system might not be blockaded for much longer." She passed over the microtapes at last.

Kirk took them calmly from her, trying not to show how eager he was for the news of his friend. But then he forgot all about keeping up appearances as he read the update story three times before he was sure he believed it.

"Spock's *suing* the Federation?"

"That's what he said at his update conference."

"And *Starfleet?*" Kirk blinked to clear his vision. "On behalf of . . . Students for Stars for the People. Who the hell are Students for Stars for the People?"

"Last paragraph," Gauvreau said. "Apparently it's a radical student organization based at Berkeley."

"Berkeley?" Kirk said in shock. "Across the bay from San Francisco, Berkeley?"

Gauvreau nodded.

"But that's almost next door to Starfleet Academy. Berkeley's been one of the most conservative universities on Earth for more than a hundred years. Why would Spock get mixed up with anything so . . . ?"

"Amateur?"

"Exactly."

"From what you've told me about him, I'm sure he has his reasons."

"I'm sure he does, too," Kirk said, rereading the update for the fourth time.

"But because of the challenge he's threatening to bring over enforcement of the Prime Directive, there seems to be quite a public outcry to get emergency relief aid to Talin."

Kirk sat back at the table, feeling overcome by the sudden assimilation of this much unexpected news. He had been so singlemindedly fixed on his goal of getting to Talin IV that he had not permitted himself to remember how much he missed his crew, and how much he cared for his friends.

"Even Spock will never be able to do that," Kirk said. "No matter what they think the trigger incident might have been, as far as the board of inquiry was concerned, the destruction of Talin IV was caused by Talin weapons and Talin politics. Neither Starfleet nor the Federation could possibly allow the Prime Directive to be broken there again."

"Maybe," Gauvreau said, "and maybe not. But my credits are on your Mr. Spock. All of them." She flipped open the screen of her paymaster terminal and hit the balance button. It came up close to zero. The ship's accounts were drained.

"There should be close to one hundred thousand credits in there," Kirk said. He had seen the cargo manifest and the insurance papers from Lloyds.

"Already transferred out to pay for our new cargo," Gauvreau explained. Should be shipping up to the spacedock within the next hour.

"What did you buy?" Kirk asked.

"Emergency supplies—medical mostly. Radiation stabilizers. Water purifiers. That sort of thing. Should come in handy when Starfleet calls off their blockade."

"You're serious, aren't you?"

"According to the updates, Kirk, I'm not the only one. There are about two hundred ships already underway to Talin. And that's not counting the additional picket ships Starfleet's ordered in to manage the traffic. Something's going to give there soon. And whatever else happens, you and I will be there along with your ship and most of your crew."

She clicked the paymaster off and shut its screen down. "Now drink your coffee, so I don't have to hear you complain about the jifficoff cubes anymore."

Kirk lifted the mug and finally savored the rich scent of the brew. *Scott hadn't given up,* he thought. And Spock was doing something completely outrageous. And if McCoy and Uhura, and Chekov and Sulu had disappeared, then the chances were more than likely that they were somewhere together, also planning something. He found himself smiling at the way things had turned out. He had decided he would go back to Talin on his own because he couldn't force any of the others to share the hardships and the risks of the journey with him. Yet they had all come to the same conclusion and set out for the same goals on their own anyway. *Even when we're apart,* he thought, *we're a team.*

Kirk sniffed the coffee. Real beans, freshly roasted, steaming hot. But even without tasting it, he knew it couldn't be even half as good as what he had had on the *Enterprise.* And would have again.

FIVE

☆

By standing to the side of the small window and almost against the wall, Spock could just see past the other towers of the student housing complex and catch a glimpse of clear sky over San Francisco. He looked into his human half for some connection with what he saw, but the blue of Earth's skies was still alien to him. He found it intriguing that he responded to the red skies of Vulcan in the same way—neither world held the skies of home for him.

Behind Spock, in the small and cluttered student apartment, five humans carried on two separate conversations—both about him. He followed their words easily while reflecting on the hundreds of skies he had seen in his travels, trying to recall which ones, if any, he had felt at home beneath.

After a time, one of the conversations became heated.

"Well, don't ask *me*," Marita Llorente said in exasperation. "Ask *him*."

"I don't think I can," Marita's companion said uncertainly. "Look at him. Isn't he meditating or something?"

"No," Spock said, and at the sound of his voice the other conversation died. "I am not meditating. What did you wish to ask me?" He turned from the window. For now, he decided that the true color of his sky was black. His home was space. He was confident he would return there soon.

Marita's companion was Penn Grossman, the young oriental human who shared these quarters with her. Spock had seldom seen a more harried or nervous creature. He had the attitude of someone who felt anything and everything which happened anywhere in the galaxy had some direct personal bearing on his life—usually negative. *At least,* Spock thought, *in regard to my presence in his life, the young man is correct.*

"Why did you have to go to the update services and tell them about the legal challenge?" Penn rocked back and forth on the worn couch where he sat beside Marita. The couch could be unfolded. It was where Spock slept. "That little grandstanding ploy could ruin everything."

Spock placed his hands behind his back, remaining impassive as he rapidly tried to recall if he had ever before heard the term "grandstanding." He guessed at its meaning from the way Penn had used it. "I assure you I was not grandstanding. It will be more beneficial to our purposes if update coverage of the General Council meeting is more intensive than normal, so that more beings will be aware of our struggle." Spock had quickly picked up the cant of Marita's organization. Typical for humans, they found romance in thinking of their political aspirations as rebellion. Many scholars on Vulcan still had trouble understanding how democracy had flourished on a planet where logic had not.

Penn's hands fluttered rapidly in front of him. "But Marita told me what happened when you saw Ambassador Sytok. He said that if the Council found out Marita would be attending the general meeting, then they'd cancel it or something so she couldn't disrupt it."

"First, I must remind you that under the terms of our agreement, the Council meeting must not be disrupted. All business which I shall present there will be conducted in accordance with the Federation's Rules of Order."

"Yeah, yeah, I know," Penn said rudely.

"Second, at no time during the update conference did I mention that Marita would be attending the Council meeting with me. All the update services reported was that I would be speaking on behalf of Students for Stars for the People to press for the repeal of the Prime Directive.

"If any of the Council members had learned of the topic of my address before it had been made public, then the meeting could have been delayed quite easily. But now that my intentions have been widely reported, the Council cannot postpone their meeting without inviting public criticism and an increased public debate on the propriety of the Directive. By holding the update conference, I have removed that choice from the Council's options and we remain in control of their agenda."

Marita clapped her hands. "Well done, Mr. Spock." She looked scornfully at Penn. "See? I told you he knew what he was doing. You should have seen the look on the ambassador's face when Mr. Spock had me do the finger-embrace thing. I tell you, this guy knows how the system works. He's just what the SSP's been needing—someone from the inside who knows firsthand how morally bankrupt the Federation is."

Penn sat back in the couch and folded his arms across his chest. "I thought that the finger embrace was something that only married Vulcans did. Or . . ."

"I assure you, Penn, that I asked Marita to attend me only to distract the ambassador from the true purpose of our visit to his embassy. Nothing else was intended by it."

One of the other three students in the cramped room chuckled. "Hey, Penn's jealous of a Vulcan!"

Penn was indignant. "I am not! It's just that . . . " He glared at Spock. "We were doing pretty good on our own. We didn't need him to come along and take over."

Spock remained expressionless though he conceded to himself that, for all of Penn's misplaced nervous energy, the young human was quite perceptive.

Marita pushed against Penn's shoulder. "Mr. Spock hasn't taken over, Penn. He's helping us. Running student rallies and uploading pamphlets is one thing . . . but Mr. Spock is the first person from the inside who believes the same things we do. The Prime Directive has got to go and Mr. Spock's the one who can make that happen." She smiled up at Spock. "Isn't that right?"

"I do not know if I can indeed convince the Council to repeal the Directive," Spock said truthfully.

"See?" Penn said, hands waving. "He admits he can't help us."

Marita stood up from the couch and gathered a stack of serving plates from a small table. "All he's saying is that he can't *guarantee* anything. He's just being truthful, Penn. You know that Vulcans can't lie." She carried the plates over to a small autokitchen set in a corner of the room. As the plates clattered in the metal-walled cleaner, Spock heard the first stirrings of the baby waking in the bedroom. No one else did.

Penn stared at Spock. "Is it true what she said? Is it true that Vulcans can't lie?"

Spock allowed a momentary half-smile to come to his lips. "Assuming that you really do not know the answer, I believe if you consider that question carefully, you will discover that no possible answer I could give would provide you with any useful information." Spock was pleased that he would not have to answer Penn's question directly. The truth was that Vulcans, as a matter of principle, strove to avoid the telling of lies at almost all cost. However, there were times when, to accomplish the greater good, it was necessary to disguise the truth. In the past, Spock had experienced no moral qualms in telling outright lies to Klingons and others who would do violence to the innocent, just as he experienced no qualms in lying to Marita and the other students involved in the SSP. Despite what they might think when they discovered his real purpose in joining them, he was not seeking personal gain. Someday, he hoped they would understand his motives, and condone them.

The student who had laughed at Penn's apparent jealousy got up from the floor where he sat. Beside him, the two other students who had been sitting crosslegged stretched out their legs. One of them knocked over a stack of music cubes. Spock noted disapprovingly that many of the cubes were not in their covers.

"So when is this other bigshot insider going to be coming?" the standing student asked. His name was Lowell and he had told Spock he intended to study law. Spock had noted the orderliness of Lowell's mind and was thankful that he was not the leader of the group. That role had fallen to Marita not because she was the best organizer among the students, but because of her unrelenting energy. The notoriety she had gained by having and caring for a child while still a student also helped attract attention to the group. It was a choice seldom made on Earth these days.

"I believe my guest is due at any moment," Spock said in answer to Lowell's question.

The young law student stood by the window beside Spock and stared out as if trying to find whatever it was that Spock had been looking at. "And he's just supposed to be another guy from Starfleet who's seen the light about the Directive and wants to make the galaxy a better place?"

Like Penn, Lowell also had his doubts about Spock's motives in becoming involved in the SSP. But unlike Penn, he seemed willing to go along with Spock, if not trust him, as long as he felt that the group might gain an advantage from their association with him—even if it wasn't the advantage they were hoping for.

"He is not 'just another guy,'" Spock said. "And he will attract even more public attention for the SSP than I."

"Hard to imagine that," Lowell said, giving up on his search out the window. "You were the first Vulcan to join Starfleet, and the first Vulcan to resign. And along the way you helped destroy a world." Lowell glanced at Spock, looking for a reaction.

But Spock gave him none. He was used to the charges and the misconceptions by now. He felt no need to correct them. There were other solutions. "I believe young Alexander is waking up," he said to Marita.

The woman turned away from her recycler and smiled at Spock. "Would you?" she asked. "You're so good with him."

Spock nodded. Since the day he had resigned from Starfleet and sought out the SSP to take his first unexpected step in his new course to correct the errors of the past, Marita and Penn had not accepted what little payment he could make for his room and board. Thus, he felt he was obliged to contribute to their lives in other ways, such as by tutoring and helping with Alexander. He excused himself to the students and went into the small bedroom.

Alexander's crib module hung against the wall near a larger bed. The walls were decorated with two-dimensional images printed on sheets of plastic and paper. Spock found it ironic that many of the images depicted pristine landscapes from other systems—not colony planets but alien worlds. He wondered if Marita could imagine what these scenes would look like if the Prime Directive did not exist. From Earth's own history, images of the fate of indigenous North Americans came to Spock. As was known now, the European colonists were not representatives of a better culture, simply a more intrusive one, and the indigenous cultures had been overwhelmed. The Federation Council was committed to ensuring that such outrages were never repeated on an interstellar scale, which is why Spock had had to be so careful and so precise in orchestrating the appearance he planned to make before them. He had no doubt that they would not be a receptive audience for what he had to say.

Alexander stopped rocking in his crib as he heard Spock enter the darkened room. He waved his stubby arms and legs as Spock appeared above him and gurgled happily as he was lifted into the air.

When Spock returned to the main room, Alexander was contentedly resting against the Vulcan's shoulder, intently tugging on a gracefully pointed ear.

Penn came over as Spock rocked the child gently, waiting for Marita to finish at the autokitchen. "I didn't think Vulcans liked to be touched by humans," he said waspishly.

Normally, when a Vulcan came into unexpected physical

contact with a human, or any being with an undisciplined mind, the crude contact-telepathy transmission of uncontrolled emotion could be distressing. But children were an exception.

"The minds of babies are seldom confused," Spock observed. "And, in fact, they can be quite refreshing." However, he did have to adjust Alexander's position against him to prevent the child from deciding to chew on the ear to which he had become so attached.

A few moments later, the visitor chime sounded. It was an old building, so Marita couldn't speak to the door. She had to walk to it and open it by hand.

Lowell was the only one to recognize the man Spock had invited to join them.

"Alonzo Richter?" the student said in awe.

The old theoretical culturalist chased Marita back from the door by waving his black cane at her.

"What about it, you little brat?" Richter sneered at Lowell. He shuffled into the room and looked around, licking his teeth and lips noisily. "*Barge g'l*, what a dump. You actually live here, Spock?" He coughed loudly.

Alexander twisted in Spock's arms to see who the new intruder in his home was. Richter stuck out his tongue at the child and Alexander began to cry.

Marita took Alexander from Spock and was jostled out of the way as the other students gathered excitedly around Richter. They all had heard his name before, even if they hadn't recognized his face.

"Dr. Richter," Lowell said, "your work is the underlying structure upon which the Prime Directive is based. Are you seriously joining us to oppose it?"

Richter frowned and made another face at the crying baby. "I'm one hundred percent behind Spock, here," he said. "And I've come a long way to be able to say that, you can be *vrelq* sure about that."

The autokitchen buzzer blared and Alexander responded with screams. Marita bounced him energetically and smiled in the face of the chaos. "The sandwich tubes are ready, Mr. Spock. Would you?"

Spock dutifully went to the autokitchen to remove the sandwich tube trays.

Richter called out to him. "And get me a bubble of ale while you're there, Mr. Spock."

Spock worked quickly and efficiently, all the time preparing for what he would say in his address to the Council, and knowing that no matter how his and Richter's plan worked out, he had to get back into space.

The buzzer sounded again. Alexander yowled. Two more requests for ale were shouted out and someone plugged a music cube into the player.

Spock had no doubt whatsoever. He had to get back into space, and quickly.

SIX

☆

Sulu jerked awake and tried to jump from his bunk as the
shipmaster's voice roared from the overhead speakers. But he
had forgotten the *Queen Mary*'s double-gee field. He heard
something crack in his neck and fell back onto the bunk with a
drawn-out groan.

"Don't complain," Chekov said from the other bunk. "At
least you can still move."

"Attention, all *tislins*," Krulmadden bellowed. "This jewel of
the luminous veils drops from warp in less than the time it will
take you to crawl to the bridge." Krulmadden sang a few notes
as if delivering a morning concert. "That is all."

Sulu rolled to his side and raised his eyebrows at Chekov,
even though they felt as if they weighed a hundred kilos apiece.
"And cadets think that *Starfleet* commanders are crazy."

Chekov slid his legs to the edge of his bunk and slowly rose to
a sitting position. "What is this *'tislins'* he keeps calling us?
Why always *'tislins'*?"

Sulu tensed his neck to keep anything from grating, and
forced himself up. At least if they ever got off this ship alive,
they were both going to have muscles like iron.

"Do you know this word?" Chekov asked.

Sulu nodded carefully. He did.

282

"Well?" Chekov said.

"I think you can figure it out, Chekov. You see, we didn't want to have anything at all to do with the slavegirls."

"So? We are gentlemen. What of it?"

"Tislins means that even if we *wanted* to have something to do with the slavegirls, we couldn't."

Chekov waited expectantly for more.

"Keepers of the harem, Chekov. Snip snip."

"Oh," Chekov said as the realization hit home. "Cossack," he muttered.

The vibration in the deck abruptly changed and Sulu heard the whine of the impulse engines coming to life. The *Queen Mary* was much smaller than the *Enterprise* and the sound of her machinery traveled through her more easily.

"We are out of warp," Chekov said.

Sulu sighed. "Time to meet this 'Black Ire,' I guess—whoa!"

Sulu and Chekov both flew from their bunks, then slammed onto the metal deck as if they had been snapped from a whip.

"Where did he buy his gravity generator?" Chekov complained. "Or more likely, where did he steal it? I have not felt one malfunction so badly in—"

"Hold on," Sulu said, pushing experimentally against the deck. The movement was far more effortless than it ever had been before on the ship. "That's not a malfunction. The field's been reset. It's so weak . . . it's like Mars."

Chekov jumped smoothly to his feet. He picked up one of his boots from the side of the bunk, held it over his head, then dropped it. "But look how fast that fell. This is not Mars normal. This is Earth normal. We are just . . . not used to it."

Sulu pushed off from the floor and was impressed with how painless the action was. It was better than being in Mars gravity. It was like being on the Moon.

"I wonder why he's reset it?" Sulu said.

Krulmadden's voice squawked over the ship's intercom. "Because our guests to be are from a weaker planet, little mammals. Your shipmaster is being courteous, oh yes, indeed."

"We're from a weaker planet, too," Chekov grumbled.

"But you are not guests aboard *Queen Mary*," Krulmadden crooned. "You are crew and courtesy is not required. Now to the bridge before I see what gravity setting for Jupiter does to your little hollow squishy bones."

Chekov sat on the edge of his bunk and pulled on his boots. "Let's hope 'our guests' remain onboard for a long meeting," he said.

Sulu wanted to say what he was hoping for, too, but he didn't think it was something Krulmadden would enjoy overhearing.

The bridge of the *Queen Mary* was arranged in a standard configuration—it was a circular deck ringed by elevated monitoring stations, with a main viewscreen mounted in front of a helm and navigation console, and a central commander's chair. But what wasn't standard was the way every surface in it had been finished with gleaming horizontal strips of gold and silver plating. Beneath the blazing blue Rigel-normal lighting, Chekov had to squint to keep from being blinded by the painfully harsh reflections from the bulkheads, consoles, and deck. He saw Sulu doing the same.

As Chekov and Sulu carefully entered the bridge from the ladderway entrance, Krulmadden whirled around in his chair to face them. *More like a throne,* Chekov thought. The shipmaster's bulk flowed seamlessly into a rippling gold chair that resembled a sculpture of an alien flower bud.

"Ah," Krulmadden said, "so *f'deraxt'l* mammals *can* walk upright like real bipeds after all."

Chekov peered around the bridge, trying to see if the infamous Black Ire had already beamed aboard. But all he saw was Lasslanlin at the helm. Chekov presumed that the other mate, Artinton, was somewhere else in the ship.

"If you are going to reset the grawity for Black Ire," Chekov said, "why not reset the lighting as well?"

"What weaklings you are," Krulmadden jeered. "But it is the least I can do for fearsome pirate guest to be." He rubbed a thick finger against a part of his chair where there were no apparent control surfaces and the bridge lighting dimmed to a more tolerable level. *Tolerable like high noon on Mercury,* Chekov thought. But at least his eyes had stopped hurting. He decided Krulmadden's unmarked chair control surfaces were the strongest proof of his paranoia yet. Even if someone managed to steal this ship from him, it would take days to learn how to run it. Though he guessed the two mates could be convinced to give up her secrets if the price were right.

"What's that supposed to be?" Sulu suddenly asked. "A gunnery target?" He sounded as if he were ready to laugh.

Chekov looked at the screen and saw a vessel that was even more improbable than the *Queen Mary.* The main hull appeared to be a leftover from the days of the old DY-500s when surplus submarine shells were reconfigured to transport cryogenic cargo through vacuum. And the warp pod slung on the back of the hull looked as if it were nothing more than a half-hearted attempt to disguise a twenty-year-old Mark II shuttle.

"That is supposed to be the ship of a fearsome pirate?" Chekov asked. He and Sulu looked at each other and smirked.

"It is good disguise," Krulmadden protested. "Who suspects that Black Ire hunts the spaceways in rundown cargo ship not worth fifty credits to spit for? But little *tislins* . . . see why Black Ire so clever." He palmed another unmarked surface on his chair and a tactical display sprang up in a corner of the viewscreen. "Lasslanlin! Full scan on *Heart of the Storm!*"

Chekov watched as the Orion mate engaged the *Queen Mary's* sensors from his station. Then he waited for the results to appear on tactical. But there were no results.

"Good stuff, yes, no?" Krulmadden said approvingly. "Full sensor block. Starfleet deflectors. Very expensive. Could hide anything." He turned back to Chekov and Sulu. "The stories Krulmadden hears say *Heart of the Storm* is delusion like *Queen Mary's* impulse pod."

"Illusion," Sulu corrected.

"Whatever. Antique outside over Starfleet prototypes inside." He widened his eyes as if they were about to burst from his head. "Warp nine Krulmadden hears, with tractor beams that reach two lightseconds, and cargo transporters that—"

A tactical alert sounded and Krulmadden popped his mouth closed and spun back to the screen. The *Queen Mary's* shuttle came into view, sliding up close to the *Heart of the Storm.*

So that's where Artinton is, Chekov thought. *But why send a shuttle over when the pirates could be beamed aboard?*

"Warp nine?" Sulu said to Chekov. "In that crate? He's got to be kidding."

"Message arriving," Lasslanlin announced. The image on the viewscreen rolled over once and a new transmission appeared —Black Ire.

"Greetings, oh noble scourge of death and construction!" Krulmadden gushed.

"Destruction," Sulu said under his breath.

"Withdraw your shuttle at once or it will be destroyed." On the viewscreen, Black Ire looked vaguely humanoid, but through the odd twists and folds of his costume, Chekov couldn't be certain. The warbling computer distortion from the translator mask he wore—a small silver cup which covered his nose and mouth—also made it hard to tell what race he was. But the pirate was a he, Chekov decided. Thick tufts of black and white hair sprayed out from around the translator. The rest of the pirate's face and head was hidden beneath a spaceblack battle helmet and featureless radiation goggles. Klingon, Chekov decided. With a ship named *Heart of the Storm,* Black Ire had to be a Klingon.

"I send transportation to you my guest," Krulmadden said, spreading his hands in an ingratiating gesture of friendship.

"Black Ire does not travel in filthy shuttles like cargo," the pirate growled. "My mate and I must be beamed aboard your ship."

Definitely a Klingon, Chekov thought.

"But noxious one," Krulmadden said as Sulu groaned at the shipmaster's misuse of the language, "my transporter is onboard my shuttle and has, I feel such shame to say, a limited range because of the great cost of the equipment. Unless you drop all your shields completely, I cannot beam you from there to here."

Chekov finally realized what the extra equipment at the back of the *Queen Mary's* shuttle had been. Krulmadden had obviously wanted a getaway vehicle with transporter capability but hadn't wanted to spend the credits for two transporters so he could have one in his ship as well.

"Black Ire is not fool enough to drop all shields for *Ur'eon* scum!" The pirate looked off to the sides. "Crew! Arm phasers! Lock on to that scow's bridge!"

Krulmadden cringed and held up his hands. "No, no, do not. Use your own transporters. Your own shuttle. Swim aboard if you wish."

Black Ire settled back on whatever he sat in and for a moment Chekov saw another figure in the background—a veiled female draped in a floor-length vest and tunic of shimmering red. She moved quickly out of range of the visual sensor.

"So," Black Ire said, "you invite us to beam aboard ourselves. Does that mean that Krulmadden would drop his own shields to us?"

Lasslanlin turned around in his chair and gestured to his board. Krulmadden ignored him.

"Alas," the shipmaster said, "but our screens have a slight malfunction and I regret to say we are unable to turn them off."

Chekov wondered how criminals could ever trust each other long enough to stay in business. If it was this difficult just to arrange a meeting between the two pirates, how long was it going to take to work out a way to transfer the Orion females to the *Heart of the Storm* once a deal had been struck? He wished he and Sulu had had another chance to talk privately so they could have worked out some way to free Krulmadden's captives. But at least they had the satisfaction of knowing they had enough information about the shipmaster's operations to set the Federation authorities onto him as soon as they got the chance.

"Shipmaster Krulmadden," Black Ire spat out, "you know

who I am, do you not? You have heard the word about me spread through space, have you not?"

"Who has not heard of the dread Black Ire, oh dread Black Ire?" Krulmadden shook his fist at Lasslanlin who kept trying to attract his attention.

Black Ire leaned closer, filling the screen. "Therefore, you know what will happen if you betray my trust in you?"

"I cannot know, for my life would not be worth living if such a thing I ever did, oh no."

Black Ire stood and placed his blackgloved hands on his wide black belt. A black cape fell from his shoulders. *Odd,* Chekov thought, *that looks just like the one I bought in the souvenir store on Rigel VIII before I met Sulu in the bar.*

"Very well, *Ur'eon* dog. You may beam my mate and me to your shuttle and from there to your ship. But if anything should go wrong, my officers will lock tractor beams onto you and drag you into the nearest star! Now lock onto these coordinates exactly so you can beam us through the opening we shall make in our shields." He punched something in on a console out of view. A blue light lit up on Lasslanlin's board.

"We receive your coordinates, Black Ire. My shuttle pilot will beam you now."

Black Ire's image winked out and was replaced by the outer sensor view of the shuttle by the *Heart of the Storm.*

Lasslanlin almost shrieked the instant the transmission was cut. "Shipmaster! Shipmaster!"

"What is it, loathsome sore?"

"When Black Ire called for phasers armed, nothing happened," Lasslanlin said. "There should have been carrier leakage through shields so his weapons officer could lock on *Queen Mary*—but was nothing."

Krulmadden rubbed at his green fleshy face with jeweled fingers. "But why would he bluff? It costs next to nothing to power up phasers for such a simple threat."

Lasslanlin looked once at Sulu and Chekov, then dropped his voice to a whisper. "But what if he has none?"

288

"What?"

Lasslanlin looked to be in pain. "What if only has a sensor block? No weapons, no shields, no cargo hold full of unsynthesized metals?"

"No cargo . . . ?" Krulmadden was clearly upset by the concept. "Then how could he pay for the greenskins?"

"Perhaps not wish to pay, Shipmaster."

Krulmadden leapt from his chair and under the lighter gravity traveled a meter higher than he had intended, though he still managed to land gracefully.

"He is a pirate!" the shipmaster said. "Why should he lie to us! All of space knows of Black Ire!"

Chekov cleared his throat. "For what it's worth, Shipmaster. I have not heard of Black Ire."

"Neither have I," Sulu added. "And the *Enterprise* was always receiving updates on pirate and smuggling operations."

Krulmadden silently picked at the emerald in his teeth. He turned to Lasslanlin. "Little snail thing, have you heard all your life of the great and terrible stories of the lonesome pirate, Black Ire?"

"That's loathsome," Sulu said.

Lasslanlin shook his head, jingling his metal earrings. "Only in past few tendays, Shipmaster. Many, many subspace transmissions."

Krulmadden pulled something stringy out from between his teeth, looked at it, then sucked it back into his mouth. "Which shows what a good pirate he must be if he has hidden his crimes so well."

Chekov figured that when Krulmadden lifted off from a planet in his shuttle, he'd be lucky to know which way was up.

Then Krulmadden boasted with pride. "Good thing this fine shipmaster has hidden a few crimes of his own!"

Lasslanlin looked more confused by his cousin than usual. On the screen, the shuttle turned smoothly, then sped for the *Queen Mary*. Artinton's voice came over the commlink.

"Guests on board, Shipmaster. Coming alongside."

"Beam them to our bridge!" Krulmadden said. "We have no secrets from Black Ire and his mate! And take care to miss nothing when you energize."

"That's the first time I've ever heard anyone around here worry about taking care of anything," Sulu said.

Chekov shrugged. He had given up trying to understand Krulmadden or any of the Orions. He found himself hoping that Black Ire would start a fight when he came onboard. At least a Klingon could be reasoned with. After a fashion. Compared with Orions.

A transporter chime started and Chekov saw the swirling eddy of materialization form in front of the helm and navigation console. As Krulmadden and Lasslanlin concentrated on the slowly forming shapes of two humanoids, Chekov moved closer to Sulu.

"We should be ready to take adwantage of whatever might happen," he whispered.

Before Sulu could reply, Chekov had left the elevated ramp and gone to stand near Krulmadden's chair.

As Black Ire solidified, Chekov saw that when the pirate had referred to his mate, he hadn't been talking about one of his officers. The second figure who beamed in with him was the woman in shimmering red. Though her face was still veiled, Chekov was struck by her startlingly blue eyes which shone out from her rich black skin. He was also struck by the way in which she stared at him.

Black Ire stepped forward and placed his hands on Lasslanlin's console. "So, Krulmadden, we meet—"

The distorted speech of his translator mask was interrupted by a second transporter chime. Chekov looked down at the deck as a small pile of objects appeared at Krulmadden's feet. Black Ire and the woman suddenly looked nervous and began patting themselves under their arms and on their backs as if they had just realized they had lost something.

The shipmaster turned to Chekov and gestured for him to pick the objects up. Obviously, he could not bend that low himself.

Chekov carefully lifted what had materialized. The temptation to try something was strong. He held four phaser mark ones, two stun wands, and an area disruptor. They all looked used, rebuilt, or surplus.

Krulmadden studied the weapons for a moment, then shook his head. He took them from Chekov and dumped all except a phaser one in his chair. Then he smiled at Black Ire and his mate.

"You try to bring weapons on board this jewel of peace. Krulmadden cries tears of loss and sorrow for the honor that has died today, oh yes."

Black Ire drew himself to his full height and held the back of his glove to his translator mask. "*Heart of the Storm,*" he barked, "lock phasers on this scow's engines."

Krulmadden glanced sadly at Lasslanlin. "Mate Lasslanlin, lock disruptor cannon on *Heart of the Storm.*"

The pirates glared at each other. Chekov was fascinated. Whatever happened next, things could not be worse than they were. Unless, of course, the *Heart of the Storm* opened fire on her own commander. And if they were Klingons, that was a distinct possibility.

"Shall we play this game, Black Ire, whom no one has heard of?"

"I play no game with garbage," the pirate scoffed.

Krulmadden brought his hands together and tapped his fingertips against the small phaser he held. "You are right, fearsome one. Krulmadden shall not play this game either." He shrugged and smiled.

Black Ire seemed relieved. He began to lower his glove.

"Mate Lasslanlin, destroy our guests' ship."

Before Krulmadden had even finished giving the order a glowing blue lance of disruptive energy flashed on the screen and the *Heart of the Storm* dissolved into a handful of spinning hull sections and a cloud of sparkling energy.

Black Ire and his mate wheeled to see the destruction of their ship on the screen. The woman put her hand to her mouth.

"No bodies," Lasslanlin said. "No crew."

"Mate Artinton," Krulmadden said, "stand off until I give you order to dock. Our guests have decided to stay and share hospitality with us. But might decide to be beamed back to what's left of their ship anytime I say." He made a shallow bow to Black Ire and the woman. "How kind of you to accept shipmaster's even kinder invitation."

Chekov applauded and Krulmadden jumped back as if he had expected an attack. "You are a fine shipmaster," Chekov said.

"You are pitiful liar," Krulmadden snorted. "You wanted Black Ire to be bad to your shipmaster and feed Krulmadden to recyclers so you and other mammal could sell the greenskins for yourself."

Chekov gave the shipmaster his most winning smile. "Is that not what you would have us do? You are a fine shipmaster and a fine teacher. Sulu and I have learned much from you." He made a bow as Krulmadden had done.

Krulmadden frowned theatrically. "Very well, I give you three percent of the Talin fissionables for being such toads. Now go get manacles for ex-pirate and mate."

"There is a better way to keep them captive," Chekov said slyly.

Krulmadden waited.

"The way you kept us captives!" Chekov explained. "The grawity field!" On the other side of Krulmadden, Chekov could see a look of sudden horror pass through Sulu's eyes.

Krulmadden shook a finger at Chekov. "You are a clever little mammal. The *f'deraxt'l* and *stator*fleet have not ruined you completely. Even if you do not like the company of greenskins, which puzzles me in great amounts." He went back to his chair and brushed his hand against a section of the inner arm. Chekov kept his eyes level with Krulmadden's, but concentrated on remembering exactly which part of the chair arm the shipmaster stroked to adjust the field. As the local gravity constant on the bridge began to climb, Chekov knew that at least the first part of his plan was going to work. Now the question was whether or not he could continue to function.

Krulmadden bounced from foot to foot. "Ah, feels good like home." He rumbled with laughter. "Let us make it feel *twice* as good!"

Chekov braced himself for four times Earth gravity. He felt the field climb higher. His shoulders sagged in on his chest as the weight of his arms increased. He had to struggle for each breath.

There was a thud from the front of the bridge and Chekov slowly turned his eyes to see that Black Ire had collapsed to his knees. His hands pressed against the floor and his arms trembled with the effort to support himself. Then the woman collapsed beside him.

"Ha ha! Is good is good!" Krulmadden sang.

Chekov staggered to Krulmadden's chair and leaned against it. He saw Sulu step back to hang on to the railing behind him. He felt his knees creak.

"Exercise!" Krulmadden laughed. "Good *Ur'eon* exercise for my little mammals. I go see what kind of weakling Black Ire is now." He bared his jeweled teeth at Chekov. "You do not go anywhere."

Chekov forced a smile past his sagging cheeks. He was beginning to see black sparkles in his vision as his heart could no longer keep blood flowing to his brain. *Now or never,* he thought, then leaned over the arm of Krulmadden's chair and reached for the hidden control surface.

But when he bent over he no longer had the strength to keep his back extended and he crumpled over the side of the chair, losing his breath with the sudden impact. The weapons on the chair seat pressed in on his face. He tasted blood and his heartbeat thundered in his ear.

Chekov blindly reached for the gravity control. He touched the smooth metal of the chair arm. Suddenly the bridge lights flared back to Rigel normal. Wrong control. He heard Krulmadden's grunt of surprise.

Desperately, Chekov slid his fingers over the chair arm. *It has to be here,* he thought. *I saw Krulmadden do it just like this.* He felt a slight impression in the smooth metal and stroked his finger against it. He heard a violent explosion of breath and realized it was his own. He had sent the gravity setting the wrong way and now his fingers were too heavy to lift.

The pressure of the chair arm in his stomach was overpowering. He could no longer take a breath. The bridge seemed to start spinning around him as his inner ears began to collapse. He heard Sulu calling out his name.

Then Krulmadden's black-maned head appeared above the level of his seat. The strength of the gravity field was so strong that even the powerful Orion had to crawl. But he could crawl. And from the look in his eyes he was also going to be able to kill.

"Bad little mammal," the shipmaster grunted. His thick lower lip hung down as if invisible threads pulled on it. "I crush you into spread for biscuits."

Chekov closed his eyes. He had no time nor strength for one last breath. *For Captain Kirk,* he thought, then put the last Wortham unit of energy he had into one final stab of his fingers.

He touched the metal of the arm. He felt Krulmadden's hot breath on his face. He stroked the metal away from him and—
—free fall.

Krulmadden whooped like a child on a roller whip and flew away from the chair, the phaser slipping from his hand. Chekov had known what was coming—had hoped for what was coming —and held on to the chair arms. With the pressure gone from his chest and stomach, he drew in a huge breath. His ears still rang and the bridge still spun but he could see once more.

Chekov looked over to Sulu. His friend had locked his arms around the bridge railing and was holding himself in place as if he were blowing in a gale force wind.

"Look out!" Sulu shouted. "Above you!"

Chekov twisted his head around in time to see Krulmadden swooping down from the ceiling of the bridge. Chekov ran his finger back along the gravity control and Krulmadden's trajectory changed as a triple field came back on.

"Again!" Sulu shouted.

Chekov got the hang of it. By flipping the gravity on and off, he bounced Krulmadden across the deck until the Orion's eyes crossed and he simply flopped from one field setting to the next. Then Chekov set the field for Earth normal, grabbed one of the phasers he had kept in place beneath him, and stood up. For a moment he wavered back and forth, still feeling the bridge move beneath him, but it was only a sense memory because Krulmadden, unconscious, didn't budge from his place on the floor.

There was a moan from the center of the bridge as Lasslanlin unsteadily tried to crawl out from beneath the helm console where he had tried to escape the wild gravity fluctuations. Chekov braced himself against the center chair and checked to make sure his small phaser was set to light stun. But even as he aimed the phaser at the Orion mate, Lasslanlin's eyelids fluttered and he fell over, out cold.

Sulu walked stiffly to Chekov's side. "Good work, Chekov. I only have one question."

"What's that?"

"Did you have the slightest idea of what you were doing?"

Chekov tried his best to look indignant. "Of course, I had it planned wery carefully all along."

"Sure you did," Sulu said, but patted Chekov's shoulder in congratulations anyway.

Then Krulmadden moaned and both men turned to him.

For a second, Chekov almost forgot where he was. Black Ire and his mate were standing by Krulmadden's vast body. They looked familiar somehow. But the woman was doing something completely unfamiliar with her eyes. She was picking at them. Then Chekov saw why. She held two blue lenses in her hands.

"Don't you think you should do something for him?" the woman asked Black Ire.

Chekov's mouth fell open. He knew that voice.

"I don't see why," Black Ire said as he reached up to unhook his translator mask and goggles. "I'm a pirate, not a doctor."

"Dr. McCoy?" Chekov stammered.

"Uhura?" Sulu gasped.

Uhura tossed her contact lenses aside and pulled off her veil. McCoy yanked his battle helmet off and left his hair in wild disarray.

"I hope you two know how to fly this blasted thing," McCoy said. "Because this big oaf just blew up my retirement savings."

"You *paid* for that hulk?" Sulu asked in disbelief.

"Do you have any idea how much it cost to buy a used spaceship and send out hours of subspace messages to build the legend of Black Ire?"

Chekov and Uhura caught each other's eye and began to snicker as Sulu and McCoy traded complaints.

"What's so damn funny, Ensign?"

"Why, nothing, Dr. McCoy," Chekov said. "I was just thinking how wery glad I was to see you, too."

For once, the bridge of the *Queen Mary* rang with the sound of *human* laughter.

SEVEN

Thunderous applause reverberated in the hallway outside the Federation General Council chamber. The large, white marble-tiled hallway itself was almost deserted, making the noise that filtered out through the double-height wooden doors oddly out of place.

Sitting motionless on a padded bench beside the speakers' entrance to the chamber, Spock waited patiently. He judged that the ovation had greeted the announcement by the delegate from the Antares Corona Worlds that her system would be supporting the new agricultural trade proposals tabled by the Federation Resource Management Board. The Antares commitment had been seen as necessary to prevent a recurrence of the bottleneck transport problems that had contributed to the near-famine on Sherman's Planet. Once again the worlds of the Federation had become a bit closer knit, and once again the Federation had become stronger.

Spock reviewed the agenda he had memorized when it had been posted that morning. After the Antares declaration, the delegate from the Centaurus Concordium was scheduled to move that the Council issue its congratulations to Hudson's World on the occasion of its fiftieth year of independence. That motion would be followed by a unanimous voice vote, and then the meeting would be thrown open to civilian petitions, as authorized by their respective official representatives. Spock had been the third speaker set for the day, though he had since learned that the two speakers who were to have preceded him had now withdrawn. He estimated that four minutes and thirty seconds remained before he would be requested to enter the chamber. He trusted Dr. Richter was capable of performing the same calculation.

Penn Grossman walked over to Spock. His new shoes squeaked on the marble floor and he wore his dress tunic uncomfortably, ruining its line by jamming his hands in its pockets.

"Face it, Mr. Spock," the student said, "he's not going to show."

"Yes, he will," Marita answered before Spock could speak. She scrunched up her face and held her baby close to her. "Won't he, Alexander? Won't he?" The baby gurgled and clapped his hands. "See? Alexander knows Dr. Richter won't let us down."

Penn took a few steps away, then turned and came back. He rubbed nervously at his short dark hair as if trying to stay awake. "How can you sit there like that, Marita? Can't you see we've been tricked?"

Spock said nothing. He had tried explaining what he had done three times already. It wasn't that Penn was not intelligent, it was that he was stubborn—one human attribute with which Spock had dealt many times, thanks to the able help of Dr. McCoy.

"Mr. Spock had his reasons for doing this, Penn. I'm not mad at him."

"But you're missing out on your one chance to talk to the Federation Council! Do you know how many billion beings are going to be watching the update tapes of this meeting?" Penn wiped his sweaty hands on the back of his tunic.

"And they're going to listen to Dr. Richter a lot more carefully than they would to me," Marita said.

Spock was impressed with the young woman's powers of comprehension. When he had broached the possibility that Dr. Richter replace Marita as Spock's associate-to-be-named, she, not Penn, had immediately understood that that had been Spock's intention from the beginning.

"That's why you took me to the Vulcan Embassy, isn't it?" she had said after the first meeting with Richter. "You knew that Ambassador Sytok would warn you not to put my name on the credentials, and that was supposed to make me understand why my name shouldn't be listed. But what you really wanted to do all along was have an open accreditation form so that *Dr. Richter* could go before the Council as your associate. And his name couldn't go on the credentials because he's under Starfleet authority, and they could have prevented him from speaking if anyone had suspected that that was what he was going to do. Damn sneaky, Spock. And very logical."

Spock had politely accepted her compliment without correcting her assumptions.

But Penn wasn't supporting Marita's acceptance of the changed situation. "Look, I don't care how buddy-buddy you want to get with this alien, but the fact is that Mr. Spock the Vulcan *lied* to you. He used the SSP as a way to gain support for this appearance. And he planned to cut us all out from the start."

"He didn't lie, Penn. He just didn't tell the whole truth."

"Big difference!"

Marita jiggled Alexander on her knee. "Mr. Spock, when you go in to address the Council, are you going to speak against the Prime Directive?"

"Yes," Spock said.

"Truthfully?" Penn asked.

"Penn, I regret to say that you have learned nothing about logic in the time you have spent with me. However, to answer your question in the spirit in which it was asked, yes, truthfully, I will speak against the Prime Directive."

The hallway echoed with the sound of the Council delivering

a unanimous voice vote. Spock calculated that now only one minute, ten seconds remained.

Marita continued. "And Dr. Richter, when he goes in there, will he also speak against the Prime Directive?"

"I do not expect Dr. Richter to say much to the Council, but his presence with me will lend great support to what I have to say."

Marita looked reprovingly at Penn. "There. It shouldn't matter who does the job, as long as it gets done. Your problem, Penn Grossman, is that you're jealous."

Penn put his hand to his forehead and stared wildly around the hall as if he had just been accused of being a Romulan spy. "I am not! Why does everyone keep saying that?"

Because it is true, Spock thought, and once again he was grateful that the students' emotional turmoil had kept them from continuing their questioning of him in detail.

Spock stood up moments before the door of the speakers' entrance swung open and a Council page appeared, dressed in a traditional gray suit and white scarf. Spock handed the page the microtape of his embassy forms.

"Please note that this form is open, giving me the right to have associates accompany me."

The page slipped the tape into the reader and read through the forms, though obviously she had been briefed on what to expect. "Are these two with you?" she asked.

"Yes," Spock said. "They will not be addressing the Council with me, but by rights they are allowed to enter the meeting with me."

"How about the baby?" the page asked dubiously.

"Well, I'm certainly not leaving him out here," Marita said.

"As you wish," the page said. She flipped up the large brass wreath which was the doorpull and a hidden mechanism smoothly swung the door open again. The sound of a hundred whispered voices came out in a wall of soft noise.

"One last thing," Spock said, just before entering. "Some members of my party have been delayed. Please let them in when they arrive."

The page glanced down at her reader again and nodded. "Sure," she said. "How many?"

"Five," Spock said. He entered the chamber.

In actual voting delegates, the membership of the Federation Council numbered in the thousands. Every world, every colony dome, every LaGrange outpost, every species on shared worlds, all were entitled to representation and the Federation took heroic measures to see that as many who wanted to take part could take part. But to streamline the running of the day-to-day affairs of the Federation, the Council split itself up into hundreds of specialist committees organized along regional lines and common concerns. Full gatherings of the complete membership occurred only rarely.

In matters of more pressing importance, it was necessary for a governing body to be able to meet quickly and efficiently, and that was the purpose of the General Council. Each block of members from local regions—usually at the united system level—selected one delegate to represent them. There were fewer than two hundred and fifty of them—more than half nonhuman, but they were the power brokers of the most successful interstellar union known in the history of a thousand worlds, and it was they whom Spock prepared to address.

The meeting chamber for so impressive a body was a simple affair, two facing tiers of benches, a communications wall, a guest area in which Spock saw Ambassador Sytok standing, and a speakers' area where those who were not members of the Council—or even of the Federation—were able to make an address.

Spock waited in that last area as the Speaker of the Council read Spock's consular civilian credentials to Sukio Hirashito, this session's Council President. Marita, carrying Alexander, and Penn, hands still jammed in his pockets, waited a few meters away, closer to the speakers' door.

The Speaker, a tall Maori wearing a traditional black parliamentary robe, returned to Spock and handed him back his papers. Then he turned to face the Council members.

"The Council recognizes Spock, citizen of Vulcan, citizen of the United Federation of Planets. Bear witness, all who are in attendance." The Speaker turned back to Spock as the subtle drone of a hundred universal translators hummed alien versions of what had been said. "Come forward, Spock. The Council waits on you."

Spock went forward, knowing that each member who sat before him already knew what he was going to say, and knowing that each of them was wrong. He began his address to the Council.

"Madame President, Mr. Speaker, distinguished members of the General Council, I come before you today to inform you of a grievous wrong which has been perpetrated on the United Federation of Planets, and by the United Federation of Planets, and which demands immediate and compassionate resolution for the sake of peace."

Startled, some Council members leaned close together and spoke among themselves. This was not starting out as they had expected—with a plea to repeal the Prime Directive. By stating that he was informing them of a wrong committed against the Federation and by the Federation, Spock had spoken the formal words generally used to give warning of a real or threatened internal treaty violation. And there had not been a serious internal treaty violation within the Federation for decades.

The Speaker of the Council walked up to Spock, sensor microphones in the ceiling swiveling to capture his voice and amplify it through the chamber.

"Spock, you were to talk about the Prime Directive."

"I am aware of no topic being entered on my credentials," Spock said. "I have the floor."

The Speaker glanced back at the President, who nodded once.

"Spock, according to the words you have used, it appears that you intend to talk to the Council about matters of treaty. That is a legal matter."

"I am quite aware of that, Mr. Speaker."

"But this is a citizen's forum intended for the debate of

general concerns. If you wish to use it as a legal forum, I must ask you to state your legal grounds or give up the floor."

Good, Spock thought. He would not have been able to introduce his next topic without that question being asked. But now the way was open.

"Mr. Speaker," Spock announced so all could hear, sensor pickups or not, "I invoke as my legal grounds the Fundamental Declarations of the Martian Colonies."

Not a member of the Council was silent. Two Tellarites jumped to their feet. The Speaker had to call to order twice to quiet the members. No one had any idea what would happen now, and that made the power brokers uneasy.

"Mr. Speaker," Spock said, "I believe I still have the floor." The Speaker retreated, walking away with head bowed.

"A founding precept of this Federation is that different cultures be allowed to progress in their own time, according to their own needs and desires. Indeed, the Prime Directive is a direct extension of this principle." There was a strong murmur of satisfaction that at last Spock had mentioned what all had assumed would be his main topic.

"However, by accepting this principle of self-determination, the entrenchment of specific inequities is inevitable. That is, those cultures that achieve a certain level of technological achievement before another can claim an unfair share of natural resources." More murmurs, this time, of confusion. Was this a talk about treaties or the Prime Directive?

"This conflict was first addressed in the Fundamental Declarations of the Martian Colonies, in which the signatory bodies agreed that, in recognition of the Colonies' inability to field a full mining force, certain sections of the asteroid belt would be set aside in trust for future exploitation by Mars as their technological capability progressed and their cultural needs developed.

"This first, interplanetary recognition of the importance of resource allocation over time, has since gone on to become entrenched in all facets of Federation law. I point out to you that there is not a member of the Federation who does not have set aside by treaty, in trust, natural resources for future exploitation. In fact, such trust allocations of natural resources are automatic upon being admitted to the Federation, and are a right of every new member."

A Tellarite held two hooves to his mouth and bellowed, "Get on with it!"

"This right, originally meant to confer mining claims, has since grown to include the right of colonization. It is recognized that worlds at an early stage of space exploration cannot afford the cost of colonizing nearby systems. However, if they delay, there is the danger that other worlds might expand around them and cut off all possible colonization possibilities. Therefore, the Federation routinely allocates colony worlds within its own boundaries for the future exclusive use of those worlds not yet ready to undertake colonization."

A page handed the Speaker a note. The Speaker read it, nodded again at the President, then approached Spock once more.

"Spock, it has been brought to the Council's attention that you are expecting others to join you in your address and that those others have not yet arrived. Therefore, the Council suspects that this disjointed history lesson which you are presenting to us is nothing more than an attempt to make the Council wait for the arrival of your missing associates. I point out to you, Spock, that if that is your intention, then you can be held in contempt of this body and asked to leave."

Spock had anticipated that this interruption would have occurred two minutes earlier. Perhaps he had caught their interest.

"Mr. Speaker, each point I have raised is a necessary step in the presentation of an important matter to the Council. I ask for five more minutes of your time to prove that this is so."

The Speaker sought clues to any future disturbance in Spock's face but apparently found none. "Very well, five minutes. No more."

Spock calculated it would take three.

"In the case of the planet, Talin IV—"

The Council chamber erupted. They had been waiting for this.

"Murderer!"

"Worldkiller!"

Other insults and curses were shouted in a variety of languages. Spock tried several times to resume speaking, but the clamor of the Council members drowned him out each time. It took the Speaker most of those five promised minutes to quiet the Council to the point where Spock could continue. The response had been far stronger than Spock had anticipated. He hurriedly made cuts in the rest of what he had to say so the timing he had worked out would still hold.

"In the matter of Talin IV, a planet which is home to a species which the Federation had predicted would be ready to attempt an interstellar colonization program within the next fifty to one hundred standard years, fully forty-eight planets within a twenty-five parsec sphere have been set aside, in trust, for their future use." He paused, but his unruly audience had already been chastised by the Speaker. The members remained silent and hostile.

"Recognizing this existing, formal arrangement on behalf of the planet of Talin IV—a planet that has recently experienced a terrible disaster—I charge the Federation to provide immediate emergency relief and long-term aid in order to help this world and its people to full recovery."

After a second explosion of clamorous protest, the President of the Federation at last stood to take part. She took a small pair of antique wire-framed glasses from a case on her desk and slipped them on as she waited for the Speaker to once again bring order to the chamber.

"Mr. Spock," she began in a voice of quiet authority. "The planet, Talin IV, is under the protection of the Prime Directive. No aid can possibly be sent to it. I am surprised by your actions. The son of Sarek should know better."

Spock stepped forward into the center of the chamber. "Madame President, with respect, I submit that the Prime Directive does not apply to Talin IV."

The President adjusted her glasses. "Spock, this act of desperation does not become you, nor does it bring honor to your world. The Prime Directive holds with all worlds which are not part of the Federation."

Spock moved closer. "Madame President, with respect, I submit that Talin IV is *already* a member of the Federation."

President Hirashito lost her composure as she gaped at Spock. "On what grounds do you make this claim?" The Speaker could no longer restrain the other members. Dozens of them began to shout similar questions to Spock.

Spock raised his voice above the din. "I submit that by virtue of the planet Talin IV having assigned to it forty-eight planets held in trust for future exploitation, that it shares in the rights and privileges of being a member of the Federation and therefore *is* a member of the Federation. *To which the Prime Directive does not apply.*"

Despite the best efforts of the Speaker and the President, the Council members did not subside until Ambassador Sytok walked out to face Spock in the center of the chamber. This time he was wearing his official garments, and the gems of his achievements gleamed in rich and colorful panels on both sides of his robe.

"Madame President, Mr. Speaker," Sytok said, raising his hand to each of them in turn. "I claim the right to speak with Spock, citizen of Vulcan, whom I charge with abusing his rights and obtaining credentials under false pretenses."

Spock ignored the Vulcan ambassador. "With respect, Madame President, the Council has not authorized my request that immediate aid be sent to Talin."

"Mr. Spock!" The Council hushed instantly at the shocking sight and sound of a Vulcan who had raised his voice in apparent anger. Sytok looked around, realizing what he had done, then composed himself. "Madame President, please allow me to address Spock's request."

"Please do," Hirashito said. She sat back down.

"Mr. Spock," Sytok began again more calmly. "I will admit that there is some logic in your request. A case can be made for claiming that Talin IV is a *de facto* member of the Federation by virtue of its property held in trust."

"Thank you," Spock said. By his admission, though he was not yet aware of it, Sytok had just guaranteed that Talin would be helped.

"However," Sytok continued sagely, "beyond that facile argument, your logic has faltered badly."

"I look forward to your correction," Spock said, adopting the words of a student to his teacher.

Sytok made his pronouncement. "You are not properly accredited to this Council to request aid for a member world, Spock." The Vulcan ambassador swung his arm around the Council chamber to include every member. "If Talin is a member and requires aid, then where are its duly appointed representatives—or its ambassadors—to make such a request of us?"

"Is that all that stands in the way of aid being sent to Talin? A formal request?"

Sytok gripped the collar of his robe in his hand. "It is enough." He turned his back to Spock and began to walk from the center of the chamber.

Spock looked back to the waiting area by the speakers' entrance door. Marita and Penn stood there with accusing looks of betrayal in their eyes. Spock had spoken against the Prime Directive as he had said he would, but only in relation to a single planet. Spock looked at Marita, knowing that if anyone in her organization would understand his intentions, she would. He motioned to her to open the door.

He saw her nod as she adjusted Alexander against her shoulder and stepped over to pull on the bronze wreath. The massive door opened slowly and Spock saw the last pieces of his presentation waiting behind it—all five of them.

"Ambassador Sytok!" Spock called out.

Sytok halted and looked over his shoulder. Then he turned

slowly and fully around. The sound growing among the Council members mirrored the ambassador's most un-Vulcan look of surprise.

Spock turned to the rest of his associates. First, Dr. Richter walked into the chamber, cane clicking on the hard marble. Then came Carole Mallett and Mario Cardinali of the FCO, both gently guiding two tall figures in sweeping gray robes which swayed with the graceful rhythms of a powerful gait.

"I present to this Council," Spock proclaimed, "their excellencies—Seerl ti'La and Orr ni'Li—"

All the Council members rose, speaking in all the languages of the Federation at once.

Spock continued, knowing that at least the automatic recorders would hear what he said for future playback. "—joint representatives of the two nation states of Talin IV known as Green and Brown—"

Mallett and Cardinali stopped when they reached Spock. Powerful, pebble-skinned arms burst out from the guests' robes to flip back their hoods.

Seerl ti'La's cranial crest bristled crazily as he flushed deep scarlet and stared at the extraordinary gathering of alien creatures who surrounded him. Beside him, flushing to a deep turquoise hue, Orr ni'Li blinked her large yellow eyes. Both creatures' heads turned back and forth with quick birdlike movements. Mallett and Cardinali kept their hands on their guests' arms, constantly speaking assurances to them.

"I charge you with kidnapping these creatures!" Sytok accused. *"Shame and dishonor!"*

The Talin linked arms, seeking protection in each other from the threatening confusion of the Council's upheaval. Spock saw the small silver speakers of miniature translators attached to their hearing membranes. He wondered how much of what was being shouted the machine would be able to translate for them. But at least from their meetings with him, the Talin knew what he was going to say.

"—who left their planet by their *own choice* and in a space vessel of their nations' design," Spock continued, countering

Sytok's charges. He raised his consular documents above his head. "To become, by the authority of these open credentials, provided by the Vulcan Embassy, the duly appointed ambassadors *to* the Federation *from* the member world of Talin. And who now respectfully ask this Council for aid to rebuild their world.

"As is their right."

EIGHT

☆

The *Ian Shelton* traveled at sixty-four times the speed of light, but to James Kirk it still wasn't fast enough. He sat at the ship's navigation console as if by pushing on it he could coax a few more kilometers per second out of her. *Three more days to get there,* he thought. He was used to ships that traveled a lot faster.

Kirk heard an avalanche of small feet behind him and braced himself for the assault he knew would follow. Nogura was the first to jump up on him. Fitzpatrick and Komack took second and third place by rubbing around his legs.

"Ah," Gauvreau said as she followed her cats onto the bridge, "the captain and his loyal crew."

Kirk edged Nogura off his lap with a helpful shove and kept the other two at bay by moving in closer to the console. He had been in a similar situation before on the bridge of the *Enterprise*, but at least tribbles couldn't jump.

Gauvreau stood at his side. "So what did you want me to look at?" she asked.

Kirk pointed to a nonstandard sensor display in the upper left-hand corner of the control board. It wasn't included in the online manuals and he hadn't been able to determine which system drove it. Up to five minutes ago, he hadn't been concerned about not knowing what it was because it consistently had shown a flat reading. But now it was displaying peak numbers.

"Whatever this is set to look for," Kirk said, "it seems to have found some."

Gauvreau looked pleased. "Welcome to the mercenary world of the freighter captain. That's my salvage scanner. It's always sweeping for lost ships, old probes, that sort of thing."

Kirk thought such a scanner might make sense farther in toward the center of Federation space. But, out in this sector, there had yet to be enough traffic for there to have been many lost ships. Besides, most of the ships passing through this region followed established trade routes such as the one the *Shelton* traveled now.

"What have you found with it?" Kirk asked. "I mean, all the way out here?"

"You'd be surprised," Gauvreau said, adjusting the salvage scanner's sweep to a finer focus. "I'm always coming across some of the old impulse-powered probes from Earth, you know, the Voyagers, the Nomads, that stuff. Remember that after four or five years of full impulse at point nine nine cee, those suckers had a fifty-fifty chance of tunneling into warp space. That's why they lost so many of them, and that's why they're still turning up thousands of lightyears away from Earth." She stabbed her finger at a locking button. "So far I've sold three to the Smithsonian."

Kirk watched the display home in on whatever the scanner had detected. "Is that another?" he asked. The scanner's readings were cruder and less sensitive than the sensors he was used to from the *Enterprise*. As far as he could tell, it might be picking up anything from an antique probe to a rogue planet.

"Too soon to tell," Gauvreau said. She stood back from the board with her hands on her hips. "Small and metallic, definitely. Could be another ship . . . but there aren't any power readings." She pursed her lips. "I got fifty kilocredits apiece for those probes."

Kirk checked the coordinates. He estimated that a five-hour deviation would put them close enough to positively identify the signal. He appreciated the fact that Gauvreau appeared to be leaving the final decision to him. *It's only five hours,* he thought. He just hoped Scott wasn't about to pull another one of his miracles and take the *Enterprise* out of the Talin system ahead of schedule.

"All right," Kirk said. "Let's change heading and track it down." He didn't wait for Gauvreau's reply. He simply entered in the new course and watched as the stars swung by on the viewscreen.

Four and a half hours later, Kirk knew enough about the salvage scanner to have it work with the main sensors and deliver a thirty percent increase in sensitivity.

"Not bad," Gauvreau said as she studied how Kirk had realigned both sensor systems to function together. "There's nothing like that in any of the manuals."

"Out on the frontier, you'd be surprised how quickly you learn to improvise," Kirk said, continuing his fine adjustments of the newly enhanced scanner. "When we get to Talin, we should try to have Mr. Scott take a look at your matter-antimatter intermix chambers. I'd bet he could get another half factor out of your drive for the same power consumption figures." He pressed the control that sent the sensor data to the viewscreen where the computer would reconstruct a visual image. "There, this should tell us what it is we've found."

A slowly expanding cloud of gas filled with spinning flat pieces of metal appeared.

"Debris," Gauvreau said with dismay. "It's got to be a ship."

"And it's not old," Kirk added. "Less than a day." The cloud of escaped atmosphere hadn't dispersed more than two hundred kilometers and the metal fragments were still close enough together to have returned the strong scanner signal the *Shelton* had detected. Kirk had the computer track and map the largest pieces of what he guessed were hull plates, then reassemble them in memory to try and determine what type of ship had been destroyed.

A wireframe reconstruction of the vessel slowly filled in on the screen.

"Merde," Gauvreau said as she and Kirk recognized the half-drawn graphic at the same time. "A freighter."

"An old one," Kirk confirmed. "The DY series." He had become quite expert in recognizing them.

Gauvreau reset the sensors for organics and got nothing. "Must have been a robot ship," she said with relief. "No sign of bodies."

But Kirk didn't agree. "Look at the oxygen reading from the gas cloud. No ship would carry that amount of atmosphere unless someone were breathing it."

Gauvreau reset the sensors again. "Scanning for lifepods and shuttles."

The sensor alarm chimed. "That's a positive contact," Gauvreau said. She squeezed closer to Kirk at the navigation board as they both worked the sensors together. The cats watched patiently from the chairs at the other, empty stations.

"But it's not a lifepod," Kirk said. "And not a shuttle, either." He punched in a new command line. "It's a waste trail . . . ?"

"Radioactive," Gauvreau confirmed. Her tone became flat. "First-stage matter."

Kirk felt a sudden burst of anger. Only one class of vessel left that unique signature of radioactive waste in its wake. "Orion pirates."

"Bastards," Gauvreau said bitterly.

"What weapons system does the *Shelton* have?" Kirk asked.

Gauvreau looked away from him. "You know it's illegal for a freighter to be armed, Kirk."

Kirk looked at her steadily.

"Photon torpedoes," Gauvreau conceded. "They're surplus but they're still at seventy percent power."

"How many?"

Gauvreau looked embarrassed. "Three."

"How do you launch them?"

"I, uh, sort of modified the forward waste-jettison tube."

Kirk nodded. He turned back to the board to trace the Orion's trail.

"Now wait just a minute, Kirk. The *Shelton* isn't the *Enterprise*. We're not taking on a pirate. No possible way."

Kirk didn't look up from the controls. "Don't worry, I know. But we have to get close enough to him so we can make a sensor ID that we can pass on to Starfleet when we get to Talin."

Gauvreau relaxed, but only for a moment. "Then why were you asking about weapons?"

Kirk laid in the new course that would take them after the fleeing pirate. *Good,* he thought, *he's almost on a direct heading to Talin himself. This won't cost us any more time.*

"I said: Why were you asking about weapons, Kirk?"

Kirk stood up from the board and stretched. "I estimate we'll be within optimal leading sensor range of the Orion within three hours."

"So?"

"Which means there's a good chance that we'll be inside his trailing sensor range within *two and half hours.*" He smiled at Gauvreau to try and reassure her. "Don't worry, it makes it easier to decide to run away when I know we've got the weapons to stand and fight."

But Gauvreau looked anything but reassured. "Tell me more about the running-away part," she said.

Two hours and forty minutes later, Kirk watched as the tracking sensors indicated that the Orion vessel was slowing and changing course.

"It's about time you started paying attention to your stern," he said, watching the sensor blip.

Gauvreau sat at the environmental station where she could control the modified waste-jettison tube, if required. "Are they coming about?"

"Not yet," Kirk answered. "We're dead in their waste trail so at this distance there's a chance we might only be a false return. They're just running a minor deviation to see if we follow or stay put. As long as we stay put, they'll think we're an echo."

"So we're staying put, right?"

"For now, we are." Kirk watched as the Orion's course

changed by five degrees, held for a few minutes, then resumed its normal heading. "That's it," Kirk said. "We're an echo. That gives us at least another twenty minutes to get closer before they'll—what?"

The sensors showed that the Orion ship had suddenly dropped out of warp to relative rest. Kirk punched at the warp cut-off switch, but by the time the *Shelton* hit normal space, the Orion vessel was going to warp three at a ninety-degree deviation to its original course.

Kirk swore and Gauvreau looked with concern at him in alarm. "What happened? What did he do?"

"He's sharper than I thought," Kirk admitted. "By pulling that maneuver, he was able to get a cross fix on us. Damn. I didn't think the Orions knew about that one."

"What now?"

"He knows we're here, so we might as well keep going." Kirk entered an intercept course and the *Shelton* jumped back to warp four.

"Why?" Gauvreau demanded. "He blew up that freighter."

"Exactly," Kirk agreed. "And I'll only take us close enough to get an ID scan and then we're heading straight for Talin. We'll still be hours ahead of him." He looked up as Gauvreau headed for the ladderway. "Where are you going?"

"I'm going to put the cats in the lifepod. Let me know if the Klingon Armada shows up."

"I'm not getting anything that makes sense," Kirk said an hour later as he started his sensor scan again. "It's almost as if they've rigged their own sensor systems to relay false readings to us."

"Why do you sound so surprised?" Gauvreau said. "Even I've heard of that strategy before."

The *Shelton's* captain was back at the environment station. This time she wore a pressure suit and orange micrometeoroid overalls. Her helmet was slung at the side of her chair. Kirk wore the same outfit. After Gauvreau had described to him the minimal power ratings of the *Shelton's* deflector shields, it had seemed the prudent course to take. The pressure suits would give them enough time to get to the lifepod in the event of sudden decompression.

"A strategy is one thing," Kirk said, sliding the sensor controls back and forth, "but to carry this off, they'd have had to rewire their comm system into their sensors. Unless they've got a couple of communications geniuses onboard, I don't see how they could have done it so quickly."

"Maybe they did it earlier?" Gauvreau suggested. "Before they knew we were here."

"Possible," Kirk said, "but not likely they'd want to limit their own comm system to just short-range transmissions out in deep space. There's something very strange about that ship. Damn it!"

"What, Kirk?"

Kirk slapped his hand on the console. "They've disappeared again . . . no . . . there . . . I don't believe it. They managed to broadcast a perfect phase delay to us so our sensors showed no return signal for a few seconds." .He turned to look at Gauvreau. "Just when did Orions get so smart?"

"Why not stop underestimating them? Let's give them some of their own back."

Kirk smiled in swift response. He liked that idea. He went to work on it immediately.

Thirty minutes from intercept, the *Shelton* blazed through space, straight for the Orion vessel. Abruptly, it dropped from warp, flipped to a full reverse heading, then vented its impulse baffles at point nine nine cee. When the relativistically compressed vapor cloud cleared from around the ship, the *Shelton* rotated slowly, stern over keel, running lights out.

On the *Shelton*'s bridge, Gauvreau unstuck her hands from her chair. The inertial dampeners of the freighter had not been able to keep up with sudden vector shifts. Neither had her stomach.

"Good," Kirk said. "Very good."

"What was so good about that? If the cats ever come out of

their kennels they won't eat for a month." Gauvreau rubbed at her face to wipe the tears of surprise from her eyes.

Kirk couldn't blame her. It had been a wild ride and he had almost been thrown clear of his chair himself. "As far as our friends out there are going to be able to tell, the *Shelton* just lost warp drive," Kirk said. "Between the exhaust venting cloud and the system shutdown and the spinning, they're going to think we're crippled."

"This is good?" Gauvreau asked.

"Trust me," Kirk said happily. "Now broadcast an emergency beacon, but cut it off after a few repetitions."

"Terrific," Gauvreau muttered. "That way no one will ever find us."

"Don't worry. They're going to come in with their guard down. We'll get our ID scan, then pop off a torpedo, then hit warp."

"I don't know, Kirk. The way they've been behaving, I don't think their guard's ever going to go down."

Kirk scratched at his neck under the tight collar rim of the pressure suit. "Don't be so pessimistic. It's not as if we're dealing with Academy graduates here."

"Is that so?" Gauvreau pointed at the screen. "Look at that." The visual screen painted an image of a brilliant streak passing by—the Orion vessel had not stopped.

Gauvreau read from her instruments. "We were flooded by sensor radiation, Kirk. They did a complete scan."

"Hold it. They're coming back," Kirk said, intently watching the course change indicators. "Ready with that torpedo as soon as I get them in memory."

Suddenly the Orion ship fell out of warp space directly beside the *Shelton*. Whoever was piloting her was fearless. Or an idiot.

"Steady," Kirk cautioned. "Get ready on that torpedo."

"It's not going to do a whole lot of good, Kirk. Look what they're doing." Gauvreau gestured to the screen.

It took Kirk a moment to realize what Gauvreau meant. Then he understood. These pirates were better than any he had ever dealt with before. They were even better than any he had ever *heard* of before. Standing off from the *Shelton* a half kilometer distant, the Orion ship matched the freighter's slow cartwheels, constantly keeping at right angles to the waste-jettison tube.

"I'm never going to be able to target them at this rate," Gauvreau complained.

"Doesn't matter," Kirk said. "I've got them in sensor memory now. Starfleet will be able to track them down and deal with them."

Gauvreau stared up at the viewscreen. "That doesn't help us now, Kirk. Their scanners are going to be able to see our warp engines power up. If we can't fire a torpedo for a diversion, we're not going to be able to get out of here."

The Orion vessel moved in perfect step with the freighter, waiting. But for what, Kirk couldn't be sure.

"Get ready on the torpedo," he said suddenly. "I'm going to use the attitude thrusters to speed up our rotation. As soon as the tube lines up with the pirate, fire."

"Torpedo ready," Gauvreau responded.

Kirk slid the attitude control forward and the Orion ship disappeared from the viewscreen as the *Shelton*'s rotation increased. "Now!"

The freighter shuddered as the photon torpedo was jettisoned. Kirk reached to engage warp drive. But the Orion ship went to warp first, moving toward the torpedo casing and the *Shelton*, missing both by centimeters. The *Shelton* remained in normal space. Its safety programs had not let it go to warp while another warp drive was in such close proximity. The Orion ship was now in normal space on the opposite side of the *Shelton*. The torpedo detonated harmlessly, a hundred kilometers away.

"What kind of maniac is piloting that thing?" Kirk asked.

"Kirk! They've got a disruptor cannon powering up. They've locked on us."

"Ready torpedo two," Kirk said. He'd dealt with maniacs before.

"If I try to fire, they'll blast us!"

"Just keep the tube open and I'll do the rest," Kirk said. He held his hands over the board, counting silently to himself.

"Torpedo ready."

". . . three . . . two . . . one . . . now!" Kirk hit two sets of controls at once. The *Shelton* lurched forward, directly toward the Orion ship. At the same time, Kirk used the forward cargo tractor beams to pull the torpedo from its tube and position it in front of the *Shelton*—without firing it.

The *Shelton* came to relative rest ten meters from the Orion ship. The hull creaked with the stress of the sudden deceleration.

"I don't believe it," Gauvreau gasped. "They didn't fire."

"Of course not," Kirk said. "Look what they would have hit first."

There on the screen, locked into position exactly five meters from each ship, was the sleek and gleaming case of the photon torpedo.

"Great," Gauvreau said. "So the first time either of us tries something, we'll both be blown up."

Kirk shook his head. "If they were Klingons, maybe. But whoever's running that ship is too smart to want to die. We'll work our way out of this. One way or another."

Gauvreau unslung her helmet from her chair and put it on her lap, keeping it ready.

The incoming light on the communications board suddenly blinked on.

"I'll handle the transmission," Gauvreau said, taking her helmet to the comm station. "You stay ready to get us out of here."

Kirk watched the screen as the close-up image of the Orion ship was replaced by a visual channel from the Orion's bridge.

"Who is the madman who commands your vessel?" the pirate commander snarled. He wore a black battle helmet, black radiation goggles, and a voice-distorting translator cap that covered his nose and mouth. "I am the pirate Black Ire and I demand that you drop shields and allow my crew to take over your vessel before I blast you into transporter dust! Surrender now or die a thousand deaths!"

Gauvreau didn't open a return channel. "Listen to him, Kirk. He sounds insane."

Kirk stood up, eyes fixed on the screen. "It's all right, Captain. I think I can handle this. Open up a channel back."

"If you say so." Gauvreau bit her lip. "You're on."

"What say you to my demand, spacedog?" Black Ire growled. "Or do you wish me to flay you open and take out your organs one by one?"

Then Black Ire's head jerked and he leaned forward staring at his adversary in amazement.

Kirk frowned and narrowed his eyes. "I admit I've been slow in getting around to that physical, but don't you think this is taking professional concern a bit too far, Bones?"

On the viewscreen, Black Ire clawed at his goggles and mask. "Jim?" McCoy said, eyes wide with wonder.

Behind him, Chekov and Sulu and Uhura crowded excitedly into view.

I knew it, Kirk thought. The four of them *were* together. And heading for Talin, just as he was.

All that was missing now was Spock and the *Enterprise*. And Kirk doubted they'd remain missing for long.

NINE

☆

Scott's footsteps echoed in the empty corridors of FCO Outpost 47. The hundred and twenty personnel who had once worked there had been recalled to Earth five days after the devastation of Talin IV and the facility had been deserted ever since. *Until last week,* Scott thought. *Everything had changed then. And maybe tomorrow things would change even more.*

"Aye," Scott muttered to the corridor, adjusting his grip on the three storage boxes he carried, "and if Lieutenant Styles had wings he'd still be a pig."

Scott continued along the corridor, remembering and savoring the look on the lieutenant's face when the *Enterprise* had survived the separation of her warp-distorted port nacelle the previous week. It had been such an odd expression of delight and regret. The delight was without question because the ship remained intact and Styles had his designs on her. But the regret Styles had felt had been because Scott was standing with him—and the twenty-being team of Starfleet experts—in the observation lounge of the *Exeter* when the separation had taken place. The chief engineer did not consider himself a mean or vindictive person, but when the *Enterprise* had remained peacefully in space before them, safely minus her damaged

321

nacelle, he had taken great joy in turning to Styles and saying in a voice which all could hear, "I told ye so."

For Scott, the separation of the nacelle had gone just the way he had expected. For the experts, it had been a terrible disappointment, especially after all the self-important trouble they had gone to in arranging for the *Enterprise* to be towed to the edges of the Talin system.

As the time for the nacelle's removal had approached, excited groups of them watched intently through the viewports as well as on the viewscreen close-ups. After the *Enterprise* had been completely evacuated, four uncrewed workbee shuttles had been attached to the ship's port nacelle with carbon tethers. Twenty-eight additional remote-controlled workbees were attached to the ship's secondary hull. The plan was that, when the two groups of shuttles pulled in opposite directions, the port nacelle's explosive bolts would be triggered to separate it from its support pylon. The experts clenched their hands together, scarcely daring to speak to each other, expectantly awaiting the brilliant rainbow flare of destruction. Scott had just felt irritated and impatient.

With the carbon tethers pulled taut and the *Enterprise* beginning to slowly drift away in the direction of the twenty-eight pulling workbees, a bright yellow flash had sparkled from the support pylon joint on the nacelle. Then, as the experts gasped—and some braced themselves as if shock waves could travel through a vacuum—the *Enterprise* had only continued to slowly drift in one direction while the twisted port nacelle drifted in the other.

One hour later, sensors showed that the warp-compressed point of the nacelle was still evaporating molecule by molecule. That led one of the disappointed experts to propose an alternate theory to account for the nacelle's slow disintegration. Perhaps, the expert suggested, the hull metal had been damaged by the barrage of fusion explosions to which it had been subjected and was simply undergoing a molecular outgassing effect similar to the skin leaching which occurred on primitive

Earth-orbiting spacecraft centuries ago. Scott had moaned, "I told ye about that, too," but by then the scientists were digging into old historical tapes, to come up with new theories, completely ignoring the now-orphaned nacelle.

At last with the theoreticians otherwise engaged, Scott had had an easy time directing the installation of the new nacelles the *Exeter* had brought and left in orbit around Talin's moon. Once the *Enterprise* had been quickly towed back into lunar orbit to undergo her final repairs, the work had gone smoothly and now, one week later, there was little left to be done. For that Scott was grateful. But not for much else.

Scott came to the doors marked Sortie Planning Center and they reluctantly slid open before him, sticking from disuse. The people working in the vast room looked up from their tables and desks piled high with microtapes and datacubes and printouts. Despite the work—and the possibility for failure—that remained ahead, Scott felt renewed to see so many familiar faces. Vice Admiral Hammersmith had been true to his word, and then some. Already more than half the *Enterprise*'s crew had been transferred back to the Talin system to assist with the repairs, and most of the rest were in transit.

Carolyn Palamas came up to Scott to take the boxes he carried. "Thank you, Scotty. We've just got the next terminal set up."

"Careful, lass," Scott said as he passed the containers over, worrying about the delicate chiming sounds he heard as the duplicate Talin datadisks inside jostled against each other.

"I know what's riding on this," Palamas said gently, then returned to her section of the vast room.

Scott watched her go, caught up in memories. There was a time when he thought they might have been more to each other than colleagues. But the events at Pollux IV had changed that and, in a way, Scott was glad they had. Otherwise, he might never have gotten to know Mira Romaine when the *Enterprise* took her to Memory Alpha and—

"Mr. Scott, I require your assistance."

Scott felt he had been suddenly transported back in time. He had missed that voice more than he had realized. "Aye, Mr. Spock, I'm coming."

Despite the four months that they had been separated, Scott had noticed no difference in Spock when the former science officer had beamed to the *Enterprise* earlier that day—other than his civilian clothes, of course. At first, Scott had been surprised when Vice Admiral Hammersmith had escorted Spock to Scott's cabin. But given what he had heard on the update channels about the trouble Spock was causing on Earth, the chief engineer had had no doubt that his former fellow officer would be returning soon to the Talin system. Even Scott knew that logic would demand that Spock be prepared to act in case the Council debate he had ignited was finally settled and the authorization was given to begin rescue operations.

Spock had not been at all surprised by Scott's continued presence on the ship, nor had he expressed any pleasure at being reunited with him. After saying hello, he had merely asked if Scott would help him reopen Outpost 47. Hammersmith had said he was happy to loan Scott out if Scott also agreed—which he had, without hesitation.

"How're ye doing, Mr. Spock?"

Spock looked up from the large desk where he worked. The terminal screen before him displayed row after row of the multicolored paint splatters that Scott now recognized as Talin script. "How am I doing what, Mr. Scott?"

Aye, Scott thought, *I've missed the voice, if not necessarily what it says from time to time.*

"I mean, are the modified terminals working out for you?"

"Yes," Spock said. "The ambassadors have been most resourceful in helping us adapt our equipment."

Scott glanced over to Seerl and Orr. The Talin ambassadors worked with a group of young humans and Mario Cardinali, the FCO outpost's ex-manager of communications. Spread over two work benches and a corner of the floor were fifty desk computer terminals, cases open, most with circuit boards removed.

One of the two Talin—Scott still couldn't tell them apart unless Orr allowed her skin to change to a blue shade—moved quickly and surefootedly around the spread-out equipment, lifting its legs and its feet high like a strutting heron. The creature was supervising the work the young humans did to convert the standard Starfleet terminals so the machines could extract information from Talin-style datadisks. The young people were university students, Scott had been told, though he felt certain that no one in university would dare dress the way that this lot did. Scott knew that students had never dressed so outlandishly when he had been their age.

The second Talin stood to the side of the equipment work area, talking though a small translator unit to a young woman who was busily arranging rations on a set of mess trays. Scott had seen many strange things in his day, but the sight of the saurian creature gently cradling a wee baby in its arms as it talked to the baby's mother ranked among the oddest. Though at the same time, the sight of the two species united in such mundane activity made him feel secure about the Federation's future. Now if only the Council would realize what the voters had realized and authorize the aid mission which Spock had fought for.

"What can I be doing for you, then?" Scott asked Spock.

"I shall require full computer access to the main communications monitoring lab. Mr. Cardinali can provide you with details."

"Beggin' your pardon, Mr. Spock, but there's not much of any communications to be monitoring in the vicinity these days."

"True," Spock agreed, "though there are eight standard years' worth of previously captured data to analyze. The monitoring room would make the process more efficient."

"I'll get on it right away, Mr. Spock." Scott saw the clouded look that came to Spock's face. "Och, ye know what I mean."

As Scott left the work room with Cardinali, Vice Admiral Hammersmith appeared in the doorway. "Ah, engineer, I'm glad I found you. Lieutenant Styles reports that the construction drones have finished replacing the master transtator nodes and that the warp generators in the new nacelles are locked in and ready to power up."

Scott hesitated. "So, then . . . what you're saying, sir, is that the *Enterprise* is ready to be taken out?"

"For trials first, of course," the vice admiral said. "The warp engines will have to be tuned over the next few weeks before she can be classified operational again. But Styles says she'll be ready to break orbit in six hours."

"I see, sir."

Hammersmith put his hand on Scott's shoulder. "We had an agreement, engineer. I brought back as many of your crew as I could, and I gave you your week—and a few days more—to try and come up with more evidence for your claim that the *Enterprise* had been attacked. Now *you* owe me the services of a chief engineer."

Scott looked back in at the controlled excitement of the workroom. *Spock* must *be on to something*, he thought in despair.

"Have you found any evidence to back your claim, engineer?"

"No, sir," Scott admitted. "But with Mr. Spock here and—"

Hammersmith shook his head. "I'm afraid Mr. Spock is here on a completely different matter. He is no longer associated with Starfleet. The only reason he was allowed through the blockade at all is because the Talin ambassadors have appointed him and these other people with him as their consular officials."

"But this outpost is Starfleet property," Scott said. He couldn't imagine Spock no longer being in Starfleet.

"Not any more," Hammersmith corrected. "This moon was held in trust for Talin IV's future exploitation and the ambassadors have invoked their right to claim it. The outpost is forfeit."

"I don't understand," Scott said.

"Mr. Scott, the repairs to the *Enterprise* went smoothly and so I had no problem assigning you to help Spock here as a gesture of goodwill from Starfleet to the Talin. However, until the Council debate over the status of Talin is concluded one way or another, there is nothing more to be done here. The Federation is more than just this one planet in this one system. Starfleet has too many ships and personnel here already. We need the *Enterprise* out doing her job and we need you on her doing yours."

"Please, Vice Admiral, I know that with just a few more days I could—"

"Lieutenant-Commander Scott, I have given you all the latitude that my orders allow. Now, you, sir, are ordered to report to Lieutenant Styles, in temporary command of the *Enterprise,* in six hours, to prepare her for operational trials and return to full duty. Do you understand, Mr. Scott?"

Scott's shoulders slumped. He had come so close only to lose again. "Aye, Vice Admiral. I shall report aboard the *Enterprise* in six hours. Thank you for your patience, sir."

"Good man, engineer." Then Hammersmith offered Scott one last piece of hope. "Of course, if you do manage to come up with something in the next six hours, I have been known to change my mind."

"Aye, sir. Thank you, sir," Scott said glumly.

Hammersmith nodded in dismissal, then entered the workroom. Scott and Cardinali left for the main monitor lab.

"What was the vice admiral saying about you trying to *prove* that the *Enterprise* had been attacked? Didn't the bridge logs show that the nuclear missiles were aimed directly at her?" Cardinali asked.

"Aye, but we weren't talking about the missiles." Scott explained to Cardinali about the unnatural pattern of damage which had been found throughout the *Enterprise*—how the most vital twenty percent of her transtator circuitry had been destroyed, but nothing else.

"And you think it's possible a focused subspace pulse was used as a weapon?" Cardinali asked when Scott was through.

"You're a communications expert. What do you think?"

Cardinali paused in the corridor and put his hand on his chin. "Theoretically, it makes sense. But I don't know anything that could generate that kind of power without setting off every energy sensor from here to the Neutral Zone. If it happened that way, then it's something that's never been reported before. And other than that, Mr. Scott, you've got me." He began to walk on.

Scott hurried to catch up with the big man's long strides. "Well, what exactly is it that you and Mr. Spock are doing for those Talin? I thought perhaps he had read my report on the subspace pulse and was coming to do some work of his own on it."

"He hasn't said anything about that." Cardinali stood in front of the monitoring lab's doors and helped them open with a strong shove. "Basically, Seerl and Orr say they were launched on their joint lunar mission because their respective governments thought something strange was going on up here on Talin's moon. I'm surprised Dr. Richter didn't suspect that it was a joint mission in the first place, I mean with their ship not carrying the colors of either nation. As far as I know right now, what we're all trying to help Spock do is find out exactly what chain of events set off that final exchange of weapons.

"Seerl and Orr want to know because they still can't believe that their governments actually went to war on their own and, I'm guessing here, Spock seems to think that if he can give the Talin the answers that they want, he can also prove that the *Enterprise* was not to blame for what happened either. But I don't know all the details."

Scott shrugged. "Well, at least we're trying to do the same thing, if not exactly in the same way." He stared around at the huge circular lab, ten times the size of the *Enterprise*'s bridge. Every one of its hundreds of screens was black.

"All right then, laddie," the chief engineer sighed, "I've got six hours to give you. Where's the 'on' switch for all this?"

One hour before Scott was to report back to the *Enterprise*, Spock entered the monitoring lab alone. Scott and Cardinali worked together at the center command console facing the master viewscreen, and did not notice his arrival until he was beside them.

Spock looked approvingly around the lab—all displays were now functional. The viewscreen flickered with a hundred focus patterns, awaiting input.

"We're ready for your datafiles anytime," Scott said.

"Please try input channel forty-five," Spock said.

Cardinali punched in the file number and ten of the smaller image areas on the master screen dissolved into one larger one. A computer graphic formed in it. To Scott, it appeared to be an illustration of the orbital mechanics of Talin IV and its moon. Also plotted on the chart were several small objects orbiting the planet, but Scott couldn't tell what they were supposed to be.

"Good work, Mr. Scott. I shall begin transferring the rest of my files here as soon as the others arrive."

"The others?" Scott asked.

"Yes," Spock said. "If my calculations are correct, they should be arriving at any moment."

"Who?"

Spock turned to the chief engineer, but before he could answer, a transporter chime filled the lab. Scott blinked as three figures took form.

Spock greeted them when the beam had faded. "Welcome, Dr. Richter, Ms. Mallett, Mr. Wilforth."

The outpost's former manager of sampling operations came forward to the command console. Behind her, the old scientist tapped his cane against the dark carpeted floor of the lab, then spit on it. "Pah. Four months later and it still stinks like *fladge* down here. Hello, Mr. Spock." He squinted at Scott. "What? You lose your *narflin* job, too, Mr. Scott?"

"Unfortunately not, Dr. Richter." Scott stood up to shake the scientist's hand but the man declined to offer it. Mallett and Cardinali hugged in greeting.

Wilforth gazed around the room with longing, then folded his hands together. "I never thought I'd see this room again."

"How are Seerl and Orr?" Mallett asked.

"Adjusting well," Spock answered. "Their guidance has helped eliminate more than forty percent of the recordings on file at this outpost from unproductive study. Apparently many of the update broadcasts which the FCO studied had a reputation on Talin for being less than truthful."

"That's something you should know about, isn't it, Mr. Spock?" a woman's voice asked.

Scott turned to see that the young woman who had been passing out rations had entered the lab. This time, she was carrying her baby herself. The Talin ambassadors walked majestically at her side, each carrying the silver tube of a translator.

"Mr. Scott," Spock said, "may I introduce Marita Llorente, organizer of Students for Stars for the People."

Marita extended her hand to Scott, balancing her baby on her hip. "And advisor at large to the Talin Embassy," she added, shaking Scott's hand with a forceful grip. "But these days, who isn't?"

"A pleasure," Scott said. Then he was aware that as Marita stepped back, the two Talin drew near. Both had extended their taloned hands in a duplication of Marita's action.

Makes sense, Scott thought. Though he had seen the Talin before, he had not been formally introduced. He reached out and took the closer Talin's hand, startled by how soft and warm the heavily textured folds of reddish skin were, and how sharp the talons were. He was more careful shaking hands with the next.

The shorter of the two was about Scott's height and spoke into its silver translator. The Talin's voice was a melodic, whispery whistle. The translator's interpretation of it was clipped and mechanical.

"Welcome to our moon," the first Talin had said.

The second Talin spoke into its translator. "You wear a manly shirt."

Scott smiled at the compliment. He guessed red might be a favorite color.

The first Talin looked around the lab and its skin rippled, then quickly changed to a sky-blue shade. Then that one's Orr's, Scott thought, the female.

"Is this the place where observation was done?" Orr's translator asked.

"Yes," Spock said. "Virtually all of your planet's communications channels were monitored from this facility."

Seerl held the translator to his wide mouth. "Yet you still have no answers."

"Soon," Spock promised.

Scott checked the time readout on the console chronometer. In forty minutes he'd be beaming back up to the *Enterprise*. "What answers, Mr. Spock?"

"The same answers you look for, Mr. Scott. Who attacked the *Enterprise*. And who attacked Talin."

"Hold on," Marita interrupted. "Talin destroyed itself. Its nuclear warheads didn't come from anywhere else. That's why the Prime Directive has got to be thrown away. So the Federation won't stand back and let something like this happen again." She looked directly at Spock. "Right, Mr. Spock?"

"Ms. Llorente, please," Wilforth said in distress. Scott had noticed the man standing at the side, trying to avoid confrontation.

Scott was bewildered by the way Marita had made her last comment. "You don't agree with that, do ye, Mr. Spock?" Had he changed over the last four months, after all?

"No, Mr. Scott. Marita and I have only agreed to disagree. I admit I used her organization's resources to further my attempts to speak to the Council about Talin IV. And I admit that I told her that I would be speaking against the Prime Directive, which is her organization's goal."

Marita shifted her baby from one arm to the other. "But what he did do was speak against the Prime Directive only as it applied to Talin. Not quite a lie. Not quite the truth. But all Vulcan."

"And you're not upset with him for that?" Scott asked.

"It's a start," Marita said. "A small step forward. The Prime Directive's grip on the Federation has become weaker because of what Spock has done in Council. Someday it will be abolished altogether."

Spock crossed his arms over his chest. "As I have said before, Marita, since the Prime Directive should not have been enforced on Talin IV in the first place, nothing that has transpired here will undermine it in any way. In the years to come, the Prime Directive can only become stronger, as a policy, and as an ideal."

Marita turned away from Spock and looked at her baby. "Well, we'll see about that, won't we, Alexander?"

As the Talin began to ask more technical questions about the communications facility, Scott motioned to Spock to join him away from the others. "I've been ordered back to the *Enterprise*, Mr. Spock, and I'm afraid that this might be the last time I get a chance to talk with you in the next few weeks."

"What do you wish to say?"

Och, someday he'll learn, Scott told himself. "I want to know if you have any proof of what you were mentioning about whatever attacked the *Enterprise* and Talin IV."

"I am working on it, Mr. Scott."

"Any chance of coming up with something in the next thirty minutes?"

"Unquestionably," Spock stated.

The answer took Scott by surprise. "What? You mean that? You'll have the answer that quickly?"

"Part of the answer at any rate, Mr. Scott." From the center of the lab, another transporter chime sounded. It was louder than before—multiple beams coming in.

"As I said earlier," Spock continued. "I have just been waiting for the others to arrive."

Scott followed Spock's gaze to the lab's center where five golden shafts of light and matter swirled into being. The sound they made was like a song.

"Captain Kirk!" Scott cried out in delight.

The last of the beams faded and Kirk looked over to Scott

and raised his hand. Around the captain, Chekov, McCoy, Sulu, and Uhura did the same.

"You're back! All of you!" Scott shouted again. Without thinking he slapped Spock joyously on the back, accompanying the action with a wordless whoop of excitement.

Spock froze in position, half bent forward by the force of Scott's blow.

"Oops, sorry, Mr. Spock, sorry," Scott said, reaching out to take Spock's shoulders, then realizing that he shouldn't, then thinking that he should. "Och!" he finally said and hurried across the room to his friends—the latest additions to Talin's embassy staff, as approved by Mr. Spock earlier that day when the SS *Ian Shelton* and RRV *Queen Mary* had reached the edge of the Talin system.

Uhura's hug was the longest and most intensely felt of the greetings Scott gave and received. He was suddenly struck by the thought that of all of them, Uhura was the one he had missed most. But the loud and joyful celebration was not the time to consider those thoughts. It was a time of feeling, not thinking.

Like a statue, Spock stood motionless apart from the crush of people as the returning *Enterprise* crew reunited with Richter and Cardinali and Mallett and Wilforth, and made new acquaintances as well.

It was Kirk who approached the Talin first. "You are the lunar astronauts, are you not?"

Chekov tried to correct him. "The word is cosmonaut, Keptin."

But Kirk didn't hear as he shook hands with the saurians. He looked from Mallett to Cardinali. "They're why you smashed through the doors of my hangar bay, aren't they? You went to rescue them before they could do anything in reaction to what they saw happen on their planet."

"It was Dr. Richter's plan," Mallett acknowledged.

"Did the doctor also work out the plan for getting them to Earth for their appearance before Council?" Kirk asked.

"Partially," Mallett confessed. "Mario and I managed to get

333

them down to the outpost and hidden before the rescue teams from Starbase 29 came into the system. Then, with all the confusion of the next few days, we were able to beam them up to the private ship from the Richter Institute which came for Dr. Richter. They stayed aboard until Dr. Richter was able to get into contact with Mr. Spock to work out the rest of the details."

Kirk nodded, "When I read the update reports of what happened in Council, I thought I detected Mr. Spock's flair for the dramatic."

"We all had a hand in what went on," Mallet said earnestly. "But no matter how it was going to turn out, when Mario and I saw what had happened on Talin IV, we knew we weren't going to let the lunar explorers die. One way or another, with or without Dr. Richter, we would have saved them."

Cardinali added, "You should have seen the looks on their faces when the Wraith matched orbit beside their ship. But it only lasted a few seconds. Almost as if they were waiting for us."

Orr stepped carefully among the humans. "We were waiting for you," her translator said. "All of our lives."

Seerl joined Orr. "But mostly since your tractor beam disturbed our mass detectors and triggered an automatic evasive orbit change."

Cardinali laughed and patted Seerl on his back. Scott was struck by how natural the gesture seemed, even between human and saurian. Perhaps that was the true legacy of space exploration, he thought. By entering a realm where *everything* was different, similarities became what was most important— cooperation, not conflict.

McCoy at last came to Spock. "Well, Mr. Spock, if I didn't know any better, I'd say you weren't happy to see me."

"I am not, Doctor." Spock's words stopped the conversations around him. "I calculated there was a seventy-five-percent probability that Cap—" He stumbled over the word, then apparently decided he meant what he said. "That Captain Kirk would arrive in the Talin system within one hundred and twenty standard days after our departure, which he has done."

Kirk acted disappointed. "Only seventy-five percent, Spock?"

"There was a twenty-five-percent chance that you would die in an accident involving manual labor or cargo handling."

"Oh," Kirk said quietly.

Scott reminded himself to ask the captain what he had been doing these last few months.

"Chekov had a fifty-percent chance of arriving here within the same timeframe," Spock continued. "Most probably in the company of Orion pirates. Sulu had a forty-eight-percent chance of doing the same."

"Why did I have less chance than Chekov?" Sulu asked indignantly.

"I estimated that there was a two-percent chance that you would, indeed, decide to become a pirate."

Chekov howled with laughter. Sulu didn't seem to want to argue the odds.

"As for Uhura," Spock said, "I regret that Dr. Richter's revelation to me that he and Mallett and Cardinali had smuggled the Talin lunar explorers back to Earth resulted in my sudden change of plans, requiring that I not contact anyone involved with the Talin incident. However, Uhura, I assumed that upon your release from Starfleet detention, you would arrive here about this time as part of the civilian relief effort."

"But what about me, Spock?" McCoy pressed. "What did you have figured out for me?"

Spock eyed McCoy warily. "Doctor, there was a five-percent chance that you would die or be seriously injured in a reckless camping accident. There was a ten-percent chance that Vice Admiral Hammersmith would change his mind about your assault on him and have you arrested."

"And what about the rest of it?" McCoy said. "There's eighty-five percent still to go. I can take it."

Spock glanced away. "And there was an eighty-five-percent chance that you would arrive here," he said quickly.

McCoy was confused. "Hold on, I *am* here. You were right. Why be unhappy to see me?"

"Doctor, there was an eighty-five-percent chance that you would arrive here *one month* from now. When I received Captain Kirk's communiqué from the *Ian Shelton* today, I admit I was quite astonished that you were included."

McCoy's smile was so wide his face seemed to expand. "Spock, you underestimated me! I'm not going to let you forget this for months! For years!"

"I know, Doctor. Which is why I am not pleased to see you."

Everyone except Spock and the Talin joined the laughter that followed. It was interrupted by the double chirp of Scott's communicator.

Scott flipped the device open. "Scott here."

"Lieutenant Styles, temporary commander of the USS *Enterprise*, here, Mr. Scott. I believe your time is up. Prepare to be beamed aboard."

Kirk's eyes darkened. "Styles?" he repeated in disgust. "That pompous, strutting napoleon is in command of my ship?"

Styles's voice came back from the communicator. "Say again, Scott? I didn't quite get that."

Scott knew it was time to make his stand. "Uh, I canna beam up right now, Lieutenant."

"And why not?"

"Uh, we've had a wee bit of an emergency down here."

"Good Lord," Styles sighed. "You've got half of Starfleet orbiting over you right now. How can you have an emergency in an FCO base?"

"Communications are out," Scott said, then dropped the communicator to the floor and stepped on it.

Kirk went to Scott and put a hand on his shoulder. "Scotty, Styles is an officious nit, I know. But he is your commanding officer."

Scott was past caring. "Aye, Captain, I know. But I've spent three months taking apart the *Enterprise* trying to find out what happened to her and it's only now that Mr. Spock's come that we have a chance of finding out. And if we can prove that we were attacked, then the vice admiral will let me stay here until we find out who did it and why. I'm sure of it."

Kirk turned to Spock. "What do you say, Spock? Can you prove it?"

"I shall so endeavor, Captain."

"Good," Kirk said quietly. "If anyone can, you can." Scott saw a change come over Kirk then. Somehow, for just a moment, he no longer had the bearing of an officer or leader, he was just one person among many, no different from the rest.

"Thank you, Captain," Spock answered. "Now, if you take positions facing the master viewscreen, I shall present the facts as Seerl and Orr have helped me understand them."

Scott half-expected to see Styles and a security team beam in at any second. But he also knew that Styles would rather sit it out in orbit for an hour or so before admitting to Hammersmith that he had lost track of his chief engineer. As long as Spock didn't waste any time arguing with McCoy, Scott figured he'd be able to see the entire presentation, or whatever it was that Spock had been working on for the past six hours.

Spock called for the first datachannel he had prepared, and the image of a Wraith shuttle appeared in a large section of the viewscreen. Scott recalled hearing about this picture. The Talin had recorded one of the FCO's sampling runs.

"Seerl and Orr tell us that on Talin this picture was officially described as a hoax," Spock said. "The perpetrators were reported to be members of an organization that believed that extraplanetary beings were visiting Talin."

"We know about this picture, Mr. Spock," Wilforth said. "We know it didn't tell the Talin anything about us."

"Correct, Mr. Wilforth, but what is more important about this picture is what it tells us about the Talin. Specifically, the sophistication of their visual recording technology. The Wraith-class shuttle was designed to be virtually undetectable. However, this image proves that the Talin were able to track such craft."

Spock asked Cardinali to open the next datachannel and a flood of images—real and artistic representations—began to move across the screen. Scott thought it was one of the oddest assortments of flying vehicles he had ever seen.

"These are pictures of other, so-called extraplanetary space vehicles which were reported in the public update media on Talin."

"But the FCO has already searched through these images most carefully," Wilforth said. "There are no other Wraith photographs among them."

"Correct again," Spock agreed. "With the Talin's help, Carolyn Palamas programmed the graphic computers to sort the images and select all those showing legitimate flying vehicles not indigenous to Talin."

"We also did that," Wilforth said.

"And these are the results Lieutenant Palamas obtained." The images on the screen—some saucer shaped, some round like balloons, others angular or rounded like winged aircraft—sorted themselves into smaller and smaller groups until nothing was left.

"See?" Wilforth said. "That's exactly what we found, too. What are you trying to say here, Mr. Spock?"

Spock walked around to the front of the command console so he could address everyone, his back to the screen. "Mr. Wilforth, it is my contention that on a planet with the proven technology to capture images of fast-moving, near-invisible, covert alien spacecraft, the fact that only *one* such image exists is not logical."

"But our computers were able to scan through every image, Spock. We found nothing," Wilforth argued.

"No, Mr. Wilforth. The FCO did not scan through every image. Only every image *available* to the FCO." Spock looked at Cardinali. "Datachannel two hundred, if you please."

A new series of pictures came on screen. Twelve of them. Each a clear and detailed image of what could only be a Federation Wraith-class shuttle traveling through the atmosphere.

"The FCO never had a chance to analyze these images because they were obtained through military sources and judged classified," Spock said.

Richter slammed his cane against the command console to

get Spock's attention. "If the FCO couldn't get these *snorled* pictures, then how the *ziq* did you?"

Spock placed a hand on the console. "The FCO did get these pictures, Dr. Richter. Unfortunately, they were obtained on the FCO's last mission to Talin—the intrusive-collection landing party sent from the *Enterprise*. Talin was devastated and the FCO outpost shut down before any of the classified and unreleased datafiles obtained during that mission could be evaluated. These pictures were finally analyzed today and as they clearly show, without a doubt, the Talin were aware of the FCO's operations on their world."

A deep voice resonated through the lab. "Well done, Mr. Spock." It was Vice Admiral Hammersmith. Scott tried to remain inconspicuous. With the vice admiral were Styles and three red-shirted security officers.

"I am not yet finished, Vice Admiral." Spock stepped around the command console to face the vice admiral directly.

Hammersmith stared appreciatively at the screen. "I tell you, Mr. Spock, when I look up on that screen and see that the Talin military had been tracking FCO missions, that tells me that you are finished. For whatever it's worth, what you've done here today is to conclusively show that whatever happened on Talin wasn't just the *Enterprise*'s fault. The blame must also be shared with the sampling personnel and director of this outpost."

"No," Carole Mallett said angrily. "I only conducted twenty sampling runs to Talin. It's inconceivable that they could have been sophisticated enough to record my operations thirteen out of twenty times!"

"The evidence is right up there on the screen," Hammersmith said. "It appears that Starfleet is going to have to re-open the board of inquiry so it can spread the blame around. Now where's Lieutenant-Commander Scott hiding?"

"Vice Admiral," Spock said forcefully. "What is on the screen is only a portion of the evidence, as you call it. Mr. Cardinali, datachannel two hundred and one, please."

A second series of images came on the screen—pictures of

wingless flying craft, long and streamlined with pinched-in midsections and deep grooves along their forward hulls. Scott tried to count them but there were too many. They didn't fill the entire screen so he knew there were fewer than one hundred, but still there were more than five times as many as the images of the Wraiths. The only problem was, Scott couldn't tell what they were.

Neither could Hammersmith. "What are those supposed to be, Mr. Spock?"

"For want of a precise term," Spock said simply, "I chose to call them sampling shuttles."

"But the FCO doesn't use anything that looks like that," Wilforth protested.

"They are not FCO shuttles," Spock said. "Neither are they from any known world within the Federation. Or without."

Scott saw Kirk's eyes fill with excitement. "Yes, Spock," Kirk said. "That's it."

But Hammersmith didn't share that excitement. He was irritated when he spoke. "Just what are you trying to tell us, Spock?"

"According to the classified records which were analyzed today, for the past fifteen standard years, the world of Talin IV has been inundated with visits by these alien shuttles. These shuttles identified and used the same gaps in Talin's radar defenses as did the FCO. However, so great in number were the aliens' intrusions that the Talin launched a vigorous program to upgrade their detection devices. The FCO's Wraiths were not recorded because the Talin were trying to specifically find them. The Wraiths were recorded by military devices designed to detect the shuttles you are seeing on the screen now—alien shuttles."

Wilforth waved his hands at Spock. "Just a minute, Mr. Spock, this isn't making any sense. If the Talin governments officially denied the existence of these extraplanetary craft, why did they then upgrade their defenses?"

Spock asked for datachannel two hundred and ten. Scott brought it online. A geopolitical map of Talin IV appeared.

Moments later, a flurry of hundreds of green dots flashed on and off across it.

"The dots represent major military outposts, airbases, space launch facilities, and nuclear power plants." Spock reached across the console and pressed a switch. The green dots were almost overwhelmed by a second flurry of flashing red triangles. "The triangles represent sightings of the alien shuttles. As you see, they are almost exclusively centered on the military installations."

Hammersmith joined Spock by the console. "Mr. Spock, there's nothing remarkable about trying to analyze military and industrial capability—no matter which Talin group was doing the analyzing."

Spock pointed at the screen. "Look at the frequency of sightings, Vice Admiral. There are far too many of them to be accounted for by any need by Talin's nations to analyze each other's military strength. I submit that these alien craft were engaged in a systematic series of provocative sorties designed for one reason only—to heighten the fear of war on Talin and to make the military and political leaders of the planet arm themselves to the point where stability would no longer be possible."

"Are you saying that *aliens* were attempting to start a war with Talin?" Hammersmith asked incredulously.

"Not *with* Talin," Spock corrected. "But *on* Talin. Preliminary tapes collected by the FCO team indicate that the incursion into polar air space, which almost brought the Talin to war while the *Enterprise* deployed satellites, was the result of provocative overflights by one or more of these shuttles."

Hammersmith shook his head. "This can't be right, Mr. Spock. It's impossible to—"

"You're wrong, Vice Admiral!" Kirk was up by Spock and Hammersmith now. "Whatever you think about the existence of any unidentified aliens, Spock is right in his conclusions. The data came from the Talin themselves. The data cannot be ignored. Someone was trying to get the Talin to destroy their own world."

"Then the Prime Directive wasn't broken!" McCoy shouted. He joined Kirk and Spock. The three of them faced Hammersmith together though the vice admiral directed his gaze solely at McCoy. Knowing what he did about the two men's last meeting, Scott wasn't surprised.

"The doctor's right, Vice Admiral," Kirk said. "The Prime Directive does not apply here. Talin IV's normal development had already been altered by the aliens' attempts to increase political and military tensions. It was right for the *Enterprise* to step in. The military exchanges on Talin were the result of extraplanetary interference. The Prime Directive compelled us to act as we did to prevent those exchanges!"

Hammersmith backed off, obviously shaken. "But to make an entire world blow itself up? Why, Kirk? What possible reason could there be to force a planet to destroy all life in a nuclear war?"

Spock reached for another switch on the console. "But not all life on Talin has been destroyed, Vice Admiral."

A new image came up on the viewscreen. It was a realtime feed of the dayside of Talin IV, transmitted from one of the *Enterprise*'s sensor satellites. Scott bristled as he saw that the insulting caption—KIRK'S WORLD—was still displayed. Behind him, he heard the Talin ambassadors make a sound of anguish that needed no translation.

The choking clouds of dust and radioactive poison which had swept the world were almost gone now. But the destruction they had brought would scar the planet for centuries, if not millennia. The land masses were still streaked black and brown. The once-white polar ice caps were gray with soot from the worldwide firestorm that had raged for weeks after the disaster. The only sign of life remaining on the planet was in the oceans now choked with the deep purple algaelike organism that had mutated and bloomed in the days after the planet's death.

"What could possibly live down there?" Hammersmith asked in sorrow and anger.

"Mr. Cardinali," Spock said, "cycle back in memory one month."

The image of the world shifted as the viewscreen presented the earlier recording. The clouds were thicker, but the ravaged land and purple-stained oceans were unchanged.

"Another month back," Spock said.

The image shifted. A brown-streaked hurricane battered the primary continent. Some patches of blue could be seen in the oceans among the purple, but more than half the planet was obscured by smoke and clouds.

"Two weeks after the incident," Spock said.

Shift. The world was wrapped in a black pall. Through small breaks in the almost solid cloud cover, fires raged.

"Two days."

The planet was hell.

"Mr. Cardinali, have the computer run through that day's recording, extracting all portions of the images that show what lies beneath the clouds to construct a composite picture of the land masses and the oceans as they appeared then."

Cardinali typed in the commands. Slowly the clouds disappeared from the image of Talin as the computer assembled the clear areas from thousands of separate shots to create a master picture of the planet's surface. Walls of fire followed the coastlines where the cities had been clustered. Forests and farmlands blazed.

Then Scott thought the computer made an error as the oceans were reconstructed. The first section cleared showed that a mutated bloom of purple algae had already appeared. More of the oceans cleared. Scott saw another bloom. And another.

He felt his flesh creep as the rest of the planet appeared as it had been that day. *The algae blooms were studded across the oceans in a regular, geometric pattern.*

"Good Lord," McCoy whispered.

"No," Hammersmith gasped.

"Exactly," Spock said without inflection. "The algaelike organism which has taken over the entire ocean ecosystem of Talin IV is not a mutation brought on by radiation. It is an artificial lifeform which is not native to Talin, and which was seeded on that planet quite deliberately. Just as the nuclear

343

holocaust was deliberately induced to ensure that the world would be made . . . fertile for it."

Scott was horrified by the atrocity that Spock had just described. He heard the Talin keen with high-pitched wails of sorrow as their translators told them what Spock had said.

McCoy's face was splotched red with anger. "Who would do such a thing, Spock?"

Spock calmly changed the display back to the pictures of the streamlined, pinch-waisted alien shuttles. "They would," he said.

Kirk's face was grim and set. "But *who* are they, Spock? *Where* are they?"

"To answer that question, we will need help from two additional sources," Spock said. He turned to Hammersmith. "The *Enterprise,* which will enable us to find the aliens . . ." He turned to face Richter. For the first time Scott noticed that the old man's face was drenched in sweat and pale with shock.

". . . and you, Dr. Richter," Spock concluded, "who have always known about them."

TEN

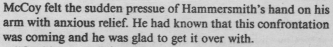

McCoy felt the sudden pressue of Hammersmith's hand on his arm with anxious relief. He had known that this confrontation was coming and he was glad to get it over with.

"Could you wait in my office?" Hammersmith asked Kirk and Spock, who walked just ahead with Wilforth and Richter. "The doctor and I will be along in a moment."

Kirk looked at McCoy, subtly asking if the doctor needed help, but McCoy shook his head. "I'll catch up, Jim." Then he and Hammersmith waited as the other four disappeared around a corner in the corridor.

"Don't worry, Dr. McCoy," Hammersmith said when they were alone. "I'm not going to ask you to apologize."

Fat chance of that, McCoy thought.

"Not that I'd expect you to, anyway," Hammersmith added. "I just wanted to know what the hell it is you think you're doing here?"

McCoy could feel every muscle in his body tense with anger. "I'm here to do what you wouldn't let me do in the first place—get to the bottom of this mess."

Hammersmith shook his head. "I didn't stop you from doing anything, Doctor."

McCoy spoke hotly. "You transferred Spock and me to San

345

Francisco. You wouldn't bring formal charges against us so we couldn't get a decent hearing. And—"

Hammersmith held up a single finger and McCoy instantly stopped talking. "Doctor, you *had* a decent hearing. Starfleet chose not to bring charges when it became apparent that Kirk was going to resign. And where else would you have wanted to transfer? Another starship patrolling on the other side of the Arm? Some starbase out on the frontier? You think you would have been able to do anything about Talin out there?"

McCoy stared at the vice admiral, not following what he was saying. "So what was I supposed to be able to do in San Francisco?"

"Dr. McCoy, I sent you and Mr. Spock back to Command, to the Council, and to the headquarters of most of the inter system update bureaus. Don't you think that was one of the best places to do something about Talin? It certainly worked out for Mr. Spock."

McCoy didn't want to believe what the vice admiral was hinting at. "Are you saying that you transferred us back to Earth *on purpose,* because we could do the most good there?"

Hammersmith's face went blank. "Of course not, Doctor. That wouldn't fall under my orders as commander of Starbase 29."

McCoy felt even more puzzled.

"Look, Doctor," Hammersmith said, lowering his voice, "I know why you slugged me back at the starbase. I know why you're feeling you'd like to do it again. And that's okay. I understand. It's because you've run out of things to say. And the only reason a person like you runs out of things to say is because you know that I'm right. And you don't like that one bit."

"Now wait just a minute," McCoy sputtered.

But Hammersmith cut him off. "No, sir, it's your turn to wait. I've already put in my years to get to this rank and I've got a few more levels to go. And the reason I've gone as far as I have is because this is what I want to do. This is how I give something back. But like I said, Doctor, I don't know what it is you're doing here."

"I'm trying to set things right."

"I don't mean here, on this moon. I mean why were you in Starfleet at all." He held up his hand again to keep McCoy silent. "I checked your record, Doctor. You were a brilliant medical student. You could have gone anywhere and had success, wealth, whatever you wanted. But for some reason, you chose Starfleet, and then you chose a starship. And I happen to know what starship duty means for a doctor. Most of the time you don't know what to do because your only patients are probably among the fittest and healthiest humans since the dawn of time. And the rest of the time you're frantic with frustration because you're facing diseases and toxins that no one has ever seen before, or even dared imagine."

McCoy didn't interrupt. He had to admit that Hammersmith wasn't far wrong. But he was damned if he knew what the vice admiral was driving at.

"Now, I know you try to make yourself out to be some sort of rebel with a pioneering spirit and that's one of the reasons you chose starship duty. But I've watched you with your friends, and I know you envy Mr. Spock for his clear-cut reasoning—no emotions to cloud the issues. And you envy Kirk's cut-to-the-heart, full-speed-ahead ability to just make a decision and make it stick. And I wonder what might happen if you let some of Kirk's spontaneity, or Spock's logic, out in yourself?"

Struck by the vice admiral's insight, McCoy tried to make his face as unreadable as Hammersmith's. But he hadn't had the practice the vice admiral had had.

Hammersmith zeroed in as he caught something in McCoy's eyes. "Or have you already tried it? Have you already done something—out of compassion, out of logic—and realized it was the worse decision you could have made?"

"I'm not in Starfleet anymore," McCoy stated flatly. "I don't have to stand here and listen to this."

Hammersmith shrugged. "I know you don't have to hear this, Doctor, because everything I've said . . . you already know."

McCoy turned to follow the others.

Unperturbed, Hammersmith kept talking. "You know, Doctor, when we had our big argument at the starbase—with all of your objections, and your reasoning, and my counter objections and all of that—there were a couple of times there when I thought that maybe you had me and I had better work a lot harder in trying to convince you what was the best thing to do—for yourself as well as Starfleet.

"But when you finally stopped talking and hit me, that was the moment that I knew you'd lost—you'd given up."

McCoy turned back to him and spoke angrily. "You didn't win anything. I quit."

"I can see you've been spending too much time with Kirk, Doctor. I didn't say I had won. Sometimes, the point isn't to win. Sometimes the point is just not to lose. And I didn't lose. Starfleet procedures required you to be transferred, so I sent you where you could do the most good, if you were interested in doing it. But to tell the truth, I never expected to hear from you again."

"I guess you don't understand me as well as you think you do, after all." McCoy's words were clipped with sarcasm.

Hammersmith stopped beside McCoy. "I understand you better, Doctor, because Starfleet and the Federation are a lot like you. We've got humans on one side, Vulcans on the other, and we're stuck in the middle trying to make everything work. And though we might not win every fight, what I can tell you is that we are never, ever, going to lose."

Hammersmith began walking down the corridor again. McCoy decided that meant the lecture was at last over.

But the vice admiral hadn't finished with him yet. "Oh, and Dr. McCoy, one last thing. I'm a very forgiving person, but if you ever try to hit me again, two things are going to happen.

"One, I'm going to have a new set of trophies for my office wall back at Starbase 29, and two, you're going to spend six months in a regen tube growing a new pair of lungs." Hammersmith patted McCoy on the arm he had grabbed the doctor by. "I understand you, Doctor. This is just so you understand me."

* * *

Spock understood why Zalan Wilforth was so agitated. It was not just that his First Contact assignment had apparently been fatally compromised from both within and without. It was the inner conflict of his two different halves that truly troubled the man. Spock could look at Wilforth and see how his suppressed human side wanted to scream and rage at Alonzo Richter for what the scientist had done. But Wilforth's other half—his Centauran heritage—struggled to avoid the confrontation altogether. The outpost's former director was trapped between wanting the wrong resolution or none at all. Spock tried to think of something he might say to Wilforth to help ease his turmoil, but he knew from experience that help like that could only come from within. Spock wished Wilforth peace and returned to observing Vice Admiral Hammersmith. The vice admiral was someone Spock thought he could handle.

Hammersmith sat behind what had once been Wilforth's desk in the director's complex. He leaned back in Wilforth's chair, reading the data that came up on the desk display. The vice admiral's body was completely relaxed, but Spock saw how his eyes moved rapidly to scan each screen of information, absorbing everything.

The datafile came to an end and Hammersmith turned to the others in the room. McCoy sat in a chair in the corner of the office, arms folded defensively. Kirk didn't move where he stood near the office's closed door. Richter slumped in his own chair, staring past his folded hands at the floor.

Hammersmith's tone was compassionate, though it hid a trace of anger. "When did you know about them, Dr. Richter?"

The scientist exhaled with a rattling sound from deep in his chest. "I suspected them . . . I *suspected* them, when I saw the first Richter Scale rating of Talin IV. That was maybe six or seven years ago."

Hammersmith rubbed at an eyebrow. "How can a Richter Scale of Culture rating indicate the presence of alien observers?"

Richter looked up defiantly. His eyes were red rimmed, his lips moist, his skin sallow. "I *invented* the thing. I know how to

349

read it." He tapped his cane on the floor once, but only weakly. "What you people don't understand is that life is the same no matter where it comes from. It has different colors, different forms, different chemistry, but what drives it is the same." He looked at Spock. "Even Vulcans have the same drives and needs and emotions. They just have better discipline than most."

The vice admiral tried to remain polite, despite the pressure Spock knew he was under. "What point are you trying to make, Doctor?"

"It's so predictable, life is. The development of culture, of civilization, I wrote an equation about it. It makes the Richter Scale work. And the Talin didn't *fit* the equation."

"How?"

Richter coughed. From the sound, Spock noted that the congestion in the man's lungs had increased since their trip from Earth. "If you had twenty years, I could teach you. If I had twenty years . . . Listen, the Talin culture was just like a thousand others—but for their level of understanding about the universe, for their technological achievements, they thought too much about the stars. They wanted to get to them too badly. Much more than most races do at their stage."

"I still don't understand, Dr. Richter," Hammersmith said.

"They saw something. They knew there was something more beyond their planet. It was like a transtator current through their entire culture—their literature, their art. And that desperation to leave their planet when their technology still wasn't ready—that skewed their entire Richter Rating." He tried to tap his cane again for emphasis but almost lost his grip on it instead. "This isn't just me blathering. Other people saw the problem with the rating, too. That's why Starfleet called me to consult. That's why they ended up bringing me out here." Everyone saw the problem, but I was the only one who knew why it was there."

Spock glanced at Kirk. He showed remarkable patience. Spock had no doubt that if another, younger, scientist were being questioned here, Kirk would be asking questions faster than anyone could follow.

Hammersmith persisted. "Why didn't you tell Starfleet what you suspected?"

Richter mumbled something to the floor.

"I beg your pardon, Doctor?"

"The Prime Directive," Richter snapped. "The bloody damn Prime Directive, that's why."

Hammersmith shifted in his chair, brows knitted. "Let me get this straight. *You* didn't want to interfere?"

"No! Of course I wanted to interfere. I hate the Directive. It slows everything down so much. It keeps secrets from us. Hobbles our research. Impedes . . ." He broke into a fit of coughing. McCoy was up instantly, holding a small medical scanner over the man's back. Before Richter could recover enough to push him away, McCoy had held a spray hypo to the scientist's arm.

Richter took in a deep breath. His congestion was noticeably lessened. "But what could I do about it?" he continued irritably, waving McCoy aside. "One scientist among many here. And all so dedicated to noninterference—to just standing back and doing *nothing.*"

This time he managed to keep his grip on his cane as he rapped it against the floor. "But the others—the aliens—*were* interfering. I didn't know why. I wasn't sure how. But that wasn't important. The Talin saw them, talked about them, tried to hunt them down. I thought that if I kept what I suspected a secret, kept the controversy over their Richter rating going, then someday the Talin would succeed. They'd capture one of the aliens' ships. Or one of our own Wraiths."

"You wanted that to happen?" the vice admiral asked accusingly.

"Yes," Richter said. "Because then the Talin would know for certain that there were other civilizations in the galaxy. And that would mean, according to the Federation's own rules, it would be time for their 'normal' development to be at an end. The Prime Directive would cease to apply and we could finally talk to them. Learn from them. Know so much more." Richter closed his eyes. Spock could see tears of frustration well up in them. "You people just don't understand how much there is to know. How little time there is to find it all out." He covered his face with his hands.

Kirk spoke gently but with concern. "Dr. Richter, what I don't understand is that if you were so set on circumventing the Prime Directive, why did you react so strongly when you thought there might be a chance that the *Enterprise* could be sighted by the Talin astronauts?"

Richter didn't look up. "If you, or the FCO, had done anything to break the Prime Directive, then Starfleet would have shut us down and sealed the system. But if those other aliens had been revealed, or the Talin had discovered us by their own efforts, then the whole planet would be wide open." He raised his head to look at Kirk. "Instantly. No wasted time."

Hammersmith studied the desktop for a few moments. "Dr. Richter, sir, do you understand that by not cooperating with Starfleet's First Contact Office, and by not following the provisions of the Prime Directive, that you might have contributed to the disaster that befell Talin IV?"

"I didn't want that," Richter said in a strangled voice.

"No one ever does, Doctor. That's why we have the Prime Directive. So we won't be in a hurry. So we won't rush in blindly when there are entire worlds at stake."

"Too little time," Richter whispered.

"For you and me," Hammersmith said, "perhaps. But not for the Federation, Dr. Richter. The Federation can afford to be patient. We're going to be here for a long, long time."

Spock waited with Kirk and Hammersmith outside the director's complex as McCoy treated the exhausted Richter.

"What happens now?" Kirk asked grimly.

Hammersmith was equally concerned. "I don't know, Kirk. With what Richter said in there, and Wilforth's admission that he thought Richter might be hiding something but didn't want to put pressure on the man . . . it's a mess. Starfleet's going to have to launch a brand-new inquiry. It's going to take years to sort out . . ." He shook his head. "I just don't know."

But Kirk wouldn't accept that. "What's to sort out? There were other aliens interfering with Talin IV's normal development so they could grow mutated algae—or whatever it is—in the oceans. That makes it an open-and-shut case."

Hammersmith glared at Kirk. "Don't tell me what's open and shut. I understand how you feel, Kirk. You lost your command. Maybe it was your fault, maybe it wasn't, but that's not the only consideration here."

"But it is! It all comes down to the Prime Directive. And with the presence of the other aliens—the Prime Directive does not apply."

"What other aliens, Kirk? You heard Richter in there. He *suspected* their presence. That's all. Suspected."

"What about the images from Talin?" Kirk asked.

"What about them? They're computer data from a devastated world. Those disks passed through an FCO facility where a chief scientist admits he was trying to subvert the Prime Directive. Those data could have been manipulated a thousand different ways. It will take years for Starfleet experts to authenticate them. *If* they are legitimate. There's nothing else that can be done."

Kirk was speechless.

Spock wasn't. "Excuse me, Vice Admiral, but I believe you are mistaken. There is another option open to us which might settle this situation once and for all."

"What, Mr. Spock?"

But Kirk saw it instantly. "Find the aliens who were interfering with Talin."

Hammersmith spread his arms. "Be my guest. If they're real, they've only been flying around in front of the FCO for the past eight years without anyone there noticing them. Care to guess how many years it's going to take you?"

"It will take approximately three hours," Spock said.

Hammersmith and Kirk stared at him.

Spock returned their stares with a quizzical expression. "I know where they are," he said.

* * *

In another office, Spock switched on the desk display and swung the screen around so Kirk and Hammersmith could see it. Then he called up input channel forty-five. A graphic representation of Talin IV and its moon appeared.

"A standard orbital map," Hammersmith said. "What does this prove?"

"By itself, nothing," Spock agreed. "However, I shall use it to plot additional information." He pressed a control on the desk computer. A small red triangle flashed on the picture of Talin IV.

"Is that a military base like the other ones you were showing us?" Hammersmith asked.

"No," Kirk said. "I know those coordinates. That's the site of the missile silo where the warhead exploded."

"Exactly," Spock said. He pressed another control. A small blue dot appeared in fixed orbit over Talin.

"That's a geostationary orbit," Kirk explained. "It's one of the sensor satellites we deployed."

"Correct, Captain."

Kirk put his hands on the desk to lean closer to the display. "Just a minute. Is that sensor satellite number five?"

Spock stood back. He had no need to explain anything more to Kirk.

"What's important about satellite five?" Hammersmith asked.

Kirk adjusted the controls so that the display rotated the image of Talin IV. "Satellite five malfunctioned. All its transtator circuitry was wiped clean."

"That's impossible, isn't it?" Hammersmith asked. "I mean, for an FCO sensor satellite? They're armored."

"It *was* right overhead," Kirk said excitedly.

"What is?" Hammersmith asked.

"That's got to be it!" Kirk adjusted the controls again. "Look here. The satellite was deployed almost exactly over the area of the missile silo installation. Whatever kind of signal went down to the silo passed directly through the satellite and wiped out its memory."

Hammersmith didn't follow Kirk's reasoning. "A detonation signal was transmitted from space?"

"No," Kirk said. "The warhead blew up long after the satellite was crippled. The signal that wiped the satellite must have realigned the missile warhead's circuitry so it would go off as soon as the Talin tried to disarm it. It must have been something similar to what Scotty used on the Talin's lunar warheads." He snapped his fingers. "Spock! If a signal of that strength wasn't focused, but was allowed to spread throughout the entire system . . . "

Spock nodded. "It would effectively block virtually all subspace transmissions, which could explain the *Enterprise*'s failure to receive Outpost 47's emergency messages."

"But where did the signal come from?" Hammersmith protested.

Kirk stood back from the desk as he watched the display draw in the final details of the diagram Spock had started. "It came from the most logical place of all, correct, Mr. Spock?"

"Exactly, Captain."

On the display, the computer showed the continuation of a straightline transmission beam that reached from the missile silo, through sensor satellite five, and from there directly to the perfect base for observing Talin IV—its moon.

ELEVEN

☆

The lunar dust of Talin's moon drifted up in a small eddy, disturbed by the vortex of transporter energy which swirled above it. Seconds later, the dust of that moon was marked by Kirk's footsteps.

Kirk peered through the faceplate of his environmental suit at what waited for him on the brightly lit lunar landscape. Spock's plotting had been precise, and it had taken the science officer only one hour to make his calculations instead of the three he had originally estimated.

"Kirk to *Exeter*." His voice sounded odd in the closed-in space of the helmet he wore. "The coordinates are perfect."

He heard the *Exeter*'s transporter technician reply. "Energizing."

Three more columns of sparkling light appeared. They coalesced into Spock, McCoy, and Uhura.

Kirk heard Uhura gasp in astonishment.

Spock immediately held up a vacuum-armored tricorder. "Fascinating."

McCoy checked his own scanners and grunted in disbelief. Then his voice crackled over the helmet speaker. "Forget 'fascinating,' Spock. How about downright impossible?"

On the barren rocks and soil of Talin's moon, beneath the blazing radiation of unfiltered sunlight and completely exposed to the hard vacuum of space, there was life.

Kirk moved forward with long, low-gravity strides to meet it.

What he approached was obviously a base of sorts. Parts of it were alien. Parts of it were understandable. Kirk could see about twenty of the sleek, pinch-waisted shuttles hidden in the shadows of a rocky overhang. Each shuttle was about ten meters long—though no two were exactly the same, and while some were parked neatly side by side, others were stacked on top of each other like a pile of kindling. The overhang had protected them from direct overhead observation by the Talin and the FCO, though Kirk couldn't understand why the rest of the base had not been detected by the FCO's long-range scans—especially the aliens. There were hundreds of them.

The aliens' bodies reminded Kirk of wasps, but with only two segments, mottled with black and glistening silver. Their basic shapes were also similar to the shuttles', though the creatures were only between one and two meters in length. They were supported and moved across the lunar soil by two sets of four spindly silver legs each. One set sprang from their forward segment, the other set from their hind segment, and their bodies were slung beneath their highest leg joints like a spider's.

The aliens' legs ended in wide flattened pads which kept them from sinking into the loose lunar soil. Kirk noticed that some of the creatures moved slowly around their base, while others scuttled back and forth faster than a human could run, sometimes springing ten meters in a single jump.

Cautiously, Kirk edged closer to the creatures as they swarmed around their shuttles and the large silver and black domes that were scattered nearby. So far, they had not acted as if they had detected him or the others, but he kept his vacuum phaser drawn and ready. He reminded himself that these creatures had destroyed a world.

Kirk stopped ten meters from the nearest dome—it looked as if metallic lava had bubbled out of the ground and frozen solid.

The creatures crawled over it and around it, their forward legs tapping soundlessly all over its surface while their hind legs propelled them. From the corner of his faceplate, Kirk saw the rest of his landing party draw nearer to his position.

"They're not in any sort of pressure suits, are they, Spock?" Kirk asked.

"Indeed not," Spock answered. "Their exterior carapaces seem impervious to the vacuum and the radiation of space."

"Are they machines?" Uhura asked. Kirk saw her working with a large, flat computer board with enlarged controls for use by personnel in protective gear.

"That's the incredible part," McCoy answered, checking his medical scanners. "They've got organic parts inside. There are pressurized pockets in them but don't ask me how. And free water. A high metabolism rate. I wouldn't be surprised if they're living off the radiation from the sun somehow."

Kirk was fascinated by the aliens' thin legs. They seemed to be made of solid metal. "Are they some kind of artificial construct, Spock? Organics built into a mechanical shell?"

"I see no indication of anything artificial in their structure, Captain. I believe that these are living creatures, either genetically engineered or independently evolved to live in hard vacuum."

"Sir," Uhura interrupted. "I am picking up a great deal of low-level radio static. And it seems to be coming from these . . . things."

"Try to localize it, Uhura," Kirk watched as one of the creatures scurried only two meters from him without slowing. It carried a chunk of lunar rock. "Any idea what kind of sensory organs they might have, Spock?"

"None whatsoever, Captain. I am continuing with my readings."

A second alien followed the path made by the first, also carrying lunar material. Then a third carrier went by. Kirk stepped forward into the pockmarked trail left by their footpads. A fourth came along and bumped into Kirk, almost knocking him over. Kirk was shaken by the unexpected force of the creature's impact, but he stayed upright.

"Be careful, Captain. Their legs obviously have great strength," Spock warned.

Kirk remained motionless as the alien that had collided with him dropped the rock it carried and raised itself on its hind legs until its segments were at Kirk's waist level. Its forward segment angled upward and its second set of legs waved out like insect feelers until they made contact with him.

Kirk heard Spock's urgent message. "Spock to *Exeter*. Lock transporter on the captain and prepare for emergency beam-out on my signal."

"It's all right, Spock," Kirk said. He kept completely still as the creature's legs tapped lightly all over him, following the contours of his silver environmental suit and the paths of the red and blue life-support tubes. "Their forward legs are their sensory organs. It's including me in its interior map of its surroundings."

The creature finished tracing Kirk, then dropped back down to its original stance, picked up its rock, and diverted around him. Relieved, Kirk placed his phaser on its adhesion patch at the side of his suit.

"How are your pressure readings, Captain? Did the creature create any punctures?" Spock asked.

Kirk glanced down at the indicator lights built into his helmet. "All readings are green, Spock. You can cancel the transpor—"

Another creature came charging toward him. Kirk braced himself for impact. But the creature smoothly swerved just as the first one had done after its examination of Kirk.

"Fascinating," Spock said. "Apparently they can communicate through the vacuum."

Kirk's next idea was impossible, but then so were the creatures. "Uhura, is there any chance that the creatures are communicating by radio transmissions?"

"I—uh, why not? I'll try to link up with one." Uhura

bounded over to where two of the creatures were stroking a small silverish bubble that appeared to have sprouted from the ground. One was exuding a dull black paste from an opening in its forward segment and then rubbing the substance against the bubble. Nearby, another creature appeared to be actually consuming rocks which had been deliberately stacked near it. Kirk wondered if he were watching the creatures process building materials.

Kirk hopped back to Spock and McCoy. "Any idea what those bubbles are?" he asked. "Or what they're made from?"

"They are composed of the same substance as the creatures' carapaces, and the coverings of the shuttles," Spock added. "Their composition is also virtually identical to that of the surrounding rocks and soils." Spock glanced down at his tricorder. "Captain, I believe that we must be looking at different versions of the same lifeform. Or at the very least, different species who share the same evolutionary past."

"Are you saying the *shuttles* are alive?"

Spock pointed his tricorder in the direction of the shuttles. "They appear to be dormant in the shadow of the overhang, but their shape and coloration are suggestive of the smaller creatures."

"Jim, I'm picking up something odd from one of the bubbles," McCoy suddenly said. "That one over there."

McCoy took two long strides to land beside a bubble almost five meters in circumference. Its surface was like the creatures', mottled silver and black, shining in some areas, dull in others.

"Bones, do you think they could be egg casings?" Kirk asked. "Like a horta's?"

"That's what I thought at first, too," McCoy said. His gloved fingers worked clumsily at the scanner he held to the bubble. "I *am* getting life readings from it, but they're different from the ones I took from the creatures themselves."

"Odd," Spock confirmed, reading from his own tricorder. "There appears to be a pressurized atmosphere inside. Well insulated, and with a quantity of liquid water."

"But what *kind* of lifeform's in there?" Kirk asked.

"Low-level plant analogue, Captain."

"Plant life?" Kirk repeated. "You're sure there's nothing higher?"

"Most certain," Spock confirmed.

Kirk pulled his phaser from the side of his suit, twisted the intensity setting on it, and fired at the bubble before either Spock or McCoy could say anything to change his mind.

A long stream of white vapor sprayed up from the small hole the phaser beam made. The vapor instantly changed to solid crystals and for a few moments it appeared to snow around the bubble. As the crystals sublimated in the vacuum, the area around the bubble slowly cleared again. The only difference now was that a thick sludge oozed from the hole, freezing as it fell to the ground in fist-size chunks. It glittered with a white gloss of fine frost, but the color of the sludge was apparent: purple.

"It's algae, isn't it?" Kirk said. "The same organism that's taken over the oceans of Talin IV."

Spock held his tricorder to the mass of thick, freezing material that pushed through the bubble's skin. "You are correct, Captain. But how did you decide this? It is not an obvious conclusion."

McCoy didn't agree. "Why not, Spock? The creatures are probably growing their food down there."

"Doctor McCoy, as both our readings show, these creatures do not require food. They thrive on hard radiation. The algae cannot sustain them."

Kirk saw a flurry of movement to the side. A herd of twenty creatures was leaping directly toward the leaking bubble. "Stand back, gentlemen. Looks like the repair crew has arrived."

The three men jumped away from the bubble just as the creatures swarmed around and over it. They quickly found the hole and cleaned the frozen algae away. Then Kirk saw several creatures, smaller and shinier than the others, who appeared at the edge of the repair team. The larger creatures formed a chain and passed the smaller ones over their bodies until they were deposited at the side of the bubble. The smaller creatures' footpads were twice the size of the larger creatures' pads and when they rubbed them over the hole, the pads began to glow white hot, melting the skin of the bubble to heal the opening.

"I hope you're recording that, Spock," McCoy said. "Because even seeing it myself I don't believe it."

"Captain!" It was Uhura calling. Kirk tried to find her silverclad form.

"State your location, Uhura," he said.

"Near the east side of the overhang, Captain. And you were right, sir—they *are* talking over radio frequencies!"

Uhura had found a large boulder on which to place her computer panel. Nearby, one creature methodically ripped apart a second. The second creature did not try to escape. A small pile of other disassembled creatures was nearby.

Uhura laboriously punched in commands on the panel. "I'm patching through their main channel to our helmet speakers, sir. They seem to be able to generate low-frequency radio waves through an organ in their forward segment. They don't have much range, but the ability is definitely there."

McCoy stepped over to examine the creature, casting his shadow across it. "How can a being evolve an organ to take advantage of radio?"

Spock answered. "Life constantly adapts to use the features of the environment in which it finds itself, Doctor. Our eyes have evolved to sense electromagnetic radiation of certain frequencies. Radio waves are also electromagnetic waves at other frequencies. It is a predictable development, however unlikely."

Suddenly Kirk's helmet speaker crackled with a confused flurry of static.

"That's their language?" McCoy asked.

"That's a raw signal," Uhura explained. "I'm going to tie it through the universal translator."

"Captain," Spock began, "since this language is completely alien, it will take the translator several hours to supply equivalent cognates. I suggest we return to the *Exeter* to replenish our consumables."

"Good idea, Spock. Then we can—"

"Strange life block food." It was the clipped, mechanical voice of the universal translator circuitry. *"Strange life block food over here over here."*

McCoy smirked. "Several hours? I guess you missed reading about a few upgrades to the translator, Mr. Spock."

"No, Doctor," Uhura said. "The universal translator shouldn't have been able to even start decoding this kind of language for hours." She held the computer board at an angle to clumsily punch in more commands. "I hate these gloves," she complained.

At the same time, the translator's voice kept repeating, *"Strange life block food over here over here. Strange life—"*

"Any idea what it means, Spock?"

"I'll let you know in a moment, Captain."

Suddenly, McCoy shouted in surprise, and Kirk awkwardly turned to see four creatures grab the doctor's legs. "Kirk to *Exeter!*" he transmitted. His hand went to his phaser. The creatures dragged McCoy through the lunar dirt by his feet, sending up a cloud of billion-year-old dust.

Then they let him go.

Kirk leapt over to him. "Are you all right, Bones?"

"Just fine," McCoy grumbled. He pushed himself up from the ground. His suit was streaked with black lunar soil. "And thank you for your help, Mr. Spock. From where you were standing, you must have seen them coming."

"I did, Doctor."

"Then why didn't you do something about it?" Kirk asked.

"The creatures were simply responding to their fellow being's call for assistance. Dr. McCoy's shadow covered the creature we were observing, thus cutting off its supply of food—the sun's radiation. As you will notice, the creature's transmission has now ceased."

363

McCoy hopped back to join Uhura and Spock. "You might have warned me anyway."

"Yes," Spock said. "I suppose I might have. Next time, Dr. McCoy."

Kirk went to Uhura. "Good work, Uhura. How'd you get such a quick translation?"

"The creatures are speaking in a language already known to the translator, sir." Uhura turned to look questioningly at Kirk through her faceplate. "They are speaking in the primary language of Talin."

"Spock, analysis." Kirk was at a loss for an explanation. The creatures could not possibly be indigenous to Talin. Neither did the planet have the genetic engineering technology to create them.

"Sir, if my preliminary conclusions are correct, then what we see here are not intelligent lifeforms. They are little more than worker insects, a group hive mentality which has worked to make Talin IV a suitable environment for growing the algaelike organism. In the absence of any language of their own, and given that they are able to transmit and receive radio messages, it seems likely that they have absorbed the Talin language by listening to the planet's radio transmissions over the years."

"Years, Spock?" McCoy asked.

"In the time that this system has been under FCO jurisdiction, no alien vessels have been sighted entering it. Therefore, the creatures have been here since before the FCO arrived."

"Sharing the same moon," Kirk mused. "And no one ever detected them."

"Since their carapaces are composed of the same material which covers this moon, it seems probable that the creatures reproduce by constructing duplicates of themselves from the raw materials at hand. The FCO's general scans would not have been able to distinguish the drones from their surroundings. I shall recommend to Starfleet that, in the future, airless planetoids should be scanned for small pockets of organic surface life contained within apparently nonliving shells."

Kirk watched as the nearby creatures finished ripping apart their victim. *No, not victim,* Kirk corrected himself. Obviously what he was watching was a part of their life cycle. No sooner were the pieces of the first creature dragged away, than another creature hurried up, also to be disassembled. One of its legs appeared to be damaged. *How efficient,* Kirk thought uneasily.

McCoy was still caught by Spock's explanation of the creatures' language. "So what you're saying, Spock, is that these things are like mindless parrots, just mimicking what they've heard?"

"Not at all, Doctor. The fact that one of them was able to complain about the shadow you cast indicates that they have also absorbed some of the language's context and meaning, just as some Earth primates have learned to use symbolic languages, though they cannot develop such languages on their own."

Kirk checked his suit's oxygen level. They would have to beam up in less than twenty minutes, and Spock and McCoy would have ample time to continue their discussion then. "Forget the details, Spock. The bottom line is that if these creatures have a language that they use, then we can use it, too."

"To do what?" McCoy asked.

"Why, Bones," Kirk said. "To talk to them."

Kirk hopped over to the creature that had complained about McCoy's shadow. It used its forward legs to grip onto a section of the creature being taken apart, then kept twisting the section around in the same direction, almost in an unscrewing motion, until it fell off. The creature being dismantled did not appear to experience any discomfort.

"Uhura," Kirk said, "can you link my helmet communicator to this one right here?"

Uhura brought her board over. "Aye, sir. Setting the frequencies now. Go ahead."

Kirk moved to cast his shadow on the creature.

The translator circuits came to life instantly. *"Strange life block food over here over here. Strange life block food."*

Kirk spoke. "Would you like the food to continue?"

"Yes food eat." Uhura's link worked both ways.

Kirk stepped aside, then, after a few moments, he blocked the sun once more. The creature went into its recitation.

"Would you like the food to continue?" Kirk asked again.

"Yes food eat."

"Then tell me who you are."

The creature didn't protest or try to negotiate. *"We are the Many."*

Kirk was relieved. He had been worried that once his questions and the creature's replies had been passed back and forth through Standard, into Talin, and then into the creature's own internal system that there would be no common ground for communication. But it appeared Dr. Richter was correct. Life was almost the same everywhere, no matter what its chemistry.

"Do you know what I am?" he continued.

"You are strange life. Give back food now." As if it were running low on energy, the alien stopped disassembling the other creature.

Kirk stepped aside and let the alien have a few more seconds of light. It began to move again.

"Do you know where you are?" Kirk was carefully proceeding only one step at a time in his questioning.

"Here," the creature answered. It apparently did not need the threat of light starvation to answer questions. Though Kirk doubted with that kind of answer that he was going to be able to get much useful information from such a basic mind.

"What do you do here?"

"Work," the alien answered readily. It twisted a leg off the motionless creature before it.

"Why do you work?" Kirk asked.

The alien did not respond.

Spock did. "Captain, if you are indeed conversing with a mind that functions at little more than an instinctual level, it will not be able to understand higher concepts such as motivation. It would be like asking a paramecium why it absorbs food. It is not a conscious decision."

"But, Spock, there has to be some conscious intelligence at

work here," Kirk argued. "Think of what they accomplished on Talin. They were able to manipulate the entire planetary defense system. They realigned warhead circuitry. Blocked our sensors and deflectors. Launched Talin missiles at us. How could they do all that without conscious thought?"

"Sir, everything these creatures did was achieved by altering the functions of electronic and transtator-based machinery. At the most elementary level, all that they did was to simply manipulate the data that passed through that equipment." Kirk heard Spock take a breath. It sounded almost like a sigh. "Captain, just as birds can fly without conscious knowledge of aerodynamics, and a virus can reprogram the complex chemistry of a living host without any awareness, these creatures can apparently provoke nuclear exchanges on a planet without any conscious knowledge of the cultures they are manipulating."

McCoy was appalled by the analogy. "There's a huge gap between flapping some wings and blowing up a planet, Mr. Spock."

"Only in degree, Doctor. As we have all seen in our voyages, given enough time, virtually any characteristic can be evolved. Given enough time, virtually any behavior can be learned."

Kirk stared at the dismemberment ritual going on before him. "They've done this before, haven't they?"

"Undoubtedly, Captain. Perhaps millions of times, to achieve this level of sophistication. Their identification of the master circuit nodes in the *Enterprise* was quite precise."

Kirk's mind reeled at the destruction that these creatures might have caused throughout the galaxy to grow food they couldn't use. He wouldn't accept that it was arbitrary action. No matter how they had evolved, no matter how their behavior had been learned, somehow, somewhere, there had to be a reason for it.

He stood in the sunlight and blocked the creature's food again.

"Why do the Many work?" he demanded.

The creature still did not respond.

"Captain, it cannot answer."

"Did you *hear* me?" Kirk said. *"Why do the Many work?"* He kicked a cloud of slowly falling lunar dust at the creature but it continued its task without pause.

"Jim, let it go. Spock's right. It's like questioning a child."

Child, Kirk thought. He stared at the creature before him, silver and black mottles covering its body. He looked at the bubbles in which the algae grew—bubbles *grown* from the same mottled substance created from the lunar rock. And the shuttles, lying dormant in the shadows—the same shape, the same substance, the same . . . skin. Spock had said they were different forms of the same species, or different species with a common ancestor. That was the answer. It had to be.

"What is your work?" he asked, changing his approach.

The creature stopped moving its legs, running out of energy in Kirk's shadow.

"What is your work?" he repeated.

The translator came online. *"To sow the seeds of life."*

"Why?"

"To grow food."

But *they don't eat the food,* Kirk thought. *They don't need the food.*

"Why do the Many grow food? What *purpose* does the food serve?"

The creature's footpads scrabbled weakly in the loose soil as it tried to crawl out from beneath Kirk's shadow. Kirk moved with it, keeping it blocked, knowing his conversation with it was preventing it from calling for help over the same frequency.

"I said, why do the Many grow the food?"

"The Many grow the food for the One," the creature finally answered.

Kirk stopped. "The One?" he said. "What is the One?"

"The One is that which consumes the food," the creature said.

Obviously the drones were not the One because what could a hive mentality know about individuality? Kirk thought. He began to feel a cold chill of apprehension.

"When will the One consume the food?" Kirk asked.

"When the One is here."

"Where is the One now?"

A burst of static rushed from the helmet speaker.

"Uhura," Kirk asked anxiously. "What did the creature say? What language was that?"

Uhura studied the readouts on her computer board. "Sir, that wasn't a language. That was . . ." She put the board down and turned to Kirk.

"Sir, the creature transmitted coordinates."

TWELVE

☆

"Let me get this straight," Styles said. "You and the *Enterprise* aren't guilty of any wrongdoing because of a colony of vacuum-breathing, rock-eating insects, which—even though they have no intelligence—were somehow able to trick the Talin into blowing themselves up?" The lieutenant did not bother to disguise his sarcasm. "You've beamed out once too often, Kirk. I always knew it would happen."

Kirk and Styles glared at each other in the director's complex at Outpost 47. Neither had forgotten their first—and last—tour together on the *Farragut*.

But Vice Admiral Hammersmith was interested in other matters. "Stow it, Lieutenant. You, too, Kirk." He glanced down at Wilforth's desk and again read the printout sheet of the coordinates of 'the One.' "How could they know our coordinate system, anyway?"

Uhura answered. "The universal translator converted the aliens' coordinate system to Talin astronomical conventions, and then to our quadrant and sector standards, sir."

Hammersmith looked at Spock. "Do you accept this as reliable data, Mr. Spock?"

"The drones had no reason to lie to us, assuming that they

370

have the capability, sir. However, I cannot vouch for what might actually occupy those coordinates."

Hammersmith swept aside the qualification. "But you do have a theory, don't you? You must have a theory."

"Yes, sir, I do."

After a long pause, McCoy said, "For heaven's sake, tell the man, Spock."

"I believe we will find a related group of creatures who will be arriving to consume the algae which the seeder drones have planted on Talin IV."

McCoy shook his head. "Uh uh. Not related creatures. There's got to be some intelligence at work here someplace. The drones' behavior is far too complex to ever have come about by chance. The One has got to be a colony ship—an alien colony ship that sent these things ahead to prepare a world the aliens can live on. The seeder drones aren't naturally evolved creatures—they're a living terraforming machine. Only they aren't making Talin IV like Earth."

Spock closed his eyes in subtle exasperation. "Doctor, if you would study the facts as have been recorded, you would—"

"I *have* studied the facts, Spock, and that's why—"

"Mr. Kirk," Hammersmith boomed to stop the altercation. "How about you? What's your theory?"

Kirk loathed the vice admiral's use of 'mister' but he wasn't going to show his anger in front of Styles. "I don't have a theory. Theories can wait until we get out there and see what it is we're dealing with firsthand."

Hammersmith nodded. "Yes, I suppose that's what has to be done."

"Good," Kirk said. "Then may I request that—"

"I'll put it into my report to Starfleet Command," Hammersmith added.

"What?" Kirk asked.

"You heard the vice admiral," Styles said. "He's going to follow the chain of command. Remember what that is, *Mr.* Kirk?"

"Styles . . ." Hammersmith warned.

"Why bother reporting it until you've gone out there and checked it for yourself?" Kirk asked.

"It's only a half lightyear away," McCoy said.

"At warp six, a ship could intercept those coordinates in less than one day," Spock added.

Hammersmith held up his hands to quiet everyone. "No one's going anywhere! Is that clear?"

"Yes, sir," Styles said smartly.

"I've got more than four hundred private vessels already stationkeeping at the edge of this system," Hammersmith went on. "Starfleet's got Greenpeace and the Planetary Society breathing down its neck. Half the galaxy is geared up to send aid to Talin IV and I don't have enough personnel or ships to keep them out as it is."

"By my estimation," Spock offered, "the Council debate should have ended by now."

"Even if it *has* ended, Spock, it's still going to take two days for the subspace relay to reach us." Hammersmith almost sounded apologetic. "And I will not allow any breech of Starfleet's lawful blockade of Talin IV until the question of the Prime Directive is resolved and I am ordered to withdraw my ships."

McCoy crossed his arms angrily. "You *know* how the Council will vote, Vice Admiral! They have no choice but to rule in Talin's favor."

Hammersmith stood up behind his desk and leaned forward on his fists. "No, I don't know that, Doctor. The Council isn't ruling on wars being started by nonintelligent aliens who say they're working for 'the One,' whatever that is. They are debating the legal question which Mr. Spock raised about whether or not Talin was already a *de facto* member of the Federation when the disaster occurred. That's a mighty big loophole in the Articles of Federation and the Council's vote on that could go either way."

Spock tried to intercede as conciliator. "I agree on that point,

Vice Admiral. However, you must be aware that when Starfleet receives the evidence we have uncovered here concerning alien intervention in the affairs of Talin, the question of the Prime Directive will not even have to go to Council. It does not apply."

"That's right, Spock. *When* Starfleet receives this evidence and *accepts* this evidence, then and only then will a ruling be made."

"The vice admiral is absolutely right," Styles said.

"Oh, be quiet!" Kirk ordered the lieutenant. "Look, Vice Admiral, you've got a dying planet down there. You've got hundreds of people willing to help save it. Let them do it. Take down the blockade."

Hammersmith was a man trapped in a nightmarish dilemma. "Kirk, believe me, I know what I've got on Talin IV. I wish I had a way out of this. But there are so many possible ways this thing could go, I don't have justifiable grounds for breaking orders. You lost your career over this, Kirk. Don't make me lose mine while there's still some good I can do here."

Kirk turned away in disgust. If Hammersmith wasn't going to help, then Kirk wasn't going to waste any more time with him. "Spock, Bones, we'll go out of system to the *Ian Shelton*. Her captain will take us out to the coordinates and—"

"The *Ian Shelton*," Hammersmith interrupted. "Is that Anne Gauvreau's freighter?"

"Yes," Kirk said suspiciously.

"She's not going anywhere. The *Shelton*'s a Federation registry vessel and Starfleet has commandeered her for picket duty."

"What about the *Queen Mary*?" McCoy suggested. "It doesn't smell too—"

"The Orion ship's been impounded," Hammersmith said. "And it's now serving picket duty as well. Face it, gentlemen, you aren't going anywhere. Every warp-capable ship is bouncing around the system turning back blockade runners."

The answer hit Kirk like a phaser bolt. "Every *warp-capable* ship, Vice Admiral? Is that what you said?"

Hammersmith nodded. It was his turn to be wary.

"Then you don't mean the *Enterprise?*" Kirk asked.

"What do you mean, he doesn't mean the *Enterprise?*" Styles blurted. "I've spent three months getting her warp capable again. She's got new warp nacelles and . . . "

Hammersmith looked thoughtful. "Brand new, unrated warp nacelles. Which have to be tuned into balance well away from the gravity well of a star so the ship won't risk hitting a wormhole."

"That means she's not warp capable *within* the system," Kirk concluded. "She's no use to you here."

"This is preposterous!" Styles fumed.

Kirk grinned. "You said you wished you had a way out of this, Vice Admiral. I think you've got one staring you right in your forward sensors."

Hammersmith smiled then, too. "But who do I have who can take her out?"

"Excuse me, Vice Admiral?" Styles said weakly.

Hammersmith sat back in his chair. "I mean, you three aren't part of Starfleet anymore. You're embassy officials, of all things."

"Vice Admiral Hammersmith?" Styles tried again.

"Chief Engineer Scott," Kirk said. "Just the officer you'd want to take the *Enterprise* out for operational trials."

"But Vice Admiral Hammersmith," Styles said, raising his voice. "You said the *Enterprise* would be *my* ship."

"Not too far," Kirk promised. "Maybe a half lightyear or so?"

Hammersmith nodded his head in agreement, a look of peace coming to his face at last. Kirk had found his compromise. "And I'll ask Mr. Scott if he'd mind taking along some observers from the Talin embassy. Thank you, Kirk."

Styles exploded. "You can't do that! You said she was *mine!*"

Hammersmith turned slowly to Styles, eyes wide. "I beg your pardon, *Lieutenant?*"

Styles stammered.

"Did you just tell a vice admiral what he could or couldn't do?" Hammersmith began to rise from his chair.

Styles was hullmetal white. He glared at Kirk. "Someday, Kirk. Someday I'm going to catch up to you and . . ."

Kirk laughed easily. "Maybe someday, Styles. But the important thing is, that's not today."

THIRTEEN

☆

The *Enterprise* coursed through the vacuum at full impulse power, racing light itself, until the orbital boundary of the system's last cold planet fell behind her.

On the bridge of the reborn ship, Lieutenant Kyle read aloud the astrogator's present coordinates. "We have left the Talin system, Mr. Scott."

Scott rose from the central chair. "Aye, and it's about bloody time." He turned to where Kirk and Spock and McCoy stood on the elevated deck by the science station. "Captain Kirk," he said proudly, holding his hand out to the empty chair. "Would you please sit down?"

Kirk stared at the conn. For almost four months he had awakened from dreams in which he was just about to take his natural place there—only to have it spin off into space without him. "I'm not a captain at the moment, Mr. Scott."

"You will be again soon enough."

Kirk shook his head. There would be time enough for that later. If there were a later.

Scott tilted his head and looked at Kirk with mock annoyance.

"Captain Kirk, you don't leave me any choice. As the duly

appointed commander of this vessel, sir, I *order* you to sit in that chair."

Kirk looked at Spock. "He can't order a civilian, can he?"

Spock arched an eyebrow. "He is the commander of the vessel."

McCoy sighed. "Well, if you don't, I will. Now get down there."

Kirk stepped down to the center deck, helped by a push from McCoy. "I'll try to give her back to you in one piece, Scotty."

"I'm sure the vice admiral would be most appreciative." Scott looked around the bridge. "Och, now what happened to the other three?"

Twelve hours later, flashing through warp space, the *Enterprise* neared the coordinates the drone had transmitted.

"There *is* an object there," Chekov said, reading the navigation board displays. He and Sulu had also been 'ordered' by Scott to take their stations, as had Uhura.

Kirk leaned forward in his chair. He had stopped thinking about how strange it seemed to see half his bridge crew dressed in civilian clothes. He only thought about what lay ahead—at the coordinates of the One.

"Sensors confirm, Captain," Spock announced from his science station.

"Well, what is it, Spock?" McCoy stood by the captain's chair, arms folded. "A spaceship, right?"

"We are still too distant to tell, Doctor. But if it is a ship, it is larger than any we have seen before."

Kirk turned in his chair. "We've seen some pretty big ships in our day, Mr. Spock."

"I believe we are about to see another."

Kirk looked back to the viewscreen. Nothing showed there yet except the computer's rendition of moving stars. "How much longer to intercept, Mr. Sulu?"

"Just over two hours at this factor, Captain."

Kirk hit the comm switch on his chair arm. "Mr. Scott, how are the warp generators coming along?"

Scott answered over the bridge speakers. "You wouldn't believe the changes they've made in them since the last pair we had, sir."

"Is that good or bad, Scotty?"

"Captain, if a thing's not broke, then why fix it?"

McCoy and Kirk shared a smile. "But can you handle them, Scotty?"

There was a long pause from engineering.

"Are you still there, Mr. Scott?"

"Aye, Captain. You want to know if I can give you more power from these bairns, don't you?"

McCoy had to turn his back to avoid laughing out loud.

"That would be appreciated, Mr. Scott."

Scott sighed. "Give me a few minutes, and I'll see what I can do."

"I can tell things are finally getting back to normal," McCoy said.

Kirk settled into his chair and gestured at the brightly colored shirt McCoy wore. "Now if we could only get you some normal clothes to wear."

Before McCoy could reply, the sound of the ship changed. She had been running rougher than before, but that was part of the break-in period her new warp generators required. However, now there was a second unusual harmonic added to the sound of them.

"Captain," Sulu announced, "our speed is increasing. Mr. Scott has boosted the power output. New estimated time of arrival is fifteen minutes, sir."

Spock stared intently into his science scope. "Captain, whatever it is we are approaching, it is not a ship."

"Then what the blazes is it?" McCoy asked. Kirk could hear the disappointment in the doctor's voice as he realized his theory was incorrect. McCoy didn't mind being wrong from time to time, it was just that he hated it when Spock was right.

"Is it a collection of lifeforms like the seeder drones?" Kirk asked. At full magnification, the viewscreen was just beginning to show a small gray swirl at its center.

"Life sensors are picking up readings consistent with the presence of drones, sir. But they don't begin to account for the mass of the object."

Kirk didn't like the way Spock had said that. Over the years he had become attuned to the subtle variations in his science officer's speech. Whatever he was seeing in his scope, Spock was startled.

"What *is* the mass of it, Mr. Spock?"

Spock straightened from his scope to look at the viewscreen. "According to all readings, Captain, we are approaching a planet. Slightly larger than Talin IV."

"Keptin," Chekov said, "the object . . . the planet . . . is changing course. It's . . . coming toward us, sir."

Changing course? Kirk thought. Then it *must* be a ship. "Spock, can you pick up what kind of propulsion system is being used for something that massive?"

"I can detect nothing," Spock said. "It has simply changed its trajectory."

Kirk contemplated the energies that must be involved in altering the course of something the size of a planet—a planet already traveling fast enough to cross the half lightyear to the Talin system in just under sixty years.

"Lieutenant Uhura, go to red alert."

"Aye-aye, sir." The warning sirens sounded and the alert lights flashed.

"Mr. Chekov, Mr. Sulu, prepare phaser banks and photon torpedoes, all tubes."

McCoy was suddenly concerned. "Is that wise, Jim?"

"Whoever is controlling that thing has sent out an advance force that destroyed a world. And they've got a propulsion system that can move a planet-sized mass around without any indication of how they do it." Kirk frowned. "It may not be wise, Bones. But it's safe."

Kirk called down to engineering. "Scotty, we're going to need full power to the shields when we leave warp. But then I'm going to want you to stand ready to get us back up to warp speed instantly, if not sooner."

Scott sighed. "The engines aren't broken in yet, Captain. If they can't take the surge, there'll be a terrible mess to clean up in the nacelles."

Kirk stared at the screen as the object in it grew. There was still no detail apparent, only a shifting gray whorl of what might be tendrils of gas. "Don't worry, Mr. Scott. Those engines are so new they're still under warranty. If they don't work, we'll send them back to the factory."

"Aye," Scott said, "but what worries me is where they're going to send us."

"Captain, we're coming up to intercept," Sulu announced. The object filled more than half the screen now. It was spherical like a planet, and wreathed in dark fog.

"Go to impulse, Mr. Sulu. Whatever it takes to stay ahead of that thing."

The ship shuddered as she dropped from warp space with a slightly unbalanced transition. But the impulse engines ran smoothly.

"Holding at ten thousand kilometers," Sulu said.

Kirk stood to see the viewscreen more clearly. If he were outside the ship on his own, he knew he wouldn't be able to see the planet-sized object at all because of the lack of light, so far from the nearest star. But the ship's sensors were able to amplify the dim starlight from all around and make the object visible on the screen. "There it is, Bones. The One."

McCoy was not impressed. "It looks like a dirty snowball to me." He turned to Spock. "How can a planet out here have a gaseous atmosphere. I thought it was too cold."

"Those swirls of what appear to be fog are not an atmospheric phenomenon, Doctor. They are drones flying around the object. By the billions." Even Spock seemed subdued by the scale.

Kirk tried to picture what that number of drones could do to a world.

"Uhura, are they transmitting anything on radio frequencies?" Kirk asked.

"Yes, sir. Too many of them for the computers to handle. I'll try to lock into the strongest one and tie it in through the translator, but I can't promise anything."

"Do your best," Kirk said. "Spock, if those clouds are drones, then what's beneath them?"

"Maybe nothing," McCoy suggested. "It could be like a beehive. In the winter, the bees form a ball to conserve energy. They hang in the hive and slowly change position so that they each only have to spend a short time on the outside of the ball being exposed to the cold."

"An admirable speculation, Doctor, though incorrect. Sensors show that the matter beneath the drones differs from them. Though our instruments cannot yet make a clear enough reading to tell us what that matter is."

Kirk watched as Sulu made some adjustments to the impulse controls. "Is it changing course again?" he asked.

"No, sir," Sulu said. "But it is accelerating. Only by a few meters per second though. We won't have any trouble staying ahead of it . . . so far."

A rush of static burst from the bridge speakers. "I've got that signal," Uhura said. "Patching it to the translator."

The static warbled, then dropped in loudness as the translator's circuits took over. *"Cold cold cold coldcoldcoldcolco—"* The speakers whined piercingly, then clicked off.

"Sorry about that," Uhura said. "Feedback on the translator. Too many similar messages coming in at the same time. I'll try to filter them down again."

Kirk watched the masses of drones writhing over the object. "What's the temperature out there, Spock?"

Spock didn't look up from his scope. "Less than thirty degrees Kelvin."

That didn't make sense to Kirk. "But the seeder drone on Talin's moon slowed right down as soon as I cast a shadow on it. How are these staying active without any sunlight?"

"Obviously, they must be receiving energy from another source," Spock said.

Uhura broke in. "Sir, I can't get anything coherent on normal radio frequencies, but there is a strong, short-range low-frequency signal coming from the object."

"Let's hear it, Uhura."

The bridge speakers hummed with a new sound, low and pulsing. "It's not like the drones' language, but I'll try routing it through that part of the universal translator."

The low pulsing noise dropped in volume. The speakers clicked. *"Hungry. Strange life. Hungry. Consume strange life. Hungry. Faster. Hungry."*

Kirk tapped at his chest. "The seeder drone said that we were strange life. And whatever that was was talking about eating strange life. . . . Mr. Sulu, is that thing still accelerating for us?"

"Yes, sir. Very slowly."

McCoy put his hand on the back of the conn. "Do you think it plans to eat us?"

"That's exactly what I think." Kirk went up to Spock's station. "Mr. Spock, is it possible that somewhere under all those drones there is another lifeform?"

"It is difficult for the sensors to penetrate the mass of drone readings. They appear to be in a layer more than one thousand kilometers thick."

"A thousand kilometers," Kirk said, turning back to the screen. "Like insulation against the cold. Living insulation." He went to Uhura. "Open a channel to the subspace frequency you're putting through the translator." Uhura nodded at him to proceed.

"Who are you?" Kirk asked. He shrugged off McCoy's frown. He had to start somewhere.

"I am hungry."

"I," Kirk said. "Not 'we.' Not a hive mentality like the drones. A single individual. *The One.*" He remembered the conversation he had had with the seeder drone. "What is your work?" he asked, already knowing what the answer would be.

"To consume life."

Kirk turned to Spock. *"The Many sow the seeds of life. The One consumes life.* They're symbiotes, Spock."

"Yes," Spock agreed. "That would make sense."

"What makes sense?" McCoy asked. "That thing out there doesn't make a bit of sense."

"Where are you going?" Kirk asked the One.

"To get food."

"Where?"

"There."

Kirk was certain he had solved it. "It's in communication with the seeder drones on Talin's moon. It has to be. And the way they damaged the *Enterprise,* they must have subspace capability, as well as radio."

"But how can you know they're in communication with each other?" McCoy asked.

"When I asked the seeder drone where it was, remember what it said. It said 'here.' When I asked this planet creature where it was going, it said 'there.' Simple concepts for simple, basic, rudimentary minds."

Chekov called for Kirk's attention. "Keptin, I am picking up a configuration change. The creature is . . . altering itself."

On the screen, the random gray tendrils of the massed drones were forming into a central vortex which covered half the area of the sphere's visible side. The outer edges of the gray cloud spun out ahead of the rest like clay on a potter's wheel while the inner surface became sharply concave, dipping in toward the hidden surface.

"Mr. Spock?" Kirk asked as a pale red glow began to appear in the deepest section of the growing planet-size whirlpool.

"The covering of drones is thinning, Captain. Our sensors are beginning to penetrate to whatever lies below."

The apparition on the viewscreen was no longer a solid sphere. It had opened up, the edges of it stretching outward like straining tentacles. The glow from the interior was brightening steadily, red and pulsing.

"It's trying to eat us," McCoy said, unusually restrained. "It's opening its mouth."

"Still accelerating, Captain," Sulu announced.

"Stay ahead of those tendrils," Kirk ordered. He turned to

Spock. "What do the sensors show, Mr. Spock? What's inside that thing?"

Spock turned away from his scope, and to Kirk it seemed as if the science officer were abandoning it. "Captain, there is no doubt that the creature is alive." Spock sounded hesitant. The deep red tunnel which had formed within the creature, large enough now to swallow a world, flashed with odd purple bolts of energy. But the bolts arced and branched in lines which followed smooth and perfect curves, not the jagged streaks of ordinary energy discharges.

"And the lining of the creature's tendrils does have the capability of consuming and metabolizing the algae that grows on Talin IV," Spock continued.

"The lining of the tendrils?" Kirk said. On the screen, the tendrils appeared to be made of red glowing gas or shaped energy. "Are the tendrils solid matter?"

Spock stood by the railing, eyes fixed on the screen. "Not as it exists in our universe, Captain. It contains subatomic particles similar to our quarks, but the ways in which those particles interact are . . . different."

"Is the One from another dimension, Spock?"

The science officer shook his head without speaking and Kirk wondered what had so deeply affected him. Then he heard the impulse engines reset to a higher power curve as the creature accelerated again.

"All other extradimensional manifestations that we have observed have shared the same basic laws of energy and matter interaction established in the first nanoseconds of our universe's beginning," Spock said. "But this creature does not share those laws."

McCoy turned to Spock. "Are you saying that thing's from another universe, Spock?"

"An earlier universe, Doctor. One that preceded ours."

Kirk stared at the thing on the screen—now a mad, spinning maelstrom of . . . hunger. A primal hunger billions of years old. A simple, basic lifeform that had evolved over uncountable eons to acquire the ultimate survival trait—the ability to live beyond its universe.

"How?" Kirk whispered. He suddenly knew how Richter felt. So little time to understand.

"Captain, for a being to be able to maintain itself during the heat death of a universe . . . for it to be able to withstand the infinite compression of a universal collapse of energy and matter . . . and for it to then survive the creation energies of the Big Bang . . . there is nothing in our science which would even begin to suggest how such a thing might be possible."

Kirk had Uhura open the channel to the One. "What is your age?" he asked, not knowing if the creature would comprehend.

"Hunger," it answered plaintively. On the screen, it twisted as if in agony, reaching hopelessly for the constantly retreating ship it wanted to consume.

"Where do you come from?"

"Consume need consume need. Faster. Faster."

"Why?" Kirk asked.

This time, the translated voice gave no answer.

"Instinct," Kirk said with finality as he stared at the screen. "As Spock said, it's like asking a paramecium why it absorbs food. It is not a conscious decision. And this is not a conscious lifeform."

Spock and McCoy watched as Kirk returned to the conn.

"Well, Doctor," he said as he sat back in his chair, "at least now you know how the One, and the Many, had enough time to develop such complex behavior. If it could survive the collapse of one universe . . . it could survive the collapse of billions."

McCoy, for once, was speechless.

"Mr. Sulu," Kirk said decisively, "take us back just beyond the distance we were when Chekov first noticed this creature change course."

The straining maw of the One receded on the screen, slowly folding closed, again encasing itself within its living cloud of insulation against the harsh environment of interstellar space. When the *Enterprise* had matched her earlier distance from it,

Sulu reported that the creature resumed its original course—bearing directly for the Talin system.

"Keptin," Chekov said, "we have passed out of phaser range. Shall I arm the photon torpedoes?"

"If it can withstand the Big Bang, Mr. Chekov, I don't think there's much we'd be able to do to it," Kirk said.

"It could not have survived in that form," Spock said. "As it exists now, it *is* vulnerable to our weapons."

"Thank you, Mr. Spock, but our weapons won't be necessary. Uhura, cancel red alert."

McCoy stormed down to Kirk. "Not be necessary? Good Lord, Jim. That thing is in contact with the drones that destroyed Talin. It's probably planning to eat the entire planet by the time it gets there."

"It's not *planning* to do anything, Bones. It can't think."

"Neither can a shark," McCoy muttered.

Spock stepped down beside McCoy. "In any event, Doctor, at the slow speed with which it is traveling, Starfleet will have ample time to return and either capture or destroy the creature."

Kirk shook his head. "Starfleet's not going to capture or destroy that creature, Spock. What purpose would that serve?"

"To pay it back for all the other worlds it destroyed with the drones," McCoy said.

"To preserve the worlds which it might destroy in the future," Spock added.

Kirk turned to McCoy. "Bones, it can't be paid back. It didn't decide to destroy worlds any more than the shark knows the difference between eating a fish or a swimmer." Kirk looked at Spock. "And there are lots of planets out there, Spock. If those drones were able to mindlessly convert Talin IV into a suitable planet for their host in less than two decades, just think what the Starfleet corps of engineers could do in *six* decades to prepare one of the Talin gas giants for it." Kirk put his hands on the arms of his chair and gazed at the screen, watching the swirling gray mass shrink to a dot. "It's a big universe, gentlemen. With worlds enough, and time for everyone."

Kirk looked back at his friends. Neither one looked satisfied but that reaction pleased him. It meant he could be sure that he had made the right decision.

There were no enemies here. Only mysteries.

The *Enterprise* came about in space. Her mission, at last, continued.

Part Four

THE NEW MISSION

ONE

─────────── ☆ ───────────

In standard orbit around Talin IV, the *Enterprise* resonated with the activity of her newly returned crew. Kirk moved briskly through the corridors as if drawing life from the energy they brought back to the ship. His ship. The new gold command shirt he wore made him feel as if he had returned home. He had.

In the main branch corridors leading to the cargo transporters, an earnest-looking lieutenant with a Starfleet Command insignia on his blue shirt jogged up behind Kirk, carrying a fat sheaf of printouts and a screenpad. He was balding and the last remnants of his curly brown hair were mussed and unruly, like the hair of someone who had been up all night. Kirk didn't care. He guessed that at least half of Command hadn't had any sleep for the past two days.

The lieutenant caught up to Kirk and had to walk quickly to keep the rapid pace. "Captain Kirk," he said breathlessly, the voice of a man in a hurry, "I'm Peter Bloch-Hansen, sir. Starfleet Emergency Rescue Office."

Kirk kept moving, no time to waste. All through the corridors other crew members ran or jogged, carrying equipment and supplies. There was so much to do. So much time wasted. He thought of Richter then, still in the *Exeter*'s sickbay. He knew what drove the man.

"Has the order come through yet?" Kirk asked brusquely.

"No sir, Captain," Bloch-Hansen said.

Kirk didn't bother to correct the lieutenant. Until the order did come through, he was still 'mister.' But no one doubted that Nogura's order was not already blistering through subspace to the Talin system. Too much had happened for even Starfleet to ignore. And when that order came, it had better include full apologies for each member of the *Enterprise* Five.

Kirk guessed it would be an easy apology for Command to make. Only Uhura's case would require Starfleet to go to the trouble and potential embarrassment of an official review board to withdraw all charges of contempt and to reinstate her. Because the rest of the Five had resigned, regulations allowed them to rejoin Starfleet service at full rank and pay anytime within six months. With a bit of bureaucratic juggling, Starfleet could even manage to keep the resignations out of the official records, as if they had never happened.

"But I do have the new figures for you, sir," Bloch-Hansen continued. He shuffled his printouts as he and Kirk weaved rapidly around the other rushing crew they passed in the corridor. "As of twenty minutes ago, there were five hundred and twelve vessels in stacked orbits around Talin IV. They'll be working in shifts to transfer their relief supplies to the *Enterprise* and the *Exeter* for mass beaming to the surface. The time/ton transfer schedules are here. . . . " He offered Kirk his screenpad.

Kirk ignored it. He kept walking. "Tell me about the Talin. Was Spock right about the survival rate?"

The lieutenant efficiently produced a printout from his bundle. He was prepared for anything. "Mr. Spock *was* right, sir. The figure is astonishing. As long as they escaped immediate blast and fire injuries, their autonomic cocooning reflex would have dropped their metabolism right down . . . uh, the life readings show just more than two billion Talin remain alive on their planet, ninety-five percent in hibernation."

Kirk stopped and looked at Bloch-Hansen with relief. That was far higher than anyone, even Spock, had hoped.

The lieutenant continued. "I estimate a complete revival program should take three years, but by that time the seeders' growth will be scavenged from the oceans."

"How's the drone contact team working out?" Kirk and Bloch-Hansen turned the corner into the final corridor. The entrance to the cargo transporter room was jammed with people, some crew, some civilians.

"The task force will arrive on Talin's moon to begin relocating the drones within a week, sir. The Talin ambassadors have given permission for them to begin seeding the gas giant, Talin VIII. It will be converted into a food source well within the next sixty years."

Kirk shouldered his way into the crowd. "Good work, Lieutenant. Let me know when the order comes in."

Bloch-Hansen stopped at the edge of the crowd. "Oh, you'll know when it comes, sir. You'll know."

As people realized who was pushing up against them, they quickly made way to let Kirk through. He passed the processing desk with a nod from the volunteer coordinators and stepped out to the open area immediately in front of the honeycombed crystal pads of the cargo transporter grid.

Nearby, Chekov and Sulu stood with Christine Chapel, checking a crate of medical tricorders. Kirk could hear the two ensigns telling the others about Lieutenant Styles's new assignment—ferrying the impounded *Queen Mary* back to Starbase 29. There was much laughter as Sulu explained how the gravity generator on the Orion ship had mysteriously been broken. It could only put out a three-gee field now, and it was tied into the warp drive so it couldn't be turned off. "I am certain the lieutenant will wery much enjoy his weighty new position," Chekov said.

Kirk looked around for Spock among the confusing stacks of boxes and knots of people. As he turned around, he bumped into McCoy. The doctor was back in his science blues.

"Have you seen Spock?" Kirk asked.

"No. He's probably hiding from me." McCoy reached out without warning and jammed a spray hypo against Kirk's arm. "There," he said when the longer-than-usual spray was done, "now you can eat plutonium for breakfast."

Kirk rubbed at the tingling spot where the radiation stabilizer had entered. "Is that going to work on the Talin?"

"It needed some modification, but M'Benga's already got the first batch processing."

"Good work, Bones. Or do you prefer 'Black Ire' now?" Kirk chuckled at McCoy's sudden look of discomfort. "How'd you ever come up with that one, anyway?"

McCoy frowned. "Someday I'll tell you about my illustrious ancestors. If I live that long." He tried to change the subject. "Has the order come in?"

Kirk looked around the huge room. It was filled with at least twenty different conversations and the hum of antigravs as boxes were received and stacked through the doors leading to the cargo hold. "Not yet," Kirk said. He suspected there would be pandemonium when it did come through. "Why do you think Spock's—"

Suddenly he felt a light touch on his shoulder. He turned to see Anne Gauvreau. Her flight jacket had a new crest proudly sewn on the front. The writing on it was in Talin splatterscript.

Kirk looked at the crates on the transporter grid. Most were marked with bold red crosses. "Is this from the *Shelton?*"

Gauvreau patted one of the crates. "Sure is. Starfleet Emergency Rescue didn't want to wait for the official word. They're buying all the medical supplies that everyone's brought in. If the supplies aren't used here, they say, then they'll still be useful somewhere else."

"These supplies *will* be used on Talin," Kirk said. There was no doubt in his voice. "So . . . until things get settled here, I suppose you freighter captains are going to be leaving this system with empty holds."

Gauvreau smiled brightly. "Not this time." She looked at McCoy and winked. "Thanks to Dr. McCoy, the T'Prar Foundation has hired me to transport twenty-six Orion females to a reorientation village on Delta Triciatu."

"Delta?" Kirk asked, raising his eyebrows.

"Seems Deltan males aren't affected by the Orion females' pheromones, so it's a good place for them to be helped to start their own lives again. And besides . . . I've always wanted to go there. . . . " Gauvreau blushed. "Look, I've got to break orbit to let another ship get into transporter range." She leaned closer and kissed Kirk on his cheek. "Thank you for making me feel I was back in Starfleet again."

"Thank you for bringing me back," Kirk said, then watched her move off into the crowd by the door. He hoped he would see her again.

Kirk turned to McCoy. "Whatever happened to those pirates?"

"In the brig on the *Exeter*. Last I heard Krulmadden was trying to buy it from her captain."

"I'm glad he's not on this ship talking to Chekov," Kirk said. He looked up with sudden interest as another crew member jostled him as she walked by with an antigrav pallet of visual sensors. It was Carolyn Palamas.

"Welcome back, Captain Kirk," she said. "The herbarium roses are in bloom again. I checked."

Kirk stumbled over a reply as she continued on without waiting for one. When he turned back to McCoy, he was greeted by a soppy smile. "Don't you start," Kirk warned.

Then McCoy looked puzzled and Kirk saw why. Spock was approaching. Like the doctor, the science officer was wearing his uniform again, tricorder hanging at his side. But he was also carrying a familiar-looking green bottle.

"Mr. Spock," Kirk said with a bemused expression, "is that whisky?"

Spock held the bottle up to read the label, as if confirming that it was true. "Yes," he admitted. "It was given to me by Mr. Scott."

"Did he say why?" Kirk asked.

"He said it was my . . . birthday present."

McCoy looked surprised. "It's not your birthday, Spock."

"Thank you, Doctor. I explained that to Mr. Scott, but he was quite emotional about it. He said, and I quote, 'Och, it dinna matter one wee bit.' And then he asked me when the party would be."

McCoy held a hand out. "Tell you what, Spock. Why don't you just give me the bottle as a token of apology and then you can stop trying to hide from me."

"Doctor, not only am I not trying to hide from you, I can think of no action on my part for which I might possibly owe you an apology."

McCoy feigned great shock. "Spock, I said there were aliens, remember? When we were talking in the shuttle at the outpost, and I said that it was obvious that the Talin were under observation by other aliens but you said, nooo, there were no other aliens. There's nothing of value in this system, you said. And meanwhile those drones *were* creating something of value —that purple sludge of theirs—right under your big pointed ears. But you didn't see it and I did. I said—"

Kirk held his hands up as if threatening to cover McCoy's mouth.

"Bones, you keep going on like that and we're all going to have to hide from you."

McCoy folded his arms and smiled smugly. "I don't care. All that matters is that I was absolutely, inarguably right and—"

"As I recall," Spock said dryly, "you suggested there were Klingons with Romulan cloaking devices lurking about."

"I said *aliens,*" McCoy insisted.

"You said—"

"What *about* the aliens?" Kirk asked Spock. "Any results from the FCO's computer analysis of our sensor readings?"

Spock and McCoy didn't break eye contact. "A classic symbiotic relationship, Captain. It appears Dr. Richter was correct when he said that life everywhere was the same—even when it originates in different universes. The computers have modeled a logical relationship between the two lifeforms: The seeder drones prepare planets with the purple food organism which then converts the entire biosphere into a highly radioactive algae analogue. When the One arrives in the system, it enfolds the planet and ingests the converted biosphere. In return, it carries some of the drones from system to system, providing energy to them so that they can survive the journey between the stars. Other drones it sends ahead on a smaller clump of accelerated matter, somewhat like plants spreading spores."

"How do they decide which planets to go to?" Kirk asked.

"I do not think 'decide' is the term to be used, Captain. The selection of planets for seeding is most likely an instinctual response, done without consciousness. I suspect that we may find that colonies of drones lie dormant in thousands of systems throughout the galaxy, waiting to be awakened by the first electromagnetic pulses resulting from an atomic explosion. That would indicate that fusion warheads will soon be developed on a given planet and that the planet's inhabitants could therefore be manipulated to devastate their biosphere with radiation, making it a suitable world for the growth of the algae. As the drones come to life and begin their instinctive behavior to create tension on the target planet, they send out signals to the One, informing it that a new planet is about to be seeded."

McCoy fidgeted with his tricorder and medikit. "I still don't see how anything could survive the death and birth of a universe."

"Especially if the physician present at that birth were—"

Kirk broke in again. "Perhaps, gentlemen, we should simply accept that there are still mysteries in the universe. Or the universes." He smiled at them. "Let's leave something for another ship to do, all right?"

Before either McCoy or Spock could answer, the page whistle of the ship's intercom system sounded. Instantly, every conversation in the cargo transporter room stopped. Only the background whir of the equipment could be heard until Uhura's voice came on.

"Attention all crew. Attention all crew. The USS *Enterprise*, as flagship for the Starfleet Relief Operation to Talin . . ." Kirk felt the hair on his neck bristle. He heard small gasps from the people in the room who also understood what Uhura had just said. This collection of ships had been given a name. The Starfleet Relief Operation to Talin. Uhura didn't have to read the rest. It was official.

". . . has just received this subspace communiqué from Nogura, Admiral, Starfleet Command: Effective this stardate, Earth, the findings of Starfleet's board of inquiry into the incident at Talin IV are rescinded. In addition, with remorse, Starfleet offers full and official apologies to—" The transporter room resounded with applause. Kirk felt hands slapping at his back. He struggled to hear the rest of what Uhura read. He had been waiting so long to hear it.

"Also, in accordance with Starfleet Command Regulations, General Order One, Talin IV is hereby recognized as a planet whose normal development has been subject to extraplanetary interference and thus is excused from the Prime Directive of Noninterference." The ship seemed to shake with the roar of the cheers which joined the continuing applause echoing through her. Uhura's voice was almost lost amid the tumult.

"Therefore, all Starfleet personnel are requested to take whatever action may be deemed necessary to repair the damage caused by such interference. Furthermore, in recognition of the General Council's ruling to admit Talin to the United Federation of Planets, all Federation citizens are likewise urged—"

It was no use. Her voice was completely drowned out. Kirk's ears rang. McCoy had cupped his hands to his mouth and was shouting deafening huzzahs. Kirk caught Spock's eye and saw his science officer smile, just fleetingly, and before anyone else could notice.

Then, as swiftly as it had begun, the joyous ovation quietened. It was not replaced by a return to the conversation and the activity which had preceded it. There was only silence. For a moment Kirk was puzzled. But only for a moment.

"Captain," Spock said, "the crew awaits your orders."

McCoy put his hand to Kirk's arm. "Now you really are back, Jim."

Without hesitation, Captain James T. Kirk stepped onto the transporter platform and faced his crew. He nodded to Kyle, standing ready at the transporter console, and gave his crew the order they waited for.

"Energize," he said.

TWO

☆

The shimmering veil of transporter energy fell from Kirk's eyes and he gazed onto a city of the dead.

The air of Talin was thick with the stench of rot and smoke. A sea breeze blew up from the distant ocean where he could see foul purple waves crash against a beach of blackened wood and the skeletons of sea creatures that had washed ashore. Even the shafts of weak sunlight which cut through the overcast skies seemed gray and dull.

Kirk stepped forward onto the ash of the shattered world that had briefly borne his name. Before him was what the sensors had determined was the largest gathering of still-functioning, uncocooned survivors on the planet. Its population numbered less than four hundred.

An old Talin female was the first to see him as he took another step in the ash. She had one arm. Her bibcloth hung in tatters. Kirk could see her bones move beneath her cracked and bleeding skin.

The female cried out weakly, a harsh discordant shriek. Behind her, other Talin slowly emerged from the rubble they had made into shelters. A few hundred meters away, he saw the long shapes of soot-darkened cocoons stacked like firewood.

Respectfully gathered for a better day which no Talin could believe would ever come.

But Kirk was there to make that day a reality. He looked all around him at the desolation and destruction. He saw the blasted stumps of buildings, shattered girders, fields of blackened crops.

And it was all a mistake. It had all occurred because there were still too many mysteries, still too many unknowns. But Kirk knew, at least, that *this* would not happen again. The Federation would learn. It would know what to look for next time. Other worlds would be saved by the painful lessons of Talin IV. The Federation would learn and from that knowledge, grow stronger.

A dozen Talin had gathered before him now. They pointed at him in wonder. Some covered their eyes, afraid to look at his alien form. Others reached out with trembling limbs, but were too frightened to come closer.

Kirk heard another transporter chime swell. He heard the gasp of awe from the crowd before him. More Talin were coming from the ruins. Some dropped to their knees as the golden light played upon them.

There were new footsteps behind him. Kirk glanced over his shoulder to see Spock and McCoy coming toward him, already opening their tricorders. A wall of medical supplies had also appeared, still shimmering.

He heard another cry from the Talin as the air filled with the pulsed harmonics of multiple transporter chimes. All around them the air danced with shimmering columns of luminous energy. And from each apparition came another human, or another gift of supplies.

Chekov stepped forward with Sulu and Uhura. Scott appeared with a pallet of machinery that could draw water from the air. Next, M'Benga, Chapel, Palamas. Everyone had returned to Talin.

Then, from the crowd of Talin adults, staring, pointing, shaking, not daring to believe that what they saw might be real, one female child stepped forward. Her skin was green and caked with mud, but her yellow eyes were clear and penetrating.

Alone among the Talin, she stepped up to Kirk unafraid.

Kirk twisted the dial on the small silver wand of his translator. He spoke into it for the child.

"My name is James Kirk," he said. "Captain of the starship *Enterprise*."

He waited as the translator repeated his words in the whistles and whispers of Talin.

The child's eyes widened. She looked up to the sky, past the clouds, as if they were no longer there. She whispered one word back to Kirk. The translator spoke it to him.

"Starship."

Tears fell from the child's eyes. She turned back to her people and shouted the word to them, pointing to the skies, to the stars that waited there.

"Starship. Starship." The translator said the word as each Talin spoke it.

The child came closer to Kirk. She lifted her arms to him and he saw then in her eyes what he had seen in the eyes of a woman long ago on Earth, what he had seen in the eyes of a Tellarite child in an asteroid only weeks ago.

Kirk took the child's hands in his and lifted her up close to him, knowing that the beginnings and the endings of things were sometimes one and the same.

But this time, he knew, it would be a beginning.

"It's all right," Kirk said. "Let me help."

EPILOGUE

THE DREAM OF STARS

The ship surrounds him and bears him through space, and protected by her, he sleeps.

And dreams of Iowa.

He is a young boy. He runs with his dog through fields of grain, full of the smells of things growing, and of life.

At night, he feels his father's hand, rough in his, as they walk into those fields.

The boy looks up and gasps to see the sky so black, the stars so brilliant. His father names them, magic to the boy's ears, to his eyes, to his heart, to something within him that he does not yet understand.

Rigel, his father says. Aldeberan, Antares.

Yes, the boy says. He has never heard them before but he is certain that he knows them all. The names continue, the grain is forgotten. His mother waits in the house nearby, lights blazing through windows brilliant as the stars.

But the boy looks up. I want to go there, he says, reaching out to them. His father's face is uplifted, too, feeling the heat of a thousand suns, seen and unseen, known and unknown.

The boy is five years old and he feels a pain in his chest with the weight of millennia, as if the whole species had moved forward to this one instant, to this one person, driving him on.

I have to go there, the boy says. I know, his father answers. He reaches down and lifts the boy high, holding him to his chest with love, holding him to look up, just that little bit closer to the stars in his father's arms. And you will, Jimmy, you will.

The boy's heart beats faster. I will, he whispers, clutching his father, afraid of the dark and the cold of night and the distance from the house, but hungry to see more. The challenge, the promise, the love he feels. All cast in him in that one night when first he looked up and knew where his destiny lay.

That night his house surrounds the boy and bears him through the darkness, and protected by her, he sleeps.

And dreams of stars.

ACKNOWLEDGMENTS

We are deeply indebted to our editors, Dave Stern and Kevin Ryan, for their ongoing support, encouragement and, most important, patience.

Once again, our "historian," Sal Nensi, has worked hard at Memory Prime to help us keep our facts and references straight and we are grateful for his fast and detailed assistance, and his friendship.

We are also grateful to Carole, Mario, and Peter, for kindly introducing us to Star Trek Toronto in particular, and Trek fandom in general.

In the almost quarter century that Gene Roddenberry's Star Trek has been in existence, a great number of writers have contributed to its canon. For this story, we have drawn on the work of many of these writers and thank them all for the entertainment and inspiration they have provided.

The character of Lt. Carolyn Palamas, the ship's A & A officer, first appeared in the television episode "Who Mourns for Adonis?" written by Gilbert Ralston and Gene L. Coon. Palamas was played by Leslie Parrish. An older but no wiser Lt. Styles first appeared as captain of the *Excelsior* in the movie, *The Search for Spock*, written by Harve Bennett. Styles was played by James B. Sikking.

ACKNOWLEDGMENTS

We would also like to acknowledge the work of Vonda McIntyre and Shane Johnson. Allan Asherman's *Star Trek Compendium* has been an invaluable reference tool as well.

Of course, none of this would exist without Gene Roddenberry's creative and ongoing vision of the future as it should be—a grand adventure.

Our thanks to all. Here's to the next 25.

J & G